I0693087

The Russian

ANN HOWES

*The saddest thing about betrayal is that it never
comes from your enemies.*
~Unknown~

T *en years ago*

Stakeouts sucked Russian ass.

Vasily Melnikov hated them and was never more convinced this particular stakeout was a waste of his time. Except for indulging in his uncle's ambition that could start a war—which he was not on board with—he'd be doing something more productive. Like working out on the basketball court or giving his older brother Dean shit.

He stretched his arms as far as the front seat of an old Toyota Corolla would allow, then twisted his spine a couple of times. It didn't do much to relieve the stiffness settling in his back, nor did it give his brain a break from the boredom. His phone battery was in the red, the radio didn't work, and there was one CD stuck in the player. A man could listen to Gretchen Wilson serenade the virtues of being a redneck woman only so many times.

He would've preferred to do the stakeout in his own car, but a bright red, newer model Mercedes didn't exactly blend in with the rest of the cars in the neighborhood.

It was beginning to get dark, the streetlamps had just turned on and his target still hadn't shown. Weighing the benefits of calling it for the day, he was about to turn the key in the ignition, when a car turning the corner at the bottom of the street caught his attention.

It was loud. The kind of loud that said it was missing the muffler on its exhaust. And exactly the kind of car that should be headed to a junkyard protected by a chain-link fence and razor wire. Vasily's interest perked up. Here came his first live eyeball of Mario Marcello, his target.

"Let's see what you look like in real life, old man."

A sixties-model vintage Mustang rumbled to the back gate of the metal scrapyard he'd parked across from since the early hours of the morning. The color was primer gray and the car had seen much sexier days, but it matched the autos Marcello specialized in. Rare, and probably stolen.

The Mustang's door pushed open. His first clue that something wasn't quite right, was Bob Marley's *Buffalo Soldier* tumbling from the speakers. Then the hair on the back of Vasily's head stood up. And this was *before* he caught a full glimpse of the person climbing out of the car.

A slim, but still curvy young woman with shoulder-length dark hair appeared. She rocked the shit out of calf-length brown leather cowboy boots and a light-orange dress that umbrellaed around her ass as the evening wind blew just right.

Two perfect ass cheeks covered by peach lacy panties were

gorgeous enough, but they were attached to long, shapely legs which took his breath away. He had a hard time pulling his eyes away from them.

"Well, hello." He moved his head a bit to get a better angle. "You don't look like a Mario."

The woman tried but failed to keep her dress under control as she walked to the gate. Vasily, not normally a fan of the wind, found himself rooting for it.

"Who the fuck are you?"

Then it dawned on him.

"Oh my God," he murmured. He'd known his target's offspring existed, of course. He'd done his homework, but clearly, he'd been remiss and hadn't done enough.

Nicky Marcello was a girl?

"Fuck me." Vasily sucked in air through his teeth as eyes remained glued on her legs. He recalled the details in his file. He hadn't focused on the kid, because he—sorry, *she*—was nineteen and just out of high school. Too young to be of any interest.

He couldn't have been more wrong. Reality just walloped him in the chest. Or more accurately— according to the sudden tightening in his jeans—his twenty-four-year-old and very interested cock.

The girl unlocked, then lifted the rusty gate with practiced ease, opening it just enough to allow the car to fit through. Then she strode back and folded those legs back into that shitty yet valuable Mustang. On the other side, she repeated the process never once looking in his direction.

There was no logical reason for disappointment to wash through him, but he felt like she should've noticed him, given his intense focus on her.

"Nicky Marcello," he whispered, his lip curling in a little grin. He'd said the name before, but this time it slipped off his tongue like crème brûlée—sweet and decadent. If he chose to savor, it would be bad for his health. Like a bullet to the back of his head bad for his health. "What an unwelcome, yet pleasant surprise. I've got a strange feeling settling in my balls that those legs are going to be the end of me."

As if she'd heard him, Nicky stopped suddenly, then looked in his direction. His heart lurched in his chest. He was already slouched low behind the steering wheel of that Toyota Corolla but as she scoped out the street, he slowly slid further down watching her just over the dashboard.

For a good fifteen seconds, she took in the neighborhood. And for those same fifteen seconds, Vasily zoomed in with his camera and snapped a few photos.

At last, she rubbed her arms and shook her head in dismissal. Then she walked back toward the Mustang and climbed in. The door shut, and the reggae riff of Bob Marley was drowned out by the engine's loud hum. Then the hum changed as she put the car into gear and drove behind a stack of squashed autos and out of sight.

"Good girl," Vasily murmured. A strange sense of pride settled around him, which made no sense to him at all. "Your instincts are on point, and mine are telling me I'm liking Uncle Leo's plan less and less. I just need to convince the old bastard of that."

His gaze dropped to his camera as he began to check out the series of photos on the display. He found one that showed her looking straight in his direction, then pressed the little plus sign to expand the image of her face.

It was even prettier than her legs.

"Fuck," he muttered. "I think I'm in deep shit."

Two hours later, Vasily sat in one of the fat leather armchairs in Uncle Leo's office. He folded one ankle over his knee, leaned back, and laced his fingers behind his head. "It's not a good idea, Uncle," he said in Russian. "There's a better way to get a scrapyard. One in a better location and one with a lot less risk."

"What risk are you talking about?" Uncle Leonid barked, his bulky arms bunched over his chest as he scowled across his desk. "I want *that* property because I *like* that location."

Leonid wasn't really his uncle, more a guardian than anything, but he and Dean called him that out of respect. The man took them under his wing when their father went missing, presumed dead. A safe presumption, as Dmitri Melnikov hadn't reappeared, dead or alive in the intervening twelve years.

Leo was short and balding with the beginnings of a gut, but the man was hard. Made so just like their father was by the Gulags in Siberia before they escaped from Soviet Russia. But fortunately for all their sakes, Leo wasn't as cruel.

Nor as wily.

"Why start a war when we don't need to?" Vasily asked. "We can't afford one right now. Our numbers are low and it's safe to bet the Italians are better equipped. Taking that scrapyard will just blow things up."

"That's the point, bro," Dean his older brother argued. He had a stupid, smug grin plastered on his face. "We're trying to get rid of our competition. Get back some of the ground we lost."

This last statement was a dig at Leo. It was under his leadership and poor decisions that they'd lost territory from the Italians. And though he wasn't looking directly at Leo, Vasily saw his nostrils flare and the mean pinch in his eyes at the subtle insult.

It should've been his first clue.

"We need to strike now," Dean added, pushing his luck.

Vasily clenched his jaw. His patience when it came to his brother was in short supply. "Were you not listening? We don't have the muscle or the weapons we need. If we take the scrapyard from Marcello, it's as good as a declaration."

"It's not our fault Marcello's partner likes to gamble." Dean threw his hands in the air. "We need to show that we're not weak-kneed pussies and let idiots like Pavel get away with owing us money."

"What are you suggesting we do then?" Leo asked Vasily before he could counter Dean's point.

"We use finesse."

"Finesse?" Dean laughed. "How do you plan to do that, brother?"

"We do what smart people do. Gather intelligence. Find their weak points and exploit them."

For once Dean had no comeback, and the room was filled with a dark silence. Vasily waited, knowing somebody other than himself would fill it.

"I agree with *Vaseely*." Leo finally stood and cracked his knuckles, pronouncing his name the way a Russian would. "Maybe now isn't the time to strike."

Vasily dropped his hands from behind his head and squinted at Leo. That was almost too easy.

"We *do* need to improve our numbers." Leo moved from behind his desk until he stood in front of Dean. "So, in the meantime, we do what he says."

"You're kidding, right?" Dean asked, his eyes moving between Leo and Vasily.

"*Nyet*. You take the partner Pavel, and Vaseely takes Marcello. Learn everything you can about them."

Dean scoffed, then shook his head. "He's already learned quite a bit about a certain Marcello female. Maybe he wants to make war between the sheets instead."

"Shut up, Dean," Vasily groaned, regretting he'd mentioned the Marcello girl as they had walked together to Leo's office. Or showing him the photos he'd taken of her. For his file, of course.

"Marcello's kid, she's a girl?" Leo focused on him, eyebrows raised.

The fact that Leo hadn't known either made him feel slightly less like a tool. But Dean, the idiot made stupid little kissy noises proving once again, though he was the older brother by two years, Vasily was the mature one.

"Sweet little apple, that one. Wouldn't mind taking a bite myself."

"Shut *up*, Dean."

The immature dick chuckled, which ground on his already frayed nerves, but Leo's scrutinizing gaze was a warning and Dean zipped it.

"You gonna let enemy pussy get in the way of business?"

Vasily bit back a growl. "Of course not, Uncle. Dean's just being an idiot."

"We'll see about that. Anyway, you got no time for pussy now. I've been thinking. We need a man in Moscow."

Moscow?

Leo pointed at Vasily with a thick, blunt finger. "You said yourself our numbers are low. I want to ally with the *Bratva* so we can expand our distribution routes and grow. Make up for our lost pipeline."

Vasily didn't even bother asking why it wasn't Dean he considered sending, as he was the older sibling. His brother had his strengths, but Dean was a hothead, and more likely to piss off an Oligarch by deflowering his daughter and getting himself killed. Dean's dimples had a way of making panties drop, sometimes to his detriment.

"Why not go yourself?" Vasily asked keeping his narrowed gaze on his uncle.

Leo shrugged, not meeting his eyes. "I can't go back to Russia. My name is still on a list somewhere, and I'm needed here. You're a good negotiator. It'll be excellent training for when you both take over."

Vasily's instincts stirred. This was the first time Leo had mentioned any interest in Moscow. Dmitri, Vasily's father had cut ties with the city completely and built this brotherhood from nothing but himself, Leo, and the few men who'd managed to make it to San Francisco after they escaped the Iron Curtain. The timing, though logical in the face of their depleted numbers did nothing to dispel the notion that something seemed...off.

But Moscow?

Vasily watched him for a moment longer, then pushed his uneasiness aside. Perhaps it wasn't that bad of an idea. Despite his Russian heritage, Vasily had never been to the country. A little sightseeing might be fun.

"When do I leave?" he asked. Hopefully not before he got to meet the Marcello girl in person. See if she was as pretty as the camera seemed to show. Even if she wasn't, her legs were worth it. Jesus. He swallowed. What he wanted to do with those.

"Soon, but first I've got to arrange it with Moscow."

"So, it's settled then? We gather information and give Pavel more time to sort out his gambling debts, and in the meantime, avoid a war?"

Leo walked to the window, turning his broad back to them, and shoved his hands in his pockets. "For now."

Vasily blew out a slow breath of air.

"I'll reconsider once we have more intelligence, so Pavel gets a little more time."

Time.

If he'd known exactly what that meant, he'd never have gone to Moscow.

But then you know what they say about hindsight.

Chapter One

There will always be scumbags. It's just the degree of scumbaggery that varies.
~Vasily Melnikov~

T*en Years Later, Present Day*

How does a man regain his soul after taking a life, assuming he had a soul to begin with?

Vasily Melnikov dragged a hand over his scruff and leaned back in his lumbar-support chair. The text he'd spent the better part of his evening waiting for had finally come.

He's ready.

He took a deep breath and blew it out slowly. The text wasn't a welcome one, but he had an example to set. He could not be seen as being weak. Weakness invited trouble, and in his world, inviting trouble resulted in innocent people getting hurt. A lesson he'd learned a long time ago.

His return to San Francisco after ten years in Russia came at a price and was accompanied by painful memories. Every small thing reminded him of her, and they were memories a man like him could not afford to indulge in. Yet all those years ago, they had been the only thing that kept the darkness at bay.

Taking another deep, calming breath, he ejected a silver thumb drive from his chrome and glass desktop. He cracked his calloused knuckles and rolled his neck to ease the tension in his shoulders. Opening the top right drawer of his desk, he retrieved a clunky silver ring that was not designed for decoration, but for doing damage. His father had used it to beat the life out of those he believed had betrayed him. One of those people had been Vasily's mother. Something he'd never forgiven the old asshole for, though it seemed fitting Vasily would be using it on a different abuser of women.

He slipped it on the middle finger of his right hand, then pushed his chair back from his desk and stood.

A moment later, there was a soft tap at his door. His second-in-command and sometime bodyguard entered.

"We good to go?" Yevgeny asked, his solid bulk filling up the doorway.

Vasily nodded and grabbed a small white bag with a big red cross from his desk. "Let's get this done. I need to go to the restaurant after."

"Would that be for business or pleasure?"

Something in Yev's tone made Vasily throw his bodyguard a questioning look. "You worried about me?"

"Nah, just that you've been distracted lately. It's been a while since I've seen you with a woman. Thinking you might have a testosterone buildup. Maybe you need help getting laid."

Vasily smirked and gave Yev's big head a shove. Getting laid had never been Vasily's problem. There were always women that were drawn to the power he wielded and the darkness inside him. Being the boss of a criminal organization had its magnetism, but he wasn't a man who wanted more.

"Need me to round one up for you?" Yev grinned. "Before your balls explode?" There was a mischievous glint in his eyes that shone past the long scar that divided his black eyebrow and continued an inch down his cheek. An ugly and permanent result of coming face-to-face with the broken end of a wine bottle.

"You better watch yours," Vasily pretended to grumble, although he took no offense. "Before I explode *them* with the business end of my boot."

He knew Yev was trying to break the tension and lighten things up before they got to the ugly shit that unfortunately needed doing.

"You're gonna have to take a number," Yev countered, chuckling. "I got several women wanting to do just that."

"Left them unsatisfied as usual?" Vasily led the way across the polished oak floors and fluffy white rugs of his office.

Yev snorted behind him. "Just left them, that's all."

This didn't surprise Vasily. Like himself, Yev had no shortage of willing women. His looks weren't conventional as his face was too craggy to be considered pretty. Standing six foot five in his cowboy boots, his height and size were intimidating to most men, but women were attracted to his swagger.

Vasily locked his office, and they crossed the short hallway to the elevator, and he pushed the down button.

The elevator dinged and a couple of seconds later, the polished brass doors opened. They stepped into a cherry wood encased box lit with soft lighting and a hidden camera that fed to the security room. After pressing his thumb to the digital button marked PG they moved swiftly down to the private garage.

"I know you don't like this kind of shit," Yev said, glancing at Vasily. "And I'm not even sure what it is we're doing with the motherfucker, but you want me to handle it?"

"No," Vasily stated flatly. "Appreciate the offer, but this is something I need to do."

"Understood."

The only way to keep the respect he'd earned from his men since taking over from his brother was to do his own dirty work. "Anything new going on?" he asked.

"A couple of the girls at the escort agency reported a social worker has been sniffing around their web pages."

Vasily quirked a brow. "Doing what exactly?"

"Messaging them, offering her services. Nothing serious as of yet."

Social workers. Vasily didn't mind them. Mostly they were overworked, underpaid, emotionally exhausted individuals trying to do the right thing. He had nothing to worry about. Everything was legal and aboveboard, and he treated the women that worked for him well. They in turn treated him well and worked for him because they wanted to, not because he forced them. When the reins had been handed to him, Vasily had given the girls the option to leave the sex business. Even encouraged them to find other means of gainful employment, but most had chosen to stay.

"Find out who this social worker is, and make sure she's not a cop."

"Will do."

The elevator pinged. They stepped onto the concrete of the private garage where Maxim, his driver waited in a late model black Cadillac Escalade. As they approached, Max exited from the front, walked around the hood, and opened the back passenger door.

"Where to, boss?" he asked in Russian.

"The business on Geary." Yev took the front, Vasily slid across the soft leather seat, and reached for his seatbelt.

The "business" was a butchery they'd acquired recently. The previous owner didn't have cash for the required upgrades demanded by the city of San Francisco and had defaulted on his tax payments. Vasily paid the government in exchange for the deed and now they had a perfect place to rid themselves of unwanted bodies.

"Very good, sir." Max nodded and closed the door.

"The facility has been cleared as I specified?"

Yev nodded but pulled his phone from his pocket anyway. "Double checking with Sasha now."

"Don't need witnesses."

"Goes without saying, boss. You worry too much."

"Hmm." Perhaps he did, but worrying was what had kept him alive.

Fifteen minutes later Max backed the Caddie into a loading bay behind a white cargo van. It was protected by two brick walls on either side, blocking their neighbor's prying eyes or any video cameras that may be pointed in their direction.

Yev led the way while Max remained behind, seating his ass on the front hood facing the street to keep watch. It was a two-story building with no tenants, but tweakers had been known to use it in the past to smoke meth.

They walked through blacked-out glass doors into a musty, paint-chipped area that used to be where meat was sold. Then to a back stairwell leading down to a basement, half of which was a giant refrigerator. The other half was where the meat had been cut and that's where they were headed.

Yev opened a heavy metal door. Entering, the smell hit him. He was a hardened man, but oxidized iron and stale urine still made his stomach churn and brought back more unwelcome memories.

He curled his nostrils and stepped onto what were once pristine white floor tiles. They sloped towards a drain. Similar tiles went halfway up the walls to meet dingy white paint. The ceiling boasted four bright fluorescent lights that illuminated the bland space.

Four other men occupied the room. Three were his soldiers, Sergei, Sasha, and Vadim. They were dressed in dark blue, plastic coveralls and black rubber wellingtons. The fourth man was the reason they were here.

Viktor Sokolov.

Vasily observed him for several seconds, taking in the man as he sat on a metal chair in the middle of the room directly above the drain. A hood covered his face, his hands were zipped tied behind his back and his ankles were restrained to the chair's legs.

Ironic.

He hadn't told his men how to control the prisoner, yet Vasily imagined the situation looked exactly as the private investigator Carmine Niccoterra had described when he'd been held prisoner by this man and his partner several weeks ago. Karma was indeed a mean bitch.

Vasily walked towards Sokolov, his heels clicking on the scuffed tile floor.

He nodded at Vadim, who stepped forward and removed the hood revealing an average face. The only thing of note on it was a long bulbous nose, which was slightly askew.

He'd ordered his men not to touch Sokolov and they hadn't, but it was clear he'd been in the chair for a while. That in itself was torture, and a large wet stain covered the man's groin area.

Sokolov grimaced at the sudden glaring light, then opened his eyes enough to squint at Vasily.

"Viktor Sokolov, do you know who I am?" Vasily asked in Russian.

Sokolov took a moment as his Adam's apple bobbed in his throat, then he nodded. A thin layer of sweat made his forehead shine.

Vasily pulled the thumb drive from his pocket. He walked to a long metal table adorned with the laptop he'd asked Sasha to prepare and placed the white bag he'd brought with him next to it. Sticking the drive into the USB port, he opened a file and set the screen at an angle so Sokolov could view it.

"We're watching a movie, boss?" Sergei asked, scratching at his shaved chin.

"Of a sort, but it's not a fun one." Then he moved his finger on the trackpad and hit start on the video that was stored in the file.

He didn't have to watch it—he'd seen it enough times. But while his men focused on the grainy cell phone video, Vasily paid attention to them as they recognized Sokolov and some of the girls being herded like sheep at auction out of a large delivery truck. He noted how their faces changed when a man with a paunch yielding a whip touched their breasts or between their legs. One of the girls spat at him.

Their rumblings grew when the fat man punched her in the face, and she dropped to the ground. Some of the girls were selected by a woman with her hair in a ponytail, and they were taken into a large, two-storied house. The remaining girls were ordered back into the delivery truck.

That video ended, and Vasily started a second one. This one was clearer. He sensed his men's anger grow, felt the air getting prickly, and saw the ugly, dangerous glances they threw at the man in the chair as they watched it. It showed the conditions the women who had not been chosen in the first video had been kept in. They were horrific and filthy. The condition of the girls when they were rescued was even worse.

Vasily also watched Sokolov.

He saw the moment hope left his face, the moment he knew his death in this room was all but guaranteed.

A stunned silence predominated the room when the second video ended.

Then Yev released a feral growl. "You fucking pile of pig shit." His fists were already tight as he moved his focus from the screen to Sokolov. He drew closer, fury making his face taught and red.

"Not yet, Yevgeny," Vasily ordered in a calm voice, holding a palm up. Yev stopped in his tracks, but barely.

Vasily turned to Sokolov. "This is what I need to know. Who are those people, and where's that house in the first video?" he asked rolling up his sleeves. Then he grabbed another chair and placed it in front of his prisoner.

"I can't tell you." Sokolov glared at him.

"You mean you can. You just won't."

"I don't know anything."

"You're lying."

"Fuck you, pretty boy." There was no vigor in Sokolov's curse, just some level of face-saving.

Vasily snorted and looked to his men. "He thinks I'm pretty."

Yev snarled. "As pretty as those girls you trafficked?"

Sokolov attempted to turn his glare to Yev. It failed, and instead only emphasized the fear beginning to shimmer in his eyes in the face of Yev's rage.

"Here's how this is going to work." Vasily sat in the chair and leaned his forearms on his thighs, hands dangling between his knees. Keeping his voice calm, he said, "You tell me who is involved in that operation. The name of that fat prick with the whip and the woman who takes those girls inside that house. If I'm convinced, you might live. We'll send you back to Russia which is more than you deserve."

Sokolov looked at him. There was a faint glint of defiance shining through his dull eyes. "I can't tell you what I don't know."

Vasily sighed heavily as if the weight of the world was on his shoulders, then he shook his head slowly. "Unfortunately for you, I know you know more than what you're saying. And unfortunately for me, this means I have to get my hands dirty. You see, your foray into sexual slavery on my territory was a stupid thing to do. And one I don't approve of."

"I didn't enslave those girls." Sokolov shook his head, but a slight hint of panic began to show in his voice, raising it in pitch. "I was just the delivery man."

Vasily's nostrils flared as he drew in a slow breath of air.

"Delivery men see a lot of things. So, let's do this one at a time. Maybe that will help. Who's the fat man?"

"Don't know his name."

Vasily struck the soft tissue of Sokolov's knee hard, his clunky silver ring taking point.

The prick yelped and what little color was left in his face turned ashen.

Waiting until Sokolov's breathing evened out, Vasily continued, "Who's the woman?"

"I don't know," he whined. "She's no one."

Another strike and another, louder yelp, this one accompanied by several knee spasms and a moan.

"Stop wasting my time. She took those women into that house to be sold. Who is she?"

Sokolov's breathing became harsher, forcing snot onto his upper lip, which mingled with the blood dribbling from his mouth. "I don't know her."

Vasily punched Sokolov in the balls. An inhuman sound spilled from him, kind of like a breathless keening and he felt, rather than saw his men cringe.

When the keening died down, he said, "How does it feel, coward? Hmm? To be out of control. Have someone do unspeakable things to your body that you neither approve of nor can stop. Those women you raped and sodomized, they're all somebody's sister or child. And now five of those women in that video work for me. So you see, I'm invested. You think they liked it?"

"No, please, I didn't rape them. That was the other men. The woman watched. She got off on it. I...I never...I only transported them."

Vasily slipped his tongue between his upper lip and teeth, then sucked. "And kept them prisoner in a dirty stable with a single blanket and a stinking Porta-potty. Women will not be traded nor imprisoned on my territory. Now, who is the fat man with the whip?"

"I don't..."

"Know." Vasily finished for him and sighed. He shook his head, then stood and looked at Vadim. "This is getting repetitive. You got what I asked you to bring?"

"Right here." Vadim patted a weighted-down pocket in the rear of his coveralls.

Vasily walked to the table and the small white bag. From it, he removed a pair of latex gloves and a clear plastic raincoat. He took his time donning the garment, letting Sokolov's imagination stew. Then he snapped on the gloves and held out his hand. Vadim reached behind his back and produced a pair of pruning shears, placing them in his boss's hand.

"What're you gonna do with those?" Sokolov's panic pitched his voice higher.

Vasily glanced at his crotch and shrugged. "What do you think?"

"No...no, please." Viktor started to sob when he saw the crescent-shaped blades. "No, fuck no."

"Cut his pants open. I'm going to relieve this prick of his prick."

Yev produced a small pocket knife from his jeans and moved closer to do as ordered.

Sokolov turned whiter. Sweat dripped from his forehead and he twisted against his restraints.

"No, no, no, *nooo*." He attempted to kick his legs, but the force against the restraints made the chair skid inches across the floor.

"Please, oh fuck, please. Okay, *okay*! Sokolov yelled. "I'll give you their names. The men are Kai and Bob."

Now they were getting somewhere. He already knew about Kai, but the fat man was still a mystery.

"Bob who?"

"I don't know!" Sokolov shook, gulping air in between sobs. "It's just Bob. I only met him once. Please don't cut my cock off."

"Then tell me what I want to know. Who is the woman?"

"Fuck, okay." Sokolov sobbed, his head hanging forward. "Her name is Mar...Mari...sol."

At fucking last—Marisol Price.

The name jived with that of the woman that had led Carmine Niccoterra into a trap. Seems she was more than just the girlfriend of the man named Kai. Silently he hoped the feds got to the bitch before he did because if he ever met her in person, it would get ugly.

Really ugly.

"Tell me more about this Bob. Any little detail will do."

"I think he owns that house. I don't know them well. I met Marisol a few times with Kai and she's not the kind of woman you spend time talking to. She scares me."

"More than me?"

"Jesus, Jesus...*please*."

"I don't think Jesus is going to help you." He slapped the shears into his other palm and pretended to study them carefully, testing the spring. After a couple of squeezes, he flicked off a piece of imaginary dirt. "You're beyond redemption. And the house is where?"

"Oh man, oh fuck it's...it's a few miles inland from Eureka."

Northern California. He nodded at that because it made sense. It wasn't too far from the small biker town of Sawmill where all the shit had gone down with Carmine and where the girls had been rescued from.

"How do they bring the girls in?" he asked, using the point of the shears to clean his nails.

"They ship them in from a tanker and drop them off at a marina. We collect them from there and drive them to the house."

"I need directions."

"There's a road off 101 that heads into trees. Lots of trees. That's all I know, I swear. It was dark when we drove in, and I had no clue where we were. I just followed some GPS coordinates. They're on my phone."

Vasily looked at Vadim questioningly. Vadim shook his head in the negative. "Don't have his phone."

Hm. He sucked more air through his teeth. How unfortunate.

Vasily moved closer and used the sharp end of the shears to tilt the man's chin. Making his eyes go cold, he stared into Sokolov's. "Anything else you want to add?"

"That's it. I swear. I'm sorry. I'm so fucking sorry. I got sucked in, I didn't know they were selling girls."

"You didn't know." Vasily raised his brows, disbelieving.

"I didn't..."

He stopped speaking when his eyes landed on Yev screwing a silencer onto a gun, then handed it to Vasily.

"What are you doing? You said..."

"I lied." Vasily pointed the weapon at Sokolov, and his men were smart enough to move out of splatter range. "First bullet I put in you is for the women you helped kidnap from their homelands, abused, raped, and sold to be further abused and raped. Got anything to say?"

"No...please."

Vasily shot him in the crotch. Sokolov screamed. The area between his legs exploded, the bullet punching a hole through the chair, destroying a tile, and embedding it into the concrete below.

Nausea crept up into Vasily's throat as blood spurted and soiled his raincoat, but he swallowed it back. Contrary to what most people believed of the reputation he'd earned, he didn't enjoy killing. However, he couldn't let Sokolov go. Nor could they keep him any longer, it was too risky. Too many of those girls' lives depended on him disappearing. While Vasily waited for Sokolov's screams to turn to pants, he pointed the barrel to his heart. Sokolov was staring at the red patch between his legs that used to be his cock and balls. It formed a fat rivulet snaking to the drain in front of his chair.

"Look at me," he ordered.

Sokolov obeyed, his breathing was labored as the blood ran from his body, yet his eyes were wide and glazed with shock.

"The next bullet is for the two women you dropped into a fire bunker in the woods, leaving them to die. One of those women, I know personally."

Sokolov remained silent, death and defeat written all over him.

"You needed to know that before you head to hell." He pulled the trigger. The bullet entered Sokolov's chest, then exploded from his back like a burst watermelon showering the wall behind. The chair toppled, and the man's head hit the tile with a dull thud. The stench of cordite, blood, and burnt flesh filled the room.

Vasily stared at what remained of the man for a long moment, feeling empty and soulless before engaging the safety. He tested the temperature on the suppressor before unscrewing it and sticking the gun in the waistband of his pants. It was warm, but not enough to burn or even be uncomfortable. He would not hand the piece back until it was thoroughly cleaned. A cleaning he'd do himself. No need to leave prints or DNA on a weapon that could come back to bite him in the ass. With that same reasoning, he retrieved both mangled bullets. Digging them out with the tips of the shears—one from the floor and the other from the wall.

"You mind cleaning this up?" he asked after removing the scrubs and gloves, then dropping them into a garbage bag and the bullets into his pockets.

Vadim nodded. "Those girls could be our sisters, boss. They deserve the justice you handed them. Federal prison would've been too easy for that prick."

Vasily nodded, but it was a small consolation for the loss of his soul. Though truthfully, his soul had been taken a long time ago. Ejecting the thumb drive from the laptop, he dropped it in his pocket. "*Spasibo*," he said to his men who were already preparing Sokolov's body for disposal.

They acknowledged, then he and Yev left the room to walk back to the Cadillac.

"Jesus, I had no idea," Yev murmured when they climbed into the back seat. His forehead was lined with anger equal to Vasily's. "The girls haven't talked about it."

"Can you blame them?"

"No."

Who wanted to relive that? He understood that kind of trauma all too well.

Yev shook his head and exhaled. "Where did you get those videos?"

Vasily glanced sideways at his Number Two. "From a source who knew I'd do something about it." He wasn't prepared to give up the name of the private investigator, Carmine Niccoterra, just yet.

It wasn't that he didn't trust Yev, he did. It was that certain aspects of that trafficking ring weren't clear yet. And until they were, he'd keep things close.

"I need a drink," he told Max as he climbed into the back seat of the Cadillac. "Take us to the restaurant."

Chapter Two

Intuition is a funny thing and it didn't strike Nicky like a comic-book bolt of lightning. More like a gradual awareness, a gentle skin prickling that raised the fine hairs on the back of her neck beneath her dark layered bob.

Still, she paused as she exited *The Happy Clam's* powder room, her hands smelling of the gardenia soap she'd washed them with. It was a silly name for a serious restaurant—a Michelin-starred one no less—but had become popular of late and the waterfront location couldn't be beaten.

The sense that something was suddenly different tickled her awareness. There seemed to be a slight change in the energy, much like when a loved one entered the room. Nothing dramatic. Nothing that caused alarm, spiked the adrenaline, or screamed *look out*!

It should've.

"Too much champagne, Andretti." She shuddered and rubbed the skin on her arms to rid herself of the sensation. "And probably not enough food."

The lights were low and *Couldn't Stop Caring by* Spiritual

Machines poured through the restaurant, infusing the diners with a pleasant mix of human happiness and mood music. She blew a soft raspberry and started through the restaurant, scanning the faces seated at neatly arranged tables loaded with aromatic food.

She noticed a couple of celebrities. A news anchor from a local channel and at a different table, a Grammy-winning drummer of an alternative rock band. Somehow, she'd managed to catch his eye. He smiled when she walked past his table, shaggy black hair, dimples, and small gold hoops in each ear on full display.

Well, that explains it.

She grinned back, relaxing somewhat. Celebrity energy vibrated at a higher level than regular humans. It's what ultimately drew people to them.

Continuing on, she was about to cross the threshold onto the patio which hung over the San Francisco Bay water's edge. Dotted lights reflected from nearby watercraft lent its ambiance and the feeling intensified.

Again, she paused. Perhaps another famous person was in their midst? It wasn't unheard of, considering the restaurant's popularity and gorgeous views of the bay. Her eyes shifted, searching the faces of the crowd when her gaze got stuck on a man. His head was tilted slightly as he appeared to be listening to somebody shorter than him.

It was dark out, and though the lighting was soft and flattering, he was kind of hard to miss. Not just due to his stature, or the way he was built, all six foot plus of broad shoulders and a lean, narrow waist. The kind of man whose presence set hearts aflutter with a casual, yet consequential sexuality. Added to that, an air of dangerous authority draped him like a comfortable jacket even though he wore none.

Nicky looked closer, trying to see if she'd recognize him, because a man like him, in a place like this would be...well, consequential.

Huh.

There was something familiar about that cock of his head, and about that stance—confident and in charge. He reminded her of...

Unbidden, the specter of a time in her past she'd struggled for long, heartbreaking months to put to rest lurched forward. It rushed up hard and fast, sucking the air from her chest.

No!

She blinked to clear her eyes, because yeah, she'd drunk her share of alcohol, but she was nowhere close to being impaired. If anything, the adrenaline shooting through her veins heightened her senses and ensured she wasn't.

Fuck, no!

It couldn't be...could it?

She needed to be sure, though only the devil knew why, because her organs felt as if they were tumbling over themselves, and her legs didn't want to work properly.

But she had to. With her heart stuck in her throat, she inched out of the restaurant proper through wide-open sliding doors. She nudged past a couple next to a large potted lemon tree strung with white fairy lights. Staying behind the lemon tree, she craned her neck to get a better look. Between them was the short man, and a mountainous one in a dark shirt tucked into jeans. He was enough of a barrier to hide behind, or to make a quick getaway should she be spotted.

Or faint.

Whichever happened first.

The hum of conversation around them was loud, but she was close enough to catch snippets of what the shorter man was saying. "I appreciate your partnership, and..." The short man said a few more words she couldn't hear, then he clapped his hands together into the prayer position. "Please, stay for dinner. I can get a table sorted quickly."

Then one of those weird, strange lulls in conversation that

sometimes occurred in crowds happened. Long enough for Nicky to hear him respond.

"Thank you, Jones, but we've had a long day."

Goosebumps erupted on her skin. Even if she never got to see his face, there was no mistaking his voice.

"Just a drink will be all."

Deep and commanding, the timbre carried the suggestion of sin, as it had long ago when he'd whispered sinful words against her neck. Even now her nipples puckered. And if that didn't confirm it, the dent in his chin, those sculpted lips, and gently hollowed cheeks did. Just a few of the things on that devilishly beautiful face she'd once been so attracted to.

And now hated.

How fucking dare he?

An avalanche of emotions swamped her, speeding up her palpitating heart. How dare he step back into her world? Where had he come from?

For ten years most people presumed him dead. But Satan, if you believed the lore, never died. There was a time she'd wished he had until she'd set his memory aside like a pair of dirty socks.

But there he stood.

Breathing.

And looking down that Slavic nose at an establishment that was now painfully obvious it at least partially belonged to him.

She wanted to scream. Hurl herself at him and do damage. Serious, deadly, *painful* damage, hurting him the way he'd hurt her.

She took a shallow, shuddery breath. Then another and counted to five and repeated the process. Her fingers itched to snatch a steak knife from the nearest table and stab him. Unfortunately, the place was too public, with too many witnesses and she had her little boy to think about now.

Vasily Melnikov, that lying, insensitive, cold bastard would remain uninjured...for now.

Without realizing it, she took another step closer, glaring at his profile. It surprised her he didn't feel its fire charring his skin.

But the mountainous man in front of her did. He turned, then placing himself directly between herself and Vasily, folded his arms.

"Can I help you?" he asked in a voice that matched his craggy, scarred face. His brown eyes were wary, but his solid stance was wide and protective.

So Vasily had a bodyguard. Lucky for him.

"Don't mind me," she uttered in a tight voice, her throat at risk of closing. It annoyed her that it didn't come out as strong as she'd like, but at least she could still speak. "Just saw something distasteful."

The bodyguard grunted, giving her a scrutinizing once-over. Once his examination was complete, he stayed put, staring her down like he didn't believe her. But bodyguards by default were skeptical and if she were him, she wouldn't move either.

"Lady, you need to step back."

Lady?

"Excuse me?" Who the hell did this mountain think he was? "Oh, I'm sorry, am I blocking your view?"

He snorted at her sarcasm, but then a stir in the air to her left, like a small tornado had touched down, shifted his attention.

A tall, emaciated woman with long platinum hair pulled up in a sophisticated ponytail approached in a flash of metallic ice blue.

Good God.

Another celebrity? This place was crawling with them.

Sunny, the svelte, yet notorious Swedish supermodel glided towards them. Her eyes, the same color as her dress, (undoubtedly contacts), were focused solely on that fucking Russian. As if still on the runway she'd made her name on, the woman paraded on heels dotted with bling and designed to impale rather than walk on. According to the daytime gossip shows, she had a thing for bad boys. Foregoing the usual endorsements of flawless makeup brands and flowery perfumes, Sunny chose dark, like her men.

Well, congratulations—she'd found Satan.

While the model's flash drew everyone's attention, including hers, it was just moments later when she noticed a tingling beginning on her scalp. It moved down her neck like a whisper of hot breath or a lover's caress.

That too was dangerously familiar.

He'd seen her. She knew because his gaze had the same arousing effect it always had when he'd looked at her before. Except this time the arousing was not sexual, it was of anger.

Taking a moment to steel herself for impact, she turned slowly and scowled directly into the silvery-gray eyes of the man who destroyed her life.

For five full seconds, their gazes locked.

Some unknown emotion flickered in his. He gave a little squint, but whatever it had been slowly changed until it turned into...nothing. She'd expected to see regret perhaps. Guilt...shock? But other than a single tick of his jaw his expression was impassive, then he blinked and shifted his attention to the oncoming bombshell.

Just like that, he'd dismissed her.

It felt like a slap to the face, and after what he'd done? Broken her and left her to piece her life back together shard by shard, each sliver slicing deeper. But then again, how could she expect anything more? The man was a deceiver. A criminal with a black heart and no space in his memory for those he'd wronged.

Tears of rage stung the back of her eyes.

Luca.

Think of Luca. He's all that matters. He doesn't deserve to have a mother in prison. Before she did something stupid, like stab him, she made a sharp turn, crunching her heel on the bodyguard's foot.

"*Blyad,*" he grunted but limped aside and gave her space.

Fuck Vasily Melnikov to hell and back.

Two could play his game. He didn't want to acknowledge her? Well, she wasn't going to humiliate or embarrass herself in a public space by giving him any more of her energy. He wasn't worth it.

Shaking, she somehow managed to keep it together and not fall off her strappy heels as she walked between happy couples and exuberant singles waving colorful cocktails like airport beacons.

"Took you long enough," Soren said as she approached their table. They'd known each other since their teens and if anyone knew the pain that man had caused, it was Soren. Fortunately, they were seated on the opposite end of the dining patio, giving her a chance to dial it back a bit. This wasn't the night to create drama.

"I thought you got...hell's bells, Nick!" Soren's eyes went round. "Uh-oh, you look like you want to kill someone."

Nicky held up one hand. "Just give me a second," she murmured and snatched her glass from the table and downed the remaining bubbly. Placing the glass down with deliberate care, she took her seat closest to the plexiglass partition. She was glad it was there as she was shaking so hard, there was nothing else preventing her from toppling into the murky waters of the bay. While her friends stared, she refilled her glass from the bottle in a silver bucket at the center of their table. Almost knocking over the candle in the process.

"Honey?" Terrence, tired of waiting, joined in the query, sending one professionally manicured brow higher on his coffee-toned face. "Soren's right. Something happen?"

Nicky pulled in a breath, and for a moment debated telling them, but this was Terrence's night. They were celebrating his new leading role with a prestigious theatre group, and he didn't need her drama. Then again, Terrence thrived on drama—it was his profession. But the questions. There would be a million and that she wasn't ready for.

"It's nothing." She waved it away. "Just thought I saw a ghost."

"The ghost of an ex-lover?" Terrence asked only half joking.

Nicky swallowed, balking at calling Vasily her lover. They'd had sex, yes, many times, but 'lover' implied feelings were involved. And as far as *he* was concerned, it was never more obvious there had been none.

"Nobody that important."

"Not important?" Soren flipped her naturally flaxen hair—a gift of her Scandinavian heritage—over her shoulder. "You're going to have to be more specific, sweetie, because I don't believe you. Point us in the right direction. I need to get a gander at who this ghost is."

"He's gone," Nicky lied. Her eye began to twitch. She just wanted them to drop it. Soren had been there when it happened, and she wouldn't be above causing a scene. First, Nicky needed to process, and armor herself. If she chose to confront him, it would be on her terms.

"Pity." Terrence chuckled. "I'd like to see the man that made you look like that, but I do spy that wench, Sunny."

Oh...*shit!*

"You can hardly miss that gaudy outfit." He craned his neck. "Doesn't she know electric blue died when Disco did?"

"Apparently it's made a comeback," Nicky quipped, grabbing the bottle of champagne to divert their attention away from the supermodel and those around her. "Who wants more?"

"In a sec, sweetie. I need to see more of that godawful outfit." Terrence adjusted his satin rainbow shirt before twisting for a better view. He stiffened mid-twist and jerked his head back.

"Oh, hold the phone!" he gasped. "Are you shitting me? *Who* is that delicious creature she's poured onto?"

Nicky pressed a finger to her twitching eye.

Soren, always on the hunt for *her* next ex, turned, then consequently jerked in her seat. After several beats, she turned back to Nicky, then back to *him*. "Is that...no fucking way. *Satan's* your ghost?"

Nicky nodded squeezing the eye that was twitching shut. It didn't help.

"Okay," Terrence demanded. "Somebody explain. Who is Satan?"

"That demon spawn you consider delicious. Our girl had multiple encounters with him—of the sack kind."

Terrence's eyes widened in glee, then he made a show of fanning his face. "I might want one of those."

"No, trust me, you wouldn't." Nicky countered, shaking her head.

"Oh, call me craven, sweetie, but certain well-endowed parts of me think I would. He's wasted on Sunny."

"Holy fucking wow," Soren murmured. "I can't believe this. I'm sorry, Nick." She reached for Nicky's hand, squeezing it. "What a bizarre coincidence."

"Again, bitches! Explain why I shouldn't be attracted to that?"

"Terrence, maybe now's not the time," Soren suggested, her eyes darting between them.

"It's fine." Terrence wasn't just her neighbor in the same crappy apartment building. He was part of her inner circle, and it wasn't fair to leave him hanging with no details. May as well get it over with. She gently extracted her hand from Soren's grip.

"Like Soren said. A long time ago he pursued me."

When she said nothing more, he gave a little head shake and flopped open palms in the air. "And this was a problem how?"

Nicky swallowed, her throat feeling tight again as the pain of that time resurfaced. "It wasn't me he wanted. I was just a means to an end."

"Oooh," Terrence groaned, his expression turning into a grimace. And he was a good enough friend he must've read her expression and didn't ask for further explanation. "Honey, I'm sorry, that's harsh. Maybe one day you'll tell me?"

Maybe, when it didn't hurt so much. "What's he doing?" she asked, to take the attention off herself. She was beginning to feel hot and prickly, like the spotlight Terrence thrived under had landed on her instead.

Terrance glanced over her shoulder, then he popped his lips. "Staring at a beautiful lady in a sexy black dress."

"Stop it."

"Not joking, honey. The man's eyes are glued to you."

Nicky froze staring at Terrence. Now that he mentioned it, the crisscrossing spaghetti straps between her shoulder blades felt like they were on fire and burning lines into her flesh. Her palms got sweaty, and she clutched her dress at her sides.

She would not turn around.

Fuck him.

"Let's do shots," Nicky said, and flagged their waitress down, who just happened to be passing. Screw the inevitable hangover. If she was going to get through the rest of this night, champagne wasn't nearly strong enough.

She looked at Terrence pointedly. "No more about me, this is *your* night. We're here to celebrate you, so let's do it."

"Amen, bitches." Terrence grinned and did a little drumroll on the table, making the silverware rattle. "Tequila it is."

An hour later when they called for the bill, their waitress politely told them there wasn't one.

"What do you mean, we have no bill?" Nicky asked looking up at her.

"Compliments of the house," she said with a bright smile. "Our management randomly picked a table for free meals and complimentary service, and yours is the winner. Congratulations."

Nicky stared at her, eyes narrowed in suspicion. "Which manager was this? We'd like to say thank you."

"Oh." The waitress waved them off. "He's already left for the evening, so there's no need."

Then before she could ask for the manager's name, so she could thank him in the future, (though she was pretty sure she'd never come to this restaurant again) the waitress scurried away.

Nicky shook her head and looked at her friends. They were staring at her.

Son of an asshole!

"Complimentary service, my ass," Soren murmured, giving Nicky a sideways glance. "Seems like Satan was feeling generous. Girl, I've got a funny feeling about this."

Funny or bad? Either one, Nicky couldn't agree more.

Chapter Three

"Bye, Buddy." Nicky dropped down to Luca's level, wincing at her pounding head. Multiple rounds of shots at *The Happy Clam* had seemed like a good idea at the time, but her suffering brain would say not so much. And it hadn't helped keep thoughts of *him* at bay.

She hugged him and whispered in his ear. "Have a good day at school, yeah?"

Fridays were bittersweet. On one hand, she enjoyed the small amount of freedom it gave her, but on the other, he spent weekends with Anthony. That brought its own bag of worries. And though he was five, it still hurt to let him go, even if it was only for the weekend. "Daddy will pick you up as usual after school. I'll see you on Sunday, okay?"

"Do I have to go, Mom?"

"You do, Buddy." She frowned and straightened his plain blue tee-shirt. "Daddy misses you. Don't you want to spend time with him?"

"He's always working. And sometimes a strange lady comes to the house."

Nicky's brows scrunched together. "What do you mean

'strange lady'?"

"She comes after I go to bed, and they make funny noises in Daddy's room. Like his tummy hurts and he wants to throw up."

Nicky bit her lip. *Hell's fucking bells.*

"Is he sick?"

She let out a measured sigh. Separated almost six months and still Anthony's inability to keep it in his pants made her angry, just not in the same way it used to. Besides the fact she got an STD because of his screwing around—okay, that she'll never forgive him for—but really? The man couldn't abstain over the weekend when his son was with him. A not so pleasant reminder her ex was a dick.

"No, honey, Daddy's not sick."

"He doesn't have cancer? Charlie's Mom has cancer and she's got no hair. She wears one of those things on her head to hide it."

"That sucks about Charlie's mom, but Daddy doesn't have cancer, I promise you. I'll talk to him, but we've got to get you inside. You don't want to be late again, right? Miss Mulligan will give me the evil eye." Nicky made a face.

Luca giggled. "That's just the way she looks."

"She does? Are you sure about that?" she joked.

"Uh-huh."

"Okey-dokey. I'll give her the benefit of the doubt, but only because you say so. Love you to Betelgeuse baby."

"Love you too, Mommy."

She laid a kiss on the top of his dark, silky head, then ruffled his over-long curls. "Have fun. I'll see you on Sunday."

"'Kay."

As she watched him skip to his class, his little blue overnight backpack bouncing on his small body, she pushed to her feet and smoothed down her chocolate-colored maxi dress.

"Mrs. Andretti?"

Dang. Only one person at the preschool called her that. The owner.

"Hey, Melanie. How's it going?"

"We have a problem." Nicky tried to pay no attention to the judgmental eye cast over her scuffed brown leather cowboy boots. In her opinion, the woman had a stick stuck so far up her ass, she could chew on it. The only reason Luca was at this particular overpriced preschool was Anthony insisted on it. "May we have a word in my office?"

God, what now? Going by her tone, it sounded serious. Nicky sighed and pushed her hair behind her ear.

"Is this about that fight Luca had last week? With the kid who took his Nintendo from his backpack?" She'd already talked to Luca about it after the phone call she got from Miss Evil Eye Mulligan.

"I'm afraid this is something different." Melanie said this holding her office door open. Nicky entered, then followed her stick-up-the-ass mince to her desk.

"Since you brought it up, I'm sure by now you're aware electronic toys are not allowed at the school."

"I am aware. He wasn't playing with it, but I'm sure *you're* aware, it was in his backpack because he was spending the weekend with his dad, as always. And that little boy had no right to go into Luca's private property."

Melanie Armstrong-Smythe sniffed, then sat. "Please take a seat."

"I'd rather stand, thank you. I don't have much time. What's this about?"

"You understand we have a code of conduct at Tiny Titans."

"Of course."

"Well, then you're aware that cursing is not allowed. Luca has on more than one occasion uttered the 'F' word which is unacceptable. He called one of the other boys in his class—and I quote—an effing moron. Except he didn't say effing."

"Oh?" Nicky cringed inwardly but kept it off her face. At least, this time it wasn't a fight.

"When I asked where he heard such language he said from his

father. Furthermore, I can attest to this as I witnessed Mr. Andretti using such language when he was on his cell phone speaking loudly enough that other children and parents could hear. Not minding Luca either, by the way."

Nicky arched a brow. "Did you bring this up with Anthony?"

"I wasn't able to." Melanie's eyelashes flickered a moment before she broke eye contact.

Chickenshit.

Although to be fair, Anthony in a mood could be intimidating, no doubt as a result of defending criminals in court for so many years, so she gave the woman a reluctant pass.

But Melanie continued, "You are aware your son is still in probationary status?"

"Yes, ma'am."

"Then consider this your first warning. I will be putting this in Luca's file, and you will be receiving written notification by mail that you have been warned. We cannot accept such behavior here at Tiny Titans. I hope we understand each other."

"In his file? Are you serious? This is preschool and he's five."

"We may provide pre-Kindergarten education, but I assure you, we are a professional organization and run it as such. We have standards, and if you don't like them, there are plenty of other children on the waiting list who would love to have his place."

Nicky's jaw clenched. What she wanted was to tell Melanie Armstrong-Smythe to fuck herself with the same stick stuck up her ass. But what she did instead, and only because she didn't need it to blowback on her son, was nod again. The last thing Luca needed was the stigma of being expelled from this preppy school.

Though she had nothing against other, less snobby preschools, she did agree with Anthony on this one thing. She wanted her son to get a head start. And Luca was secured the place simply because they'd placed him on the waiting list when he was eighteen months old and made a sizable donation.

"Understood. Have a good day, Melanie." She adjusted her hippy-style purse strap and turned to leave.

"There's something else."

"There is?"

"There's the matter of his tuition."

"What about it?"

"You are two months in arrears."

What? Her jaw dropped. "It hasn't been paid?"

"You must be aware that we cannot allow that to continue. Either the school is made whole, or Luca will have to vacate his place."

"Wait, I don't understand. How can it not have been paid? Nobody informed me of this."

This was Anthony's responsibility, according to their separation agreement. Had they informed him?

"Are you sure?"

"Absolutely, Mrs. Andretti. You were sent an email, and hard copies were mailed to the address on file."

Shit. She must have missed it. "I'll sort it. Thank you for telling me," she murmured feeling sick to her stomach that had nothing to do with her hangover.

"The thing is it needs to be paid by no later than today."

Nicky's eyebrows shot to the roof.

"Today is the first of the month and tuition is due the first of every month, and since you're already two months behind and if it's not paid today that would make it three. Which is unacceptable and grounds for expulsion."

Nicky squeezed her eyes shut and pressed her fingers to her temple. She could do some serious harm to Anthony for putting her in this position.

"I'll make sure it gets paid," she said. Even if she had to clear out her savings, which wasn't much.

A heavy ball of bitterness sat in her gut as she walked back to the parking lot. With her focus on her internal tirade, it took her a minute to notice the man on the opposite side of the street. He leaned against the driver's-side door of a red truck, his ankles crossed.

His vibe was so menacing, it set her antenna to high alert. Hocus-pocus aura readings were Soren's thing, and if her friend were here, she'd say this dude's aura was so dark, it bordered on black. Nicky would have to agree.

He nodded when she made eye contact and something in the way he did told her he was there for her. Paranoia, and perhaps intuition, had made her feel like this once before like she was being followed. Weirdly, it was after Vasily had disappeared. But then her father had just been arrested and incarcerated and she'd written it off as the cops hoping to catch her doing something illegal.

This was probably Anthony having her watched again.

She considered approaching the man and telling him where to get off, but what if she was wrong? Antagonizing him wouldn't be smart. Beeping the locks on her Audi, she slipped into her seat. After relocking and keeping one eye on the man against the truck, she opened her phone and found Anthony's number.

The man turned slightly as if looking at something, or someone further down the street and it was then she noticed he had large holes in his earlobes where ear gauges should be.

"What do you want?" Anthony asked by way of greeting—or was it grunting? He sounded exactly like he was in the middle of boning somebody. She knew this having been on the receiving end of said boning for a significant portion of her adult life. "I'm busy."

"Well, then dear ex-husband, why bother answering?"

He grunt-laughed. "I'm not your ex-husband yet, Nick."

Yeah. Unfortunately. And the purpose of answering mid-bone was to remind her that though she'd been celibate during their separation, admittedly not out of choice, he certainly wasn't.

Fine, if he didn't care, cringe factor aside, why should she?

"I just got reamed out by Melanie."

"Who?"

"Tiny Titan's owner, Anthony."

"Dammit, what the fuck did you do now?"

"Oh, my God! *I* didn't do anything. She reamed me out for *your* bad behavior. Like cursing in front of the kids. If he continues, it's more grounds for getting kicked out of the school. Not a great example you're setting for your son."

Anthony's loud sigh reached across the cellular waves, and there was some kind of shuffling noise in the background. Nicky listened closely and determined it was a woman complaining. Probably one of his legal aids, but hopefully not Gail, his receptionist. She was the only person in his office Nicky liked or even talked to.

"Give me a minute," she heard Anthony say to the anonymous woman. "I'm talking to my wife."

Nicky put her hand to her forehead and shook her head. He was unbelievable. Hopefully, her phone call had made him lose his boner.

"What do you mean *more* grounds?" His voice rumbled in her ear.

"Well, let's see. According to Melanie, we're three months behind in tuition."

"What...*fuck*."

"It needs to be paid today, Anthony. Otherwise, they'll boot Luca from the school."

There was a heavy silence for several long seconds. Then he muttered, "I'll talk to her."

"Just watch how you do that, please. You'll put a target on Luca's back. He doesn't need that."

"You want my help or not?"

Not really, but it was Antony's problem to fix, so she ignored his question. "Also, while I have you on the phone, you haven't paid child support either."

"Well, if you came home, you wouldn't need child support, now, would you?"

Oh, good God. She looked at the ceiling of her car. "We're not starting this again. We have an agreement, and you're the one breaking it."

"You'll get it when I'm ready to give it to you." There was another muffling noise and then Anthony's voice from a distance. "What're you doing? Where are going?"

Then the female voice. "You're talking to your wife."

"Yeah, so?"

"Jesus, Anthony!" The woman said. "I'm not into..."

"Anthony!" Nicky hit her phone on her steering wheel several times to get his attention. Though hearing one of his women ditch his ass mid-bone was semi-amusing, she didn't need to hear it.

"*Anthony!*"

"What?"

"You owe it to your son to pay on time. It's not fair to Luca I have to juggle things like this. When you don't pay, I work extra hours, which means I must pay Faviola for extra babysitting. It's a lose-lose for me. I need you to follow through on both the tuition and child support. Preferably before you pick him up."

"All right," he grumbled. "I'll transfer the money in a minute."

"Thank you."

There was silence and she was just about to hang up, when he said, his voice contrite, "Come home, Nick."

Did he really just say that? She couldn't stop the eye roll and it hurt her still suffering brain.

"Are you serious?"

"We can make this work."

She scoffed. "And you think answering the phone while you're getting laid is a good way to make it work?"

"I always answer when you call. She's nothing and I wouldn't need her if you come back."

His bipolar mood swings were nothing new, and he'd used this tactic before. Made her believe, and she'd fallen for it.

"This garbage no longer works, Anthony." She hung up.

Damn him!

She tossed her phone onto the seat next to her, then slapped her steering wheel with both hands several times.

Why did this upset her still? It shouldn't. She'd fallen out of love a long time ago when the cheating began after Luca was born. But there was a time he'd been her hero, the man who'd saved her from heartache, and she mourned the loss of that man. She also mourned the loss of her marriage because it hadn't all been bad. But whatever it had been, was long gone.

Pinching the bridge of her nose, she squeezed her eyes shut trying to stop the tears. Several rolled down her cheeks anyway and she let them fall. Let them cleanse her. After a moment she swiped them away with her thumb, then took several deep yoga breaths.

He was not going to wear her down. It didn't matter how hard things got, it was her nature to fight. Maybe now it was time to finally get that lawyer.

The red truck was still there, and the man had moved into the driver's seat. His face wasn't visible through the glare on the window, but it didn't need to be. She could feel him watching her.

Quickly, she thumbed a text to her ex. *Call off your damn watchdog!*

Without waiting for an answer, she retrieved her phone from the passenger seat and placed it into her purse, then turned the Audi's engine over. Thankfully it was paid off and in her name. One less thing he could take from her.

She hit the drive-through coffee bar, ordering an iced caramel macchiato and a banana. Next on her list was their weekly grocery shopping, and after lugging that upstairs to her second-floor apartment, she unpacked. Then sat on her purple velour couch that she'd scored for relatively cheap at a consignment store. It was good quality and matched her lavender walls.

Marley, her fat, one-eyed ginger cat, lay on the backrest swishing his tail at the disruption. Nicky ignored him and fired up her laptop.

Researching divorce lawyers was tedious, but she persisted until she had a list of ten names.

She started calling. It was after the fourth "I'm sorry, ma'am, I'm not taking any new clients at this time," she got it and flat out asked, "Is it just me, Mr. Garcia, or are you full for everyone?"

"I'm sorry, Mrs. Andretti," the man answered with a long sigh. "I have been informed if I represent Anthony Andretti's wife, *I* will no longer *have* a wife."

What?

"Are you kidding me?" Her mouth dropped open. "You're going to let a lying piece of crap criminal lawyer threaten you into *not* taking me as a divorce client? That can't be legal!"

"Not just any criminal lawyer, ma'am. I'm aware of some of Andretti's clients. They're unsavory specimens and I'm really sorry. It's just not worth the risk to me or my family."

Well, fucking fuck.

"Fine, and thanks for at least having the testicles to let me know. Nobody else would."

She didn't bother to finish the last of her sandwich as her appetite had disappeared with her hopes of finding a decent lawyer. So, she called Soren.

"I need help."

"Tell me something new, babe," Soren chuckled.

"This is new." Nicky twisted then lay back on the plush orange cushions on her couch and propped one arm behind her head, and one calf on her knee. "I need a divorce lawyer. A good one."

"OMG!" Soren yelled, and Nicky winced at what it did to the remnants of her hangover. Marley, mewled above her, seeming to agree with Soren's exuberance.

"Finally, the woman has grown some sense. What changed your mind?"

"Child support, or lack thereof." Nicky toed off one of her boots and let it fall to the floor. "I can't afford this shit anymore, but the sad thing is I can't afford a lawyer either. I'm also starting to reevaluate leaving Luca with him, Sor. He told me this morning he didn't want to go to his dad's."

"Why not?"

As Nicky removed her second boot, she explained the reason and shared the talk with Melanie in her office.

"I mean," Soren said, "that just reiterates what we all know about Anthony. What an asshole answering the phone while he was doing his bitch. Girl, he's just trying to get a rise out of you."

"Yep, figured as much." Marley stretched, then crawled from the backrest to the armrest of the couch and curled his body around her head. She tickled his favorite spot behind his ears.

"But you don't need a lawyer," Soren added. "You need a barracuda. One who specializes in taking men like Anthony to the cleaners. We could start a GoFundMe campaign."

"I'm not doing that."

"Why not?"

"Because I'm just not. That makes me sound like a charity case."

"Okay, we'll put that on the back burner for now."

How about the never-burner? Nicky sighed and pulled a navy-blue fluffy throw blanket over her legs. "I just want what Luca is owed."

"Nick, if you think like that, you're not going to get what *you're* owed. Pre-nup and terrible separation agreement be dammed. I'm still pissed at you for that by the way. Taking less than what he should be paying."

"You know why I took less." She just wanted out and agreed to the first number Anthony threw at her, even if it was low-balled. Getting away from him was more important than the money.

"Yeah, well, he's a rat-bastard, cheating scumbag and doesn't respect fair. But he will respect *fear* and if you get really lucky maybe somebody, like Satan will off him."

"Jesus, Soren! He's the father of my kid, I don't want him dead. I just want him to pay up."

"A girl can dream, right? Satan must be good for something."

"And you say I'm the one who needs help," Nicky scoffed. "Listen, I gotta go." Because she really couldn't handle talking about Vasily. Seeing him again had really messed with her and she didn't need more reason to think about him. "We'll catch up later, yeah?"

After she hung up, she tried to take a short nap, but when that didn't work because of a certain fucking Russian, she showered, and dressed for work at Chuck's Bar. Her shift started at seven but Zander, her boss never minded if she got there earlier. A few extra dollars in tips would be a good start to her divorce fund.

If she could ever find a lawyer to represent her, that was.

Chapter Four

"Hey Barney," Nicky called above Tom Petty's *American Girl* to her silver-haired co-worker, then she bent to stash her purse in the cabinet under one of the bar's registers.

"Yo," he answered. His voice was gruff, like an ex-biker's, which is exactly what he was. He came along with the bar when Zander bought it and had become a permanent fixture, decorating the place with his rough charm and no-nonsense attitude.

"Good thing you're early," he answered. "Ass on deck, we're low on beer." Then using his chin, he pointed at three people at the end of the bar. "Dude in the leather jacket needs a Jack and Coke and the two ladies next to him want cosmos. One order."

"Sure thing."

Nicky fluffed her hair, checked her lips in the mirror behind the bar for any lip-gloss smears, then grabbed her apron from a hook and tied it behind her back. "Is Zander working tonight?"

"Got company." Nicky grinned at Barney's succinctness. The man never wasted words and often, all she'd get was a small but effective body action for an answer.

But Zander not working meant a busy night, and busy nights

went fast. As she mixed the drinks, she eyed the current clientele, spotting several regulars and a few unfamiliar ones. Chuck's had once been a biker bar and was now technically a dive bar, but her boss had turned it into the coolest one in the Tenderloin. By hosting good bands and not skimping on the alcohol, he attracted a mix of the after-work crowd and follow-the-band crowd. If the current situation was any indication, tonight would be a good one, and over before she knew it.

After serving her order, she pulled several drafts and made Moscow Mules, White Russians, and a Long Island Iced Tea. By the time Barney finished unpacking six cases of beer and changed a keg, the band was about to start and the place was buzzing.

It was almost midnight when her phone vibrated in her apron pocket. Being in the middle of a large order she ignored it. As she was finishing, it buzzed again, then pinged with an incoming text message.

It was from Anthony. *Meet me in the back parking lot.*

Was he kidding? What was he doing there and who was with Luca? She stared at her phone for several seconds, then thumbed a reply. *Where's Luca?*

You need to get him. Out here. NOW.

Oh, man! Anthony was in a mood and that behavior didn't need to come inside. Not only did she like her job, she needed it. Zander was an understanding boss, more than most, but she wasn't going to push Anthony into messing things up any more for her. She finished her order then she moved to Barney's side of the bar.

"I've gotta take a quick break."

The motorcycle brother of days past dipped his chin and looked at her from beneath his thick, bristly brows. "You want a bathroom break, there's no need to ask."

"It's not a bathroom break."

His brows squiggled together. "What's up?"

"Anthony's outside and Luca's with him. I need to find out what's going on."

"Past the kid's bedtime."

She gave Barney a look. "I hadn't noticed."

"Cupcake." He stepped away from the pink-haired girl with multiple face piercings he was about to serve and flipped his bar towel over his shoulder. "Don't go out there without backup. Give me a minute."

"Barney, no. You can't leave the customers."

"Then get Petey."

"Petey can't leave the door."

His lips went flat, and she knew he wasn't pleased. "Let me call Zander to cover."

Nicky put her hand on his forearm which was hard and ropey from all the years of swinging heavy crates loaded with bottles of alcohol. "You said Zander has company. Please don't call him. I'll be fine. You know it's nothing I haven't dealt with before." Nicky glanced at the impatient pink-haired woman who was giving her the stink eye and tapping a stubby black fingernail on the bar. "Take care of your customer. I won't be long."

Again, Barney's bristly brows pushed together and deepened the grooves between them.

Nicky squeezed his arm. "Please."

"All right," he relented with a growl. When she let go of his arm, he pulled his phone from his pocket and placed it under the bar next to the unwashed glasses. A rarity, as Barney thought cell phones were an unnecessary intrusion in his life. The only reason he had one was because Zander insisted. He gave her a pointed stare. "Text if you need me."

She sighed in relief, then nodded. "Thanks, Barney."

Maybe Luca was sick. He'd been fine when she left him at school, but kids got sick quickly. A couple of late-night trips to the emergency room with a high fever had taught her that hard lesson.

She undid her apron and hung it back up before shoving her phone into her bra.

Chuck's had a small, but decently lit lot behind it for staff parking and Zander's truck, his Harley, and an ancient, purple VW camper that belonged to Zander's woman.

Using the tip of her boot Nicky shoved a rubber doorstop in place to prevent the back door from closing all the way. If things went south, she didn't need to be accidentally locked out.

The change in light took a moment for her eyes to adjust, but it wasn't difficult to spot Anthony leaning against his Porsche, ass to hood, smoking one of his Marlboro Reds. He'd double-parked in front of a red, sporty Mercedes she assumed belonged to Zander's guest.

If his text didn't give it away, the jittery leg bounce and clenching jaw were all the signs her ex was coked to the gills.

"When I say now, Nick," he gritted out between clenched teeth. "I mean now."

"I was working and came out as soon as I could. Where's Luca?"

"Asleep."

He stayed silent but she could feel his eyes on her while she peered in the window at her son strapped in his car seat. Luca's head lolled to the side and his eyes were closed.

"You're driving him around while you're coked? God, Anthony? What are you thinking?"

"I gotta deal with a client. I can't have him with me."

"A client at this time of night?"

"This is my job, Nick."

"And this is mine!" She swung a hand at the bar. "Who is this client that's more important than spending time with Luca?"

"Don't ask. You don't want to know."

Of course.

Anthony's standard answer. Well, in the past, she didn't. He'd represented her father in his trial, along with other small-time criminals, but since then his practice had grown and his clientele had become a lot less desirable.

"Luca said that you're always working. He also heard you having sex, by the way. If you can't abstain, can you at least keep it down when he's there?"

"He said that to you?" Anthony's eyes widened. To his credit, he at least had the sense to look a little horrified.

"He didn't say those words exactly because he's five, so use your imagination. But you can't be getting drunk or high when he's with you, either."

Anthony's gaze took on a mean squint. "The day you left me was the day you lost any right to tell me what to do, Nick." He brought the cigarette between his thumb and first two fingers to his mouth, took a drag, then dropped it and ground it out with his shoe. "I hear you've been calling divorce lawyers."

Already?

Man.

Obviously, one of his so-called colleagues spilled. Or more likely one of their female legal aides or assistants. Anthony was up there on the good-looking spectrum, with thick, dark curls, full lips, and the same beautiful brown eyes he'd given to their son. Women found him irresistible when he turned on the charm. She had.

"And *I* hear you've been telling lawyers if they represent me, bad things will happen to their wives."

He lifted his focus from the mangled cigarette butt and took his time raking his eyes over her body. "You haven't given me much choice, so what was I supposed to do, Nick?"

She sighed. "I don't have time for this. I need to get back to work and I thought you had a client you needed to get to."

He glanced at his wristwatch, the one she'd given him for their second anniversary. It wasn't a Rolex, but it still cost her more than she made in a month's tips, and she'd bought it with love. Now she wanted to pawn the damn thing.

"I have a few minutes," he said, but then he paused as if trying to get his words right. His tone changed, from that cranked-up anger to something that sounded like sorrow. "We can't go on like this. At least I can't. So, what's it gonna take, Nick?"

Nicky tilted her head. "I don't understand."

"What's it gonna take for you to come back?"

She stared at him, and while she stared, that stupid twitch in her left eye started, but she resisted the urge to press it with her finger.

"I'll stop," he said, filling the silence. "No more women, no more coke, booze, whatever. You tell me, and I'll do it."

How many times had they done this, and how many times had she believed him in the past? She was embarrassed to admit too many, but she'd done it for the sake of their child.

"You've said that before."

"I know, but I mean it this time."

"You always mean it in the moment, Anthony, but the problem is the moment never lasts. Anyway, I think we're well past that."

"We can have that second baby you've always wanted."

Oh, that was low.

It was true she did want another child, longed for one actually, but to bring that up now? He almost sounded desperate.

She shook her head. "No."

"You're not divorcing me."

"Anthony—"

"You're fucking not!" He slammed his palm onto the top of his car. She jumped. Then he stepped towards her and leaned in until he was inches from her face. "You got that? Remember those vows you took...till death do us part?"

She took a step back and her rear bumped up against the trunk of the Mercedes. "You took vows too. Forsake all others. Remember *that?*"

He blinked. "So, I fucked up. I'm human and I'll always fuck up. But so did you, Nick. After Luca was born you had no time for me, and you gained weight and got those stretch marks. I asked you to take care of them and you didn't, because you didn't give a fuck about what *I* wanted. So can you blame me for looking at other women?"

She scoffed. Fifteen pounds after having a baby was hardly gaining weight, and Luca was a colicky child, needing constant attention. She'd been exhausted, but it didn't matter. She could've done everything perfectly, he would've found other excuses. The fact that he used those to justify his womanizing was just insulting. And shallow. It showed exactly the kind of man he was. It had, however, devastated her self-esteem. She shook her head in hurt and disgust.

"It was more than just looking, Anthony, and you know that."

"It doesn't mean this has to end."

"It already has."

Those eyes she'd once thought beautiful and soulful glittered and hardened.

She moved sideways, away from the Mercedes, but he grabbed her arm, then pinned her with his body to the car. His free hand slid slowly over her chest, almost like a caress, 'til they reached her breasts.

"Stop!"

Then he squeezed. "You always had such great fucking tits." His fingers left her breast, moved up and circled the front of her neck, and began to tighten. "You need to figure something out, Nick. These tits are mine, and I'm not letting you go."

"Anthony," she choked out, trying to wiggle the arm caught between their bodies free. He pressed his pelvis to hers, the outline of his growing cock rubbing against her stomach. "I said, stop it!"

"A good fucking should remind you of what we had. How about it, Nick? You and me against this car."

With her air cut off, her vision blurred. His hand was big and strong and tight around her windpipe. *Christ, why hadn't she listened to Barney?* Anthony was going to rape her right here in the parking lot. She had no doubt, as it wouldn't be the first time he'd violated her.

Then Anthony grunted.

Cold air rushed against her body as he suddenly jerked away. She was too focused on trying to breathe to compute what happened, but why were there two figures in front of her like she was seeing double. Lack of oxygen did that, right?

Only, one figure was taller.

She gasped, sucking air until her throat spasmed, making her cough. Blood rushed back into her head and her vision cleared. Anthony was flat on his back. The other man had one foot on his throat and a large gun pointed at his face.

"Don't move," her rescuer directed at her in a voice so cold it made her shudder. Amber light illuminated the planes of his face like a beautiful avenging angel.

Or a devil. Depending on your perspective.

Her stomach flipped and her heart thundered in her ears. Twice in as many days, she'd come face to face with her own personal hell. How could the universe be so damn cruel?

"You all right?" he asked, his tone flat as if this was just another uneventful day in his life. But then again, pulling a gun on a man in a parking lot was probably the kind of thing that normally filled Vasily Melnikov's day.

She nodded, her breath hitching as she stifled another cough.

"Good. Now straighten your clothing."

What? Nicky looked down in alarm. Her skirt was hiked up around her waist showing her panties. They were good panties, thank the gods, with pretty black lace trimming the legs and the waistband, but not the sort of thing she wanted Vasily to see. Not anymore.

Quickly she ran her hands down her skirt and smoothed it into place.

Vasily was known for his ice-cold, dead-calm demeanor, and

back then she'd never actually seen that side of him. So confronted with that lean, powerful body barely containing that crackling violence did something to her monkey brain.

And it wasn't good.

Knowing what he was capable of, and what was associated with the Melnikov name, she understood one wrong move could turn very deadly. The air thickened with tension and long seconds ticked by as he flayed her with his eyes. She swallowed.

"Mommy?" Luca's little boy voice was pitched high with fear and it shattered the heavy silence. "*Mommy?*"

Vasily's gaze jerked from hers and went towards the window. "There's a kid in the car?"

She nodded. "My son." Her voice came out croaky so she cleared her throat but that turned into an inelegant cough. When she was able to speak, she said, "Can you put the gun away please, before you scare him even more?"

Something flittered across his face, disturbing that stoney expression. With an almost imperceptible headshake, his gaze shifted from the car window to settle back on her. "What the hell are you doing bringing a kid to a bar?"

Of course, he would think that. He was wrong, but why should it matter to him what she did in her private life? Nor should she care that he thought she was a degenerate mother, but somehow she did.

"I work here."

Vasily continued to scrutinize her with narrowed eyes, like he didn't believe her. "You work *here*, at my brother's bar?"

Wait a minute.

She tilted her chin in question. Was he saying... "Zander is your brother?"

"Technically he's, my half-brother. Same father, different mother."

Nicky stared, holding onto her surprise like a lifeline, processing this new information. Then she scoffed. God, how little she'd known of him. It made her feel even more foolish for wasting her time and heart on him. But it would also explain what he was doing here and in some weird way, that was a relief.

"Well in that case, yes. I work for your half-brother. Now *please* put the gun away."

His nostrils flared, then he tilted his head in that arrogant yet sexy way, and a shiver rippled through her as her body remembered.

"Not doing that until I know what's going on here."

Anthony had remained silent this whole time, but he chose this moment to butt in. "What do you think is going on here?"

"What I saw was a man with his hands around a woman's neck." He paused, but his gaze remained pinpointed on Nicky, and the point of that pin pricked like a million little needles.

"I didn't get the feeling it was consensual," Vasily continued, his voice like gravel. "Was. I. Wrong?"

Nicky could no longer tell if that icy anger was directed at her or Anthony.

Nor could she answer.

To do so would risk Anthony sustaining more damage than he presently was. And though that would be satisfying, her son would be a witness and it wouldn't help her in the long run.

She chose not to answer. "Can I get my son out of the car, please? He needs me."

Vasily's eyes moved to Luca's face staring through the glass. Perhaps it was a trick of the light, but they seemed to soften as they lingered for a moment before coming back to her. He gave a single nod.

She tried the door handle, and of course, it was locked. "I need his keys."

Vasily made a go-ahead gesture with his free hand and while she dropped to her haunches to search her husband's pocket, she felt his gaze linger on her.

"Let me up," Anthony said, his voice strangled from the pressure of Vasily's shoe. He attempted to shove it away which caused the Russian to increase the pressure.

"When she's done. In the meantime do nothing stupid. I have zero desire to harm you in front of a child, but it won't stop me. Understood?"

Anthony grimaced in answer.

Nicky pressed the fob and the Porsche's locks popped up. She pushed to her feet, then yanked the door open and crawled onto the back seat to release her child from his straps.

"Mommy," Luca's voice hitched as she embraced him. "That man is scary. Why's he got a gun?"

"Shh, it's okay, baby. It's okay." God, she hoped it was. Vasily's cold anger was frightening enough for her, she couldn't imagine what it must feel like for a five-year-old. "Look at me." She pulled her head back so she could make eye contact with her son while keeping a gentle hand on the back of his head. "It's okay, it's just a misunderstanding." Then she turned to look at Vasily, who was still watching her like a hawk and implored him with her eyes. "Right?"

While his lips remained pressed together, he lifted his chin just an inch and grunted. "Hmm."

"Who is he, Mommy?" Luca wrapped his arms tightly around her neck, and his skinny little boy legs around her waist, clinging hard.

"He...um." How on earth did she answer that without making the situation worse? Turns out, she didn't have to.

"I'm the man who helped your mother. You don't need to be afraid of me."

"Then why you got a gun on my dad?"

Vasily stared, his jaw ticking and for a very brief moment she got the impression he was processing. She swung her legs out and with Luca still in her arms climbed out the Porsche. Her skirt again rode up her thighs. Not a practical item of clothing for the current situation, but she wasn't above using her legs for garnishing good tips. When a girl had a living to make, she needed to use what assets she had.

"Yes, please, for the love of crickets, I'm begging you to put that away."

Vasily's gaze dropped to her legs, then she saw his Adam's apple bob. Heat spread up her cheeks as she remembered how much he'd once enjoyed them. The way he'd run his hands up her thighs as he whispered in her ear what he wanted to do with them.

But that was then.

Now he preferred the likes of emaciated supermodels. Why that annoyed her, she refused to acknowledge.

"Name?" he demanded.

Was he serious?

She looked at him in confusion. Then it dawned on her that perhaps she and her friends really had just been lucky winners of a complimentary dinner the previous evening and he didn't recognize her.

"Nicky."

"Not yours, Dominique." He tilted his head toward Anthony. "His."

Her breath caught in her throat as she felt like someone kicked her in the chest. No one else used her full name, and hearing it on his lips after all this time sent shivers through her body and made her heart pound even harder.

"Anthony Andretti," she muttered breathlessly.

"Let me up," Anthony spluttered again, still fighting against the weight of Vasily's shoe. "Get your foot off my neck."

"You going to do something stupid, Andretti? Make a further idiot of yourself in front of the kid?"

A guttural noise came from Anthony that Vasily must've taken to be a confirmation, as he relented, and removed his foot. Then he stepped back keeping a wary eye on him.

"Fucking asshole," Anthony murmured the moment he was

on his feet. He rubbed his throat and then cleared it. "You got no business stepping between me and my wife."

"You made it my business when you put your hands around her throat."

"Um?" Nicky murmured.

Shit!

Still holding Luca, Nicky placed herself between them. The Russian needed to leave before things got even more out of hand. Before her brain short-circuited, or before Anthony started to assume things he shouldn't. His anger was one thing, but his jealousy was another entirely and something she could not handle right now on top of everything else. Hopefully, he didn't recognize the Russian.

"I appreciate your help, but he's right. This is a personal matter."

"I agree," Vasily said, the full force of that silvery glare landing on her for a long, intense moment. "It is."

Fuck.

This wasn't happening. He was not going to turn this around on her, but she'd forgotten how electrifying being so close to him was. How her body reacted whenever they made eye contact for any length of time. She'd always gotten the feeling when he did that, he could see right into her. Stupid. But the pulse pounding in her throat didn't understand or care about stupid.

I'm grateful, truly," she said, swallowing. "But I can take it from here."

"Daddy." Luca whimpered against her throat. Her son being witness to all that transpired seemed to have a momentary effect on Anthony. His face softened, and he ruffled Luca's hair before he hugged him still in her arms, and then dropped a kiss on top of his head.

Something inside of her cried. *This* was a side of Anthony she'd cared for, but that man barely existed anymore. This was reinforced when he met her gaze over Luca's head. She tensed, her arms tightening around her boy because some sort of verbal abuse would surely be forthcoming.

"What's your deal with him?" Anthony thumbed in Vasily's direction. "Something I should know about, Nick?"

God.

She remained silent because there wasn't anything she could say.

But Anthony knew her, and his face twisted into an ugly mask. "Don't pretend there isn't. I can smell something's going on." Anthony then looked at Vasily, his chest puffing up. "What are you doing here, at my wife's place of work? You fucking her?"

"Anthony!" she snapped, covering Luca's ears. "Watch your language."

"Your time is up, Andretti." Vasily's words practically dripped icicles long and sharp enough to pierce. "Get your ass in your car. Leave. Before I do something all of us will regret."

They locked eyes, like two rams about to face off, each assessing the other. Somewhere behind the chemical-induced dysfunction of Anthony's brain, his survival instinct must've kicked in because he backed off.

The new intensity of Vasily's cold anger raised the hair on her arms and if she'd thought he was scary before, he was now utterly terrifying. Not daring to move, breathe, or blink, she waited.

Moments ticked by, then Anthony finally held out his hand, but he didn't look at her as she dropped his keys into his open palm. He walked backward for a few steps, turned, and rounded the front of his car. Before he opened his door, he paused. "I know who you are, Melnikov, and if you think this is over, you're wrong." Then he looked at Nicky. "Not by a long shot."

She exhaled slowly, but held her stance, unwavering.

Anthony climbed into the Porsche, and a moment later it purred to life. He gunned the engine, then drove out of the lot through the narrow alley on the side of the bar.

She couldn't see the far end of the alley where it met the street, but it was apparent when he left the property. A horn beeped, probably because Anthony cut some poor soul off when he entered the late-night city traffic.

Frozen, she clung to her son. Luca whispered in her ear. "Mommy, you're squeezing me. I'm going to pop."

"Sorry, baby." Loosening her grip, her eyes flickered up to Vasily. He was watching her, his expression unreadable. The ice had melted but left something in its place that thickened the tension in the air.

"You okay?" he asked, his tone gentle.

Hell, no. She was far from okay. And she had things to say about what he'd done to her dad, and what he'd done to her. But that wasn't going to happen in front of her son. If she opened her mouth now, she wouldn't be able to stop. So she kept it shut and started to walk away.

"Dominique, wait!" There was enough command in his voice that despite what her brain and sanity demanded, her legs stopped in their tracks. Along with her breath.

She waited but did not turn around. Vasily closed the distance until he was in front of her, then reached into his trousers pocket. Removing a black leather wallet, he extracted a white business card. He held it out for her between two fingers.

She shook her head.

His silent gaze demanded she accepted the card, but when it became obvious she wasn't going to relent, those sculpted lips flattened, and his attention shifted to Luca.

"Hang onto this for your mom. If either of you need help for *any* reason, you call me. Hear me, little man?"

Luca's eyes were wide, and it seemed to Nicky some sort of silent message passed between them, and to her surprise, Luca nodded and took the card.

After he did, and after another moment of whatever passed between her son and Vasily, his gaze returned to her. Somehow they were closer in proximity, but she couldn't tell which one of them had moved. Perhaps it was both. He smelled clean, like a Caribbean breeze and a touch of whiskey, and the gods forgive her, but she remembered his smell. Remembered what it had done to her senses in the past and, like a recovering addict faced with their drug of choice, she wanted more. It took all her strength to jerk away from that raw magnetism, the undeniable tug that had pulled her in so many years ago.

Clinging to her boy as if her sanity depended on it, she forced one foot in front of the other until she reached the back exit.

Don't look back.

Don't look back.

Of course, she looked back, and he was still there, one leg cocked at the knee, one hand shoved in his pants pocket. His expression wasn't the satisfied smirk she'd expected but it was one she was familiar with.

I'll see you, it said.

Oh, he had that right. But when that moment inevitably happened, it would be on her terms, and when she was ready.

With the only thing Nicky had left going for her still in place —her resolve and her determination—she shut the back door and took her son upstairs to Zander's apartment above the bar.

Her heart and her head would just have to wait.

Chapter Five

Of all the damn dive bars!

To anyone watching his gaze appeared to be focused on the woman sitting on the wooden barstool next to him, but Vasily's mind was on the parking lot of Zander's bar. His big toe bounced a rhythm to Gin Wigmore's *Kill of the Night* against the black leather of his shoe.

"Are you still with me?" Kat Lewis asked, jostling his knee with hers. "You've got that *I'm somewhere else* vibe about you."

He grunted. Nicky would bump his knee when she'd thought his attention had wavered. In all honesty, she'd had him riveted. It had been his defense mechanism—acting cool and slightly distanced to avoid coming off as an infatuated tool—when in reality, that's what he'd been. Any man putting his hands on her or getting too close had the rare distinction of pushing him to the edge. Last night had proven that was still true.

After ten fucking years.

He could not afford those feelings again. They'd almost killed him last time, yet they'd resurged like a drunken Russian on a rampage.

"Earth to Vasily!" Kat bumped his knee again, this time harder. It made the ice in his whiskey tinkle. "Where did you go?"

Back to hell.

"You called me, remember?" Kat said, a smirk curling up one side of her lips. "This is your meeting."

"Yeah, sorry." He shifted his position on the barstool and resumed bouncing his big toe to quell the storm raging inside of him.

Despite her closeness to him and the intimate way their arms almost touched, Kat wasn't a woman he'd fucked in the past. Instead, they had a long friendship and a productive working arrangement.

"You all right?" she queried, her hazel eyes worried. "You have dark circles smudging those pretty grays. What's bugging you?"

A woman who shouldn't be. "You familiar with a man named Anthony Andretti?"

"Who?"

"Criminal lawyer in the city." Yeah, so he'd done some googling. Sue him.

Kat took a sip of her gin and tonic, then swirled the liquid in her glass. "Oh, *that* Anthony Andretti. Only what I've read in passing. That he represents some...shall we say, reprehensible people. Why are you interested in him?"

"He abuses his woman and I want him neutralized."

Kat chuckled behind her glass. "Neutralized, huh? Or do you mean neutered?"

"Hmm."

Interesting thought.

"And this particular woman he abuses—she the reason for those dark circles?"

He glanced at Kat sideways, causing her to tilt her head. "Aah... she is." She placed her glass on the polished brass of the hole-in-the-wall downtown bar and then angled her neck to look at him.

"Tell me about her. Must be pretty fascinating to have one super-model dating mob boss's undies in a knot."

"What?" His eyebrows came together.

"I read the smutty headlines in the web mags. *Sunny's New Sunrise Man.* Not to mention, your photo with her draped on your arm is splashed all over the internet."

Jesus. "I'm not dating her, and never plan to see any sunrise with her. She introduced herself to me, and that was it. One of her entourage must've taken that photo."

"Well, whoever did, they got her good side. She's gorgeous, no?"

He shrugged. "If you say so." He honestly didn't get the appeal. Five seconds and he'd pegged Sunny as self-absorbed and privileged. He'd known plenty of women like that in Russia—spoiled rotten Bratva princesses with more bling than sense—and had no desire to pursue that. Anyway, his mind had been on a particular brunette who'd just blindsided his ass and ripped his chest cavity wide open.

When he didn't elaborate, Kat tilted her head and watched him over her lime garnish. "And this other woman is?"

He remained silent, just pursed his lips. His old FBI friend knew him well enough to deduce his non-answer was a confirmation.

"There's only one woman I know of that…" Suddenly Kat inhaled, then lifted her chin. "Oh my God, it's *her*, isn't it? The one you left behind!"

Fuck.

He should've left well alone. Kat was smart and he'd been the asshole who brought up Andretti. Their eyes caught for a beat, and he didn't like what he saw in Kat's. Pity was not an emotion he did well with.

"You sought her out. I thought you weren't going to do that."

"I didn't." He blew out a breath. "We sort of …just bumped into each other."

Twice.

"I suppose that was inevitable. San Fran's a big city, but not that big. How's she doing?"

"Still married."

And angry, which he didn't understand. Sure, things had been left unsettled between them, but time had a way of softening old grievances. Her raw hatred had churned his gut like sour milk. Which begged the question, the one that had kept him up for the past few nights. What had happened after he left? Perhaps he hadn't gotten *all* the intel he should've. After Vasily had returned from Russia, he'd spent his time fixing Dean's fuckups, and he'd had none to dwell on the past. Not that he was the kind of man who dwelled on the past, but he'd be lying if he hadn't thought about finding Nicky. Just to check on her.

"And let me guess, she's married to this Andretti character," Kat asked.

"Hmm." He ran his tongue over his teeth and sucked.

"Jesus, Vas, are you sure you want to travel that road again? Remember, I was there, and I know what it cost you last time."

Yeah. But what had his stepping into her situation last night cost *her*? Men like Andretti didn't like to lose, but unfortunately took their losses out on their women.

"I've possibly made a bad situation worse."

"And knowing you as I do, you can't help inserting yourself into bad situations."

That went without saying. Her kid had taken his card so that was something. Perhaps it wasn't the first time he'd witnessed his dad with his hands around his mother's neck. A circumstance he unfortunately related to.

Papa, don't kill her!

Vasily cleared his throat and pushed back at the old memories.

"But that's not why I invited you for a drink," he said. "I need help."

Using the swizzle stick in her drink, Kat stabbed the lime twist at the bottom of her glass. "After what you did for me over there?" She shuddered. "Always."

Kat's parents were Russian, and with her ability to speak the language, she'd been recruited by the FBI in college. Her job had been to honeytrap his old boss, Aleksei Federov, and accumulate intel on his drug-running and money-laundering operations. She'd discovered how they connected to his businesses in the US. Being a fellow American, Vasily noticed tiny nuances that had given her away, but instead of outing her to Federov, they'd become allies and helped each other. When her cover was about to be blown, Vasily had risked his life to deliver her to the US Embassy in Moscow.

"But what can I help you with?" she asked.

"There's a sex trafficking operation taking root in Northern California."

Kat sighed and shook her head. "There's always a new one."

"I have a video, raw footage with some faces operating that ring. They prey on Russian and Ukrainian girls wanting a new life, drawing them in, drugging them, then shipping them in modified containers. Somewhere in the Pacific, they load them onto a smaller boat, then land at a marina near Eureka."

"Containers all the way from Russia?" Kat's eyes got big. "That's weeks of sailing time. How brutal."

Yep.

"Some girls are brought to a brothel, others are sold via auction on the dark web. I want this stopped, Kat. Before more girls are brought in and it becomes an even bigger problem."

"You know it's like whack-a-mole? You knock one back, ten more pop up."

He grunted, acknowledging that fact, but he didn't have to allow it on his territory.

"I'll do what I can," Kat said. "But you can start by giving me your source. I'd like to explore that angle first."

"That's a hard no. This isn't going to court."

"Vas..."

"No!"

"Shit." Kat looked away for a moment and blew out air. "Why not?"

"Some of those girls in the video are under my protection," Vasily answered. "They don't want to testify, deal with the government or risk being sent back and killed. I have their trust, and I'm not going to violate that."

"There's this little thing called witness protection, Vasily."

"These girls can barely speak English. No matter where they go, they'll stick out so that's not happening. I need your assurances, Kat."

She looked at him for a long moment not saying anything. Then her shoulders dropped. "You feel that strongly?"

"They've been through hell." He rubbed the scruff on his face. "They're happy and secure where they are now."

"If anyone knows what it's like to go through something like that, you do. I won't deny that. But things are fluid and change. Maybe we'll discuss that option again later?"

"I make no promises but until and if we cross that bridge, assurances woman." He held her eyes, letting her know he wasn't fucking about.

"Okay." She grimaced. "You're a tough shit and a pain in my ass, but you've got it."

He didn't allow himself to feel relief. He trusted Kat and wouldn't provide her with the intel if he didn't, but it was risky. For both of them.

"*If* they choose to leave the country," he continued, "they will need passports so they can go where they want."

"You drive a hard bargain."

"Not as hard as what they've endured. If you can't help with that, I need to know now."

"The only thing I can promise is I'll do what I can to make it work. Your intelligence is invaluable and has helped me way more than anything I ever did for you in that Russian hell hole."

"That's not true." Vasily's face softened. If it hadn't been for Kat's suggestion to Aleksei that he could be useful, he'd be dead. But this was purely selfish. He wanted those fuckers off his territory and it irked him to admit he couldn't do it by himself. So why not use the power of the U.S. government even if it was through a back door and not strictly legal.

"Of course, I'll help, and we'll get them. In time. I'm just glad you're on my side."

He chuffed. "Likewise."

"If that's it, I gotta head out." Kat took a last sip of her gin and tonic, placed the glass on the bar in front of them, and slipped off her stool. "Bad guys to catch. Never ends."

He rose too, leaned in, and kissed her cheek. Then from his pocket removed and handed her a USB copy of the video he'd shown to his men and Viktor Sokolov.

"The man in the video, the fat one, his name is Bob, no last name. The woman is Marisol Price. The house is in the trees off a road near Eureka where they take the girls. I want that location."

She tilted her head up and smiled, knowing better than to ask where she got that little tidbit of intel. Not that he'd tell her. "I'll do my best. Until next time."

He watched her for a few seconds as she walked away like any man would, as did several others in the bar. She had an attractive ass, but he didn't have designs on it. Metaphorically speaking, however, they'd always taken care of each other's. She'd proven that in Russia and here.

He texted Maxim, his driver, to meet him at the curb outside the bar, then he used the restroom. Washed his hands and splashed cold water on his face, then stared at his reflection, noting the dark circles Kat pointed out.

Fucking Nicky.

She was still so beautiful.

He took a deep breath then wiped his face with a paper towel and tossed it into the garbage.

Five minutes later, he slid across the Cadillac's leather seat. "Take me to Christina," he said in Russian before Max could ask.

Max studied him through the rearview mirror. "You all right, boss? You look tired."

He almost rolled his eyes. *So everyone keeps telling him.* "How is your daughter?" he asked to take the attention off himself.

"Good, sir. She's doing well in school." Max's smile was bright and full of pride. "She wants to be a lawyer."

Hopefully not a mob lawyer. "She deserves a good future."

"Thank you, sir."

"Hmm."

They drove in silence until they arrived at a fifteen-floor multi-zoned building downtown owned by the Melnikov Organization. His import-export business had a store on the ground floor. Above that, were the administrative offices. Several other floors were used to store inventory, and the rest were rented out.

But his destination was the top floor. Dean, his brother, had sold sex and ran that business as a brothel. Vasily changed it into a fully licensed escort agency and instead of sex, he sold 'companionship.' It was legal and regulated, and the women who worked for him were independent contractors and their own bosses.

Today was his monthly check-in with Christina, a woman who was once a prostitute under his brother, but now ran the agency for Vasily. She vetted the clients, dealt with complaints, and acted as Mama Bear when the women misbehaved.

Christina's apartment was at the far end facing the Bay's eastern side with a view of the city of Oakland.

"Vasily." She waved him in with a smile, then led him to a black glass desk that was situated in front of a window that spanned the entire length of her apartment. She wore a white button-down blouse, a chunky silver chain dangling an oval-shaped topaz around her neck, and a pair of sweatpants. Nobody saw the bottom half on a Zoom interview.

"Perfect timing." She flipped her long auburn hair over her shoulder as she sat. "I have this month's numbers."

Vasily seated himself on the other side of her desk while she turned a flat computer monitor so he could view the spreadsheet on its desktop.

"We look really good. Best we've ever had."

"Think the babysitting services are helping?" Vasily had put the women Carmine Niccoterra had brought him from the trafficking operation to work as nannies. It was the whole reason those girls were duped into the sex slave trade in the first place—with the promise of jobs and a new life in America. He was just giving them what they came for.

"I do." Her eyes widened. "It's genius and I wished we'd done it sooner. The women can relax knowing their kids are well cared for when they're working. Those girls, Vas...they're super sweet and grateful. None of our women regret hiring them."

"Any of them express any desire to branch out into the trade?"

"Not yet."

"Good." He wanted to keep it that way, although it was ultimately their choice.

"I know you're not keen to expand, but I gotta tell you, I'm getting referrals every day. How do I tell them no? A lot of these women are desperate, some even with expensive educations. They have massive student loans and just want to pay rent or give their kids a better life."

He sighed. When he took over, he'd offered the women their freedom. Some of the girls had left the sex trade voluntarily, but others had begged him to reconsider. At their suggestion, he now owned an escort agency. Being an escort was a legal, safer alternative to working the streets, which is what they would've ended up doing if he'd followed through.

"Let me think about it. The girls had their check-ups this month?"

"I've scheduled Dr. Ronnie for tomorrow and the following day. Most of them already have appointments. Just a couple I'm waiting to hear back from. This is another one of the changes you've made that has been good for everyone."

He nodded, her unspoken subtext clear. Dean had handled the women with brute force, many of them addicted to the product he'd supplied for the clients, for which they were then further indebted. Worse, his men had used the girls as well, but Vasily had stopped that. It had almost caused a war within the organization, but he'd eventually changed their minds once they saw the profits rolling in and their payouts getting bigger. Those same men were now their drivers and offered the girls protection on their 'dates.'

"Any of the women serviced a lawyer by the name of Anthony Andretti?"

Christina pursed her lips and shook her head. "Not sure. Let me check. You got a photo?"

He pulled up the one he'd taken the previous evening when he'd had his foot on Andretti's neck and texted it to her. The asshole was good-looking. He wouldn't have to pay, but that didn't mean he wouldn't on occasion. Some of the girls specialized.

She squinted at the photo, then typed on her keyboard, clicked through a few pages then shook her head. "He's not in the system, at least not under that name." Christina sat back in her chair. "Who is he?"

"Doesn't matter. If he books one of them, let me know."

"All right." Closing out the page, she leaned forward again and rested her elbows on the glass top. "Yev tell you about that social worker?"

He nodded. "She becoming a problem?"

"Not yet, but maybe I'm just paranoid. She's a little too persistent for a government employee, don't you think?"

Christina had a point. Although he admired persistence in

general, this wasn't one of those times. "How is she contacting the girls?"

"Through the website with private messages asking personal questions. Mostly about where they came from, if they had family, etc."

Jesus—red flag. His eyes narrowed. "I'll look deeper into it."

They discussed business a little longer, then he left. He had second thoughts as he exited the elevator and walked towards the import-export business.

This so-called social worker may very well be legit, but she could be a bigger problem than what Yev could deal with. Not that he doubted Yev's abilities and his knowledge of how the internet worked, but he did have his limits.

He needed a professional, someone with extensive investigative experience and IT knowledge.

He knew exactly who that was—Carmine Niccoterra.

Chapter Six

"Thanks for watching Luca on such short notice, Dad." Nicky leaned in and kissed Mario Marcello's cheek, the bristles from his silver goatee, tickling her lips. "Anthony had a last-minute trip he couldn't get out of, and I need this shift."

It was the following evening after the incident in Chuck's parking lot and she studied him in the fading light. Her dad hadn't gained back some of the weight he'd lost after his heart attack, and she was mildly worried. Recuperating in a prison sick bed didn't help, nor did prison food, but thankfully he'd finally been released on parole a few months before.

"Well, his loss," her dad replied, his long-time smoking habit evident in a deep, scratchy voice. "I'm always up for a night with my boy." He rubbed the top of Luca's head, fluffing his curls into a dark fuzzy cloud they liked to call his 'fro. "What say you, grandson? How 'bout popcorn and a movie?"

"Yes!" Luca yelled, completely unperturbed his hair now stood on end and met his grandpa's high five.

"In the meantime, why don't you go find some cookies in the jar next to the sink."

"Cookies?" Luca bounced on his toes clutching his little fists in front of his chest. Nicky's heart expanded and filled with joy.

"Chocolate chip and snickerdoodles."

"Savage! Can I, Mom?"

Nicky snorted. *Savage?* Where did he learn this shit? Probably at school from other kids with teenage siblings. "Go ahead."

Luca bounded up the two stairs of her dad's Class B RV. It was old, its white paint job and faded blue stripe beginning to peel, but he kept it clean and mostly shiny. His years in prison had turned him into a minimalist and an organizational neat freak. The vehicle rested in a no-frills, concrete slab RV park south of San Francisco, but she didn't care. Her dad was out of prison. She'd offered her couch, but he wanted his privacy, and she couldn't blame him, as he'd spent over nine years sharing a tiny cell with another human.

Regardless, Luca would be safe from Anthony's drug-infused midnight drives. Since he hadn't returned her texts, she presumed he was still dealing with his 'client.' Whatever that meant.

"Okay, so what's the real story," Mario asked when Luca was out of earshot. "Why isn't he with his dad?"

She gave him a quick run-down of the previous evening. "I don't know what's happening, Daddy, but Anthony is getting worse. He says he wants me back, but I can't. And I didn't want to say this in front of Luca, but I'm filing for divorce. And after last night's stunt, driving high like he did, I'm going for full custody."

Her father eyed her for a long time before finally speaking. "Hate to say it, but you should have done it a long time ago."

Nicky dug the point of her black cowboy boot into the ground, "So everyone keeps telling me."

"It's my fault. Shoulda hired a different lawyer."

"C'mon, Dad." Nicky chuckled, rolling her eyes. "It wasn't all bad. When Anthony represented you, he was my hero." At the time, the wounds from her shattered heart were still fresh. Anthony's persistence had finally worn her down and her rebound relationship turned into a marriage.

Mario scoffed and shook his head. "That's what I'm talking about. Anybody else you wouldna married him." He exhaled, his face showing his regret.

"We can't go backward, Daddy." She gripped his upper arms over his plaid shirt—which were kept firm due to the muscle it took to handle his Fatboy Harley. Silently, she thanked the gods he no longer had any connection to the stolen car-parts business. Something he perhaps *should've* taken the perp walk for, instead of for something he didn't do. "You're out now, let's just keep it that way."

Mario pulled her into a hug. "I'm worried about you, girl. Anthony's an ambitious punk with a short fuse. You file for divorce, he'll fight ugly."

"He already is."

He stilled, then pushed her gently away. Both eyebrows were raised.

"Don't look at me like that. I'm a tough girl. I can handle this and don't need you worrying about me."

"Don't matter how tough you are, you're still *my* girl. And you're the mother of my only grandchild, you got more sense in your head to know I'm gonna worry no matter what."

Yep. She had to concede his point. Nobody told her how much every little thing worried her when it came to the tiny human she'd incubated. Like when he got stuck with a vaccination needle and screamed at her. As if she'd betrayed him for protecting him against the nasty diseases that affected humans. Babies didn't come with a how-to manual. Perhaps that's why her mother bailed when she was a baby.

"Not gonna let you down again," her dad continued. "I'll help you through this. You wanna come here after work? I'd feel better knowing you're not alone."

"I'll be fine." She shook her head. "But there's something else you should know." She took a deep breath and let it out. "Vasily's back."

Mario did not look surprised. Which in turn surprised her. Her head angled to the side. "You knew."

"Heard he's been back a while."

"And you never told me?"

"Didn't want to open that can of worms. Wondered how long it would take for him to start sniffing."

"He didn't, Dad. It was pure coincidence. *I* ran into *him*."

"Sure about that?"

"Yes! Anyway, why are you so calm?"

"Whatcha mean?"

"You're not planning on doing anything stupid, are you? You can't violate your parole," she warned. "He's not worth me losing you again."

"Not planning on nothing, Stick. My freedom and being around for you and Luca are more important. Ain't nothing gonna bring back that lost time, and I've done enough. Not going back in."

She studied him, looking for any of his old tells. Like the slight narrowing of his right eye or the finger tap against the front of his jeans. There were none unless he'd learned to control them while he was inside.

"You sure?" she asked, not entirely convinced.

He shrugged. "Spent too many years being bitter and angry, look what it got me."

A heart attack, she knew. But, this was good news, if true.

"Mommy?" Luca called from the RV's door. "How many cookies can I have?"

"One. Then after dinner, it's up to Grandpa."

Her father chuckled. "Make me the bad guy."

She bumped his shoulder with hers, grinning. "You're not going to listen to me, anyway. It's on you how much of a sugar demon you want."

She walked towards her son. "Hey Buddy, gimme a kiss, I gotta go to work."

She leaned in and hugged him, holding on for several seconds longer than she would normally. "You and Grandpa have fun, but do me a favor though?"

"What?"

"Set a good example. Don't let him eat too many cookies, okay? You know, because of his heart?"

"'Kay, Mommy. I'll try to be good and 'sponsible."

"No try, remember?" She looked him dead in the eye.

"Uh-huh, like Yoda. There's only do. I got it."

"Excellent." She smoothed a strand from his forehead, her fingers lingering in his dark curls. "Love you, Buddy, now give me a smooch."

Luca left a wet smack on her cheek, and she walked back to her dad and hugged him too.

"See you, Pops. Thanks again."

As she drove away Mario flashed her his low two-finger salute, then turned to go inside.

Traffic was light and she made it to the bar with time to spare. All things considered, she had a good night and after closing, offered Barney a ride to his home three blocks away.

"Nah," he said. "Nice night, gonna walk. See ya tomorrow, Cupcake."

She blew him a kiss through the window, then made the short drive to the outer edges of the Tenderloin. Her neighborhood, though close to the up-and-coming South of Market district, or SoMa, hadn't yet been touched by gentrification, making it still affordable.

Marley jumped off the couch as she crossed her threshold, doing figure-eights around her legs until she picked him up and draped him over her shoulder.

"Miss me, handsome?" He purred in her ear as she checked the deadbolt.

"Gotta put you on a diet, fatty. Cut out some of those kitty-crack treats, yeah?" Marley gave a soft mewl in protest.

"Okay, never mind." She didn't mind him being chubby. It was a far cry from how she'd found him, one eye hanging from his skull and skin ravaged with mange near the dumpster at Chuck's. "You deserve to be fat and lazy in whatever years you have left."

She walked to her room, sat on the edge of her bed, and gave his behind a gentle shove. He hopped off her shoulder and then took up a spot on her pillow, making biscuits until he was satisfied. Nicky showered then pulled on a pair of short cotton pajamas and poured a glass of Zinfandel. Motörhead's *Whorehouse Blues*, bumped around in her head, and mumbling the lyrics she ventured back to her room.

Marley was on a credenza below her window, growling and looking like an orange pincushion.

Something primal prickled her skin as she put down her glass on her dresser then moved to the window and pulled the curtain back.

WHOOMPF!

The light outside suddenly brightened, then her window rattled in its frame.

"Holy shit!" Nicky jumped back at the explosion. Marley flew off the credenza, scattering a small vase filled with fresh flowers. She couldn't tell if it was her yell or the explosion that sent him into her closet.

A yellow-orange ball of fire, like a mini sun, lit up the parking lot, and it only took her a second to realize it was her car that had burst into flames!

"Oh my god! *No.*"

She gasped and grabbed her hair.

Fuck!

Then she ran to the kitchen and snatched her phone from her purse. Stabbing at 911, she put it on speaker and scrambled for her boots.

While the dispatcher took down the address and details, she

pulled on a hoodie sweatshirt, shoved her cell into a front pocket and ran down the stairs. She stopped at the first door on the right.

"Terrence!" She lifted and banged the discolored brass door knocker while using her boot to pound at the bottom of the door, loosening a few green paint chips in the process. "Terrence, get the fuck up, we got a fire in the parking lot."

She crossed the hall and did the same on her babysitter's door and then last, Creepy Bill, the maintenance man.

"Yo, Bill, we got a fire."

"Fire? Fuck." Creepy Bill brushed back his thinning hair, eyes wide and still glassy from God knows what substance he'd imbibed.

"Move it," she yelled while breaking the glass of the extinguisher case with the little hammer attached. By the time she'd freed it, Terrence emerged with his hair wrapped in an orange scarf. "What's the fuss, honey?"

"Holy hell, Terrence, did you not hear?"

"What?" He yawned.

She reached forward and yanked the purple plugs from his ears. "Shoes on, right now! My car's on fire and we have to stop it from spreading."

Terrence's eyes widened until his black irises were surrounded by white. In any other situation, it would've been comical.

"Fuck, *fire*?"

She turned to look over her shoulder at her maintenance man still standing at his door, frozen in his spot. "Yes, Bill. Fire. Get an extinguisher and make sure Favi and her mom know in case it spreads. They haven't answered their door."

With the extinguisher in hand, she ran out through the breezeway to the parking lot.

"Oh, shit no," she cried. The ragtop of Terrence's '63 Beetle was starting to burn. Forgoing her car, which was a loss no matter what, she focused on the VW.

"Beebee?" Terrence wailed from behind her, hands pressed to his horrified face. "Oh my God, my Beebee!"

"Get the other extinguisher and dose her down. She'll survive."

Bill arrived with Favi and Mrs. Escobar, but since his dark blue Chevy work van was not in danger of catching alight, he herded everyone to the sidewalk. Terrence took care of Beebee and Nicky moved to Mrs. Escobar's ancient Honda Odyssey giving it a preventative squirt. Then getting as close as the heat radiating off her car allowed, she aimed what remained in her extinguisher on the Audi.

When Beebee was under control, Terrence added the last of his to help just as the first fire truck arrived. Tenants from neighboring buildings scattered when they pulled into the parking lot entrance.

She wiped the sweat from her brow with her sleeve as the fire department made quick work of what was left of the fire on her Audi.

"You okay, honey?" Terrence asked putting an arm around her shoulders.

"I don't know. I suppose I will be in a bit." Mostly she was exhausted—emotionally and physically, yet her head was spinning with questions.

"What's your guess?" she asked.

"Thinking it might have something to do with a pissed-off soon-to-be ex-husband."

She gave him the side eye. "Possibly. But I'm sorry about the Beebs." She laid her head on Terrence's shoulder. "I hate that she's collateral damage. But why would Anthony do something like that?"

He jerked his head to angle it towards her. "If not him, then who? Surely not that beautiful specimen, your Russian mobster?"

Fucking wow.

She hadn't thought of that, but she didn't have time to explore it, as the police had arrived. The best-looking one happened to be an old high school buddy. He sauntered over.

"This yours?" Officer Dwayne Lee said by way of greeting, pointing at the Audi's carcass—nothing but seriousness on his handsome Chinese American features.

"Sure was."

"What happened?"

Nicky shrugged. "I got home from the bar, poured a glass of wine, and boom, my car's on fire. Thankfully I waited to fill my tank, can you imagine?"

Terrence shuddered next to her, and Dwayne grimaced. "Ugh. Think you could've left a cigarette burning in the car?"

"I don't smoke, Dwayne." *But Anthony did.*

He wrote in his little black book for a minute before looking at her car. "Window is broken. Was it like that before?"

"It is?" Nicky ducked lower and squinted at the blackened shell covered in white foam. Indeed, there was a football-sized hole in the back passenger window.

"Would you look at that?" She glanced at Terrence. "It definitely wasn't broken when I parked this evening."

"I'm guessing then, that broken wine bottle on the backseat isn't yours?"

"Bottle?" Nicky shivered in her sweatshirt, despite the heat still radiating from the metal frame. "You mean someone tossed a Molotov cocktail into my car?"

"Looks that way. Anyone got a grudge against you?"

"Besides Anthony?" Both brows moved towards her hairline as she gave him a pointed stare. "He's a pretty vindictive schmuck, but I don't think he's stupid enough to do something like this. He'll lose his law license."

The cop grunted. "Could've had one of his despicable clients do it for him. I'll check it out anyway."

"Um, there's the other possibility," Terrence offered, sticking his hip out.

"What other possibility would that be?" Dwayne looked at Terrence.

"A certain Russian mob boss that once had a thing with our little missy here."

Dwayne looked at her from beneath his lashes, chin dipped. "Melnikov...seriously?"

"I didn't say that," Nicky hedged and vehemently shook her head. "Nope."

"Well until you do, I'm not exploring that alley. Melnikov is one scary individual, and if I don't need to interview him, I'm not going to."

"You don't need to. It's not him." At least she didn't think so. Surely, he had enough mob boss stuff to keep him occupied, so why would he waste his precious time on her?

Dwayne took further details and after talking to the Fire Chief, and a representative of the ATF, Terrence hooked his arm in hers and walked her inside. "Poor Beebee," he groaned. "My baby got burned."

"Beebee's a tough old girl. With a little cosmetic surgery, she'll be good. My Audi, however." She sighed. "What the hell am I going to do?"

"Drink to her demise? I'll grab the mixings for some cocktails and bring them to your apartment. I don't think either of us is going to sleep any time soon, do you?"

Not the way her head was spinning. "Sounds perfect. I never got to drink my wine."

She checked in with Dwayne and the ATF agent one last time. Neither needed her further, so she ambled upstairs to meet Terrence.

Three hours, one bottle of Zinfandel, and a mild hangover later, she woke to Marley sitting on her chest. His cold nose was pressed to hers, his one accusing, amber orb glaring.

"God, cat," she groaned, rubbing her eyes. "It's barely daylight." Being one of those individuals that once her eyes had opened, she couldn't go back to sleep, so she rolled out of bed and stuck her feet into purple fuzzy slippers. Then she filled Marley's food bowl and prepared a pot of coffee. As it brewed, Nicky glanced out her window.

Yep—it hadn't been a bad dream. There was a blackened rectangle in her parking spot where her car should've been, bordered by the remnants of white foam. But situated perfectly in the middle of the rectangle, there was something else. It stuck out because it was stark white against the black soot. Something wasn't right and it made the hairs on her arms stand to attention. What the hell *was* that?

Still in her pajamas, she prepared a cup of coffee with milk and sugar, then went down the stairs and stared at the item. It looked like a business card.

Like the one Vasily had given Luca.

But there was no way it would have survived the blazing hell that had taken her car. What was it doing there? The skin at the back of her neck prickled as she continued to stare at it for several more seconds before bending to pick it up.

With her heart pounding, Nicky went back up to her son's room—and froze. A card lay next to her son's Superman lamp. She compared the two pieces of paper containing just a phone number. They were identical. One had grubby little boy fingerprints on it, and the other was slightly worn like it had been in a wallet a bit longer. But there was no mistaking they belonged to the same man.

The implications slammed into her, leaving her breathless.

Vasily Melnikov had set her car on fire.

Why?

Chapter Seven

Later that afternoon, Nicky forced a smile and stopped herself from tapping a naked fingernail on the shiny glass-topped chrome reception desk manned by an elderly gentleman. "I need to see Mr. Melnikov, please." She kept her tone friendly, even if that wasn't how she was feeling.

Though taller than her, the gentleman weighed less by several pounds, reminding her of Lurch from The Addams Family. Gaunt, and lanky with a sallow complexion and hollow cheeks that suggested illness.

"Do you have appointment?" he asked in a rough Eastern European accent.

"Sorry, no I don't."

"Fill information here." He pushed a large iPad toward her.

While she completed the digital form, he made a call using the desk phone, mumbling in what she assumed was Russian. Only because she understood what *da* and *nyet* meant.

When he hung up, he pointed to a long, black bench against the window. "Take seat. Someone be here soon."

"Can't you just tell me where to go? I don't need an escort."

"Take seat," he repeated with a little more emphasis. "Yevgeny come soon."

Alrighty then, she growled inwardly and popped her lips. She'd just wait for *Yevgeny*. Probably another sickly old codger with a sour attitude bent on keeping her from harming a certain Russian. And because he told her to sit, she paced, clicking her boot heels on the polished tiled floor.

The building was downtown, and it had taken effort to find which one. Google in all its worldly wisdom hadn't been very forthcoming. There wasn't much information about Vasily's businesses other than an import-export enterprise and no hint of where he resided. His online presence was virtually non-existent except for the splash he'd made by dating Sunny. Yeah, she'd seen the photo. It had not improved her mood in any way, which was borderline bitchy to begin with.

What he saw in the emaciated supermodel was beyond her, but whatever—each to their own.

After arranging for her dad to keep Luca one more night, she'd called Terra at Provocative, the exclusive lingerie store she worked at. Besides Zander (who she definitely wasn't going to ask), Terra was the only person she suspected might have that information. She could've just called the bastard, but what fun would that be? Anyway, she wanted to look him in the eye when he lied to her.

"It's a lovely day at Provocative," Terra had given the standard greeting. "Who are you seducing today?"

"Terra, it's Nicky, from the bar."

"Yo, Nickalicious. Whatup?"

Despite her annoyance at having to go to so much trouble to find the stupid Russian in the first place, Nicky allowed herself a small grin. She hadn't yet gotten to know Terra very well, but what she did know, she liked. She was the perfect woman for Zander.

"I need a favor, but you have to swear you won't tell that man of yours."

"Why's that?"

"It's about Vasily. We have history and I don't want to involve my boss."

"Ooh," Terra had chuckled. "Like booty call history?"

"Uh..."

Terra giggled harder, and its throaty sound performed a miracle and made Nicky feel slightly less murderous. "Just giving you a hard time, babe, because yeah, he's def booty call material if you're into dangerous dudes. Which he is, as I'm sure you already know. What's the favor?"

"I need to know where he lives."

"Somewhere downtown, but I don't know the building. Hold on. Helen might."

"Wait...no, don't..." Ah, fuck! The fewer people who knew, the better.

"Yo, Resnick," Terra called before she could stop her. "Where's Vasily's crib at?"

Oh, good grief.

"Say it a little louder Terra, I'm sure there are people on the street who didn't quite hear."

"What's that?"

Nicky sighed, then held her phone to her forehead and shook her head. This probably wasn't the smartest idea, but she was pissed enough her anger trumped her logic. "Next time you're at the bar I'm spiking your drink."

"As long as it's tequila. But seriously, why do you want to know?"

"I have something of his." It wasn't technically a lie. His business card qualified as something. "I want to give it back." More like shove it up his very attractive Slavic ass. Hopefully, she'd survive the experience and leave this building relatively unscathed.

"Sounds delicious."

Sounds deadly.

Before today, she'd never considered that she just might have a death wish. Nonetheless, Helen was a fountain of information but only on the promise Nicky paid a visit to Provocative to scope out their bra inventory.

So here she was, and she checked the card again, just in case she missed it the first fifty times—still no suite number. And no sneaking past Lurch to find her way to whichever floor. Smoothing her lavender dress and checking the tasseled cinch below her breasts was firmly tied, she approached the desk again.

"Hi," she said. "I realize I don't have an appointment, but it's important I see Mr. Melnikov. I'll only take a couple of minutes of his time, then I'll disappear. Like the wind." She curled her fingers up, then popped them wide—in a *poof* motion. "If you could just let him know, I'd appreciate it."

The concierge ignored her. Instead, he directed a pointed, bored-out-of-his-ancient-skull gaze to the right of her shoulder.

"Hello," she said, but he continued to ignore her. Nicky wiggled her fingers. "I'm over here."

"Ms. Andretti," a gravelly voice directly behind her said, making her jump.

She turned on her boot heel and—oh, surprise—if it wasn't the mountainous bodyguard! The man was so big, he took up a lot of space and air, yet he'd silently snuck up behind her without her noticing. Did he float there?

Nicky glanced at his cowboy boots peeking beneath his jeans. Nope, his feet were firmly attached to the ground, and he was much scarier looking in daylight than when she'd seen him at *The Happy Clam.*

"I'm Yev," he said, smirking at her expression. "I'll escort you upstairs."

"Right," she muttered, chewing on her lip. "Of course, you will." She was beginning to question the wisdom of coming here. Vasily had this mammoth for reinforcements and she had her single self. Was it too late to chicken out? What if he made her disappear as he had disappeared for ten years? Yet, despite her heart racing, she followed Yev across the lobby, through a second, smaller lobby with a single elevator.

The Mountain pressed his quarter-sized thumbprint to a nickel-sized digital pad. It made a surprisingly pleasant ping, then the elevator doors swished, and he gestured with that big bear paw that she should step inside.

But her feet balked, seemingly stuck to the floor. Heart thumping, she looked at The Mountain. He returned her look, with thickly lashed brown eyes, and perhaps she'd begun to hallucinate from all the testosterone, or he felt sorry for her, but his expression relaxed. Almost as if to say *it's okay.*

Isn't that what the spider said to the fly, moments before...?

Forcing herself to breathe steadily, Nicky gathered her courage and entered the elevator. The Mountain pressed another button that had no markings on it, and they rocketed to wherever. The entire trip up, he eyed her with idle curiosity that weirdly enough didn't creep her out, but told her absolutely nothing. Did they teach those blank expressions in mobster school?

Whizzing to a stop, a soft, electronic female voice announced, "Penthouse." She refrained from rolling her eyes. Naturally, he had the penthouse.

Yet another lobby, though this was much less glass and chrome —more sage green walls, dotted with sconces bearing orchids, lush ferns, and in the center on the marble floor, a fountain. Artfully distressed doors with small square windows led to a large rooftop balcony, but her escort ignored those and nodded for her to continue through. She preceded him into a lounge area past an angel spewing water from its mouth.

"Wait here," The Mountain said. "He'll be with you soon."

"Holy *wow,*" she whispered as soon as he disappeared through another door. This one was arched and flanked by two long shelves loaded with expensive-looking books. She dropped her purse onto a cream-colored couch and straightened her dress, mostly to rid herself of the moisture collecting on her palms.

The view beyond the floor-to-ceiling windows stretched across the north and east bay, featuring both iconic bridges: the Bay Bridge and the Golden Gate.

Okay, wait a hot second!

She wasn't here to be impressed. In fact, she refused to be. The man had made his ill-gotten gains while her dad rotted in prison for something he didn't do. Not to mention blowing up her damn car!

She held onto those thoughts and the anger they aroused when the fine hairs on her nape stood up.

Her chest was suddenly void of air.

How did he do that? How could she feel him before she could see him? Her eye began to twitch, but instead of touching a finger to it, she pressed her lips together and kept her expression neutral. Taking a steadying breath, Nicky turned to meet his silvery gaze. There was no smile on his face, but his expression wasn't hard, or cold. If she had to venture a guess, he almost seemed pleased as he leaned against the arched doorway, arms folded, looking as rich and masculine as the leather-bound novels surrounding him.

He lingered for a long moment before straightening. The man oozed power, and it preceded him, rolling across the room, and crashing into her like a runaway city bus. For a moment she had an intense desire to make an escape, to forget about her stupid car. That's what insurance was for, right?

"Dominique," he drawled in that deep, sexy voice that had always inclined to render her helpless, lulling her into a state of hypnosis where all she could do was focus on him. Like a poisonous viper just moments before it struck. Then his mouth tilted up ever so slightly. "To what do I owe this unexpected pleasure?"

"Don't call me that," she said. The way he said it was too disarming, too charismatic, and...too distracting.

"Why shouldn't I call you that? It's your name."

"My name is Nicky."

"Not to me," he said quietly, almost gently.

Daylight only enhanced his beauty, highlighting the dark honey tones in his neatly cut hair. He wore jeans, that though they fit as if they were cut specifically for him, were a little loose. They were topped with a white short-sleeved tee-shirt that stretched across his abs, and showed every ridge on that washboard stomach.

And he was barefoot.

Why was that so attractive? It sort of humanized him and made him seem less intimidating, though that was surely a ruse. After what he'd done, there was nothing on this earth that should make him anything less than the cruel mob boss that he was. Nicky swallowed.

He continued forward, pausing a few feet in front of her, and shoved his hands into his pockets as if to keep them tethered. This drew her attention to the way his muscles bunched—and ink she'd never seen. Not all of it was visible, but she made out bars intertwined with barbed wire that circled his right biceps. It was simple, black, and contrasted to his lightly tanned skin—striking.

"I suppose I should thank you for paying for our tab, but I'm confused, and not sure what that was." A disarming tactic or the beginnings of a bribe?

A short chuff left his mouth as he gave an amused shake of the head. "Simply what it appeared to be. A gesture of goodwill. A way of reaching out, considering our earlier encounter felt a little... antagonistic to me."

Nicky's eyes narrowed. "There's no goodwill between us, Vasily. That train has left the station, and no amount of *gestures* will erase what you have done."

He studied her for a beat longer, then his head tilted to the side. "Now I'm the one who's confused. Our time together was short, I'll admit, but it was memorable, Dominique." His eyes dropped to her breasts and lingered a beat before coming back up to rest on her mouth. "And what I remember was good."

So that's the way he wanted to play it—pretending what he did to her family didn't happen? How far would he go with this gaslighting charade? Parts of her wanted to find out, but other parts wanted to get this over with. Then he threw her a fastball.

"You've filled out quite...interestingly."

Her head moved back an inch. *Interestingly?* Was that a back-handed compliment, or a judgment? Yeah, so she was no Sunny. Like any woman who'd pushed out a human, she'd developed certain curves and flaws. But fuck, she wasn't Marley's fur-ball throw-up either.

"And you haven't changed at all. Still doing the mob thing, I see."

His lips twitched and something flittered through his eyes. They'd once lain naked on her bed wrapped around each other chuckling while they watched The Big Bang Theory. That look reminded her he'd once had a sense of humor. How much of that humor had been at her expense, though, knowing what he was about to do to her father?

She straightened her spine and fished the card from her dress pocket. "Enough of the pleasantries. I'm not here to catch up. I'm here to ask you something. Can you explain this?"

He squinted at her sharpened tone, but then his gaze dropped to her extended hand.

"What is it?"

"Take a look, you tell me."

Again, holding her gaze for seconds longer than necessary, he reached out and retrieved it from her, his finger sliding along hers.

She jerked her hand away. A hot, highly inconvenient, and just plain wrong surge of electricity swept through her.

How could that still happen when she hated him so? Clearly, there was something wrong with her. But that's how it always was with them. All it took was a gentle touch, a heated look, and a flick of the tongue on his lips before they crashed together and tore each other's clothes off.

"My business card," he uttered in a slightly puzzled tone before giving it back to her. "I gave it to your son. So what?"

"Yes, well, a funny little thing happened to my car last night."

A brow arched. "Dare I ask?"

"You could, but you already know, don't you?"

His jaw spasmed as he looked down his nose. "Is this a trick question, Dominique, because again, I'm confused."

"Stop playing games, Vasily."

That flat, smooth brow furrowed. "I don't play games, but I do hate repeating myself. For the sake of clarity, I'll say it in different words. I don't understand."

"Playing dumb isn't a good look on you." She took a step closer. Lifting her chin, it came within inches of his dented one. "But since you *are* playing dumb, let me be crystal clear so there is no misunderstanding on *my* part. You blew up my car."

Highly charged seconds ticked by, and within that time, his brows came together while her heart pounded in her throat.

"Don't be ridiculous."

"Ridiculous? Pardon my Russian, but fuck you, Vasily."

Something hot flashed in his eyes. She couldn't tell if it was anger, or something else.

"Careful," he growled. "I don't care for being accused of something I didn't do." He then lowered that voice and brought his mouth close to her ear. "Word of warning." His breath seduced her cheek, making her hyperaware of his warmth and his clean man smell. "You're in my home, this close to me, don't say fuck unless you mean to be."

Holy shit.

Her lashes flickered. Images of their naked, hot, sweaty bodies surfaced from her memory, sending heat twisting down between her legs. A flicker moved across his face and the way his pupils dilated and went liquid told her he remembered too.

"Stop lying." Her voice came out breathlessly and it pissed her off she was so weak that a memory could throw her so off course.

"I'm not lying."

"Then what's *this*?" She waved the card inches from his nose.

In a flash, he grabbed her wrist, then spun her until she was bent over the backrest of the nearest couch and his hips were pressed firmly to her ass.

"If you're trying to provoke me, it's working," he said, his tone low and gravelly next to her cheek. His breath was hot against her ear and made the flesh on her entire upper body prickle, hardening her nipples. "Be careful what you wish for."

Shit.

Shit!

"That Italian temper always gets away from you, doesn't it?" he murmured. "Though I have to say I didn't complain then about your passion, and I'm enjoying the position you're in now."

"Fu...go to hell."

His chuckle was mirthless, but deep and dark and rolled through her body in a rumble of desire, because no matter how damaged his soul may be, how angry she was at him, or how much she hated him, he was also very magnetic. And her body didn't care about any of those things, it only remembered the insane sex they'd had.

"You learn quickly, I'll give you that." He rubbed his stubble gently along her jawline, sending shivers to her toes and back.

This couldn't be happening. Her head couldn't allow her body what it wanted, and she hated how good it felt to have him wrapped around her.

Somewhere deep inside she found the strength to buck and wriggle beneath him, making him suck in air between his teeth.

"Stop," he growled, tightening his hold on her. When he let his breath out it was shaky and sent tendrils of desire curling in her belly.

"Tell me why you're really here." His voice was husky, and his breathing was faster.

"I just did," she whimpered.

Damn her body.

Damn the pleasure she knew he delivered. And damn his

dominance. She shuddered beneath him. It was one of the things she'd loved and craved when they were together. The way he took charge, and how she willingly submitted to his demands. A fire raged through her blood making dark spaces within her tingle and her panties damp. If he didn't let her go soon, she'd lose all dignity and self-respect.

She could feel his heart thundering against her back, and his cock nestled between her ass cheeks had grown hard. He slipped a knee between her legs, forcing them apart. "Am I going to find any electronic recording devices taped to your skin?"

Holy hell, she hadn't even thought about that. "Are you crazy? No!"

Those strong, slender fingers slid into her hair. Getting a good grip, he pulled her head back gently and turned it so he could look into her eyes. His were a dark gray and burning. "I don't believe you."

"It's the truth."

"Nevertheless, I'm going to search you. I suggest you behave while I do, or things are going to get out of control faster than you think."

Sweat popped up on her upper lip as his body heat seeped through the fabric of their clothing into her skin. "I'm not wearing a wire," she swallowed, "and I don't have any weapons."

The planes of his face were taut, harsh almost, and his breathing was heavy, like that of a man on the edge.

"Then are we going to be able to have a reasonable conversation without you getting snappy with me?"

"That wasn't snappy, Vasily. As you said, I'm Italian. I get excited. If I ever got *snappy*, you'd never see it coming."

He exhaled a long breath. "I'm trying to give you the benefit of the doubt, but that's not a good answer, Dominique. How can I trust you won't blindside me now?"

God!

Her stupid mouth. "Because I came here to talk to you, not kill you."

"That's yet to be determined."

Un-bunching his fingers from her hair and adjusting his foot outwards, he pried her legs further apart, keeping her off balance. A rough palm wrapped around the inside of her leg just above her knee. In a slow achingly seductive path, his hand moved up her inner thigh. The combination of heat and sensation against her sensitive skin made her shiver.

"What are you doing? she gasped.

"Checking you're not wired."

"I'm not!" Her voice sounded as panicked as she felt.

"Forgive me if I don't believe you."

God, what had she done? Perhaps on some weird psychological level, she had wanted to provoke him. That she wanted *this*. But now she had it she didn't know how to deal with his hands on her skin. Nor the fact her panties were getting soaked.

After an eternity, yet at the same time too fast, he switched legs. Repeating the slow, heated trail up the other, his thumb scraped the edge of her lace-trimmed panties. She squeezed her eyes shut and smothered a whimper.

No man had ever made her feel this deep, urgent need to be touched. To be wanted. Because there was no doubt parts of him wanted her. Every long, hard inch of his thick cock pressing through his jeans told her so. His fingers lingered for several beats before they vanished, leaving the area cold...and aching.

"Satisfied?" she asked, mortified by the breathless crack in her voice.

"Not even close." There was a similar hoarseness in his voice and God forgive her, but she both loved and hated that it gave a weird sense of depraved pleasure.

This was wrong!

Yet, why did it feel so right, so natural and so impossible to resist? Their chemistry had always been like rocket fuel, only more combustive, now more so than ever.

He leaned in closer. Tension rippled through him as his warm breath fanned her ear and neck. "I'm going to ask you again, Dominique." His voice was strained. "Why are you really here?"

What was he expecting her to say? That she still wanted him? She'd never admit it, but she didn't have to. *He knew.*

A moment passed. Then another. Her heart pounded, and her breath came in shallow and fast. His abs pressed against her back went taut, then with a suppressed groan he started a slow, but steady grind against her ass.

She shivered.

He slipped an arm around the front of her shoulders, and keeping her close he straightened, pulling her with him from the backrest. Then the hand on her wrist slid over the back of hers, intertwining their fingers. He nipped her shoulder tendon. Not hard enough to hurt, but enough to send a jolt of pleasure straight to her sex.

"Tell me to stop," he whispered, his voice uneven, as he grazed down her stomach.

She couldn't. The words wouldn't come out, and no part of her body wanted him to. As she trembled against him, he cupped her jaw and angled her mouth until their lips touched lightly, their breath mingling.

"Look at me," he demanded. "I want to see your eyes."

She couldn't help herself, and when she opened hers, their gazes locked. His pupils were dark and large, the expression within hungry.

His mouth took hers, tasting of whiskey and the wild, crazy, mind-blowing sex she remembered. Against her will, her body melted into his as their tongues tangled and tasted each other, in a slow but intense game of chase and explore. When he broke for air, he moved his mouth to her neck, his scruff gently scratching her skin. Forbidden tendrils of desire thrilled her body, as his hand on her stomach moved towards the hem of her dress—to her thigh and underneath the soft cotton fabric.

She dropped her head back onto his shoulder knowing where he was headed, and this knowledge fucked with her on so many levels especially because she couldn't find it in her to stop him.

Rough fingers controlled hers and together, their hands slipped under her panties, then down till he cupped her, pausing and teasing her. Every cell pulsed, needing more stimulation, more friction. A whimper escaped her as his lips moved against her neck, then her sanity returned.

What was she doing?

They were about to hit the point of no return when she shoved his hand away as if it belonged to Satan himself.

"No!"

"What?" he croaked, lifting his head from her neck.

"Let me go." Humiliation and shame filled her. Using both hands she peeled his arm from around her shoulders. To her relief, he stepped away and scraped a hand through his hair, exhaling sharply. Then his mouth moved into the semblance of a bitter smile, or was it a grimace?

"You owe me a car!" she blurted.

He stared at her as if she'd completely lost her mind. "I'm thinking I owe you a lot more than that, but why a car in particular?"

"Did you not see your card?" She pointed to it lying on the silken oriental rug.

Not bothering to look at it, he stared at her, jaw ticking. The sound of his breathing, still harsh breached the small amount of distance between them. It matched her own and moments passed when neither of them did anything, just faced the other.

"We're back to this," he responded, finally. "I fail to see the significance of it, but yes, I see my card."

"I found it in the middle of the burnt-out rectangle where my Audi used to be."

"Maybe your son dropped it?"

"He didn't." She dug into her pocket and pulled out the other card. "Because this is the one you gave him. It was still on his side table next to his bed."

His brows came together. "You found a second card?"

"That's what I was trying to tell you before you accosted me."

The sound of air being drawn through his nostrils filled the space between them, then his face went hard as he impaled her with that silver gaze.

Fuck.

She'd handled hard-ass men all her life, her dad and Pavel, his partner being two. Most of the time it was bullshit bluster and she'd learned when to stand her ground. But since she couldn't tell if this new shift in temper was directed at her, she surmised it wasn't a time to toss attitude. He looked scary as hell and ready to snap her neck. And she rather liked her neck the way it was.

"If what you say is true, that *is* a problem," he clipped.

The light had changed. While they'd been *otherwise occupied*, the sun had fallen, penetrating the thinning marine layer. Golden rays bounced off the surrounding high rises giving the world outside a warm, angelic glow. Pity all that ethereal ambiance didn't reach inside his pristine apartment.

"For me, it's not *just* a problem," she said. "It's a reality. I'm without a car and I've got a kid."

"I'm aware. What I'm not aware of, is where's your husband in this cake mix?"

"That's none of your business, nor is it the point, is it? My car is gone..."

"Jesus, Dominique." He glared at her. "You really believe I'd do damage to your property?"

She regarded him hard, swearing that was a flash of pain she just saw flicker through his eyes. "You're seriously asking me that question?"

"Considering I have yet to hear a reason why you're accusing me, yes, I am. So humor me, and explain it."

"Someone threw a Molotov cocktail onto the back seat of my car. Are you telling me you didn't do it?"

"I didn't, nor did I give the order for anyone else to do it."

"Then who did?" she asked, allowing her skepticism to show in her voice.

He gave a single shake of his head. "If I had the answer, I'd tell you. But I don't. And now, you should leave."

"That's it? That's all you have to say?"

"What else do you want me to say?"

He was unbelievable. To stand there in righteous indignation acting like he'd never ruined her life.

"How about sorry?"

"For what?"

"Oh, let me think. For putting your hands on me uninvited. For letting me believe something that wasn't real. Or...oh wait." She put on a surprised expression. "I know! How about running away like a coward after framing my dad for something he didn't do? Something he spent time in federal prison for."

Vasily was like a statue as he studied her—emotionless and as hard as one. Seconds ticked by until the silence between them screamed.

This was useless, and she scoffed in disgust. He'd never admit to any wrongdoing, nor apologize for what he did. What was the point in humiliating herself any further? A sick sense of disappointment lodged in her throat, and tears of anger burned the back of her eyes. She grabbed her purse from the couch and adjusted the strap on her shoulder.

"One." His voice stopped her from taking the first step to the elevator. "What happened between us Dominique, was as real as it got. For me, anyway."

Her breath failed.

"Two," he continued before she could fully absorb that information. "I'm not going to apologize for taking my safety seriously. Something you should've considered before you came here. Three, I did not run away. Circumstances prevented me from contacting you once I'd left."

Circumstances? What fucking circumstances?

"And fourth. I framed your father *how* exactly?"

Oh.

The man was good—there was no doubting that. He looked genuinely perplexed but surely that was a ploy. A mobster move designed to keep her off-kilter. Whatever, she was done. He'd insulted her intelligence enough.

"You think I'm stupid. Fine. You're entitled to your opinion, but you'll never make me believe you had no part in what happened."

He watched her as she walked to the elevator, making no move to stop her, but his eyes burned with an intensity she didn't understand. It didn't feel hateful, it felt...questioning. They stayed on her until Nicky stepped inside the small space, and she fought to keep the unshed tears at bay as she descended.

Downstairs, the Mountain was talking to Lurch behind that chrome and glass counter. She felt their eyes on her too as they watch her walk to the revolving doors that led to the street.

Outside she pulled up the rideshare app and put in her destination, hoping to put this place behind her for good. Hoping to forget about that fucking Russian and all his bullshit. None of it was worth keeping those old wounds open, nor being reminded of the crippling heartache he'd caused her that had taken her so long to get over. Coming here had been a huge mistake and she should've known better.

Her car arrived, and only once she'd strapped herself in did, she finally allow the silent tears to fall.

Chapter Eight

The pain of watching Nicky walk away was almost unbearable. Despite that he'd told her to leave, he wanted to run after her and stop her, and ask her more questions. Try to understand what she meant. But if he let his emotions get in the way, as they had already done, he'd lose control and do something stupid. She had that effect on him.

How could she think he'd framed her father? What the hell was she talking about?

That ugly feeling that he'd not been fully informed after he'd returned from Russia was never clearer. Granted, he'd had other priorities to focus on at the time, which had taken all his skill to finesse, but there was no excuse for Dean to lie to him. Stepping on that damn plane to Moscow had been the absolute worst move Vasily had made in his life, but the far-reaching consequences as a result of that action were still becoming apparent.

Fucking Dean!

He wanted to slam his fist into the window, but he scraped his hands over his face, catching a hit of Nicky's lingering scent—a heady mix of sultry feminine heat and something darkly exotic, like the orchids in his foyer.

He inhaled, then let out a soft growl, ignoring the ache in his balls.

Jesus, the woman got under his skin and pissed him off beyond measure, but he'd never wanted to fuck anyone more. He'd never been so close to completely losing it. That had been a problem back when he was younger and apparently, it was still a problem now.

Moving to the bar across the room with his jeans tighter than they needed to be, he removed a tumbler from beneath the mahogany counter. Adjusting himself into a more comfortable position, he poured a finger of whiskey and tossed it back. Silky fire slaked down his throat before he placed the glass back on the wood and pulled his phone from his pocket. After he pushed the number, he pressed the phone to his ear.

"Yev."

"Boss?"

"What's she driving?"

There was a short pause, then his man cleared his throat. "I saw her climb into an Uber."

"Hmm."

That didn't really confirm anything. Many people used Uber in the city as parking was a nightmare, but it was at least one indication she might be telling the truth. "Her car was allegedly set on fire last night. I want you to find out what you can."

While he pulled a stool out from beneath the bar, he gave Yev what details he had, then hung up and made another call. Carmine Niccoterra answered after the second ring.

"Need some information," he said by way of greeting.

"Course you do," Niccoterra said, snark thick in his voice. "No way you'd call just to say hello. That would be too friendly and it's not like we're becoming friends or anything, are we asshole?"

Touché.

Vasily snorted at the man calling him out for his rudeness. "Hello, dickhead."

"Well, wonders never cease." Niccoterra's chuckle was genuine and tickled his ear. "You can be friendly. If you're calling about your social worker, I don't have anything yet."

"Not that." Vasily picked up the bottle of whiskey and poured another finger into his glass.

"Then about our mutual problem?"

The Italian of course was referring to Viktor Sokolov but was savvy enough not to mention the dead prick by name, should anyone uninvited be listening. It had been known to happen and even with Kat, his FBI friend on his side didn't mean it wasn't happening now. One of the many reasons he hated phones.

"Again, not that, but since you mentioned it, it's no longer a problem."

"I won't deny that's a relief. Those kinds of problems become bigger problems if they are allowed to get moldy and spread."

"Nothing quite like bleach as a disinfectant." And great white sharks, which were in abundant supply near the Farallon islands just a few nautical miles from the Golden Gate.

"I have a couple of other things I need help with."

"Must be a tricky couple of other things if you're asking me. Not like you haven't got a whole organization of tough assholes to call on."

"It's that." Vasily pushed his fingers into his hair and scratched his scalp. Carmine Niccoterra's private investigation skills were the best he'd come across. And in the process of their working together on their human trafficking problem, he'd discovered he liked the man. Respected him even more, which said a lot in his world. Talking directly to Dean would've been preferable, but his incarceration made that difficult, and right now he needed immediate answers.

"What do you know about my brother's waitress, Nicky?"

The silence on the other side was heavy. So heavy, he could almost hear the Italian's brain churn over.

"First thing you have to be aware of I know Nicky, and I like her. Second thing you have to be aware of, I've known Zander a lot longer than I have you, which by default means I like him a lot more than I like you. With that being said, and with the clarification I'm only going to divulge what is probably common knowledge, I could answer a few of your questions."

Vasily hunched over the bar and leaned on an elbow, a million questions swirling around in his head. "I just need a little gap-filling."

"Like what kind of gap-filling?"

"History gap-filling." He tilted the tumbler and swirled the amber liquid inside, admiring the legs it left on the side of the crystal. "You familiar with her dad, Mario Marcello?"

"Marcello belonged to the Cadora crime family back in the day. Ran a scrap metal yard fencing stolen car parts. He went down for murder two and spent time inside for allegedly killing his partner, Pavel."

Vasily's chest constricted. *And there it was!* He straightened in his stool, took a deep breath, and rubbed a hand over the area of his heart. It didn't do much to relieve the pervasive tightness.

"Allegedly?"

"Marcello was framed."

Fuck. He gave a slight shake of his head. "How long was he inside?"

"One short of a dime."

Nine years! Almost the entire time Vasily had been in Russia. Nicky wasn't a kid when it happened, a mature nineteen-year-old, but still young to technically lose her only parent. He knew firsthand how much that hurt and what that did to a person.

"I'm surprised you're asking me about this," Niccoterra's voice carried his skepticism. "Don't kill me for this, but considering who you are, I'm having a hard time you didn't know this happened."

You and everybody else.

"I was in Russia when it went down." A sharp, unfamiliar

pang of guilt stabbed at his gut. "Certain things that happened then were beyond both my knowledge and control."

There was a long pause, in which he felt the air around him settle and his fingers tightened around the glass.

"That's perhaps something you need to discuss with Dean then." Niccoterra's tone was guarded, and his next words proved why. "It's no secret the prosecutor and several San Francisco cops were deep in the Melnikov pocket at that time."

A long blast of a muted car horn punctuated the man's speech and Niccoterra mumbled a curse. "Anyway, with enough green slipped to the right people to tamper with evidence and back up bullshit charges, it isn't hard to frame a man."

Vasily rubbed the back of his neck and sighed. Even if he hadn't secured a couple of San Francisco's finest himself and backed the campaign of the then deputy district attorney, he would've believed it. All it took was the right individual with just the right amount of money problems and bingo, they were in your pocket.

"Smart money said your organization was behind Marcello's conviction," Niccoterra added. "Was the smart money wrong?"

Doubtful. But until Vasily heard it from Dean's mouth, he remained open-minded. But not hopeful. Leonid, his uncle, had wanted Marcello's scrapyard for reasons of his own, and Vasily had been foolish to believe he'd dissuaded him from acquiring it. If he remembered correctly, he'd been assured of it.

The scrapyard wasn't in their property portfolio, but thinking about it now, what if that assurance was merely semantics?

"What happened to the scrapyard?" he asked Niccoterra.

"Marcello sold to a real estate developer to pay his legal fees. Andretti handled it."

So, after all that, Leo got outbid by a damn land developer. What irony. But the old, familiar anger he'd carried for so long burgeoned in his chest like a toxic mushroom, making him curl his fingers around his glass. He'd been played for a fool by both Dean and Leonid. And if Leonid, that toad-dicked bastard, wasn't already dead, Vasily would've killed him again—with his bare fucking hands. Dean, his actual flesh and blood was lucky he was incarcerated. Because any way he looked at it, this new information wasn't boding well for his brother.

Vasily poured another finger of whiskey into the tumbler and sniffed its aroma, allowing him to focus his mind on something else than the betrayal before he sipped. "Speaking of Andretti, what do you know of him?"

"I know Nicky dumped his ass."

An unexpected surge of relief rushed through his body and as it mixed with his anger, it mellowed it somewhat. He shouldn't care if they were exes or not, yet he did. That vixen was no doubt set on this earth to cause him trouble and fuck if she didn't excel at it. But it had always been the kind of trouble he enjoyed, his blue balls notwithstanding. He shifted in his seat.

"And he has ugly clients." Niccoterra's tone was laced with a warning. "Scraping the bottom of the barrel kind of clients. Not people you'd ever want to mess with. Well," he chuckled. "I'll take that back. *You* may want to mess with them, but the general population sure as hell doesn't."

"Do you know of any client that if Andretti stepped out of line, they'd threaten Nicky in his stead?"

A thick silence only filled with muted traffic noises followed his question. "What are you talking about?"

He gave the Italian the short version of what Nicky had said about her car and his business card found at the scene.

"Sounds like you're being set up," Niccoterra said, confirming what he also believed.

"But the question is why."

"Exactly." And where had that second card come from? He didn't just give them out to anybody.

With nothing more to be said, they disconnected the call. Vasily scraped a hand through his hair, then slid off his barstool to walk to the window. It was getting dark out and the colorful city lights twinkled on. The streets below were gridlocked with traffic —red taillights, and white headlights moving at a snail's pace. The same traffic Niccoterra was no doubt stuck in. And maybe Nicky.

He couldn't help wondering if she'd made it home. Then he shook his head at his idiocy. Of course, she had. The woman had survived ten years without him, why wouldn't she now?

He slid his phone into his pocket and headed through the arched doors between the bookcases. Into a more formal living room, dining area, and kitchen, with kick-ass lacquered slabs of natural oak countertops—the main reason he'd bought this apartment. Beyond that, down a long hall was his master suite and three guest bedrooms, each with their own bathrooms and multi-million-dollar views.

Besides his penthouse, there was an additional smaller apartment that Yev shared with his dad, the building's concierge. Then the security room, his private gym, a rooftop pool, and his office.

Vasily had the entire floor, much more space than he needed. But this suited him as he didn't need or want neighbors.

In his bedroom, he sat on the long black couch at the foot of his bed and opened his laptop, then went through the motions of requesting an in-person visit with his brother in Pelican Bay prison.

In light of what both Nicky and Niccoterra had told him, Dean, that traitorous little asshole, had a lot to answer for.

Chapter Nine

Two days later Vasily stepped off the private jet at Del Norte County Regional Airport, three miles north of Crescent City and home to Pelican Bay State Prison.

The rented Mercedes Yev had organized for him was parked a little more than twenty yards away, with the rental agent still sitting inside. He couldn't blame him, it was unseasonably hotter than Hades with the temperature in the high nineties. After the cool, foggy air of San Francisco and the private jet's air conditioning, moisture popped on Vasily's brow. He collected the keys from the agent, adjusted the driver's seat, fixed the mirror, then drove the additional fifteen minutes through the majestic Redwoods of Northern California that towered over Highway 101. Finally entering through a gate bordered by razorwire-topped fencing, he approached a stark concrete building.

The contrast was depressing as hell.

Inside he showed his ID and handed over his phone and keys to a weary prison guard who put everything in a sealed plastic bag and stuck them into a small locker. He was searched, given a number, then directed to wait in a high-ceilinged room with long, narrow windows covered by bars. He was at these windows staring at the bland concrete yard with only a few empty wooden bleachers when Dean entered.

His brother's appearance shocked him. It had been a few months since he'd seen him and he was thinner, his cheeks sunken with smudges beneath gray eyes so similar to his own. Dean's were dull and red-rimmed. Their faces were alike, but Vasily inherited their dad's cleft chin while Dean got the panty-dropping dimples from their mother. His drab blue prison garb did nothing to offset his pallor.

Even furious at his older brother, he wished he could hug him. Perhaps it was for the best, he might just strangle the bastard.

They took seats at a small table with its legs bolted to the floor. The plastic chairs were uncomfortable—designed no doubt to keep visits short.

"Do you ever think about Mom?" Dean asked first thing, his tone uncharacteristically melancholy and reflecting his appearance. Even his voice seemed thinner, minus its rich quality from before.

There were several other prisoners in the room doing exactly what they were. Entertaining, if one could call it that. Vasily sucked his tongue against his teeth, before giving a slow nod. "Of course."

"And that day?"

The day their father killed their mother.

"I try not to." Though now of course he would. Along with those thoughts, he'd suffer the inevitable nausea and unsettled stomach that always seemed to accompany them. *Christ.* If this was what was at the top of Dean's mind, no wonder he looked like shit.

Did he care?

Yeah, he fucking did.

They were silent for several seconds. Vasily attempted to shove the memories down into the pit they belonged in while searching his brother's face. "*Brat*, why are you bringing this up?"

"Still miss her." Dean smoothed the edge of his palm over the corner of his eye, erasing the suspicious wetness that had gathered there. "The hot chocolate she made on rainy days, you know? With the marshmallows she hid because Papa didn't want her to make us soft."

"And whipped cream," Vasily added. Too much sugar, but fuck they'd loved it. Every single second of it.

"And her roast chicken. What I wouldn't give for some of that now."

Vasily's mouth watered at the thought, despite the sickness in his gut. Those were the good memories, the ones he held onto.

"Why didn't she leave, bro?" Dean asked.

Vasily had asked himself that very question too many times to count, turned it around in his mind, and always ended up with the same answer. "Dmitri would've found her."

"I wish she had, and taken us with her. Think we'd be as fucked up as we are now?"

"Who knows." And honestly, he didn't. Their mother's submissive, gentle nature had never been a match for Dmitri's ferocity. Perhaps if she'd been more of a fighter, she might've lived longer. It was one of the things that had drawn him to Nicky. Her feistiness, and from what he'd seen of her recently, she hadn't lost it.

"She might still be around if she had."

"He would've found her," Vasily repeated. "Perhaps she'd known it would've been worse if she'd left."

"Worse than her face being flattened to a pulp? Jesus. I've been dreaming about it. Can't get that vision out my head." Dean's Adam's apple bobbed as he scraped both palms up his cheeks, then clutched chunks of his overgrown shaggy hair. "The blood, the smell, the *sound* when her skull cracked."

"Dean, stop!"

"Hate him," Dean said between clenched teeth. "Hate he took her from us. Hate who he was. Hate every fucking thing about him. Then I realize bro when I look at those walls in my cell and the reason I'm here, I *am* him. I don't just have his name, I'm exactly like Dmitri Melnikov."

Vasily exhaled. "You may share the same name, but that doesn't make you him." It had been their mom who'd anglicized his name and called him Dean so as not to confuse him with his father.

His brother's physical appearance made more sense now. Not that prison didn't do things to a man. The lack of fresh air, mental stimulation, and the knowledge he was surrounded by vile assholes, some of who'd done worse shit than he had. Self-realization was a bitch.

"You were always stronger," Dean went on. "It hurts to admit it, but since prison is about reflecting, I can't lie to myself. You at least tried to protect Mom. I fuckin' froze! Like a weak little pussy. Deep down I always figured he'd kill her. Just thought that if it came to it, I'd have had the guts to kill him first."

Vasily cleared his throat of the growing lump. There was a watery glint in his brother's bloodshot eyes, which he suspected mirrored his own.

"You forget, *brat,* you did defend her. We both did and got the living shit kicked out of us."

"We shoulda told someone."

"Who...Leonid?" Vasily's scoff was full of skepticism. "He wouldn't have done anything. He was so far up Papa's ass he could lick his intestines. Anyway, looking back I'm betting he knew."

Dean nodded.

Why's he bringing this up? A weird itching sensation spread across his skin and Vasily scratched his forearm over his shirt. He loved his brother, screwed up as he was, but this self-reflecting thing was heading into uncomfortable territory. Not that he wasn't used to being uncomfortable, but this was a level he tried to avoid. "You're not planning on doing anything stupid?" Like off himself. Suicide by prison guard, whatever that may entail.

He studied Dean closer as he looked across the room toward the barred windows, a distant look in his eye. "I had her."

Every single one of the fine hairs on the back of his neck stood up. He knew by Dean's softening tone he was no longer talking about their mom. But he didn't need to ask. He knew.

Dean's mind was on Shelley DeLuca.

"She was mine. All I had to do was keep her."

By *keeping her*, he was pretty certain Dean didn't mean as a prisoner after he kidnapped Shelley. Highly doubtful he could've kept her, but he wasn't going to piss on his brother's mood further by mentioning her recent engagement to Gianni Cadora. There was no point, except to be cruel. Anyway, he suspected Dean already knew, due to the genuine remorse and sadness etched into newly formed lines around his mouth. Along with a far more worrying emotion—depression.

"I'm just like Papa, bro. I have this rage, this *madness* inside me. I can't control it. I belong in here."

"You belong in a psych ward where you can get help. I'm working on that. Your lawyer is requesting another hearing so you can be evaluated by a shrink. Get the meds you need."

"Tell my lawyer not to bother. Don't need any meds."

"Jesus, Dean. I'm trying to help you. A little cooperation?"

"You're wasting your time, bro."

"Then just play along."

Dean sighed, then slumped forward onto the table, his thumbnail digging into the plastic. "All right."

Damn.

Vasily was at a loss. For once he didn't know what to do. Usually, his presence would cheer Dean up enough that he faked it. He almost considered not broaching the reason he came, but at the very least it would change the subject.

"I gotta ask you something and I need you to level with me."

"About what?"

"The scrapyard."

A wrinkle formed on Dean's brow, but he noted the worry that flitted through his bloodshot eyes. "That was years ago, bro."

"It's relevant, and I need to know what happened."

"We didn't get it." He emphasized this with a shrug. "You know that, otherwise that land would be in our assets right now."

"I'm talking about what happened to Pavel, Marcello's partner."

Dean's thumb stilled. Then he sighed and closed his eyes for several seconds.

Vasily waited him out. He knew if he gave his brother enough space, he would eventually fill it, which he did.

"Short version is Pavel changed his mind about selling. Leo didn't like it. Things got outta hand. Cops got a tip and found his body in a car ready to be crushed."

"That's it?" Vasily's jaw ticked.

"Pretty much."

"I said level with me, Dean."

Dean straightened but avoided his eyes. His voice soft, he said, "Marcello bought the rap."

The pit he'd had in his stomach since Nicky confronted him yawned wide open.

They'd done it!

They'd framed Nicky's old man!

His nostrils flared. "Explain. It. To me."

There was another long silence while his brother chewed on the inside of his lip, seemingly fighting some internal battle.

"Dean," he gritted out between clenched teeth. "How did Marcello go down for it?"

"I planted evidence." Dean closed his eyes again, his throat bobbing. The very throat Vasily had a sudden urge to wrap his fingers around and squeeze. Except it would do his brother a favor by putting the little prick out of his misery.

Instead, he kept his hands to himself. For now. "What evidence? Give me the long version."

"Bro..."

"Just do it. Since you're in the mood to reflect, indulge me."

Dean made a noise in the back of his throat and covered his face for a moment. "It happened the week after you left for Moscow. Leo never had any intention of letting the yard go, and somehow Pavel had come up with the money he owed us from gambling. I couldn't reach you and Leo was out of his mind with fury. I went in pretending to look for parts. I asked to use their bathroom and found used tissues in the trash. I'd seen Marcello sneezing and blowing his nose, so I figured they were his. There was also a brush. I snagged some hairs that still had the little bud on them. Then, when we dumped Pavel, I planted the hairs on his body. His knuckles were already roughed up because that short son of a bitch fought, so I smeared the snot from the tissues onto them. It was enough. Shouldn't have been, but it was. I always thought the forensics would be iffy and that he'd get off. That fuckin' prosecutor we had in our pocket was too good and the jury found him guilty."

Vasily sucked in air, his upper lip curling with the effort to control his rage. "Any of that shit could've been Nicky's, you fuck. Did you think of that?"

"It wasn't."

"But you didn't know that at the time."

"The hairs weren't long enough, and she wasn't there that day."

Vasily clenched his fists for several seconds, before pressing his palms in the prayer position against his forehead. Slowly, he counted to five, waiting for the ice to resume flowing through his veins. It took longer than it should've.

"I wanted to tell you, bro," Dean said. "I wanted nothing more than to give you a heads-up on what Leo was planning, but *I couldn't reach you*."

That much was true. He'd been stripped of his possessions, his passport, and all forms of communication, then thrown into a dank cell to rot and die.

"I didn't know yet that Leo had betrayed us, and I had other things on my mind. Like, I was getting worried about you, and tried everything I could to reach you."

Short of actually going to Moscow. But truthfully, he was glad Dean didn't, as he would've ended up either dead or in a dungeon himself. Fucking Leonid.

"An innocent man went to prison." And Nicky had spent ten years hating him.

"You gotta know I'm sorry," Dean added, his voice tired. "Even if I didn't give a shit about Marcello, I gave a shit about you. And I knew you gave a shit about *her*. Something I now realize the depth of."

"I'd have liked to kill Leo myself."

"I know, but I didn't know you were still alive.

Nobody did.

"They'd told us you were ambushed. The car you were in blew up. The body they showed us...it was burnt beyond recognition, but it had your ring."

One exactly like the ring he'd beaten Viktor Sokolov with. The only difference was the inscription on the inside that included Vasily's name. Leo had sent a lackey to Russia to collect what was supposedly left of Vasily, an unrecognizable burnt corpse. But they never figured out who that corpse belonged to because they'd cremated what was left of the remains and scattered the ashes over the San Francisco Bay.

"Leo played the part of a grieving uncle well. I never fucking suspected a thing."

But unknown to Leonid, Aleksei Federov, his partner in Moscow was a greedy, ambitious turd. And greedy, ambitious turds made stupid mistakes.

Like eventually trusting Vasily.

"I don't blame you for that," he added rubbing his eyes with his thumb and index finger. How fucking could he? Dean had no idea he was Federov's prisoner. Leo didn't even know. But it had taken Kat's manipulations, and Vasily faking full Stockholm syndrome—doing whatever it took—*and it fucking took*—to earn that small modicum of trust and eventually his freedom.

Vasily pulled in a long breath and sat back in his seat.

"Tell me about her," Dean said.

"Who?"

"Marcello's girl. This is about her, right? That chick for whatever reason was always your kryptonite."

"Like Shelley is yours?" he countered.

Dean's face sobered, his lips flattening into sad lines, then he looked at the ceiling. "Women make us weak, bro."

Or keep you alive. Depending on your perspective.

"I wonder if that's what Papa thought when he killed Mom. That it would make him stronger if she was gone. He could never control himself when it came to her."

"Maybe. Men who obsess tend to blame the object of their obsession."

"Like I did with Shelley." Dean gave him a pointed look. "See? I'm exactly like him."

Vasily met his stare. Obsessing tended to run in their blood, though he'd never allowed it to take control, as his brother and father had. "At least you realize it. That's a big step forward, *brat*."

He looked over at the couple at the next table. The woman was crying, wiping her blotchy face with a sleeve, and smearing her makeup. The inmate sitting across the table from her looked helpless like he had no words left to offer.

This place was depressing enough for visitors, he couldn't imagine what it was like for its occupants.

A loud buzzer sounded. Their half-hour was over.

"Until next time. Stay out of trouble, yeah?"

He was several steps away when Dean called, "Bro!"

"What?"

"Mom doesn't have a headstone. There's nothing to show she ever existed."

"Except for us."

"She needs more. Somewhere with a view."

"I'll think about it."

"You do that." Dean pointed at him, then said words he hadn't heard out of his mouth in a long time. "Love you, man."

"Love you too, *brat*."

"Life's short and unpredictable. If Marcello's girl is it for you, don't waste any more time on bullshit. Tell her what happened to you."

Could he?

It had taken him years to stop thinking about her, and about what could've been. The emptiness in his soul he'd experienced when she'd been taken from him, like half of him went missing. Though he'd never tried to replace her, there had been women. None had filled that hole. None had made him feel alive or made his blood race the way Nicky did. Could he put his guilt on her?

Never.

He watched Dean leave through a door on the far end, a couple of other prisoners behind him. A deep sense of darkness settled over him, one he couldn't shake.

As soon as he got his phone back and stepped into the fresh air, he called Derek Granger, their lawyer.

"Make that psych hearing for my brother an emergency. Bribe whomever you need to and have Dean put on suicide watch."

Chapter Ten

"**M**r. Melnikov!"

Zander's young bouncer stuck out his hand, his cheerful voice wasn't enough to hide that he seemed close to having a panic attack. Vasily noticed the way Yev glared at him for daring to shake hands with his boss and he almost laughed.

It was the night after he visited Dean, and looking around Chuck's, Vasily saw the wagon wheel chandeliers and rusty motorcycle rims attached to the walls matched the invitation he'd received from Zander.

"Petey." He nodded, taking the kid's palm. Petey's grip was firm which earned a point in his favor. When they let go, Vasily tilted his head toward the man next to him. "This is Yev, my plus-one."

Petey acknowledged Yev with wide eyes and a chin nod but did not offer his hand. Neither did Yev, and it was probably a wise thing. Yev could've crushed his if he felt so inclined, even if the kid was well-built and bigger than average. Broken hands were not conducive to good bouncing, nor would Zander appreciate it.

"Zander's working the bar if you're looking for him," Petey

said, his voice finding the appropriate deferential tone. "We're expecting a big crowd. Have you seen Terra sing?"

"This would be my first. Mind if we come in?"

"Oh, shit, no sir." Petey's eyes widened even further as he must've realized he was blocking the door. "Of course not." He stepped sideways and bumped into a potted palm tree which teetered for a second, but then settled. Even under the yellow fluorescent lights that spelled out the bar's name, Vasily observed the kid's color rise.

Petey's hand came out holding the stamp. Normally Vasily would have no issue freezing someone with just the force of his gaze for even attempting to touch him with such a thing. But this wasn't his world or his establishment. It was Terra's music video debut, and if Vasily wanted to improve his relationship with his half-brother, that meant supporting his woman and not humiliating his employees.

Fortunately, Petey caught himself and pulled his hand back. "Sorry, sorry, force of habit."

"Hmm." Vasily jerked his head at Yev. "If you can find a spot on his arm that isn't already inked, give my stamp to him."

To Yev's credit, there was no shift in his carefully etched expression at his boss's blatant attempt at fuckery.

"That's okay," Petey said, holding the stamp up in surrender. "It's not like I'm going to forget who either of you are. Enjoy your evening, gentlemen."

The band wasn't playing yet, but the room was loud and two bodies deep at the bar. The Black Key's *Gold On The Ceiling* punched at Vasily like an old but familiar foe. If he was the kind of man inclined to dance, he'd move his feet to the beat. But he wasn't, so he eased through the crowd with Yev on his six and spotted a few familiar faces. Gianni Cadora and his woman, Shelley. Carmine Niccoterra and Helen were deeper inside at a table chatting to the Italian's uncle, Billy The Barrel. He'd get to them eventually, but the first order of business was to greet his brother and host for the evening.

"Yo," Zander called over the music from across the highly polished oak surface. His dark, wavy hair was pulled back into a doubled-over ponytail. "You're becoming a regular. Twice in a week, I've seen your ugly face."

"Here for Terra, dipshit. How could I say no to a personal invitation from my favorite female soon-to-be family member?"

"Your *only* female soon-to-be family member." Zander's grin broadened, his pride glowing from him like an incandescent bulb. "Considering our other brother's options are not good. Scotch?"

Vasily nodded and was interested to note that Zander didn't contradict him—he confirmed what he already knew to be true. Zander and Terra were relatively new as a couple, but anyone with half an eye could see they complemented each other. Their chemistry sizzled, practically setting the room on fire when they were together. Something he was genuinely happy for. At least one Melnikov family member got to break the streak of misery that plagued those whose veins carried their blood.

"I see you brought protection." Zander's chin pointed at Yev. "Pretty safe crowd here tonight. If you don't count looney tunes Helen that is."

Vasily's lip twitched. He knew exactly of what his brother spoke having had his own run-in with *looney tunes* Helen. The little redheaded spitfire had faced him off at a funeral. The woman, half his size, had reminded him that Terra was a sister and not to be messed with. He'd liked her immediately.

"Yev's driving. Thought I might relax and indulge a little. Partake in the goodies."

"As long as the goodies are willing and not already taken," Zander smirked. He reached up and pulled a bottle of whiskey off the top shelf. "Plenty of single women who might find your ass passable, though I can't see why."

Vasily flipped his brother off. They chuckled. He'd meant

partaking in alcoholic goodies, but speaking of—where was Nicky? While his gaze swept the room, he pulled his wallet from his pocket.

Zander passed his scotch, and a pint of beer for Yev then waved off Vasily's credit card. "On the house in honor of my woman, but feel free to tip my staff." He pointed to a large, black ceramic jar situated by the waitress station. Taped to it was a square of white paper with *tips encouraged* written on it.

"Enjoy." Zander double-tapped the bar top with his knuckles, then grinned. "We'll talk later." His brother moved to take an order from a pink-haired chick giving him moon eyes.

Vasily leaned his hip against the rounded wooden edge of the bar. Though he'd had dinner at Zander's apartment situated on the third floor of the same building, he'd never been inside this particular room and made note of the exits. The one they came in, and another through a pair of red swinging doors marked off limits. The second, he assumed led to the storeroom and the back door leading to the parking lot. The same one he'd exited to find Anthony Andretti with his hands around Nicky's throat. His nostrils curled at the memory.

Then as luck would have it, he saw her. In the far back corner, two millimeters from a dude spitting his order into her ear.

He sucked in a breath, and that weird heat flare happened in his chest. The same overwhelming thing he experienced every time he saw her. And exactly like the first time he'd pinned eyes on her at her father's scrapyard driving that shitty primer-gray Mustang. It never diminished, instead each time he saw her, it seemed to get stronger.

Just her profile was visible. That sexy hair was tucked behind an ear that had a silver hoop dangling from it. Her bangs fell loose, and at sort of an angle, partially covering the side of her face, making his fingers twitch with the desire to brush those glossy strands back.

Then the dude checked out her tits.

Granted, they were pushed up and offered a generous hint of cleavage, but then the schmuck licked his fat, ugly lips.

Vasily growled. His fingers curled into a fist as he resisted the impulse to march over there and punch him in his too-perfect nose.

Yev, ever vigilant to changes in Vasily's demeanor grew tense and leaned closer. "Boss, we got a problem?"

Vasily kept his attention on the fat-lipped schmuck. It wasn't enough Nicky constantly invaded his head, but now a man checking out her tits made him...*uncomfortable*?

What the hell was wrong with him?

Fuck. He knew what was wrong with him. His feelings for her hadn't changed and until she was his again, men looking at her, or attempting to touch her would continue to be a problem.

Yev followed his line of sight, then a moment later his lips did a little dance like he was trying not to smile. "Didn't know she worked here. A lot of shit's starting to make sense now."

Vasily ignored Yev and took a large swallow of his whiskey, finishing most of it in one gulp.

Why hadn't she stuck to cars? Gotten a job at another scrapyard or a garage for that matter? Large, inanimate metal objects didn't threaten his cool *or* check out her body when she worked.

Somebody squeezed his arm.

"Yo." Terra smiled and reached up to kiss his cheek. He leaned into it, allowing his face to crack a small smile. She looked stunning in motorcycle boots, tight skinny jeans, and a pink cropped top that showed off her belly. Her defining feature was her long reddish-gold curls which she'd teased up high like Madonna back in the day. Made sense if you took into consideration that her band covered songs from the eighties.

"You made it," she said, excitement in her voice. "I know this isn't your scene, so thanks. Really. Mom would be happy you did."

He felt a tug in his belly. "Yeah, she would." Terra's mom had been one of the women in his stable and he still felt the sting of her untimely death. "Rebecca was proud of you."

"I know. Terra cleared her throat. "But it's nice to hear it, so thanks for verbalizing."

"So tell me about this video," he said.

"You know Rory?" She pointed to a man on stage with shaggy blonde hair fiddling with some music equipment. "He wrote the song and tonight will be the first time we sing it in front of an audience before we stick it on social media. Helen's in the video." She grinned and tapped his arm in a light punch. "You missed out there, dude. Carmine's staked that claim, and now you'd need a damn crowbar to pry those two apart. My God." She made an astonished face. "They're like bunnies in the springtime. It's embarrassing."

He snorted a laugh. He found Helen adorable, though her fire-cracker nature was more suited for someone like Carmine Niccoterra. Yet another happy couple still in the throes of a new relationship. What the hell was happening to the world?

And just because Vasily couldn't help himself, he jerked his chin at the object of his endless fantasies. "So how's she working out?"

Nicky had moved to a table with a man who looked and dressed remarkably like Steven Tyler, a blonde who seemed slightly familiar, and a colorful, yet slight African American man grooving to the music in his seat. Nicky laughed at something the Steven Tyler lookalike said, her gorgeous indigo eyes sparkling. Vasily felt his groin stir.

"Nickalicious?" Terra arched a brow. "Oh, that's right. She mentioned you two have history."

History? So that's what she was calling it? Not a relationship, not an affair, not the best fucking time or sex of his life? Sex so phenomenal no other woman had ever come close to measuring up. But *history*.

Hmm.

"We've interacted."

"*Interacted*, huh?" Terra squinted at him, her expression a mix of snark and skepticism. "What exactly does that mean? I'm sensing there's a whole lot more in that there statement."

No shit.

He almost regretted bringing Nicky up, but then Terra's attention was drawn away by her drummer twirling a stick and tapping out a short rhythm on a shiny bronze cymbal.

Terra looked back at him. "Showtime. My band's gonna do a set first to warm up the crowd before Rory and I sing. You're sticking around, right?"

"Of course."

"Excellent." She made a gesture of chewing her fingernails and gritting her teeth. "Ohmigod, I'm so nervous. Wish me luck and pray I don't fuck this up."

"You'll be fine," he said, giving her shoulder a gentle squeeze. "Get your butt on stage, you've got people to entertain."

Terra giggled and tossed her mass of curls over a shoulder as she turned from him to jog up the stage stairs.

Lifting his glass, he drained the last sip of his whiskey. He was in the process of considering a second when his gaze lifted and clashed with Nicky's.

The impact was a punch to his gut.

Her eyes weren't friendly. It shouldn't have unsettled him, considering what he now knew about what his brother did to her father. But it did.

He watched her suck in a breath. Watched how her cheeks hollowed and those pretty lips, glossy with some kind of product pushed out a bit.

He needed to get her alone. Explain. Make her understand he'd had nothing to do with what happened, but he had a feeling given her current indications that was going to be difficult. No matter, he was a patient man. Ten years had passed. A few more days wouldn't make much of a difference. Somebody tell that to his aching balls.

Nicky looked away, grimacing as if she was in pain, or as if his image burned her retinas.

Fuck!

A low rumble happened in his chest. Fuck the few more days. What he had to say couldn't wait any longer, and before the evening was over, he was determined to tell her the truth, one way or another.

Terra's band broke into their version of *Brass in Pocket* and people headed to the dance floor, including Helen. This left a seat open at Niccoterra's table.

"Yo," the Italian greeted him, dragging his eyes off his woman. Helen had the Steven Tyler lookalike by the hand and was pulling him to the floor. She then commenced dancing with her arms in the air like her fire-cracker fuse had been lit slow burn style.

Billy The Barrel stood to shake his hand. Like his moniker, he was large, round, and to those in the know, deadly. The last conversation they'd had in Vasily's office a few weeks ago hadn't been so amiable, so the handshake surprised him.

"Hear you're doin' good with our girls," Billy shouted over the music, referring to the women they'd rescued from Viktor Sokolov. "You're keeping your word. For that, you got my respect."

Vasily acknowledged the compliment with a solemn nod.

"But, I still got my eye on you." Billy did that snake-eye thing with two stubby fingers, pointing first to himself, then to Vasily.

Understandable, and expected. He nodded, as he would do nothing less if their positions were reversed. Waiting for the older man to reseat himself, he then took the empty one Helen vacated next to Niccoterra.

Terra and her band did their thing, while Vasily watched Nicky do her rounds. Taking orders, filling orders, delivering orders.

Avoiding him.

Until finally she made it to their table because Billy beckoned her over. She took everyone's order—except Vasily's. Then she collected the empties and was about to step away when he wrapped his fingers around her arm, just above her elbow. The muscle beneath his fingers tensed, but he held on until she looked at him.

"Oh hello, Mr. Melnikov." Her expression was innocent and wide-eyed. "Didn't see you there in the dark."

Mr. Melnikov?

He clenched his jaw and tapped a big toe inside his shoe.

"You need a refill?" Her smile was fake and her tone dripped enough saccharine it almost made his teeth ache. "What're you drinking...tequila, rum, strychnine?"

Nicky knew damn well what his preference was. She'd once given him a bottle of his favorite whiskey, and they'd drunk it together in front of the fireplace in her apartment. Then they fucked as if there was no dawn forthcoming. He didn't know it at the time, but for him, there had been no further dawns worth taking note of after that night for a very long time. Yet the memory of that night, her smell, and the feel of her sexy body beneath his had stuck with him and helped him through the cold, miserable days that followed.

Right then, the song ended and Helen bounced back to the table. He stood, and without letting go of Nicky's arm, gave Helen a quick peck on the cheek. Then turning his attention back to the damn vixen vexing his fucking life, he leaned in. "I need you to take your fifteen minutes."

"My break?" She shook her head. "I'm not taking my break. I've got orders to fill."

"They can wait. What I have to say to you can't."

Her brows raised an inch. "You want to be the one to tell Billy The Barrel he needs to wait for his drink? Go ahead."

To which he smirked. Twisting towards the table of hardened assholes he said, "I need a moment of the lady's time. Drinks will be delayed."

He caught a glimpse of Carmine's lips quirking and Billy's eyebrows jumping before he focused again on Nicky. He leaned in close to her ear. "Walk," he ordered.

"If I walk anywhere it's to fill this order." She glared at him, her chin lifting in defiance. "I've got nothing to say to you."

His dipped. Their faces were suddenly close enough that it wouldn't take much to close the distance between their lips. For a moment, Vasily wanted to, even considered doing it, but then Nicky glanced at the table and took in their audience. It wasn't just Niccoterra's table, but several around them that found their conversation fascinating.

"Unless you want to air our business in front of everyone," he cautioned into her ear, "I suggest we go somewhere private."

She swallowed, her delicate neck moving with the effort. The urge to caress the silky texture of her skin, and feel her warmth was compelling. A pulse just below her jaw raced, but there was no trace of fear in her eyes. Just apprehension, but it went a long way to confirm this thing between them wasn't one-sided.

He knew it. She knew it, and dammit, he was going to use it to his advantage. But then that vexing again.

"What business?" she challenged, jutting her chin forward. "If you're going to apologize for screwing up my life, you don't need a minute. You can do it right now."

His gaze bored into hers, then he reached down and took the tray filled with empties from her.

"What are you doing?" she protested, trying to hang on. A little tug of war ensued until an empty beer bottle toppled.

"Dominique, let go!" he growled.

She made a frustrated noise in the back of her throat. "Dammit, what gives you the right to order me around." But she let him take control of her tray before the whole damn thing toppled and caused a mess.

"Follow me." He walked to the bar and placed the tray on the waitress station, ignoring Zander's questioning gaze. Vasily shot him a *don't even start* look.

"Vasily!" Nicky exclaimed, holding her ground.

"If you want an apology, *follow me*." Damn woman. Why was she so difficult? None of his men gave him this much trouble.

"I'm thinking I shouldn't." She folded her arms and stuck a hip out. "Not if you're going to try to search me again. Anyway, don't you have metal detectors or people for that?"

His lip quirked because he did. And he'd explicitly ordered Yev not to come within an inch of her. Another man, even his body-guard touching any part of her made him want to get violent. So fucking shoot him!

Her pretty lips pursed. "You had no right, you know."

"I did what I needed to do." He placed his hands on her shoulders and spun her around, guiding her towards the alcove next to the bar and that pair of red swinging doors. Extending an arm, he shoved the heavy wood aside and they stepped through into a small passage that led to the storeroom. A few extra feet further, he stopped next to a stack of beer crates and spun her again.

The space was well-lit. The yeasty tang of spilled beer and something harder, maybe tequila, permeated the air. But they were alone. And her beautiful face was a foot away from his.

With her back to the crates, she blinked up at him. Anger and something like conflict flashed in those deep blue eyes.

He was a stoney son of an asshole who'd—with just the chill in his gaze—withered men much harder than himself. But facing *this* woman, with *that* expression he found himself crumbling. She made it impossible for him to stay stoney or look away. The individual blue facets of her irises, some almost purple and some a slate gray drew him in deep, sucking at the very essence of who he was.

"What do you want from me?" Her voice was just above a whisper, and a little shaky as she watched him through her lashes.

You, he thought. *I want you.*

Still.

Again.

Now.

But that would have to wait as he had some explaining to do. "What you said about your dad being framed is true."

"This is not news."

"It was to me."

She stared at him, the gears turning in her head before she shook it. "No. The only thing that's news is you admitting it."

He exhaled a short breath through his nostrils. Nobody said this would be easy, and he understood her reluctance to believe him, but it didn't diminish his frustration. She needed time to process, and he'd give it to her. Along with a few more details when she was ready. "I can't take back what happened, Dominique. I wasn't here and I didn't know until I confronted Dean three days ago. He confessed to framing your dad. He didn't do it alone and you should know the other person involved is dead."

Her eyes widened. "Shit, did you kill him?"

"Sadly, no. But what I want to do, is make the situation right. For you and your dad."

"It's too late to make it right. My dad's already spent nine years in prison, and anyway, why should I trust you after what you did?" Despite her obvious attempt to fight them, tears brimmed in the corners of her eyes. His gut twisted with the pain so clear in her gaze, and though it ripped him apart for people to know what happened to him, he knew he'd have to tell her eventually. But only if he couldn't convince her otherwise. Some secrets needed to stay secrets.

"Why should I believe *anything* you say?"

"I know you believe you have every reason not to." He softened his tone. "I get that. All I ask is you give me a chance to prove it."

She sniffed, something working in her eyes. Then she straightened and made to move past him. "We'll see."

No. Fuck. They weren't done. He could not let her walk away. "Any chance your ex set your car on fire?"

Her brow creased. "Why are you asking me if Anthony would do that?"

"After what I witnessed in the parking lot?" He scoffed. "Why wouldn't he?"

Her gaze flicked towards a couple of beer kegs to his side, which suggested she agreed with him but wouldn't give him the satisfaction of admitting to it. "I have no proof it was him."

"Just suspicions." When she remained quiet, he said, "Look at me."

"No."

"Why not?"

"Because I don't want to hurt my eyes."

He chuckled. Even when she meant to insult him, her obstinance was one of the things he'd always loved about her. Half the time it made him hard, as it was beginning to now.

"It's not funny!"

"But it is." He placed a hand on the beer crate just a couple of inches from her head and leaned in closer. She didn't protest, and neither did she tell him to move. It was a good sign. Especially when her chest moved a little faster.

"Motherhood suits you."

Finally, she looked at him, her eyes widening. "Oh, no!" Slapping her hand onto his chest, she took a deep breath. "No, no! *Shut up* complimenting me. Just shut up talking altogether." She shoved at him, but he didn't move. "I need to get back to work."

"Not yet."

She was so fucking magnetic, it physically hurt to keep his distance. Every part of him strained to be closer, yet he managed to keep inches between them. Just a few, yet too many at the same time.

"I just want to talk." He added a little silk to his tone and allowed his mouth to tilt slightly upwards. "There's no harm in that."

"This isn't talking." She closed her eyes for several seconds, and her expression softened. As did her voice. "Whatever it is you want from me, Vas, I'm asking you to un-want it."

Vas.

His heart skipped a beat. He drew in a long, slow breath, and stared at her before exhaling. His name on her lips in that sweet, breathless way undid him. Like she'd punched him in the gut but in a good way. Angling his head down again, until his mouth was millimeters from her neck, he whispered, "Say it again."

"What?"

"My name." His breath fanned her skin. A quiver ran through her as he snaked an arm behind her waist, pulling her closer.

She didn't resist. "Why?"

"Why what?"

"Why are you doing this?" Her voice was husky and sounded a little short of breath. "Don't you have a supermodel to harass instead of me?"

He pulled his head back to look at her. "No."

"Then why?" she asked again.

"Because I want *you*." Because she haunted him. Because he couldn't stay away and wanted to fix the bad that happened in the past. "That hasn't changed."

Their eyes locked as her fingers on his chest curled into his shirt just above his thundering heart.

"Oh, Jesus." She shook her head and bit her lip. A tiny sob wracked her chest. "This is so wrong."

Wrong, but in all the right kinds of ways. His mouth hovered next to hers, and he waited, just breathing. She closed her eyes, and at first did nothing. After a few more hesitant seconds, she let out a shaky breath and turned the last inch toward him.

He traced his tongue over the crack of her mouth, begging for entry until she opened just enough he could slip his tongue in. It was hesitant, but he didn't care, it was an opening, and more than he was expecting. He captured her bottom lip, the plump, juicy flesh trembling between his. Sucking it in, he pulled on it gently. She opened more for him, and it gave him access to her tongue. He slid his over hers, beginning a dance that sent tendrils of lust, and want, and need straight to his cock. He tugged her soft, warm curves closer into the flat planes of his body, slowly grinding against hers. The kiss turned hungry, deep, and hot. Aching for her, his hand at her back slid down and gripped her ass cheek over her skirt and he pushed a knee between her legs. Grinding harder against her, he got the much-needed friction his cock begged for. He was so tightly wound, his body humming, he almost came like a teenager getting his first hand job.

She gave a little moan when he started to pull her tee-shirt from her skirt. He needed to touch her beautiful skin, but she stiffened and pushed against his chest.

Turning her head, she broke the kiss. "No!" Then renewed her effort to shove him away. "This isn't happening. Not again." Her cheeks were flushed bright, her eyes glistening from unshed tears. "You're no good for me, Vasily. And you're no good for my dad. I have a life, a kid to raise, and a job to do. None of it includes you, so stay away. Just...just stay away."

Vasily stilled, every cell in his body already feeling her loss. He took her words in. Absorbed them. Hated them. Denied them. But simultaneously he found a kernel that kept him hopeful, one he could work with.

She'd responded.

It took effort, but he stepped back, jaw ticking and breathing hard through his nose.

Nicky straightened her clothing and hair, then wiped her eyes with her knuckle.

"You know you made a mistake," he said, his voice cracking a little. He cleared his throat.

"Mis...mistake? What do you mean?"

He dropped his gaze to her nipples pushing through her black tee-shirt.

Her neck moved as she swallowed, and he was pleased to note her chest rose and fell as fast as his.

"You feel it too, Dominique. The same way you did in my apartment and the same way you did all those years ago. There's something undeniable between us and if you think I'm stepping back from that, you're out of your mind."

"I'm not denying *that*. That's always been the fucked-up thing about you and me. What I'm denying is *you!* You don't get to come back into my life and screw it up again. My son means every-thing, you understand? *Everything.* There's no room for your mafia bullshit. This is crazy." She shook her head. "I'm not talking to you. Not about this, not about Anthony, not about anything. And I'm most definitely not doing this." She circled a finger between them. "You can forget it."

Before he could say there was no chance of that happening, Zander stepped into the storeroom. He stopped, arms folded, stance wide in full big-brother protective mode. "All cool here?" He directed a hard stare at Vasily.

Vasily returned his look, about to tell him to mind his business, but Nicky took advantage.

"Peachy," she said wiping her cheeks again, and pushed past Vasily, her shoulder brushing against his chest. It left a heated trail, which immediately went cold when they broke contact. His gaze followed her as she exited.

"You harassing my employees now?" Zander stepped closer, squinting.

Though taller than his brother by an inch, Zander was broader —his muscles came from years of kickboxing. Vasily's came from the streets of Moscow. They were equally matched, but he still experienced the occasional dull throb of a broken nose, courtesy of the man standing in front of him.

"Just clarifying something." Normally he wouldn't explain

himself to anyone, least of all his younger brother. But this wasn't his normal, and if he wanted Zander to back off and understand the situation, he needed to offer him something. "Dominique and I had a...thing ten years ago. Shit went down and I was trying to clear it up when you interrupted."

Zander's brows rose above those golden eyes. "Dominique? Nobody calls her that."

"I do. Always have."

Zander searched his face and must've found what he was looking for because he almost smiled. "Well, fuck me. Isn't that interesting? A thing, huh? Is that what they call it now?"

Vasily snorted.

"Look, man, none of my business," Zander continued, his face getting serious again. "And there's nothing I'd like better than Nicky finding a little happiness, but if your intentions aren't good, stay away. She's like a sister. Her ex is unpredictable and I don't want shit blowing back on her. She doesn't deserve it."

"Then we think alike, little *brat*. Blowback was never my intention. As I said, I was just making a few truths known."

"Understood."

Right then the first chords of a bluesy guitar lick leaked through the swinging doors.

Zander's face lit up. "Time to support my woman. Jesus." He blew out a long breath and scraped his hands over his thick dark hair. "You're in for a treat."

Vasily matched his grin. This was a side of his brother he didn't know, and he had to admit, he didn't hate it. Following Zander into the bar he passed the tip jar, then pulling out his wallet, he flipped the leather open. It was loaded with a wad of hundred-dollar bills he kept as bribe money. He separated ten, then folded and pushed them through the slot at the top. After which he turned his attention to one of several large screen televisions placed in strategic corners of the room.

A scene played out. The video flickered in that old home movie cinematic way. Terra, twirling in the sand on a beach, playing with a short-legged, wide-as-a-beer-keg, ugly-as-fuck bulldog. She wore torn jeans, a flowy pink top, and that mass of reddish blonde curls lifted in the breeze. As it came to a close-up of her face, the sunlight caught her gold nose ring, and the song began.

Though Terra and Rory, each armed with acoustic guitars performed along with a drummer and a guitarist, they did so against the backdrop of the video.

He didn't catch all the lyrics, but he got the gist. A bad breakup, misunderstandings, two aching hearts longing for each other and never coming back together. And he sure as hell got a full appreciation of Terra's voice. Sexy, a little scratchy—feminine but with an edge that forced him to listen—and forced him to emote. The song could've been about him and Nicky. The painful hollow in his chest deepened.

When it was over, there was a brief silence before the room erupted. People jumped to their feet in applause whooping and hollering. Vasily glanced at his half-brother. Tears of pride glinted in Zander's eyes. Terra hugged Rory and high-fived the other band members before stepping to the edge of the stage. Zander met her as she launched herself into his arms, her legs wrapping around his waist.

Fuck.

A long, slow blast of air left him, making the hollow in his ribcage expand.

"Congratulations," he said to Terra, as he managed to squeeze in a hug himself. "You got a hit on your hands."

"You think?" Excitement lit up her face as she beamed at him like the spotlight she'd just been under. "God, I hope it goes viral."

"It will," he assured her just as Helen descended on her, squealing. "Go," he urged her. Enjoy your moment. I'll check in with you later." Anyway, he had someone else he needed to check in with more.

Nicky had taken Zander's place behind the bar, abusing a

stainless-steel shaker like she wanted to give it a concussion. He watched her do this. For a couple of reasons. One, to see if she'd look at him. She did. Two, because he found it impossible not to.

This woman was his drug. Tempting. Addictive. And fuck him if he hadn't fallen off the wagon. The barrier she put between them would be temporary. If it killed him, he'd crumble that wall and convince her somehow that she needed him.

But that wasn't happening tonight.

Chapter Eleven

The following day Soren pulled her BMW into the passenger off-loading zone at San Francisco International. Nicky unloaded her bags from the trunk and balanced them on the rim while Soren snagged a luggage cart and wheeled it over. When it was close enough, Nicky shifted them over and slammed the trunk shut.

"Enjoy the conference, honey," she said, turning to give Soren a quick hug. "I wish I was going with."

"I bet. Between getting half-strangled and your car blowing up, a change of scenery would be exactly what you needed. Not to mention space from a certain Russian gangsta." Soren made silly little kissy noises, then giggled like a schoolgirl. "And I'm not even going to mention the almost sex in the storeroom, am I, babe?"

Nicky snorted and rolled her eyes. "For goodness sake, there was no almost sex." Soren was joking but now she regretted spilling her guts on the drive to the airport. However, bottling it up had never worked for Nicky and if anyone could help her make sense of it, Soren could.

"Aah!" Soren feigned surprise, propping a perfectly manicured hand against her breast. "No sex? So that explains your mood?"

She chuckled again, then zipped her hot pink designer hoodie against the brisk wind. "Save it, woman. This is me, your not-so-easily-fooled best bitch. That man, stinking hot as he is, happens to be bad news and you're drawn to him like a kamikaze moth to a flamethrower."

Nicky sighed. Okay, there was no denying her lady parts were drawn to him. She'd definitely be lying if she didn't admit—even if it was just to herself—that she hadn't thought about having sex with him. What woman wouldn't? The man was sexy as all fuck, and he smelled so damned good. But that didn't mean her head had to be drawn to him, right? As long as she could control her thoughts, or get his words out of her mind, all was golden.

Because I want you.

The problem was it wasn't golden. No matter what she did to distract herself, she couldn't forget Vasily had said those words. They played around in her head on an endless loop, but Soren didn't have to know that. Nor about the seriously large amount of tips she and Barney had made at the party. No doubt Vasily was partially responsible for that too and Soren would call it a bribe.

"Anyway, I'd better get going," Nicky muttered before Soren missed her flight. "That airport cop is giving me the squinty eye. No chatting in the drop-off zone."

Soren scoffed and indicated Nicky's standard work uniform, short black skirt, low-cut black tee-shirt, and cowboy boots. "That dude doesn't care if you linger as long as he can ogle your legs. But you're right, I don't want to be last in the security line."

"Thanks for the loan of your car." Nicky accepted the keys from Soren and gave her a quick kiss on the cheek.

"No sweat, sweetie. See you Wednesday."

Nicky slid into the driver's side and adjusted the seat back, checked the mirrors, and set the car in motion. With a double honk and a final wave to Soren, she entered the roundabout and threaded through the early evening traffic back to the city to start her shift at Chuck's.

The bar was busy. And if she didn't count kissy flashbacks that sent the butterflies in her stomach into a tizzy each time she went into the storeroom, the night was uneventful. It was well into the morning hours when they closed and Barney set the alarm. Then Nicky gave him a ride to his apartment.

"Enjoy your days off, Cupcake." Barney opened the BMW's door. "Got plans?"

"My insurance came through, so I get to go car shopping. Yay," she deadpanned.

Barney chuckled as he exited, then tapped the BMW's roof before shutting the door again. Generally, she loved to listen to music but Soren's taste in hip-hop wasn't for her, and having had an evening full of a live band, the silence was welcome.

Except the silence gave her time to think. Fuck that damn Russian. Fuck his beautiful face and fuck him for giving her so much to think about.

Because I want you.

Gah!

She tapped her hands on the steering wheel as her heart tripped over itself. What was he doing? He seemed so earnest in making her believe he was telling the truth about having nothing to do with framing her dad.

Was there some truth to it?

Surely, he had better things to do, so why would he waste his precious time if there wasn't? And she wanted to believe the man she'd once given herself completely to wouldn't do that to her family. But then why the radio silence afterward? She'd left countless voicemails, and none had been returned, so what else was she supposed to think?

As if she didn't have enough confusion ruling her brain.

Nicky parked and pressed the fob twice to ensure the BMW's doors were locked, then walked through a rusty gate to the lobby of her building. The gate's lock had been broken since before her time as a tenant and never replaced. It creaked as it opened.

Crossing through the breezeway with a single flickering light fixture, she collected her mail and as she set foot on the first step, a looming figure appeared at the top.

Fear shot through her as her heart jumped into her throat.

Then her maintenance man's face came into the dim light.

"Son of an asshole, Bill!" She blew out a harsh breath. "What the hell?"

His eyes widened. "Uh, jeez, hey," his voice faltered in a way that made her wary. "It's you."

"What're you doing up here? You scared the crap out of me."

"Thought I saw someone that didn't belong come up here." He scraped an oily lock of hair back from his face. "Just checking everything was good. You know, after your car catching fire and all. Wanna be extra careful."

"I see." Although she really didn't. He hugged the railing as she passed him, but it didn't deter his body odor from assaulting her. Like the man hadn't showered in a week or knew that washing machines had been invented, contrary to the existence of the two ancient coin-operated contraptions in the basement. Her nostrils flared in disgust.

"Have a good night," he called, turning the corner towards his unit.

"Uh-huh." The cloying, armpit smell caught in the back of her throat and she suppressed a gag. It lingered near her door. Number four, the only other unit on her floor was closest to the stairwell, so why was his smell so far down the hall? It was also vacant, so no need for late-night maintenance. But there was a fire door at the end of the hall leading to another set of stairs at the back of the building. Perhaps he'd been checking that?

Or, he was creeping on Faviola, Luca's babysitter again. Hence his name—Creepy Bill.

To her relief when she unlocked and pushed her door open, Favi was asleep on her purple couch, her long, dark hair spilling over the edge of the orange cushion. The television was still on with an episode of *Arrow* playing. Everything looked as it should, and Bill's smell wasn't on the inside of her apartment, thankfully.

She walked to her babysitter, touching her shoulder lightly. "Favi."

"Mmm," Faviola mumbled sleepily and smacked her lips.

"I'm home, honey."

"Hey, Nicky." She sat up, pushing her hair out of her face and rubbing her eyes.

"Everything okay—Luca go to bed on time?"

"Yeah, he did fine, though he wanted me to read to him for longer than normal. And he wanted the light left on."

"No worries. He's going through a phase of hating the dark, so I don't mind." Nicky pulled her wallet out of her purse and separated three twenties from her tips, then handed them to Favi.

"Was Bill up here bothering you?"

"No." Favi pushed out her plump lips. "Why?"

"Just passed him on the stairs, is all."

"Kinda late for maintenance, no?"

Indeed.

Favi gathered her rainbow-colored, hand-knitted Poncho. Strangely, the colors matched those of Nicky's rug. They often joked that if she dropped it on the rug, they'd never find it. She also grabbed her purse, then shoved the cash Nicky gave her into a side pocket.

"Let me walk you down," Nicky said. "Just in case Bill is still out there."

"'Kay."

"You good for babysitting Wednesday?" Nicky asked as they descended the red stairs to Favi's first-floor unit.

"Same time as usual?"

"A little earlier. I must pick Soren up from the airport before I head to work."

"No prob. I got a big final and I need the study time. You

know my mom and how loud she has the TV? I can never focus, even with headphones on. See you then."

Nicky made sure Favi turned the lock on her apartment door before she jogged up the stairs again. After locking her own dead-bolt, she moved towards the kitchen when she noticed Favi's note-book on the floor next to the couch. Dropping her purse on the counter, she went to retrieve it when a knock sounded.

She opened her front door. "You forgot your note…"

A figure in a dark hoodie charged forward pushing hard against the wood. It knocked her off balance and Nicky stumbled, then fell on her ass, jarring her spine.

"Oh, fuck no!"

"Shut up, bitch," a man growled in warning as he kicked the door shut behind him. "Or I'll cut you." It was then she saw the knife, its long, curved blade glinting in the kitchen light. She rolled onto her knees and attempted to scramble to her feet, but he stepped closer. Then shoved her hard back onto her back. He crouched over her and waved the weapon inches from her face.

"What do you want, who are you?" Panic crept into her voice as she tried to scoot backward, but she bumped against the break-fast bar.

Where was her pepper spray?

Shit!

Her purse was on the counter. Out of reach. Was this who Bill thought he'd seen? This nightmare of a stranger?

"Move or scream, I'll fucking waste that pretty face. Got it?"

Nicky swallowed, nodding. "I don't have much cash, only the tips I earned tonight but you can have it. Let me get it, it's in my wallet." God, she hated how her voice sounded, weak and shaky, and scared.

But she was!

Scared out of her mind.

"I'm not here for your stupid money," he snarled.

"If...if it's drugs, I don't do them. I have nothing here. Other than over-the-counter meds."

A low, menacing laugh left that ugly slash of a mouth set in a canvas of acne-scarred skin. It sent chills down her back. The man dropped down to his haunches off to her side, bringing the blade even closer to her face. He was about her height but had at least an extra forty pounds on him. She pressed her head back as far as it could go against the breakfast bar. There was something familiar about him. Something greasy and evil, that slithered just out of reach around the edge of her memory.

"I'm not here for drugs either, bitch."

"Then what do you want?"

Please, not her body.

Perhaps he was looking for someone else? "I think you have the wrong apartment. Who are you looking for?"

"Ah, bitch, I'm in exactly the right place. You're gonna give that asshole a message."

Her eyes went wide. *Which asshole...Anthony?*

"He does what we want, or things are gonna get worse for him." He smiled, showing yellowed teeth that hadn't seen a cleaning ever. "And for you."

Worse things than that giant skinning knife at her throat? "You want me to give Anthony a message?"

"Anthony?" This time his laugh was a bark, his foul breath violating her. It was all she could do not to wrinkle her nose. "You stupid cunt. I'm talking about your *Russian* boyfriend."

"My...?" She gasped. *What?* He thought Vasily was her boyfriend?

Black, empty eyes stared at her a moment before slithering over the rest of her body like a cold, slimy eel. His hood had fallen from his face, exposing loose holes in his ears where perhaps once ear gauges had been. It struck her then. Oh, good God, he was the man in the red truck! The one outside Luca's school!

"Get up." He pushed to his feet and grabbed her arm, pulling her up with him.

"You've been following me, why?"

"Because I can."

"And my car? Oh, my God, it was you. *You* set fire to my car!"

"Just for starters." He leered, pinching two fingers of his free hand together. "A little hint of all the shit we can do to make your life not so pleasant."

We.

He kept saying *we*. What did that mean? Were there more of them outside?

The man looked her up and down, licking his lips, and something changed in his eyes. It could've been the light, but they got blacker, leery, and hungry.

She didn't like that look. The hair on her arms rose and cold terror rushed through her.

"All right." She gripped her skirt, bunching it between her fingers. "I'll give him the message. Please don't hurt me."

There was no point in screaming. Nobody downstairs would hear her, and she'd risk waking Luca. Whatever this pig was going to do to her, she would not have her boy witness it.

"Oh, you're gonna give him that. But if I hurt you or not, I haven't decided." He sucked air between his teeth. It made a moist, bubbling sound. "Like you said, I've been watching you. Your man has fucked with what's ours so I'm thinking I'm gonna fuck what's his."

Oh no. It was one thing to think something, but to have this punk say he meant to do her harm, possibly rape her, was another altogether.

"You're mistaken if you think he's going to let you get away with harming me." *God, she hoped that was true.* "He'll slice off bits of your flesh while you're alive and feed them to the dogs."

The man edged closer, snickering. "I'm the one with the knife, lady. You'd best shut up." The sharp point pierced the skin in the dip of her neck. The pain made her suck in her breath as a hot trickle of blood ran down her skin.

"What's so special about your cunt anyway, that you're Melnikov's latest fuck toy?"

"My cunt has teeth." She snarled with fake bravado. "It bites."

His eyes went wide in shock a moment before he cackled an ugly laugh. "You got fight. I like that even if you are just a little whore."

"What makes you think I'm a whore?" If she could just keep him talking, she might think of a plan.

"I seen you go to his apartment, you been fucking him behind that piece of shit lawyer's back."

Oh, God.

She knew going to Vasily's had been a mistake, but never thought it would come back to bite her ass like this. She needed a weapon, and the closest was in the kitchen—a knife—but then she'd be truly trapped inside that small space. It wasn't looking good.

"Yeah, well then you should ask him what's left of his dick."

His face came closer, his breath foul. Old alcohol and whatever he'd just eaten—some kind of fish. Her stomach roiled and for the second time that night, she fought not to gag. And if the knife wasn't between them, she'd have bitten his nose off.

"What's one more cock in that wet cunt? You're going to spread those legs and I'm gonna *tear you up* on your nice, comfortable bed." Twisting the blade so the flat side faced the floor, he placed it under her chin, then grabbed her hair and yanked her head back. "Bedroom?"

Jesus, how had her life come to this? What had she done in a past life that karma decided this is what she deserved?

"That way." She swallowed, the fear finally taking over. Silently she thanked Favi for remembering to close Luca's door. "Please... don't do this, it's not going to end well."

"We'll see how it ends," he ground out, tightening his grip on her hair. Inside her room, he said, "Turn around. Do it slowly."

She turned, and he let go of her hair to move half a step back. "Unbuckle my belt." When she hesitated a second too long, he pressed the blade deeper. It nicked her and fresh blood spilled from beneath her chin, down her neck and chest, running between her cleavage—the coppery scent mixing with his body odor. Tears of frustration and fear formed in the back of her eyes, spilling over.

With shaky fingers, she manipulated his belt buckle until it came loose.

"You know what to do," he grunted and pumped his hips. His breath was coming faster now. "Push my pants down."

She did as he ordered until they were low on his hips. "Take my cock out. You try anything with my balls, I'll fuckin' slice you. Hear me?"

Her vision was blurry with unshed tears, but she was no virgin. She knew her way across a man's torso. Reaching down, she hooked her fingers into the elastic band of his underwear and pushed.

He was already hard. His dick sprang free, the ugly, swollen purple head leaking. Still holding onto her hair, he turned the knife around and cut her clothes. Starting with her top, the curved point left a red scratch on her skin. She fought hard not to hiss at its fiery sting.

Then her bra. It popped open, exposing her breasts. He stared and gave a disgusting groan that made her want to vomit.

How could this be happening?

How could this pig violate her and there was so little she could do—except try to formulate a plan, find an opportunity to fight back, and somehow live through it?

And hope Luca didn't wake up in the process.

Skirt and panties were last, then she was completely exposed— just the remnants of her tee-shirt and bra hanging from her arms. Twisting the blade, he put the flat edge against her mound and pressed. The sharp edge nicked her inner thigh causing her to give a small whimper.

"On the bed."

Again she obeyed, moving slowly, awkwardly, to avoid cutting herself further. His face was inches from hers, breathing hard, emitting that foul, fishy breath. She sat on the edge with her knees as close together as the blade would allow.

"Move back," demanded, nudging her with the weapon. It sliced into her inner thigh flesh.

She hissed at the burn, biting back the tears. "Okay," she cried, "but please move the knife. You don't want to damage the goods, right?"

He grunted at the red stain smearing her thigh, but he moved the blade and allowed her to position herself in the middle of the bed.

With his jeans halfway down his thighs, he began to stroke himself, leering at the space between her legs. "Fuck, yeah," he breathed. "Wider." Humiliation smothered her. The need to scream and squeeze her legs together was strong, but she obeyed. Then her eye caught something on her nightstand. It wasn't much, but it could help...if she could get it.

"Do you have a condom?" she asked.

"What?"

"A condom."

"Are you crazy, bitch?"

"For *your* protection. You said yourself I'm Vasily's fuck toy. STDs, you know? They're no joke, trust me."

"Shut up and spread those fucking legs." But she got to him. She saw the uncertainty flicker through those horrible black irises.

"There's one in my bedside dresser. That one." She glanced at it. "Second drawer."

He glared, but he switched the knife to his other hand pressing it against her ribs, underneath her breast while he reached over. It was just beyond his reach, forcing him to lean further. Yanking it open, he stared at the contents. "There's nothing in..."

She kicked him in his stomach.

Wheezing, he staggered to the side, tripping over his jeans still hanging around his knees. Nicky reached for the fingernail scissors behind the lamp.

"You bitch!" He grunted, eyes wide. Then he regained his balance and lunged forward. She jammed the sharp end of the nail scissors into his neck, just as an orange streak shot from her closet. The cat yowled as he launched at the man, crawling up his torso, and digging in his claws.

The man screamed.

Marley yowled again as he sunk his teeth into the man's scalp and his scream got louder. It was high-pitched like a whistling kettle, but he dropped the knife!

She couldn't tell which sound was more frightening. The cat's yowl or the man's scream. They both raised the hairs on her skin.

"Help me!" he screamed, trying to fend off her cat. "Get this fuckin' thing off me!" He bumped into the wall and the nail scissors dislodged from his neck and dropped onto the carpet. With nothing stopping the flow, blood sprayed out like a scarlet fan. Some landed on her face, hot and disgusting. Marley was wrapped around his head and the harder he tried to remove the cat, the more the feline dug in.

Her would-be rapist's feet got tangled in the clothes on the floor and he tripped, his half-mast jeans hindering his ability to recover. Stumbling, he slammed hard into her closet, pulling the doors from their tracks. At the last second Marley sprang from the man's head, landing near her feet with his hackles raised like he'd stuck a claw into a light socket.

The man screamed again—or he tried to. Blood bubbled from his mouth and more flowed from his neck. "Pleath" he moaned, reaching out his hand.

It was then she realized she'd hit his carotid artery and probably killed him.

Holy fucking shit!

She'd only meant to stop him. This asshole was going to die in her room—his blood soaking into her carpet.

Grabbing her ripped skirt from the floor, she dropped to her knees and tried to put it on his neck, but he slapped at her hand. It was weak, and his face had lost all color.

"You idiot, you're going to die if I don't stop the bleeding."

"Youtheone...gonedie." He gasped for air, but each attempt only created more frothing, which in turn created more gasping and blood spitting. "Mathol's gonna kill you."

Mathol? What the hell is a mathol? But she didn't have time to figure that out, and she slapped his face. "Hey, don't die. You can't die, you piece of shit."

He made one last gulp, then the blood pulsing from his wound slowed. One more weak pump, then it stopped completely. Black eyes stared at her, but they were no longer seeing. His heart had stopped, and the life had gone out of them.

"Oh fuck, *fuck.*"

No!

She rocked back on her knees, her hand against her open mouth. Staying in that position for several moments, staring at his corpse, she hoped she was wrong. That he'd move. But he never did except for a small leg twitch. It was over.

"Oh, no."

Staggering to her feet, she reached for her dresser for support. Then caught sight of her reflection. She was covered in blood. Not just her face. There was a long gash along her ribs, below her breast that she hadn't even realized was there, leaving her lower belly slick with blood. It stung.

Her breath hitched. "Ow, damn."

"Mommy?"

Oh God, Luca.

"Mommy, why are you bleeding?"

"Oh Jesus, baby, don't look. Don't come in here." Turning her back to her son, she tried to shield him from the man in her closet. But it was too late.

"Is that Daddy?"

"No, baby, it's not. Out please."

"Who is it?"

"It's just a stranger."

"Did he cut you?" Luca pointed to her side.

Don't panic. *Don't* panic. Focus on getting Luca out of her room.

"Honey, would you get my purse, please? My phone's in there."

"Mommy." His little face screwed up in anguish.

"Honey, I'm okay, just go." She stifled a sob, but she was shaking. "I need you to be strong and brave. Please get my purse and find my phone. But stay in the living room. I'll be there in a moment."

"Okay." His little voice came out strangled, and cut right through her, worse than her wounds. God, all she ever wanted to do was protect her son. Why couldn't she even do that?

When he went, she gritted her teeth and peeled off the remains of her tee-shirt. Some of it had stuck to the cut below her breast. She used it to wipe her face and hands, and most of the blood on her torso. Then she put on an old pair of gray harem pants she never wore anymore and a loose lavender top. She knotted it so it stayed away from her skin yet covered the remaining blood. The rest could wait. Her son couldn't.

Marley was licking his paws, his fur still puffed out like an orange troll.

"Oh God, cat. Thank you! But I need you out of here. Can't have you stepping in any more blood." The feline complied when she used her foot to nudge him out of her room. Then shut the door behind her. Luca waited at the end of the hall, his face scrunched in fear. She dropped to her knees, ignoring the stinging pain between her legs and from her ribs as he held on tight. She squeezed him back, just as tight. Adrenaline and shock made her shake and the tears flowed freely. A million thoughts raced through her mind, and not one made sense. She couldn't think except to hold her child's warm little body. Her little anchor.

After a while, she stood and wobbled to the kitchen. Her wounds were still seeping, and Luca helped her with a bowl and filled it with warm water. As she wiped the blood away with paper towels, her son watched, his face tight and pale. Then they moved to her couch.

"Phone please, honey."

He handed it to her, but her fingers were still shaking, and she dropped it. Luca picked it up from the floor.

First, she tried her dad—no answer. Not surprising as he took his hearing aids out at night. Then Anthony. Again, no answer, and again not surprising. Soren was out of town and Terrence was on tour. No way in hell was she waking Zander. She didn't want to involve him in his brother's shit and Barney had no car and didn't do Uber.

Then there was the man who'd caused this.

But she would not leave her child with a virtual stranger in case she got arrested, because fuck dirty cops. What if they assumed it was just a plain old domestic violence thing? No social services worker would take her kid away from her. Calling the police could wait a few hours until daylight when her dad would be awake.

"May as well get comfortable, Buddy. Get your comforter and cuddle with me on the couch. We can watch whatever you want on TV."

"'Kay."

While her son did that, she tried to control her shaking and not focus on the pain, all the while pondering her decisions in life. Like why had she once fallen for a man connected to the Russian mafia?

This was all his fault.

Chapter Twelve

"You will watch."

"No, Papa," I cry, pushing at him. "I don't want to watch."

Smack.

Ow. My lips mash against my teeth and blood fills my mouth. I spit it out.

"You're big boys. Soon big men. Big men control women."

"Leave her alone, Papa." Dean placed himself between his father and his mother. "She didn't do anything wrong. Don't hurt her. Please don't hurt her!"

"Stupid boy!" Papa's arm rears back and punches Dean in the face. My brother drops to the floor, holding his head, blood spewing from between his fingers.

"No!" Mom screams. "Don't hurt them! Go, boys. Vasily, help Dean and get out. Go, now!"

Her face is bruised and swollen. Blood runs from a cut above her eye and one arm hangs at an awkward angle. There's a gap in her mouth where a tooth used to be.

"Go, go!"

But, I can't. I can't leave her. I run at Papa again, trying to push *him away from her, but he dodges, grabs the collar of my shirt, and swings me around. Then he kicks me in the stomach. All the air leaves me and I can't breathe. I can barely move.*

I watch Papa bring his ring from his pocket and put it on his middle finger.

"No," I wheeze. "Don't do it."

"She's junkie whore! Like all women. Junkie for money, junkie for cock. She needs lesson." His tone becomes even more menacing. "You will watch."

"Noo!"

Thunk!

Dean screams. Or maybe it's me. Or both. Mom collapses on the table, her body twitching and blood pooling around her head.

Then she's still and an unholy silence fills the room. Too much silence. Papa stares at her for a long time, his jaw working in that way like he was chewing gum. "Junkie whore," he spits. Then he leaves.

"Mom." I crawl to her. "Open your eyes, Mom. Please."

Please.

Mom.

Vasily jerked awake.

"Ugh, damn!" He brought his forearms over his face with his elbows pointing to the ceiling. Grimacing and breathing through it, he waited for the images to fade from his memory and for his heart to slow. When it finally did, he sat up and wiped the sweat that accumulated on his brow, then chugged water from a tall glass he always kept next to his bed. It helped wash away the nausea sitting at the base of his throat. A darkness weighed on his chest, heavy and foreboding, like a lead blanket. Experience told him he was done sleeping.

He kicked the comforter from his body and sat, legs over the edge, elbows on his knees.

He hadn't had the dream in a while, but it was inevitable since his conversation with Dean and his request for a headstone. He didn't see the point. It was just a dead chunk of rock, whereas his mother lived in his heart and his fucked-up memories. Once they were dead and gone—which could be sooner rather than later—there would be no one left to visit it or care for a headstone. A neglected one was worse than none at all.

He stood, then proceeded across the thick, soft rug to the bathroom and relieved himself. Washed his hands, splashed water on his face then stared at the reflection of the tattoo he hated but didn't regret. It was a reminder of what he'd done to survive. And who he'd fought to protect. Every one of the twelve bars represented a month he'd been enslaved by Aleksei Federov. And each barbed point in the wire entangled around those bars represented a small step towards his freedom.

He flipped the bathroom's light switch, flooding the past in darkness, and approached the windows. The city before him, adorned with the new crescent moon, blinked and sparkled. He stared at its yellow glow when his phone rang.

He turned to look at the device on his side table. This could not be good. It never was when it rang at four in the morning. Taking a few steps closer, he glanced at the unknown number.

"Yes," he answered.

Silence.

"Who is this?"

"Um..." The voice was small, young, and hesitant. *A child's voice.* "You said if we needed help I should call you."

Jesus!

A slow chill prickled down his spinal column, kicking that sense of heaviness he'd woken with into dangerous territory.

"Hey, little man. You got a problem?"

"Yes," his voice wobbled.

"You want to tell me what it is?"

"My mom's hurt. She needs help."

His heart lurched and his throat went dry. "What do you mean hurt?"

"A man cut her. She was bleeding."

His eyes went wide.

Cut her? *Fucking* cut *her*?

He suppressed a growl. "Is the man still there?"

"Yes. But I think he's dead."

Vasily scraped a hand through his hair at the kid's tight, quivering voice. *Focus.* How bad was Nicky cut? "Let me talk to your mom."

"She's asleep and she doesn't know I'm calling. Nobody else answered the phone and I don't know what to do."

"Does she need an ambulance?"

"She said she didn't want one, but there was a lot of blood."

"Okay, Luca. Do you know your address?" He was already walking to his closet to get dressed.

"Mom made me remember it in case of 'mergencies."

Smart, Nicky, he thought, pulling on a pair of jeans.

"Give it to me."

The kid recited the street name and number in The Tenderloin, and he couldn't help curling his nose at it. What the fuck was she doing living there? Why wasn't her asshole ex paying for a better neighborhood?

"Hang tight, little man, and take care of your mom. When I get there, I'll text you so you'll know it's me knocking on your door."

"'Kay. Please hurry." He sniffed. "I'm scared."

"I'm on my way." As soon as he hung up, he called Yev.

"Boss," his bodyguard answered, his voice gruff from sleep.

"Get dressed and meet me in the garage. Three minutes."

Then he pulled on socks, and boots, retrieved his gun from his bedside table, and shoved it into the waistband of his jeans.

Thanks to very little traffic, eleven minutes later, they drove into Nicky's neighborhood. It wasn't as bad as he expected. No junkies or drug dealers prowling the streets, and other than her building needing a paint job and better lighting, it looked clean.

Yev dropped him off first, then found parking while Vasily entered her building which was guarded by a useless gate. It groaned open and he proceeded to the second floor. A single fluorescent light flickered, creating an atmosphere that could've come from a horror movie. Perhaps they were walking into one.

He stopped outside Nicky's door, his heart in his throat as he listened. The only noises he heard were the soft footfalls of Yev rejoining him. Pulling his phone out of his pocket, he sent a quick text to Luca. *I'm outside. Open up.*

A few moments later he heard a scraping noise. Then the peephole went dark. Several seconds passed before the lock disengaged and a wedge of light appeared.

"Hey, little man," Vasily said softly, taking in the boy standing on a chair dressed in blue pajamas. There were images of a character with blades coming from his hands and blots of dark, bloody stains on them. The kid looked so small, his eyes were haunted and bloodshot, and it made his chest constrict. "Your Mom okay?" he asked. Though he wanted to rush inside and see for himself, he didn't want to scare the kid any more than he already was.

Luca shook his head and then climbed off the chair. There were more scraping noises as he pushed it aside to let him in. "Is she going to jail?"

Jail?

Christ. What happened here?

Nicky lay on her left side on a purple couch propped up by orange and lavender pillows. They matched the lavender walls, and a random memory popped into his head. That was her favorite color.

One palm heel was pressed against her forehead. If the kid was pale, she looked ghostly. Tension lines and dark circles lay stark beneath her lashes.

Then he saw why.

Her top was knotted just below her breasts. A long red line about eight inches ran along her ribcage, another from her navel upwards, disappearing under her top. A third was at her throat.

Judging by the mass of bloody paper towels and cotton balls laying on the coffee table next to her, she'd attempted to clean her wounds.

"Stay guard outside," Vasily said to Yev. "Anyone suspicious shows up, tap on the door." Then he shut and bolted it.

A fat orange cat sat on the backrest above her, swishing its tail. He could've sworn the look in the animal's single eye as he approached was a warning. With his own wary eye on the feline, he gently touched her arm. Nicky jumped awake, then pressed a hand to her side, hissing.

The cat growled. The hairs on Vasily's neck raised.

After a moment of blinking and staring at Vasily, like she wasn't quite comprehending his presence, Nicky asked, "What are you doing here?" Her voice was raspy and thick with exhaustion.

"Luca called me."

"What?" Her gaze landed on her son, her brows corrugating. "Did I fall asleep?"

"I'm sorry, Mommy, but I was scared." His little face crumpled, and a tear ran down his pale cheek. "I thought you were dying and I didn't know what to do."

Her face softened. When he continued, his voice cracked, "You needed help, and I'm too small. And nobody else was coming."

Vasily blew out air, admiring the kid. He was wise beyond his years. He reminded him a little of himself at the same age. Though he hoped the kid wouldn't grow up so jaded.

"It's fine, baby." Nicky smoothed her son's dark locks back from his forehead. "I'm not going to die, and you're not in trouble. I'm just a little surprised, is all."

Luca sniffed, then nodded before scooting behind her legs on the couch. It shifted as he found a position next to her. Nicky flinched as if this caused her more pain, but she didn't stop him. Then the kid covered them with a blue superhero comforter.

Vasily clenched his jaw. He'd done the same with his mother once when her ribs had been broken. The memory was even more raw now after his dream. He dragged his gaze back to Nicky's face, trying to ignore that his ribcage felt two sizes too small.

"Why haven't you called the police or an ambulance?"

"I can't get a hold of anyone I trust. If something happens to me, I need someone to take care of Luca."

Of course. And a hospital emergency room wasn't a place for a child alone at four in the morning, which was why he guessed she hadn't gone there either.

"Anyway, it's probably good you're here," she said, pushing her hair away from her face. "This involves you."

"What do you mean?"

"My bedroom." She made a weak attempt at pointing down the hall. "See for yourself."

Bedroom? He didn't like the sound of that.

Nostrils curling, he hesitated only a moment before he walked to where she pointed. It was obvious which door she meant. Hers didn't have a painted sign with yet another superhero that read *Luca's room* stuck to it.

When he opened it, he didn't know what he was expecting, but it sure as hell wasn't the metallic stench coming from a massive blood puddle soaking into a beige carpet. Or the person slumped over in all that blood with his jeans halfway down his legs.

What the fuck was this, a date gone wrong?

For a second he contemplated that, hating the fact another man was in her room.

Pull your shit together, asshole.

This wasn't about him or his petty jealousy. He inhaled, cleared his head, then focused on what was in front of him. He examined the room from the doorway. It was colorful and vibrant, like the rest of her apartment, with a mix of—what did they call it, boho chic? She had a silky rust-colored scarf pinned above her bed, then he noticed the blood-spattered walls and closet doors. And the smears on her comforter that seemed to be made of big mismatching colorful squares of fabric.

A fucking blood bath. Careful to avoid treading in it or touching any surface he stepped closer.

Who was this prick?

Along with vicious-looking scratches and puncture wounds on the man's face, his only distinguishing marks were gaping holes in his ears and acne-blemished skin. Somehow the last two rang a bell, but he couldn't grasp it.

With his jaw ticking, he took photos of the dead dude's face and carefully checked his pockets, finding nothing, not even a wallet. Then his attention caught on something under her bed.

A hunting knife and items of clothing. Her work clothes—sliced in half. He growled, clenching his fist till the joints in his fingers cracked. It took effort to not punch anything. A lot of fucking effort. He breathed deep for several seconds, then instead of hitting the wall like he very much wanted to, he hit a contact in his phone.

When she answered he clipped, "Ronnie, I need you. Bring a sewing kit."

"How bad?" his on-call OB-GYN asked through a yawn, not wasting time. She'd received this call before, back when he'd first taken over from Dean. Before he brought in real protection for his women and changed the rules.

"Not sure. She's not one of my regular girls and it's not your normal injury."

After he hung up, he texted Nicky's address to Ronnie, then stared at the ceiling picturing ice baths in Siberia.

Aleksei Federov had once taunted him to take a dunk in a long pool cut into the ice in the middle of winter. It was supposed to be for the rest of the men's amusement as he had assumed *the soft American* would wimp out. Instead, Vasily counter-dared him to a race. It was a bold move, risky. He could've been shot on the spot, but in the face of the other members of the Bratva present, Federov had been unable to refuse. Vasily had let him win, but only just. He'd earned begrudging respect that day—and not just from the men—but Fedorov himself. It was one of the first tiny steps towards earning his freedom.

He shuddered at the remembered chill, but it had achieved its goal, which was to cool his blood.

Walking back to the living room, he sat on the edge of the coffee table facing Nicky.

"Hey, little man," he asked of Luca, "would you mind giving me a moment with your mom?"

Luca looked to Nicky, who nodded. "Put the kettle on for me please, Buddy. I could use some tea."

The moment Luca climbed onto the counter of the breakfast bar, she focused on Vasily, her face drawn. "Well?" she asked, keeping her tone low, but there was a measure of accusation in her voice.

Well, he had an accusation of his own. He hated he had to ask, but he couldn't resist. "He was uninvited, I'm assuming?" Dick move, yeah, but so the fuck what. He needed to know.

To her credit, Nicky didn't roll her eyes, which is what he would've done at his bluntness. She only narrowed them. "I don't know him, but I'm thinking *you do?*"

He studied her face. The woman was serious. What the fuck?

"He said he had a message for you," she added. "That you have something of theirs, and they want it back. If they don't get it, worse things will happen to me."

He studied her, his brows pulled together. "You sure it was for me?"

"He was very specific, Vasily. He called me your 'fuck toy' and he thought I was your latest whore."

Whore? Fuck toy?

He didn't know which of the pejoratives pissed him off more.

Vasily inhaled, then looked at the orange fur ball eyeing him with menace. Its tail flicked back and forth angrily.

Regardless, both meant one of two things. The piece of shit had been following her and had seen them together. Or he knew what she'd been to him in the past.

What if it was both?

He was a man who didn't scare easily, but that scared him. The ink tattooed into his arm itched, but he resisted the urge to rub it.

Then he asked the question he didn't want to, the words barely making it out his mouth. "Did he rape you, Dominique?"

"No," she whispered blinking hard. "He tried." A sob wracked her chest and a few tears escaped, but she wiped them away. "That I could almost endure, but if he'd killed me, what would've happened to Luca? I couldn't have that."

"Dom," he said softly, swallowing down the lump forming in his throat. His need to protect her was primal and not unfamiliar. It almost overwhelmed him. Everything in him wanted to take her in his arms, hold her, kiss her, but he held back only because he didn't trust he wouldn't injure her further. "You did what you had to."

She reached for his forearm and curled her fingers around his wrist. They were cold, no doubt from shock, but he welcomed the touch.

"Can you make him go away?" she asked, her voice barely above a whisper.

His stomach sank. He hated denying her, but he had to. There was no other option. With reluctance, he said, "I can't do that."

"Why not?" Her face crumpled.

At another time he wouldn't have hesitated. But the circumstances were different now. There was a child involved.

"This goes against every instinct of mine," he answered, "but there's no way to avoid it. We have to call the cops for your son's sake. If I made that piece of garbage disappear, Luca would have to keep it secret for the rest of his life and it would be no good for him. He'd never be able to speak about it to anyone. You don't want to do that to him."

"Shit." Nicky wiped away a few more tears. "You're right, I'm not thinking straight. But what if the cops don't believe me?" Her voice shook making clear how afraid she was. "What if they think like you did, that he was a date, and I lost my mind. I could get arrested and they'd take Luca from me."

"You're not getting arrested. I'm going to make damn sure you don't."

"You can't guarantee that, Vasily. There are some really dirty cops in this city. Believe me, I know."

Yeah, unfortunately, he did too. But if any of those dirty cops showed up, they'd know she was under his protection.

Or they'd have to deal with him.

Chapter Thirteen

Ronnie arrived first, carrying a black leather medical bag. Minutes after introducing her to Nicky, two cops showed up. Vasily left the doctor to attend to Nicky in Luca's bedroom and met San Francisco's finest at the front door. One he'd dealt with in the past—Dwayne Lee—and his partner, a small, husky blonde woman. Neither was on his payroll.

"Mr. Melnikov." The Asian American cop eyed him, suspicion clouding his otherwise clear black eyes. Though Lee's demeanor was professional, it was obvious he was less than pleased at Vasily's presence. They had met before when Lee interviewed him after Dean had kidnapped Shelley De Luca.

The cop asked him several questions, then while the two uniforms did their thing, and Ronnie did hers, he kept the boy company on the couch.

Luca sat crossed-legged, his face pinched with worry. The big, ginger cat nestled on his lap licking between its toes, and Vasily swore he saw traces of blood in its claws.

"Hey," he said bumping Luca's leg gently with his fist. "You did the right thing by calling me. That was smart."

The cat meow-yawned in agreement.

"Who's this compromised critter?" Vasily pointed at the fur ball.

"Marley."

"Marley as in orange marmalade?"

Luca's face scrunched. "I don't know what that is."

"It's like jam, only not as sweet."

Luca shook his head at his pathetic attempt at a joke. "Like Bob Marley. 'Cause if we don't brush him, he gets dreadlocks."

Vasily's lip twitched. "And let me guess, your mom likes Bob Marley's music?"

"Uh-huh."

"What happened to his eye?"

"When Mom found him, it was hanging outside his head. The vet said it was too 'fected to put back in, so he took it out. He had to wear a cone around his neck until it was better because he kept scratching it."

"Hmm." Vasily wasn't a cat person, but considering the blood in its claws, and the scratches on the dead prick's body, he suspected it had done its part in protecting Nicky. He decided this one deserved respect.

"I heard Mom say she might be 'rrested? My dad says when people get 'rrested they go to jail." Luca's bottom lip quivered. "Does that mean she will too?"

Vasily swallowed hard. Consoling a kid was beyond his scope of experience, and he took a second to search for the right words. "What your mom did is called self-defense. It probably won't mean she's going to jail. But I'll get her a lawyer that will make sure she doesn't."

"My dad's a lawyer. He tries to keep people who've done bad things out of jail. Mom's not bad." The kid's voice got tight as he fought off tears. "Mom's good and I don't want her to go."

Vasily exhaled. "I don't want her to either, so I'm going to make you a promise. I'll do my best to make sure you'll both be fine."

The kid sniffed, then wiped his nose on his pajama sleeve. The cat mewled, snuggling deeper into his lap. Its purring was loud and oddly soothing.

Watching them, how they snuggled together, finding comfort in each other, the same way the kid did with Nicky earlier, gave Vasily all kinds of unfamiliar, domesticated feelings he had no business having. He cleared his throat.

"Just a heads up, the cops might ask you questions. If your mom can't be with you, I will, but don't answer any without her giving permission, okay?

"'Kay."

Vasily held out his fist and Luca bumped it with his smaller one. "We'll get through this, little man. I promise."

Right then Ronnie left the bedroom. Her lips were pressed together in a tight line. The hollowness in his stomach grew as he stood to get her report. They were promptly joined by Officer Lee who must've heard her close the bedroom door.

"I've given her medication for the pain, so she'll be asleep soon," she said with caution, eyeing Lee as she spoke. "And very lucky to have come away with relatively mild injuries considering the weapon the subject threatened her with."

Lee nodded, but said nothing, waiting for her to continue.

"It could've been *much* worse. Your partner is taking a preliminary statement and photos. When you've seen them, and heard what Nicky has to say, you'll know what I'm talking about."

"I'm only interested in the facts, ma'am. Nothing more."

"Doctor," she responded.

"Doctor Ma'am." Lee deadpanned back.

Ronnie smirked, then turned to Vasily giving him a *this guy* look before focusing back on Lee. "I will give a full written report, which will stand up in court, *if* necessary. Though it's pretty clear to me that the perpetrator's death was justifiable."

"Understood," the cop acknowledged. "But we'll be making that determination after our investigation."

"Regardless she should not be formally interviewed until she has a clear head." Then she turned to Vasily. "I need a moment with you."

"Of course."

When Lee didn't move, she turned to him. "Alone."

The cop narrowed his eyes but nodded. "I'll continue fact-finding then, while you have your moment. But I need your contact info Doctor Ma'am."

"It's Ronnie if you must know."

Lee looked her over, then offered a smile. "I must."

After she gave him her card, he made his way to the bedroom. Vasily waited until he could no longer see the cop. Then he motioned for Ronnie to step outside of Nicky's apartment into the breezeway. He didn't want to talk in front of the boy.

"How is she really?" he asked.

Ronnie smoothed a few honey-blonde strands behind her ear that had escaped her ponytail. "Shaken. None of the cuts are too serious, but they could've been." She took a breath, then released it slowly. "There are a few on the insides of her thigh, Vasily. And one close to her femoral artery. That asshole held *that* knife between her legs. It's how he controlled her. If he'd gotten too excited, or careless, she could've been the one to have bled out."

He processed that.

Having seen a man bleed out after his femoral had been nicked, he knew exactly what Ronnie meant. This new information threatened to set fire to his gray matter and while he turned it around in his head, his big toe jumped in his boot. The thought of a skinning knife violating one ounce of Nicky's precious flesh made him want to not just kill, but torture the rest of the schmucks involved in this mess.

Slowly.

He gritted his teeth. "It's good she took care of him, then."

"I can't say I disagree with you." Ronnie looked at the floor for a moment, before meeting his eyes again. "She's going to go through it. She's brave but in shock. I don't know what your situation with her is but be gentle. Nicky's going to need that most of all."

Their situation?

He blew out air. He knew what he wanted, but that was still to be determined. "Got it," he growled.

Ice baths.

In Siberia.

Footsteps sounded on the red-painted stairs at the end of the breezeway. They both turned to look as a tall man appeared. Ronnie stiffened, her eyes widening.

Vasily reached for his weapon and stepped in front of Ronnie.

Shit!

He'd given his gun to Yev out of caution before the cops showed. Guns and cops in the same space together were not a recommended combination. A moment later he saw the gold star attached to the top pocket of the man's leather bomber jacket. And then he recognized him, allowing him to relax—somewhat.

The detective checked him out with the same hard skepticism he was sure mirrored his own gaze. The kind that had seen the worst humanity had to offer and trusted no one.

"Fetzer," the cop said, touching his badge, like he didn't remember. "Homicide." Then he looked past Vasily, his tired gaze landing on Ronnie.

"Damn," he muttered and shook his head. "What the hell are you doing here?"

"Oh, great." Ronnie rolled her eyes. "Of all the goddamn homicide detectives in this city, it has to be you." She waved a hand at the cop. "John Fetzer, meet Vasily Melnikov."

"We've met," both men said in unison though neither offered their hand.

"You're working for the mob now?" Fetzer asked of Ronnie, one brow arched.

"None of your business, John."

"Actually Veronica, if you're here in an official capacity, it is."

The two stared at each other. Though the man was undoubtedly unhappy the doctor was here, there was something else layered in those deep brown eyes. Something Vasily recognized. The man cared, more than he was letting on. He gave an inner smirk. Strange how he knew that look.

"How do you two know each other?" Ronnie asked.

"I'll leave that up to him to explain," Fetzer answered, glancing at Vasily. "I've got a job to do. But before you leave, Melnikov, I need your statement."

Vasily nodded, and with that, the man pushed open the door to Nicky's apartment and went inside. Ronnie eyed Vasily, brows lifted high. "Well?"

He could ask her the same question. And he would, just not then. Ronnie having dated a cop wasn't on top of his agenda. "He recently investigated the murder of one of my girls."

"Oh, that's right, Rebecca! I remember now."

The man had been fair and done a good job too. Vasily hoped it hadn't been a one-off because he'd hate to have to use the full force of his power to keep Nicky safe.

But should it come down to it, he wouldn't hesitate. He'd done it before.

Chapter Fourteen

Pain seeped through Nicky's consciousness, waking her. Some places hurt more than others, like her inner thighs and the area below her breast, and she didn't quite know what to make of it. Why did she hurt so much?

She blinked at the constellation pasted on the ceiling; Orion with Betelgeuse being the most prominent. Not in real life, but because it was Luca's favorite star. All the others on the ceiling were a light, luminescent green, whereas the Big B, as they called it was a light, luminescent orange.

She was in Luca's bed?

Why...?

Then it all came rushing back. "Oh, shit!" she gasped at the images of the man in her head, his smell, and the sharp pain of his knife against her flesh flickering and disjointed like a badly edited movie.

Holy fuck, she'd killed him!

A human being.

Groaning, she pressed her hands to her face. Last night wasn't a bad dream or even a bad movie. It was her questionable, fucked-up reality. Despite having come to this reality, and besides the physical pain, a strange calm settled over her.

Was that weird? Shouldn't she be freaking out? Feel something —horror, anxiety, anything? Other than her bladder, that was. The need to pee was almost painful.

Uncurling herself from Luca's warmth, she winced as she sat up.

Wait.

She sniffed.

Coffee?

Anthony...? No, he didn't have a key and Luca was fast asleep next to her so no way he'd let Anthony in. Surely, she would've felt him leave the bed, her mom's radar being what it was?

It must be her dad then. Or perhaps she was having olfactory hallucinations. Whatever Vasily's doctor had fed her, they were heavy-duty. Some drugs did that, right?

However, that heavy-duty shit was beginning to wear off. With her hand to her ribcage, she smothered another groan and inched out of bed, careful to not disturb Luca. He was squished into the corner against the wall, his feet pointed to where her head had been. Poor kiddo would need to skip school and Melanie, the principal from hell could kiss her ass.

Pressing her hand to her side, she shuffled to the bathroom and did her thing, brushed her hair, and washed her face. The face cloth took care of the smudged raccoon makeup, but it did nothing to clear her eyes—which were glassy and still a little red.

Lifting her top, she checked her wounds. The one below her boob needed five stitches and a bunch of butterfly bandages and was sensitive to the touch. The others were shallower and would heal on their own. Nicky shivered at the cool air hitting her skin as she readjusted the knot in her top so the fabric wouldn't catch on her stitches.

Sighing at her reflection, she flipped the light switch and shuffled to the kitchen. Where she froze.

Vasily leaned against the Formica counter typing something into his phone. The zipper of his jeans was engaged, but he'd left the button undone, allowing them to hang a little lower on his hips, showing a small section of flat, enticing muscle covered by smooth flesh.

He looked up, his silvery gaze was still soft and relaxed from having just woken up. "Morning," he drawled.

"You're still here," she blurted.

A small, lazy smile tilted one side of his lips. Her breath stopped short, and a multitude of butterflies took flight in her stomach.

God, she'd always loved that smile.

What it lacked in showing teeth was multiplied a thousand times in sex appeal. He'd given that smile when they'd woken together a moment before he wrapped himself around her and kissed her which inevitably led to hot morning sex. Unfortunately, even in her current ragged state, it still had the power to unravel her.

It should not.

What it should do is piss her off. Remind her of the predicament she was in and what the hell did Vasily have that other people wanted back?

"Somebody had to stay," his sexy morning voice broke into her internal bitch fest. "Who better than me?"

She got the feeling that wasn't a question, more like a directive, and to be honest, she wasn't completely against it. He'd handled the cops for her and called a doctor, saving her a trip to the emergency room. A girl couldn't ask for much more, except for none of it to have happened in the first place. But it had and such was life.

He'd pushed his sleeves above his elbows, and as he shoved the phone into his back pocket the muscles in his forearms rippled and flexed. In response, something else rippled and flexed in that very lonely space between her legs.

She checked herself—this was ridiculous.

Instead of staring at those unbuttoned jeans and his sculpted forearms, she focused on the full pot of freshly brewed coffee and pushed her bangs out of her face. The man was too beautiful even with his hair all sleep-mussed and she was in no possible shape or the right mind to entertain those feelings. Especially with the remnants of those drugs still in her system smothering whatever inhibitions she might have. Then again, at least her body was feeling something, unlike the weird, but not unwelcome calmness in her mind.

"Not that I'm ungrateful, but why?" she asked.

"After what you'd been through? Not advisable for you to be alone. No telling if somebody else had intentions of entering your apartment and finishing whatever that asshole started."

"I...well, thank you."

"No problem. Coffee?"

"Please."

He unhooked a mug from beneath her cabinet and somehow, he'd picked her favorite. It was white with lavender sprigs painted on with a chubby bumblebee buzzing around them. The words *Bee Happy* in fancy calligraphy tracked a circular path around the inside.

Vasily poured from the decanter, and she noted the veins in his long, slim fingers. And perhaps she was still too drugged to consider why it seemed completely normal that he served her coffee in her kitchen. Taking a step to the fridge, she opened the door and attempted to remove the milk.

It was an attempt only because he gripped her wrist as her fingers curled around the plastic handle.

"Stop." He glanced down, his gaze like a soft warm glow resting on her midriff. "You'll pull your stitches."

It was then she remembered her entire abdomen was on display. Not only was her top knotted loosely under her breasts, and she was braless, but she'd rolled her harem pants to below her navel. Butterfly bandages, stitches, and *stretch marks* were all exposed.

Fuck herself.

He hadn't seen that part of her body in ten years, and the first time he did, it was like this? Her face heated and sweat popped on the back of her neck beneath her hair.

For the first time, she wished she'd listened to Anthony and had her stretch marks lasered away. Granted, they weren't terrible as stretch marks go, but they were there.

Why was she thinking these things? Why wasn't she throwing things at him? No matter what he'd done for her, it was still his fault she was in this situation.

Wasn't it?

"It's just milk and not that heavy."

"Hmm."

Seconds ticked by as they stared at each other. The heat from his palm seeped into her skin and made her feel slightly drunk. It warmed her from the inside, making it clear no matter how much she wished it wasn't, being around him was both exhilarating and unsettling.

But also dangerous.

"I suggest you let go before I give into the temptation to kiss you," he said, softly. His gaze had turned dark, and some kind of battle was happening in there. What he was fighting she didn't want to speculate about, but it seemed to pull her closer. As did the low timbre in his voice. "You're in no shape to handle the things I want to do to you, so do as you're told."

Nicky blinked. "Okay," she whispered, releasing her grip because she couldn't breathe right, or think right when she was so close to him.

Vasily drew in a hard breath, and with his jaw ticking, retrieved the milk from the shelf. Wrapping a big hand around hers holding the cup, he kept it steady and poured a little into her coffee.

"Almost like old times."

Too much like old times. But she couldn't handle that right now. "Please don't do that."

"Do what?" He closed the fridge and turned to face her.

She swallowed. "Our past is off-limits."

"That's where I disagree, Dominique. We have a lot to discuss about our past and the sooner, the better." The full weight of that gaze stayed on her, and though still soft, there was something else in there. She couldn't put a name to it, but she wanted to believe it was something good.

"My house, my rules."

"Hmm."

That "hmm" may have sounded like an agreement on its face, however, she got the distinct feeling it wasn't. She added two spoons of sugar to her coffee then moved around the breakfast bar to the small wooden table in the tiny dining area she'd made off the kitchen. It was technically part of the living area and though the breakfast bar was adequate, she liked to sit at a table with Luca when they ate.

Vasily followed and took the chair opposite her, sipping his coffee.

"Thank you for coming when Luca called," she said to break the tension, which had become even thicker. "In hindsight, I don't think I could've handled that on my own."

He squinted at her. "You're welcome, but I'm sensing a *but*."

Indeed. There were many *buts*, most of them she was no longer sure of. She straightened the midnight blue runner on the table and pushed the matching wooden salt and pepper shakers together.

"I haven't forgotten who you are."

"I'm kind of counting on that, Dominique." His head tilted as he said this, and his statement was so loaded with innuendo, it made her inner muscles clench. "I want you to remember what we were."

"Or that you just left," she added quickly, and with a little more emphasis. But it was mostly a reminder to herself there was a reason she'd called him Satan. "If what you say is true, about you not being part of framing my dad, why didn't you call?"

"I couldn't."

"You couldn't? They don't have phones in Russia?"

"Something happened to me when I was there I'm not prepared to talk about yet."

"Something *so bad* you couldn't use a cell phone?"

"Yes." His eyes were intense as he gave a slow nod. "Do you seriously believe that if I could've reached out to you, I wouldn't have?"

"I don't know what to believe. All I know is what happened to us, and it happened right after you left. My dad had been arrested for killing Pavel and was sitting in a county jail waiting for his trial. And you were just gone. No explanation. What was I supposed to feel, or believe?"

"Dom." He put his hand flat on the table and slid it closer to her. "I understand why you're hesitant to believe me, but I assure you, me leaving had nothing to do with you...or us. And I had no idea what Leo or my brother were doing to frame your dad." He paused for a beat." Please. I'm asking you to trust me, or at the very least, trust your gut."

Trust her gut?

"You knew me then, and of what you knew, is there anything that tells you I would betray you that way?"

She was at risk of losing that weird calm and with every second he spent sitting across the table, her heart battled with her logic to change her perceptions of him. And it wasn't due to the power of his sex appeal. It was something more that spoke to her on an instinctive level. And the truth was, at the time there was nothing to indicate he'd betray her. No little red flags, no little gut triggers that people sometimes explain away.

Nothing.

She pulled her gaze away to look at the living room windows.

She wanted to trust him, but fear kept eroding that desire. Their relationship before had been so intense, but at the time she hadn't been vulnerable. Now she was. What would it cost her if she let him in again?

She was suddenly exhausted and needed space from this conversation and her emotions. It was too much all at once.

"I need to call Luca's school," she said. "They get pissy if you don't follow the rules and I'm already on the gray list."

"Gray list?"

"We haven't been kicked out yet, but I think they just need one more excuse and I don't want to give it to them. It's a good school, and I want Luca to have the best."

"What do you mean one more reason?"

"We're not of the right...*class* of people they prefer."

Vasily's eyes glittered, but he said nothing. Until she started to rise from her chair.

"Stay seated," he ordered.

"I need my phone. It's on the table next to the couch."

Vasily pulled his from his pocket, unlocked it, and held it out to her. "Use mine."

"I don't know the number."

"Google it."

"It would just be easier if—"

"Dominique, I said google it."

She sighed as she didn't have the energy to fight about it and took the phone from him. Their fingers touched and a bolt of electricity charged between them. It left her breathless, forcing her to take a moment to find the icon and search for the school's number.

"Tiny Titans, how may I help you?" the secretary answered.

"Hi, this is Luca's mom. He's not coming to school today, he..."

"You know you're supposed to report illness before the start of the school day, Mrs. Andretti."

"I know, he—"

"Hold please."

"What? No, I don't want to hold—" Ugh. She'd already been cut off, and the sound of the alphabet song played in her ear. She never understood that. It was the parents that called, not the kids, so why not something more adult? Like AC/DC's *Highway to Hell*, or something? It would be more appropriate, right?

The music cut off. "Mrs. Andretti?"

"Yes, I just want to—"

"This is Melanie, the principal."

Nicky sighed." I know you're the principal, Melanie. You don't need to remind me. Anyway, I don't know why she put me through to you. The reason I'm calling is—"

"Luca's tuition has still not been paid and you have been given enough opportunities and warnings to remedy it to no avail."

What?

She pulled the phone away from her ear and looked at it like she was imagining what she was hearing. She shook her head because no.

"You know what, Melanie, that's bullshit because I checked and *I* never received warnings or any kind of communication from the school, so what you say is incorrect."

"Mrs. Andretti, all communication was directed to Anthony at Andretti legal dot com as well as physical copies sent to your home address in Pacific Heights as indicated in all the school files."

"I changed that address with the school secretary months ago. If your files are not up to date, that is not my fault."

"It's no longer relevant as Luca is suspended immediately. We need the space for a child whose parents can pay."

"Again, what do you mean it hasn't been paid?"

"The transfer failed."

"Failed?" Her left eye started twitching. How was this possible?

"Yes, Mrs. Andretti." The woman's icy, clipped tone cut into her eardrum. "It failed, as it did not arrive in our bank account."

Nicky growled, but she sucked in her temper. "Well, I'll come down today and pay in cash. How much is due?"

"Four thousand, seven hundred and fifty dollars. But it's too late. The money is still owed, but this kind of behavior is not tolerated at Tiny Titans. We can't make any exceptions. What we do for one, means we have to do for all others, and we can't run our school like that. I'm afraid Luca is no longer—"

Nicky hung up before she exploded. As it was, her blood was boiling. Carefully, she put Vasily's phone down and pushed it away from her with the tips of her fingers to avoid slamming it to death on the table. Tears of anger stung her eyes. If the direct deposit failed, there wasn't enough money in Anthony's account. But how could that be? He was a fucking lawyer who billed at...what did he bill at? She no longer had any idea. But where had the money gone? To the house and the cars? Women? Cocaine?

"Mom," Luca's croaky, sleep-filled voice caught her off guard. "Do I have to go to school?"

"Hey, Buddy." Nicky turned slowly in her chair, wincing at the pulling sensation in her abdomen. She held an arm out in invitation for a hug. "Come here."

Luca snuggled in.

"Oof, gently. Mommy hurts."

"Sorry."

"No problem, baby." She kissed his sleep-mussed hair, inhaling his familiar, slightly sweaty child scent and relishing his warm little body pressed to hers. "You did everything perfectly by the way. Thank you for being so strong and for taking care of me."

"Welcome," he mumbled.

"Morning, little man," Vasily said, clearing his throat.

She felt Luca's head move against her breast. "Morning Mr. Parking Lot Man."

Vasily chuckled, a sound that went straight to all kinds of places it shouldn't have. "You can call me Vasily."

"Morning, Mr. Vasily."

"Just Vasily, no mister."

"'Kay." He snuggled closer, then looked at her. "Mom, I'm hungry."

"Course you are, it's way past your normal breakfast time. And you've earned a special one this morning so you can have anything you like."

"Even French toast?" His sleepy brown eyes widened with excitement.

She nodded, smiling. "Even French toast." Then after a further squeeze, she let him go and moved to get up.

"Let me," Vasily said, already beginning to stand.

She paused, looking at him. Luca was too.

"You know how to make French toast?" Luca asked.

Vasily snorted, pushing his chair back into position under the table. "Do I know how to make French toast? He pointed to his chest. "My French toast is so good, it will blow your socks off."

Luca giggled. "I don't have any socks on, but Mom puts cinnamon in the eggs."

"I'll put whatever you want in it."

"Within reason," Nicky added quickly, her ovaries palpitating. What the hell was happening? Ovaries were not allowed to respond to a man who had broken her heart once already. An image of a miniature Vasily running around causing mayhem popped into her head. God help her, she wanted another child, and suddenly the urge was so strong, it took the wind from her.

She blew out a long breath and rubbed her still-twitching eye. There was nothing she could do about her ovaries, however.

"Within reason, like your mom says." Vasily lifted Luca and deposited him onto her counter. His sweater rode up, showing off inches of hard abdominal muscles from beneath his unbuttoned jeans. "But I'm going to need your help to show me where everything is."

"Uh-huh."

"Okay, first up." Making sure Luca was settled, he adjusted the waistband of his jeans and pushed the button through its hole. "We need a pan."

Nicky stood, before the butterflies in her belly took flight, and her world burst into flame.

Good grief, who turned up the heat?

She pushed to her feet, then schlepped to her room, and placed her hand on the door handle. Immediately she snatched it back and gasped.

There was a man in her room.

A dead man.

She got that awful, twisted feeling in her stomach that happened just before she threw up. But the body was gone, right? She vaguely remembered the coroner removing the corpse before she finally gave in to the drugs the doctor had given her.

Nicky shut her eyes and swallowed the excess saliva in her mouth. There was no choice in the matter, it had to be done. She needed clothes. Opening the door, she pushed it slowly, eyeing her space.

Someone had the foresight to open a window, and the smell of blood wasn't too bad. On further inspection, she noted the knife was gone too. So was her comforter, but not the blood on the carpet. The entire carpet would have to be gone for that to happen.

Great.

No way her security deposit would cover the cost of replacing the floorboards and a new carpet. Yet another expense she couldn't afford. Stepping carefully around the stain, her heart in her throat, she grabbed the first dress her hands touched and a pair of boots. Then, with clean underwear and socks from her dresser, she exited her room to the warm, cinnamony smell of French toast cooking and went to Luca's room to change.

The dress was one of her favorites. Black, with a long-sleeved, loose-fitting bodice and a flowy skirt that swirled around her legs. She'd just buttoned it up in the front and shoved her feet into her cowboy boots when the yelling began.

Chapter Fifteen

Nicky rushed from Luca's room and found herself confronted with the worst possible scenario.

"Oh my God, *Daddy!*" She positioned herself between Vasily and her father, a palm facing each of them. Both had their guns pointed at the other over her shoulder. "Put your gun away!" She turned to face Vasily. "You too!"

Vasily's nostrils flared as he sucked in a deep breath, his head tilting just a little to the side. The tension in the room was combustive, ready to explode with the smallest spark. To make matters worse, Marley hissed from his position on the couch, looking like an orange troll on crack. And further worse, Luca sat frozen, wide-eyed, and cross-legged on the breakfast bar watching the whole damn thing.

Fuck her fucking life!

Just what she needed. More damage to her son from a shoot-out in her living room.

"I'm not putting it away," Mario argued, eyes wide and eyebrows twitching. "Until I know what the hell he's doing here!"

She glanced back over her shoulder. "He's here because I needed him."

"What?" he yelled. "You look like shit. Why do you look like shit? What did this jackass do?"

"*Nothing!*" She slapped her forehead. "He did nothing. Just put it away and I'll explain everything." Looking back at the Russian, his cheeks were hollowed, those lips pursed in anger. "Vasily, please!"

After several beats Vasily lowered his weapon, pointing it at the floor, yet never once taking his eyes off her dad.

"Thank you." She swallowed, her voice coming out croaky. She was shaking, she wanted to throw up and her left eye twitched like crazy. Pressing a finger to it, she faced her father. "Now your turn, Daddy."

"Give me one good reason I should let this backstabbing, motherfucking framing asshole out of my gunsight," he rumbled.

"Because I asked him to be here." Okay, *slight* embellishment, but not important. "Something happened last night, which is why I called. Vasily was the only one to answer the phone." *Lucky for him.*

"You called him?"

"Well, I called you first, but you didn't answer."

Mario had the decency to look chagrined and softened his voice. "Didn't have my hearing aids in."

"I know." She nodded.

"What happened?"

"I'll tell you in a minute, but you should be thanking Vasily, not trying to kill him."

Never mind carrying a weapon that violated his parole should shit go further south!

Holy hell, her heart. It was lodged inside her throat and beating so hard she was pretty sure it was going to explode.

Mario's gaze darted between herself and Vasily, but his face slowly lost some of its psycho Mr. Bean look, his expression morphing into something more concerned.

"Take a seat, Pops. Please." She pointed to the table with a trembling finger.

Mario removed his black leather biker jacket, hung it on the back of a chair, and took a seat. She directed her gaze to Vasily. "Now you, please."

Vasily shoved his gun into the back of his jeans, then moved to the couch. He sat, knees wide apart, forearms resting on them. Waves of tension rolled off him and she took note of how his nostrils flared. Never a good sign. It was moments like this she questioned her ability to be a good mother. What other five-year-old had to deal with the crap Luca had in the last twelve hours?

No.

She pinched the bridge of her nose. That particular rabbit hole was not one she needed to go down now. Her main priority was to keep these two men from losing control of their trigger fingers. Considering the way they eyed each other, physical harm was still a distinct possibility. For that reason, she kept herself between them.

She turned her attention to her son. "Luca, baby, I need you to go to your room. You can take your breakfast with you, and when you're done eating play games on your Nintendo. But use the headphones, okay?"

Her amazing child nodded, his eyes still wide, and she couldn't imagine what he must be thinking. Something she'd have to check in with him about later and made a mental note to do just that. But Luca rolled onto his stomach and slid off the counter, then grabbed his plate. The moment she heard his door shut, Nicky turned to her dad.

"Daddy, have you taken your heart pills this morning?"

"What does that have to do with anything?"

"Just yes, or no?"

Mario grunted in the affirmative. Nicky blew out a breath, then sucked in another big one and blew that out too. She was still shaking, but her heart had slowed a little, so she proceeded to fill her dad in on her attack and the reason Vasily was there. To her surprise and immense relief, he listened without shooting or breaking anything.

"You're damn lucky Dwayne answered the call," Mario growled. "He's a good man and a good cop. He ain't one of the dirty ones." At this, he narrowed his eyes and cut Vasily a glance. His subtext was clear, and not missed by either herself or the Russian.

Vasily's focus remained cool. "If he was dirty, there's no chance in hell I'd have allowed your daughter to even give the bare minimum of a statement due to her condition. As it is, I've arranged for a lawyer to accompany her to the appointment with Fetzer this afternoon."

Mario grunted.

"Daddy, there's another matter. I can't stay here."

"I can arrange for a safe house," Vasily said before she could go further.

She turned to look at him. "A safe house?"

What did that mean exactly? Maybe it was just her, but she's seen enough television to envision a prison-like structure some-where out of the city. Concrete fences twenty feet high, armed guards, and vicious dogs. Or the alternative, some weird cabin in the remote woods, no running water or cell service, and *vicious dogs*.

No thank you.

"I have a job and Luca has..." She paused as she *was* going to say school, but that point was now moot. "It's okay, I can stay with my dad."

"Hate to break it to you, Stick," Mario retorted, frustration clouding his voice. But I live in a camper van smaller than your kitchen. You're not thinking straight. It's one thing to have my grandson overnight, but three people living in that thing indefi-nitely? One of us is gonna get bitchy and it ain't gonna be me."

"Daddy!"

"Am I wrong?"

She rolled her eyes. *Unbelievable.*

"And I don't have a bathtub."

True.

She loved her baths, especially after a tough night on her feet. One of the reasons she'd picked this apartment was for its deep, slope-backed bathtub, *and* she could afford the rent. But she wasn't an entitled princess who cried when her nail polish got chipped. She didn't even wear nail polish and she could do two-minute van showers until this was over.

"And how is Luca going to get to school?" Mario continued. "Your car's burnt to a crisp, and he can't be on the Harley."

Now would not be a good time to tell him Luca had lost his place due to Anthony's negligence, but she didn't have to. Vasily saved her from answering.

"I agree with your dad." His tone was cool and measured. "It's not secure, and you can't stay with your friends either. You need full-time, qualified protection. I have the location and the manpower."

"At a safe house?" Nicky asked, only half sarcastic.

"Much as it pains me to agree with him, Stick, and believe me it pains me real hard in places I'd rather leave unmentioned, you *do* need protection."

She blinked. "Two minutes ago you were ready to shoot him, risking your parole and now you're taking his side?"

"You think I'm thrilled with this idea?" Mario raised his palms in the air. "It don't mean you gotta go wherever he's suggesting or accept his protection. Just give me time to come up with an alternative."

"This is a waste of time, and it's not up for negotiation," Vasily cut in. "You've been targeted because of your association with me. Until this is over, you are my responsibility."

Her dad bristled, his jaw set hard. "She's my fucking daughter, my fucking responsibility."

Uh-oh.

Vasily didn't move, except for the purposeful shifting of his gaze from her to her dad. Not even his facial expression changed. Yet that simple act, the authority he exuded had the effect of raising the tension in the room.

"Oh, for fuck's sake!" Nicky stated before their trigger fingers got itchy. "I am a grown woman and nobody's responsibility except my own." She paced the living room, pressing a hand to her side just below her wound. It had started to throb again, probably due to her elevated blood pressure. "And it *is* up for negotiation."

"If not a safe house, Dominique, then my apartment. Those are your choices."

A deep rumble left Mario's chest, but she ignored it.

"Your apartment is filled with all those expensive books and whatever else little kids like to get into. I have stitches in my side and can't be chasing after Luca every five minutes, nor can I afford to pay for anything he may damage."

"Wait one fucking second," Mario barked behind her. "Expensive books?" Her stomach dropped as she realized her mistake.

Her face screwed up. Oh... *man.*

"How do you know he has expensive books?"

She'd slipped up big time, but there was no way she could lie to her dad. He knew her well enough to see right through any deception. Turning, she faced his questioning gaze, those thick Italian brows raised as he waited for her answer.

"I went to Vasily's apartment after my car blew up."

"You went where?" he yelled.

Heat radiated from her face.

"Jesus fucking Christ!" He stared at her, eyes wide and full of betrayal like she'd dumped his Harley into a crusher. Then he jerked out of his chair scraping a hand over his graying goat-tee. "Never mind," he said, grabbing his jacket. "I don't want to know. You're an adult, you sort this out. I'm going to the corner store to cool down...and buy some smokes!"

"You're smoking again?" Her voice came out squeaky.

"Not yet, but I may just fucking restart."

"Daddy, no. You can't, not with your heart!"

Mario ignored her as he marched to the door.

"Daddy, *wait...*" But he'd already slammed it behind him. Letting out a long, unsteady breath, she stared after him.

Wasn't that just peachy?

Add that to her list of shit to worry about. She blamed herself. If she'd insisted on using her own phone to call the school instead of Vasily's, she would have checked her notifications sooner and texted back that she was all right, avoiding all this.

Nicky exhaled, putting one palm to her forehead, and the other rubbing the back of her neck.

"How did it come to this?" she asked of Vasily, shaking her head.

He watched her with cool scrutiny, his gaze impenetrable. If only she could read him better. But she knew this much. He was a man who only allowed people to see what he wanted them to know. Which, to be perfectly honest wasn't very often and never a lot. Something that had both intrigued and bothered her in the past.

"Though I suppose I should at the very least thank you for not shooting him," she said. "He's a giant splinter in my ass, but I do love him."

"Forget it," he murmured. "If I were in his shoes, I would've done the same. I get that he's uncomfortable with my presence."

Uncomfortable? Nicky let out a short laugh that sounded like a whimper. Uncomfortable didn't even come close. "Just so you know," she pointed at him, "Italians like to hang onto grudges."

"So do Russians." He smirked. "I think we invented the concept."

"Well, I'm glad you find that funny. My point, however, is even after what you did for me last night, don't expect much from my dad in the way of forgiveness for what happened to him."

"Understood." He paused for a moment. "What about you... have you forgiven me?"

She stared at him as she pondered his question. "I haven't made up my mind yet. If you want me to believe you, you're going to have to be completely candid, and so far you haven't been."

"I've been as candid as I can be, and as for the rest, I will, in time."

"In time? Well, then we're in a catch-22, aren't we?"

He nodded slowly, acknowledging their conundrum. "If you can do what I asked you to do earlier, listen to your gut, perhaps we can get there sooner."

His phone buzzed and he checked the message. "Yev is waiting outside, and your lawyer will be here soon. You should get packing. Once you're done with the interview at the police station, you're heading to my apartment."

Her brows pinched together. "Yev?"

"He'll drive you."

"But why's he already outside?"

"He's been here since last night keeping an eye on things and he's backup if we need it."

Nicky paused her pacing. "Backup? Okay, my brain is still fuzzy, so forgive me. Why do we need backup?"

"I'm guessing your attacker wasn't working alone." Vasily's gaze pinned her, the look in it made her hands turn clammy. "I won't know for sure until we get an ID. If he's a lone wolf and not connected to anything, things can go back to normal. But he said *us*. That I had something that belonged to *them*. This implies more people are involved. He knew where you live, so we must assume whomever he was referring to does too."

Of course. She didn't know why she hadn't processed that. This was way more serious than she'd initially thought, like *criminal organization* serious. "What exactly do you have that they want back?"

"Not sure."

She gave him a skeptical look. "Got a theory at least?"

"None that I care to share at this moment."

"Seriously?" She glared at him, her mouth slightly open. "I mean, how many things do you have that belong to other people, Vasily?"

That steely gaze narrowed in a way that should've warned her to watch her tone. In any other circumstance, she might have heeded that look, but in her messed-up mental state, her brain overlooked it.

"Don't give me the bullshit mafia-boss garbage. I was almost raped, Vasily! I have cuts all over my body and my son had to do things no five-year-old ever should."

Something happened then.

Suddenly everything she'd kept a lid on for the last twelve hours bubbled up. The danger they'd been in spun her emotional dial to high. Her mouth opened, then closed. Her body began to shake as a memory torpedoed through her mind.

"Oh God," she gasped, clasping a hand over her mouth. "Oh God, he made me touch...he put..." Each phrase was punctuated with a sob, her chest heaving as it came rushing back. Breathing became hard.

Vasily shot from his seat on the couch and closed the distance between them before she could take another breath. Wrapping one arm around her shoulders, the other cupping her head, he pulled her in, making sure her uninjured side was to his torso.

"It's okay. I'm here." His heart thumped a steady beat beneath her ear as the hard warmth of his strong arms and chest enveloped her. "Let it out," he murmured. "Let it all out. You're safe. I'm not going to let anything else happen to you." Hot breath seeped into her scalp as he pressed his lips to her hair.

She clung to him, sobbing. Allowing the tears to flow and the poison to spill from her soul. It felt so natural and good to be in his arms. To be the one held and comforted for a change. She melted against him, absorbing his strength and his warmth.

The roll of paper towels she'd used to swab her wounds was still on the coffee table. Vasily dipped as he reached for it and broke off a few sheets, handing them to her. She wiped her nose and after a while, she became aware of his comfortable, earthy smell. It was clean with no trace of cologne. Just him. Calming and pleasant, and safe.

Slowly she regained a little more of herself. But the more composure she acquired, the more aware of him she became—his lips whispering words in Russian against her hair. She didn't understand them, but it didn't matter. What did, was his breath on her scalp, his body pressed to hers. It felt right and good and she didn't want to let go.

She looked up and their eyes locked. His were concerned, unshielded, and for a moment he allowed her to see into his soul.

"Dom," he murmured softly.

The single word caused his chest to rumble against hers, sending all kinds of pleasurable vibrations through her. The hand cupping her head slid down to her neck, then up into her hair, gripping it. Forcing her to keep looking into his eyes. They turned softer, yet darker. "I'm going to keep you safe. Please trust me."

God, she wanted to trust him. Wanted that more than anything. And she would with her physical safety, but what about her heart? Another shattering because of this man would likely kill her. The fact he was back in her life was already hard enough to handle. Love and hate being two sides of the same coin had never been more obvious.

Her eyes dropped to his lips, and she licked hers.

He drew in a sharp breath, then growled. "Don't do that."

"Why not?" she asked, feeling him harden against her side. A surge of lust rushed through her at how the tables were suddenly turned. Funny, how for one select moment she held the power. "You should let me go, then."

"I don't want to." He looked down at her, his gaze seeming

almost tortured. "And yeah, it's going to hurt, but now is not the time to pursue this."

Releasing a breath, he looked away, then his arms slipped from her, and he went to the window. The coolness left behind after his warmth was lacking.

She stood, not moving, wanting him back but not daring to make the leap.

He was right.

Now wasn't the time to pursue what her body wanted. What the aching spot between her legs desperately needed. Instead, she reached for another paper towel, wiped the traces of tears from her face, and found the couch. Before her legs got any wobblier.

She needed to focus on something else. Anything. Her phone was close by, on the little table next to the couch. Grabbing it, she checked her messages, and finally, read the texts from her dad. *Stick, what's going on?*

Kiddo, call me.

One from Soren. *Honey, did you butt-dial me? Conference is great. Lots of hot men. Wish you were here.*

Understatement of the year.

And zero from Anthony. Figured, though she might need a good criminal lawyer referral from him. Just because Vasily's lawyer was available for this interview didn't mean it was a good idea to keep him. A sigh of frustration escaped her, as she pressed Anthony's number. It went straight to voicemail, so she called his office.

"Hey, Gail, it's Nicky."

Anthony's receptionist was the only female member of his staff she talked to. The others? Well, she was pretty sure he'd had carnal relations with most of them. "Is he available?"

"Hey, Nick. I was just about to call *you*. Anthony is a no-show this morning and he's not answering his cell."

Shit. Nicky's brows came closer together.

Then Gail's voice changed to a whisper, but it was amplified like she'd cupped her headphone mic. "There are new clients here that are not so happy and they're not the kind you want to make not so happy, you get my meaning?"

Boy, did she. More referrals of the criminal type. "That's strange, no?"

"You think?" Anthony was many things, but being late for a client meeting was never one of them. Punctuality was one of his few redeeming qualities. "I'm getting a little worried," Gail said.

So was she. He'd often let her stew by making her wait several hours to return any messages but always got back to her. Especially if one was from their son.

"Okay, when you hear from him, please have him call me. It's urgent."

"Will do." Gail broke the connection. When she looked up, Vasily was watching her again, his face back to showing no expression. Yet there was an enigmatic something in his eyes that she didn't know how to catalog.

"Just FYI, I have a bathtub," he said, a tiny smile playing on his lips. "Several, in fact."

Satan.

He'd asked her to trust him, and he'd also promised to keep them safe. What other option was she left with? Her dad, though acquainted with some serious people, they were not the kind he was allowed to associate with due to his parole conditions.

"All right." She swallowed and dropped her phone into her dress pocket. Then she brushed her bangs aside. "Since this mess has to do with you, I'm afraid you're it." She took a deep breath and let it out through pursed lips. "Your apartment it is."

Fuck the consequences. Since Anthony was MIA and Luca's safety was paramount, her dad would have to deal.

As would she—and not with just her legal or safety matter. She'd have to deal with her messy, mixed-up emotions too.

Chapter Sixteen

W hen her dad returned from the corner store, Nicky noted with relief the lack of cigarettes in his pocket, and he didn't smell like he'd snuck a smoke either. Fuming and silent, he stayed with Luca who was engrossed in a game on his Nintendo, while Vasily escorted Nicky downstairs. He helped her into a black Cadillac Escalade.

This did not decrease her anxiety or stop the sweat from popping on the back of her neck.

A silent, yet solemn-faced Yev sat behind the wheel and gave her a nod in greeting. According to Vasily, the man had spent half the night and morning guarding her place and although he looked a little stubbly, he seemed alert and smelled pretty good too. Like fabric softener and spearmint gum. Kinda unfair, really.

In the backseat sat another, just as serious-looking man, only he wore a well-fitting suit and had a black briefcase placed between them.

"Derek Granger," Vasily introduced him. "Your lawyer."

He was a few years older than Vasily, probably late thirties, with wavy brown hair and just a smattering of gray at his temples.

"Hi, Derek." Nicky took his offered hand. Granger's grip had just the right amount of firmness, and he had a pleasant face that came along with an athletic build and a relaxed smile. The kind that would make it easy to forget he was a mob lawyer. But mob lawyers knew their shit, didn't they? Since Vasily was still walking free, that reality eased her anxiety by half a notch.

"Take care of her," Vasily said to both men, his tone serious. With a last, lingering yet reassuring glance at Nicky, he closed the door of the car, tapped the roof, and stepped away.

Why did men do that—tap the roof?

She watched him walk in his loping, easy way to yet another Cadillac Escalade, this one white. He slipped into the back seat and then they drove in the opposite direction.

"We don't have much time," Granger said, regaining her attention and making her blush for staring. "Tell me everything that happened last night and don't hold back. Warts and all. I want the smelly parts no matter how bad you think it may be."

So, she did, but it took longer than the ride. Yev circled the block until Granger was satisfied. The fact he was thorough and seemed to care helped to calm her.

At the police station, they were escorted to a bland room with mirrored windows. They waited a few minutes before Detective Fetzer joined them and sat on the opposite side of a long utility table. The cop had a way of moving that was confident and purposeful, yet his soulful brown eyes were bloodshot and tired. His hair was disheveled and his tie was slightly askew. Nicky couldn't help wondering if he was adopting the Columbo effect—the bumbling, yet wily television detective of old, only minus the ratty beige raincoat.

It was as she waited for him to get settled that she noticed the camera in the corner facing her. A blinking red light indicated it was on.

They went through all the preliminaries, name, date of birth, and other personal details. Granger had a habit of playing with his pen—twirling it between his fingers. But his cutting, no-nonsense knowledge of the law aided by Doctor Ronnie's photos and medical report sliced through the red tape with surprising ease. So much so, her palms were no longer sweaty.

Fetzer rubbed his scruff and took a sip of coffee from a black mug decorated with little red hearts and *Hottest Detective Ever* scrawled in cursive on the front. It made her want to smile, but she suppressed it. The man may be a badass cop, but clearly, he had a humorous side. Or maybe it was designed to make a suspect relax their guard a little. Nicky cleared her throat.

With his gaze on the paperwork, Granger flipped through the pages. "It's your testimony then, Mrs. Andretti, that you've never met the man who attacked you before?"

"Yes, as I mentioned last night, the only time I ever saw him before was outside my son's school."

The detective tilted his head slightly as he scrutinized her. He waited for several long moments before speaking. It made her palms sweat again. "And why do you think he was there?"

"At the time I thought my ex had him following me, but that wasn't the case."

Fetzer dipped his chin. "What was the case?"

She paused for a moment and glanced at her lawyer. Granger nodded for her to proceed. "He came to my apartment because he said he wanted me to pass on a message for Vasily Melnikov."

"And that message was that Melnikov had something of theirs and they wanted it back?"

"Yes."

"And you have no idea what that something is?"

"No." Now that she thought about it, perhaps Vasily not sharing his theory with her had been a good thing.

Fetzer opened the file before him and removed an eight-by-ten mugshot. He pushed it forward across the desk. "Fingerprints indicate his name is James Falk of Redding, California. Have you heard that name before?"

"James Falk?" Nicky squinted at Fetzer, then shook her head. "No, I've never heard that name before."

"Do you know *anyone* who is associated with James Falk?"

"Detective, how would I know if anyone is associated with him?"

Fetzer gave a small smile.

It was then she realized the shrewd detective had pulled that Columbo thing, and thank the gods, she'd passed.

"Would you look at the photo please?"

Nicky wrinkled her nose and hesitated a couple of beats before she dropped her eyes to the mugshot. She sucked in a breath. The face staring back at her seemed to seep pure evil. And that evil had made her touch him in intimate ways she didn't want to think about. The little hairs on her arms raised and she rubbed the sensation away.

When James Falk had attacked her, there were loose, fleshy tunnels in his ear lobes. In the photo, those holes were filled with black gauges. His hair was also longer with greasy bangs that hung over his brow, but the eyes were the same. Dead and black, they were burned into her memory logs. She shuddered.

Both men looked at her.

"I don't know him," she whispered. Nausea crept up her throat, but she swallowed it back.

Fetzer grunted. "This is what I don't understand. Falk has a record and was recently released on a five hundred-thousand-dollar bond from Shasta County Jail."

"Shasta County?" Granger asked, eyes narrowed. "In northern California?"

"Yep."

"That's a big bond." Her lawyer tapped his hand with his pen. "What the hell's he doing way down south in the Bay Area? A violation of his bail agreement, surely?"

"That's what I'm thinking," Fetzer agreed. "And why jeopardize that agreement by paying an unwelcome visit to Mrs.

Andretti? Doesn't make sense, does it?" The detective stared at her for a minute. "Any ideas?"

Nicky swallowed. "No, detective. No ideas."

"Well, that is something I aim to find out. As soon as I've had a chance to read his file." He tapped the paperwork in front of him with an index finger, but his eyes remained on Nicky. As if to say *you better not be lying.* Fortunately, she wasn't.

"You asked about known associates," Granger said. "Are there any names in that file you care to share, Detective? Perhaps give *us* a better idea who this man was."

"Let's see…" Fetzer rummaged through some papers until he found the one he wanted. He took a moment to read. "Looks like our perp has a half-brother by the name of John King. Goes by the alias, Kai."

At that Granger's pen stilled between his fingers for half a second before resuming. Nicky glanced at him. His expression remained the same, but she sensed him tense. "John King?"

"Either of you know him?" Fetzer looked up from the file, his gaze bouncing between them.

Nicky shook her head, then looked at the lawyer, curious for his answer.

"It's a common enough name," Granger said, shrugging. "Must be thousands in the country."

Fetzer closed the file and pinched the bridge of his nose before leaning back in his chair. Given the dark circles beneath his eyes, she almost felt sorry for him. It seemed the man had been up all night working her case.

"If you have nothing else to share that's all for now," he said. "You're free to go, but please be available for any more questions we may have."

The lawyer stood. "All questions for my client regarding this case will be directed to me." He extracted a black card with gold embossed lettering from his wallet and passed it to the detective.

"She's not under arrest, Granger." The detective rolled his eyes and stuck the business card into a pocket on the inside cover of her file. "She's free to speak for herself and given the perp's rap sheet and probable bail violation, it's looking pretty good for Mrs. Andretti."

"And I'd like to keep it that way." Granger's eyes bore down at the cop. The look in them was determined. "Directly to me. Clear?"

"As crystal." The detective smirked.

"Later." The lawyer placed his hand on the middle of her back, giving her a gentle nudge toward the exit before the cop could say anything else. They left Fetzer in the interrogation room and passed through a busy area of uniformed cops and regular civilians until they hit the street.

"Okay," she said to Granger when they stepped out of the building onto the sidewalk. Yev waited double-parked, engine running in the shadow of a tall building opposite the police station. "Who is this John King person? What was his alias...Kai?"

Granger looked down at her from his considerable height but remained silent.

"What are you not telling me?"

"Let's get to the car."

She avoided his attempt to escort her across the street, stepping aside to dodge some idiot going too fast on one of those rented motorized scooters.

Granger cursed at the fool's back as he almost clipped his briefcase.

"You know something, and I deserve the truth about what's going on here," Nicky insisted.

"And you will. When it's time."

"Are you really my lawyer, Mr. Granger?"

"What do you mean?" He frowned.

"I mean are you representing me or Vasily?"

He sighed and turned his head to face the Cadillac. "I'm representing you both."

"I'm thinking that's a conflict of interest."

"It doesn't have to be. You have a common goal and my orders from Mr. Melnikov are to make sure your interests are represented. That's what I'm doing." He glanced at her. "Discussing this outside the police station isn't the best place to do so."

Shit.

Where was her brain today? He was right about that. Dirty cops and all. Call her a conspiracy theorist but who knew if they had listening devices outside their building for unsuspecting suspects blurting their truth?

This time she allowed Granger to take her elbow. He waited for a gap in the traffic and led her across the street, then assisted her into the SUV—making sure she was comfortable before shutting the door. He climbed in next to her and as she fastened her seatbelt, she studied him while Yev pulled into the traffic.

"Okay, spill."

"All I can say at the moment is Falk's brother, John King, or Kai as he's more commonly known, was a human trafficker."

Human trafficker?

A blast of air left Nicky's lungs. She pushed her hands into her hair and gripped chunks of it.

Human fucking *trafficker!*

That man had been inside her home, feet away from her son! What if he'd killed her and taken Luca? There are sick people who do horrible things to children.

God!

She'd managed to staunch it back in the interrogation room, but now saliva suddenly filled her mouth and she muttered, "Stop the car!"

"What?" Yev glanced at her through the rearview mirror.

"Stop!"

Wide-eyed, he put his foot on the brake and a moment later she fumbled for the door handle, hearing both men curse at the same time. Ignoring them, and the cacophony of car horns behind them, she stumbled from the Caddie, barely making it to a metal city garbage can when the few bites of cold French toast she'd consumed for breakfast came up. Hot tears prickled her eyeballs. Her stitches stung from her clumsiness and the pressure. She put a palm to her side to help quell the pain.

Moments later, a large hand nudged her, then a handkerchief appeared. It was white and crisp, and she took it to wipe her mouth. Next, a cold bottle of water appeared, the seal still intact.

Grateful, Nicky looked up. Yev's face was stoic as he held it out.

"Thank you," she mumbled, breathing hard. Cracking the seal, she rinsed her mouth out and spat into the garbage bin before taking several sips.

"You good?" Yev's gravelly voice was calm, yet it showed his concern. "Boss will have my head if I let you collapse on the side-walk, so tell me now if you're going to faint."

She pushed her hair from her face. "I'm okay."

If a little shaky— her permanent condition lately. She looked at the soiled handkerchief, wondering what to do with it.

"Toss it," Yev ordered, reading her expression. "I've got plenty."

She nodded and discarded it into the garbage can. Yev followed her back to the car—his hand at her elbow ready to catch her should she wobble. As he waited for her to climb in, he seemed to be taking stock of her condition.

He was intimidatingly large, but despite his size, the man was quite attractive. Solid, and in his act of kindness, even the scar across his sooty brow seemed less menacing. He also had beautiful lips which were pursed as he studied her. She assumed it was with worry and not annoyance. An annoyed Yev probably wouldn't be a good experience for anyone.

Granger was typing something on his phone with his thumbs, but he paused for a moment as he watched her settle. His expression mirrored Yev's concern.

"Just needed a moment," Nicky said, her voice hoarse. "To process the human trafficking information."

Granger huffed out an ironic laugh. "That was a moment, I'll give you that." Then he got serious again. "You're in good hands, Nicky, but if you'd prefer another lawyer, I can refer you to someone else."

"Let me think about that, but you know, maybe you can help me with something that wouldn't be a conflict of interest with Vasily."

"What's that?"

"I need a divorce lawyer."

Granger lifted a brow. "Divorce is not my specialty."

"No one will take me as a client," she said, digging into her purse for her lip gloss as her lips felt too dry. "My ex seems to have scared away most of the decent ones in the city and I'm starting to scrape the barrel, which is not what I need. I need someone really good."

"Your ex is Anthony Andretti?"

She gave a small, ironic smile. "Hole in one."

He responded with a slow, thoughtful nod. "I may know a couple. Let me get back to you."

"That would be very much appreciated."

After making a detour to Target to pick up a new booster seat for Luca, since the last one she owned had gone up in flames along with her car, Yev pulled back into the traffic and a few minutes later they approached her small apartment complex. Her parking spot was shared by Soren's BMW and her dad's Fat Boy Harley parked directly behind the Beemer's trunk. She, therefore, directed Yev to park in Terrence's vacant spot as BeeBee, the ragtop Beetle, was still in the shop getting her post-fire makeover.

After he parked, the bodyguard helped her dad bring down suitcases filled with their essentials, her laptop, and Marley, the one-eyed wonder. Luca hopped into the back of the car and sitting on his knees, directed Yev on how to strap in his car seat. The cat showed his thoughts on the matter by sticking his pink butthole against the wire door of his carrier.

"That all of it?" Yev asked her, wrinkling his nose at Marley's indecent display.

"Think so." She checked to ensure the car seat was properly installed, then turned to Luca. "Strap yourself in, Buddy. I just need to talk to Grandpa for a second."

"'Kay, Mommy."

She closed the door and turned to her dad who stood at the entrance to the parking lot, arms folded, helmet dangling from one thumb. She walked over to him. "Daddy."

"Stick." His clipped tone and lack of eye contact left no doubt he was still pissed. Deep down, she couldn't blame him, as underneath that anger she knew he was worried.

"Daddy, please don't be mad. It's not what you think."

"What do I think? That you're fuckin' around with the enemy?"

"No—"

"For fuck sake, girl! He used you. Tossed you aside like toilet paper. For all we know, he's the one who beat the life out of Pavel."

"He said he wasn't involved and he wasn't even aware it had happened. He was out of the country at the time."

"And you believe him?" Mario's tone suggested she was missing a few lightbulbs in her chandelier.

Did she?

There was that small, damaged part of her that screamed she shouldn't. Yet there was also that growing part of her that told her she absolutely should. She'd yet to see anything in his eyes or any action to tell her otherwise.

Her dad huffed. He turned his head away, then shook it, muttering something under his breath. Turning back, he addressed her directly. "I'm disappointed, girl. Thought you had better sense than that. Not to mention loyalty."

He put his right index finger on her chest bone, where her

heart was, and looked her dead in the eye. His brown eyes were almost black with anger, sadness, and a few other emotions she didn't want to name. "He's a Melnikov. You can't *ever* trust them."

"But can you trust me?"

He blinked. "I'm not sure I can."

"Then *where* do you want me to go, Dad?" She spread her fingers in the air before touching them to her temples. "You want me to keep Luca trapped in a tiny hotel room for God knows how long until you can arrange something better? What if that never happens? Neither you, nor any of your old friends—the ones you no longer are allowed to associate with—have the muscle Vasily has. And that's what I need right now. Muscle."

His sharp intake of breath inferred she'd scored a point. Several maybe. He was still a strong man, but he was only one man and prison had aged him.

"These people, Daddy, they're no joke. I'm not taking any risks. Not with your parole or our safety."

His eyes narrowed at her determined tone. "This goes to hell like it did last time? This," he tapped her chest above her heart again, "gets ripped to shreds *like it did last time,* don't say I didn't warn you."

Then he tapped his own heart.

His silent implication sliced through her, worse than the wounds she'd received from her assailant, making clear that her heartache was his heartache too. And as a mother, she understood that. A parent was only ever as happy as their saddest child.

With that, he walked away and threw a leg over his Harley. He didn't look at her when he put his helmet on, or when he started it. And he especially didn't look at her when he pulled out of the parking lot without his two-fingered sideways salute.

That missing salute bothered her most of all.

With her heart heavy in her chest, and her eyeballs stinging, she swallowed. God, she hated disappointing him. It hurt to the bone to do so.

When she turned back to face her life, the mountain was watching her. He was back to expressionless as he waited for her. She wiped the tears from her cheeks before crossing the parking lot and climbing inside next to Luca.

"Mom," he said, kicking his legs, oblivious to the turmoil in her head and her heart. "Mr. Vasily has a pool on the roof. Can I go swimming?"

"Sure, honey," she murmured only half listening when Yev shut the door. "Why not?"

They may as well take the perks of luxury penthouse living along with the unwarranted punishment from her dad.

The way her life was going lately, she had a feeling the worst was yet to come.

Chapter Seventeen

Granger's update was concerning, but things were beginning to make sense.

The man who'd attacked Nicky was directly connected to another dead man. One Vasily had killed himself a little over a week ago in their defunct butchery. Viktor Sokolov.

Sokolov had been partners with James Falk and his brother. And all were involved in human trafficking.

Hardcore shit.

Vasily leaned against the plexiglass barrier on *The Happy Clam's* outdoor patio and shoved his hands into his jeans pockets. Looking across the bay, he allowed the brisk marine wind to temper him. The plaintive cry of seagulls and barking sea lions situated on nearby wooden piers did little to drown out the noise in his head.

At least one thing had become clear. With his lawyer's update, he now knew what James Falk thought Vasily had: The five girls Carmine Niccoterra had rescued, and Vasily now employed as babysitters. Under no circumstance was he handing them back to Falk's surviving cronies.

But there was one speck of light that brightened the abyss. At least three of those traffickers were dead.

Which left two that he was aware of. The woman, Marisol Price, and the fat man named Bob. The same two people Vasily had observed in the video Niccoterra had given him, which he in turn had given to his FBI contact, Kat.

Marisol fucking *Price*.

That name kept coming up, but who the hell was she?

Vasily laced his fingers, cupped the back of his neck, and drew in a deep lungful of salty air. He let it out slowly, then repeated the process. After he'd done this several times, he called his brother Zander and filled him in on Nicky's situation.

"Is this retaliation from her ex?" Zander asked, his tone hostile and clipped. "I told you Nicky didn't need blowback and it pisses me right the fuck off that she has now received said blowback."

"Calm down, little *brat*." Vasily kept his tone measured even though his anger equaled his brother's. "Your indignation is righteous and well deserved, but I doubt this has anything to do with Anthony Andretti directly."

At least he hoped it didn't. But if it did, he'd take great pleasure in killing the man himself. "Andretti seems like the kind he'd follow up on something like that and so far, there's been nothing but crickets from the man."

"Crickets?"

"Silent as the grave."

Which Andretti would find himself in, sooner rather than later, should it come to pass he was indeed involved in Nicky's attack.

"Huh. Must say that does strike me as counter to the man's personality given what I know he's already done to her."

Done to her? Vasily's brow furrowed. He knew of the strangling attempt, but what else was there? "What does that mean?"

"The prick slammed a beer bottle in her face. Left her with a black eye, a swollen lip, and that little chip in her tooth."

"Jesus." Vasily's fist clenched inside his jeans pocket as he struggled to keep his newly found calm in check. He put that knowledge away into a box inside his brain to be unpacked later.

"Anyway," Vasily added. "The point is, she's unavailable to work for the foreseeable future. Until this mess is sorted, I suggest making arrangements to cover for her." And hopefully, Nicky would make the decision never to go back to the bar for work. He didn't oppose her working, least of all working for his brother if that's what she wanted, but couldn't she do it in an environment where drunken fools didn't get to ogle her legs and tits?

Who the hell was he kidding?

Men would ogle her drunk or not, but his jealousy was something else he'd have to unpack later.

After he disconnected from Zander, he received a text from his driver that Carmine had entered through the side entrance of the restaurant. It led directly to the patio.

"Yo," the Italian said when he joined him, leaning his elbows on the protective barrier.

Vasily turned from watching a cruise ship docking at one of the famous, touristy piers and faced him. "You familiar with James Falk of Shasta County, half-brother of a man named Kai?"

Niccoterra squinted at him, those light green eyes hardening at the mention of the names. "I captured Falk myself when I was up north. He had an open warrant on his ass, a failure to appear in court and I called it in." Niccoterra shoved his hands into his hoodie pocket and hunched his shoulders against the cool marine breeze. "I handed him over to the local authorities, though the fucker deserved much more than jail after what he did to Helen. Why do you ask?"

"He's no longer in jail."

Surprise made Niccoterra's jaw slacken. "What?"

Vasily's big toe beat a pattern inside his boot. At this rate, he'd wear a hole in the leather and bruise his toe.

"That human garbage attempted to rape Nicky last night, something he thankfully failed at."

The silence emanating from the Italian was so thick Vasily could almost grab it. "She okay?" he finally asked, anger graveling his voice.

Vasily nodded once. "She came away with a few cuts, but otherwise unharmed. At least physically." Fresh heat flooded his veins, raising his blood pressure a few points. "But I want to know how he got out. According to his rap sheet, he shouldn't have."

"That makes two of us. Where's he at?"

"The morgue."

The Italian straightened. The wind tugged at his dark curls, blowing them across his face, but that hard, green gaze remained solid on Vasily's. "Well, I suppose that's one positive. Need I ask how?"

Vasily indicated they should walk back inside the empty restaurant. The staff had not yet begun to arrive for dinner preparations and although they were alone, the marine breeze would carry their voices to the rest of the establishments on the waterfront.

Inside, instead of taking a seat at a table, he continued to the bar. Quirking an eyebrow at Niccoterra, he asked, "Drink?"

The man nodded.

Vasily grabbed a bottle of whiskey from the top shelf and two tumblers. He poured a couple of fingers into each of them, then pushed one over.

Carmine sniffed the amber liquid before he sipped, his expression remaining hard as he listened to Vasily state the details of Nicky's attack.

"I need to know how that schmuck made bail and who cash-rolled it," Vasily finished, the sense of urgency to catch the fuckers biting as sharply as the alcohol he consumed.

"Can only have been a dirty judge," Niccoterra responded, rubbing his jaw. "A judge that perhaps makes use of the services a sex slave might provide. No other reason a felon like that should make bail. The warrant I called into the locals wasn't the only failure to appear in court on Falk's record. The man's a menace and a danger to society."

"Hmm."

There was a nugget of truth in the Italian's statement. Before Vasily had taken over from Dean, his brother had several so-called upper-echelon members of society in his grip. Judges, politicians, and even a priest had been known to frequent the pay-to-play parties Dean had hosted.

"Just speculating here," Carmine said, "but from what you've told me about your previous relationship with Nicky, and considering she was their target, I'm guessing that whoever these fuckers are, they've had eyes on both of you for some time now."

Indeed. Eyes Vasily had failed to notice. Which meant whoever those eyes belonged to was no amateur. The knowledge brought a sense of déjà vu. In Moscow, he'd never mentioned Nicky's name. Except for once, unwittingly, to a fellow prisoner who'd shared his cell before that prisoner disappeared. Vasily presumed the Bratva had killed him, but perhaps he'd been there to spy.

Hey American. Who is Dominique? You cry for her... in your sleep!

He'd never told that prisoner who she was, but Federov had figured it out. At the memory, his nostrils curled, and he rubbed his tattoo under his sweater. A cold sweat broke out on the back of his neck. "Anything on the social worker hassling my girls?"

Niccoterra took another slug of his whiskey. "Checked the website connection. Went deep. The username attached to the emails does not belong to any agency that has anything to do with social work."

Vasily's stomach dropped as he looked at the bottle of whiskey on the bar. "Which means she's not a social worker."

"But neither is she a cop." Niccoterra stabbed the air with his index finger. "If she were, their IT department would have it set up right with at least the appearance of a social agency of some kind."

"Why would someone fake being a social worker to get at my girls?"

"Million-dollar question."

Vasily left his glass and the bottle on the bar and walked around to take a seat on a stool near the Italian, propping one boot on the footrest. "Something else is bothering me, and I don't know if it's connected."

Niccoterra's gaze lifted from the glass he held to catch his own." "What's that?"

"Nicky's ex seems to be MIA."

"And you give a shit, why?"

"A man doesn't respond to an urgent voicemail from the mother of his kid, either he's complicit in what happened to her or something's wrong."

"Could be on a bender? It's been known to happen."

"Having witnessed the man being chemically impaired, I can believe it, but I still want him located. Nicky has enough to worry about and doesn't need to waste brain cells on him."

Carmine chuckled. "Instead, you want those brain cells focused on you."

He sucked his teeth and didn't deny it, but he took another sip of the amber liquid in his glass, letting the faint spice and oaky taste linger on his tongue before he embellished. "I need her taking care of her son. That little man witnessed something he shouldn't have and needs her attention focused on him."

"Very noble of you."

"He's a good kid." Vasily shrugged. "He took care of his mother and held it together. I want to make sure she can do the same for him." He rubbed his stubble, focusing his thumb on the dent in his chin.

"Any way we look at this situation, it's going to get ugly. As soon as Falk's death is discovered by his people, I expect retaliation. We have to find that house in the video, the one in Eureka before that happens. I don't want whatever girls Falk's people might still have captive moved to a different location before we can get them out. It's been over a week since we got that intel from Viktor. Time is getting away from us."

"Badger, my man, is working on it and the sense of urgency isn't lost on him. He was there, Melnikov. He saw what went down." Niccoterra gave Vasily a sharp glance before he leaned forward and snagged a toothpick from a small container on the bar and rolled it between his fingers. "Property records indicate no owners by any variation of the name Bob or Marisol Price. We're checking into rental properties and those owned by shell corporations in the area, nothing there yet either. There isn't much to go on and that video footage is crude. But when we do find that house, what's the plan?"

Vasily's mouth hardened into a straight line. "We take those slave-trading motherfuckers out. *All* of them."

Niccoterra nodded, his face pinched. "Problem is, we don't know who all of them are yet, do we?"

"Not yet."

Vasily chose not to mention he also had Kat working on the problem. There was no need to divulge he had a contact in the FBI. Often it created more questions he didn't want to answer.

"Are you in?"

Lines formed between Niccoterra's eyebrows. "Hell yes, I'm in. And so are my men."

Vasily placed his forearms on the bar and steepled his fingers. "We should keep this tight. The less who know, the better. My men know the risks and they've gotten to know the girls you rescued from Falk's people, which makes them invested."

Niccoterra's lip curled. "I have my own personal beef with that black widow bitch, Marisol *fucking* Price. If that's even her real name, which I'm seriously doubting. I'm betting she uses aliases, but I haven't managed to connect her to any yet. Bitch is smart."

There was a small divot in the polished wood where his glass stood. Vasily focused on it for a few moments, before squinting at the Italian.

"Smart enough to set up anonymous emails pretending to be a social worker?"

Niccoterra met his eyes, then nodded. "The thought has crossed my mind. Too much of a coincidence *a social worker*"—he made air quotes— "shows up and starts poking around the same time all this shit starts. My gut is telling me they're the same. That Price woman is the center of everything."

Vasily agreed. He'd gleaned that from Viktor Sokolov before he killed him. But again, who was she? Where did she come from? And who else, other than the fat man, was involved?

The Italian tipped his head back and poured the rest of his drink down his throat. Placing the empty tumbler on the bar, he stood. "Is there anything else?"

Vasily shook his head. "Just the whereabouts of Anthony Andretti and who bankrolled Falk's bail. As for the rest, I'll be in touch."

As Niccoterra left the restaurant, Vasily called Yev. "Are they getting settled in the apartment?"

"I presume so."

Vasily hugged his phone between his shoulder and his ear as he ran a cloth under the faucet beneath the bar, then he squeezed out the excess water. "Aren't you with them?"

"On an errand. I've got Sasha watching them."

"Explain."

"Seems we forgot the contraption the cat shits in. Nicky wanted to go back. I told her no, so now I'm at the damn pet store and don't know what I'm doing. Know anything about cats, boss?"

Vasily chuckled. He wiped the bar clean of a small whiskey stain while picturing Yev staring at his cowboy boots and scratching his dark head. The man could kill a person fifty different ways with his little finger, yet he was intimidated by the bathroom needs of a one-eyed feline. Granted, that particular feline was scary. He would not want to step on its tail given the damage done to Falk. But the thought was still amusing.

"Don't forget one of those shit-scooper things."

"Shit scooper?" Yev's voice rose a couple of notes.

Vasily let out another chuckle. "Like a small shovel with holes."

"If I'd known this, I'd have just gone back to her apartment."

"Why didn't you?"

"The pet store was closer." This was said in a tone that implied it should've been obvious. "Didn't think it was a big deal. It's a cat, how hard could it be?"

"Exactly. And while you're at it, stock up on treats. That little furry asshole has earned them."

"*Blyad*," Yev grunted, then hung up.

Fuck indeed.

The first of the restaurant staff arrived for the evening setup. He chatted with a few and asked about their families, then Max drove him across town, dropping him off in the parking lot at the private elevator to the penthouse. The moment he stepped through the arched doorway between the bookcases, music welcomed him into his home. Some chick singing something about something that wasn't her name. It was quite catchy, actually. He chuckled. Seems Nicky figured out how to pair the penthouse's internal speaker system with her playlist.

But that wasn't all he noticed.

The tangy essence of garlic and spices greeted him like a welcome hug.

She was cooking!

He had a housekeeper who cooked and kept him fed with mostly traditional Russian cooking, but this was different. It smelled like home, and if it tasted as good as it smelled, he may not want Nicky to leave.

Tossing his keys onto a small credenza, he eyed the orange fuzz ball taking up residence on his pristine cream couch. The cat surveyed him, that amber eye glinting at half-mast, daring him to boot him from his perch—his front paws flexing and curling, making little ticking noises as he clawed the fabric.

Vasily gave it a chin tip. The cat shut its eye in a slow blink. *Smart choice*, it seemed to communicate.

Yeah, well, he didn't need any more enemies than the ones he already had.

Luca lay on his stomach close to the windows in a sliver of dying sunshine, drawing with bright colorful crayons. He was singing along to the music. "That's not my name, that's not my name..."

Vasily bent and ruffled his dark, curly hair.

"Hi, Mr. Vasily," the kid responded with the gap-toothed grin five-year-old's tended to have. "Mom's making lasagna."

Lasagna?

Jesus.

One of his favorites and when was the last time he had some? His stomach growled, and following the aroma, he found pasta, different cheeses, onions, and garlic bulbs on a wooden cutting board. And his personal domestic goddess minus her sexy cowboy boots, but plus an even sexier silver toe ring.

He wouldn't call himself chauvinistic, but this particular shoeless woman cooking in his kitchen did things to him—her pert, round ass gently bouncing to the rhythm of each stir of the pot. He had a compelling urge to lift her onto the lacquered slab of oak topping the kitchen island and take her. His cock didn't disagree.

Top ten on his bucket list.

He blew out a breath and cleared his throat.

Siberian ice baths.

Freezing Siberian ice baths.

"Hey," she said, looking over her shoulder, wearing the same sweet smile that had always made him a fool.

"I hope you like lasagna, or mind me taking over your kitchen?"

"What's to mind, but should you be cooking in your condition?"

"I popped some of Ronnie's pain pills so I'm feeling *noooo* pain. Anyway, cooking keeps my mind off things, and I had a craving for carbs. Comfort food, you know?" She patted her ass. "Though this won't be thanking me for it."

His eyes dropped again to that particular enticing body part, thinking he liked her ass any way it was—especially naked.

"I'm surprised you pulled all this together so fast."

She shrugged. "Yev picked up a few ingredients and the rest were already here."

His brows came together.

Reading his look, she waved at the open oak door on the far side of the fridge that matched his custom-made, wooden counters and kitchen island. "Well, apparently somebody stocks your pantry and freezer."

He chuffed, feeling mildly foolish. "Ludmilla." He didn't mind cooking but had no reason to. In the months he'd owned this apartment, his experience in the kitchen was a triangular pathway from the fridge to the microwave and the coffee contraption.

"Ludmilla?" Nicky stopped stirring, her smile disappearing.

"My housekeeper."

"Oh."

Though she tried to hide it, her relief was obvious—and adorable. That very small display of insecurity and perhaps jealousy made his chest warm, and her even more irresistible.

"She cooks, and what I can't find to eat in the fridge, I have delivered."

"Well, as long as I'm here, there's no reason for Ludmilla to cook."

"Hmm."

He stepped from behind the island and walked towards her, digging the idea of Nicky spending time in his kitchen. "You cook like this every night, you'll make me fat."

She dropped her eyes, giving him a long, slow eye fuck, of which he felt every single hot inch in his groin.

"Somehow I doubt that." Her voice carried a breathless quality that made the pulse in his throat thump, and his zipper dig into his cock. "Though I must warn you, Nonna Marcello's recipe can be deadly. She put cream cheese on the noodles."

Cream cheese?

Those indigo eyes, soft and flirtatious peeked at him from beneath her lashes, but his gaze was fixed on her mouth, and those slightly parted lips. The woman was talking about cream-fucking-cheese when he was about to burst out of his pants.

For the love of Russia.

It didn't stop him from moving closer. Taking Nicky on that center island ticked up several notches on his bucket list. As the blood left his head and settled in his cock, he was painfully aware it would have to wait for another day. She was in no shape for what he wanted to do and for that reason only, and that Luca was in the next room, he reigned in his balls.

"Got things to finish up," he murmured, his voice sounding like he'd thrown back a bottle of cheap Russian vodka.

A rogue section of her bangs fell across her eye. She pushed it back with her pinkie. He fantasized about taking that pinkie into his mouth and sucking on it. Swirling his tongue around and tasting both her and the food she'd prepared. Which would lead to him tasting other, more intimate parts of her. His pants got tighter.

He leaned in and put his lips to the spot just below her jaw and ear. "How long 'til dinner?"

She shivered. "It still has to bake," she murmured, her cheeks pinking at the unbridled hunger in his voice. "Take your time."

Take his time?

Fucking hell, he wanted to take *her*. But, to prove he still had his testicles in check, he murmured, "I intend to when the time is right."

Then before he lost his shit, he spun on his heel and left the kitchen—*to take his time and finish things up.* And while he did that in his state-of-the-art shower, his palm and shower gel would just have to do.

No question about it—he wasn't letting her go. All that remained was to convince her to stay.

Chapter Eighteen

The lasagna was a hit.

Vasily and Yev consumed two large helpings each, after which Nicky insisted Yev take a plate for his dad who was still working the desk downstairs. It was a small peace offering after acting like an angry, entitled wench when she'd first come to this building to confront Vasily. Something she now felt bad about.

Yev didn't argue and offered a nod of appreciation when he left with a still-warm square of lasagna and several slices of garlic bread.

As she started to clear the dishes, Vasily stopped her, circling his hand gently around her wrist.

"You're pale and exhausted. I've indulged this long enough, but now you need to go to bed and rest."

"Let me just do the dishes..."

"Not your job." He looked down at her from his considerable height and gave a pointed stare. "Ludmilla comes tomorrow, and she'll deal with the kitchen. I want you to sleep, and heal, and don't worry about Luca. I'll take care of him."

"Vasily, he's my child. I should be..."

"Dominique, he'll be fine," he said in a tone that left no room for argument. "I'll make sure he brushes his teeth."

"I also need to pee," Luca piped in from his perch at the kitchen island, looking up at Vasily.

Vasily reached out and rubbed his head, ruffling his curls. "That too."

Out of energy and adrenaline, she gave in. "Thank you."

Vasily let go of her wrist, and where his hand had been, she felt a chill. With a strange twist in her belly, Nicky kissed her boy. Why was the man being so domesticated and why did it feel so pleasant?

"You do everything Vasily says, okay?"

"'Kay, Mommy." Luca grinned at her, then with a last glance at Vasily, she shuffled to her room. Taking one of her prescribed pills Nicky crawled into bed and within moments her wounds and her exhaustion caught up with her. She welcomed oblivion.

Over the next few days, Nicky and Luca settled into a new routine. She heard later that Mario's concern for his grandchild got his head far enough out of his stubborn ass to assert rank in the babysitting hierarchy. Nicky suspected her dad's offer was much to the relief of the rotating Russian badasses that Vasily assigned to keep an eye on Luca. Although, one accompanied Mario and Luca on whatever excursions they took.

Each night Nicky got the rundown on Luca's day when he cuddled with her in the king-sized bed in one of Vasily's guest bedrooms. Intimate details on the superhero movie they'd seen and how he'd helped Grandpa work on his Harley. Luca was proud to announce he now knew the difference between a torque wrench and a regular one.

Though she was happy her dad spent time with Luca, it hurt that Mario hadn't forgiven her for accepting Vasily's protection. But he had yet to come up with a better alternative.

Stubborn old coot.

By the third day of succumbing to Ronnie's meds and sorting the jumble in her head about killing a man, Nicky'd had enough.

"Okay, bed." She patted the velvety beige comforter that complemented the dark polished wood of her bed. "I'm breaking up with you, but since you're so damn comfortable, we can still be friends."

Slipping out from between cream sheets—of which the thread count probably matched what she made in tips in a month—she checked her messages.

Don't forget to pick me up, a text from Soren read. *Flight arrives at 5.50 pm.*

Shit!

She'd forgotten all about that, and Soren's car was still at her apartment. She checked the time on her phone—3.33 pm. She could shower and still have a little time to spare.

Sending a quick text to Favi to cancel their babysitting appointment, she then checked her other messages. Lots of good wishes from Terra and Helen, even one from Terrence. His theatre tour in Cincinnati had a constant full house and he'd met a new man.

Yay for him.

But there was nothing from Anthony. She tried calling him again, and as always, got his voicemail.

Frustrated, she texted Gail, his receptionist. *Anything?*

The response came a few minutes later. *Oh, sorry, should've told you. Got a text ordering me to cancel his appointments. Says he's dealing with an important out-of-town client and may be out of cell range.*

Out-of-town client?

Nicky's brows pinched together. The same one he'd given up his time with Luca for? And where the hell was he that he was out of cell range?

Instead of continuing the conversation by text, she called. "I hate to ask this, Gail, but is it really a client, or is he just spending time with his new someone? Or is she both?"

"Nicky...uh, God." Gail sighed into her headphone mic. "This is making me uncomfortable. I know he cheated on you and I'm so sorry for that, but he's still my boss. I can't gossip."

"Honey, I'm not asking you to gossip. I'm just trying to find him. It's unusual for him not to respond to any of my texts or messages, especially those about Luca."

Gail groaned, then there was a pause. "Yeah, there's a woman," she admitted. "And she *is* a client, but you *did not* hear that from me. I'm not even sure if that's the one he's with, but I'll try to contact him again, although every time I have called, it's gone straight to voicemail."

"I know. My calls too."

This woman, client or otherwise, must be pretty important for Anthony to risk being out of touch with his practice. Although she couldn't quite square it with his begging her to take him back just a week or so ago. But Anthony didn't like to lose, and she'd taken that begging as a manipulation technique to see if he *could* get her to change her mind—just for funsies.

Regardless, this wasn't like him.

"I'm a little worried, Gail. What if one of his shitty clients has done something?"

Gail scoffed. "You mean like kidnap him?"

Or worse. "He has received threats in the past."

"I suppose, but until he tells me otherwise, I'm not going to worry. I'm sure he's fine."

They disconnected and Nicky sat on the edge of the bed and tapped her head with her phone.

Maybe she should just let it go. Maybe Anthony was finally moving on. But then why did she have this niggling feeling that something was wrong?

She made a frustrated noise, then crossed the dark-stained hardwood floors to the bathroom. Vasily's giant oval-shaped bathtub was tempting.

But, her stitches.

Skirting past it, she eyed the display of expensive body washes, shampoos, and scrubs with longing. Selecting one with lavender and jojoba oil, she took a careful shower instead.

When she left her room, Luca was with the other big, but slightly less scary-looking Russian she'd met on the first day they'd come to the penthouse. He had black hair, black scruff, black clothing, and very serious black eyes. For some reason, they would not meet her own. They sat in front of the living room windows at a small table playing a game—the backdrop of the city skyline at their profile.

"Mom," Luca called when he saw her. "Sasha is teaching me to play chess." He held up a piece, grinning like Pooh Bear who'd discovered a treasure trove of honey. "This is a knight and I just captured it from him. I'm busting his balls."

Her brows rose.

Three days and her son was already sounding like a mini gangsta?

Good grief.

Blowing out a raspberry, she cupped her hands under his chin. Then she kissed the top of his head. "Language remember, Buddy."

"Oh, sorry. And Mr. Vasily says he'll teach me how to swim like a big kid. Isn't that dope?"

Nicky scratched her head and scrunched up her face.

Busting balls...dope?

"Speaking of Vasily, where is he?" She directed this to Sasha, who found the pieces in front of him far more interesting as his gaze flickered up only for a second before returning to the board.

"Office," he mumbled, then picked up his phone from its place next to the discarded chess pieces and started typing.

Nicky was unable to decide if his unwillingness to look at her was rude or just...Russian?

"Perhaps you'd like a break?" she asked. "I can take over from here."

"Mom, I wanna finish the game."

"That's fine, Buddy, but what does Sasha have to say?"

Sasha placed the phone back down, his gaze locked on the board. "We finish."

"Okay then." She stroked Luca's hair from his forehead, trying not to take the rejection personally. She'd missed doing things for him and to have someone else take over her parental duties felt weird. "Finish the game. I'll be in the kitchen if anyone is looking for me."

Be grateful. She smacked her lips at her general funk. *Luca is learning something new.*

In the fridge, she found raw steaks, a variety of vegetables, and freshly squeezed orange juice. She poured a glass and sipped it while nibbling on a smear of blue cheese and a whole wheat cracker when Vasily walked into the kitchen.

He wore narrow-legged charcoal trousers that showed off strong, muscular thighs and a dove gray button-up shirt tucked in. Along with the silver buckle in his belt, the casual elegance of his outfit made the silver-gray in his eyes pop.

She loved a man in well-fitting dress pants, especially when they hugged his slim hips giving just a hint of the magnificent package they contained.

Panther-like he approached, his gaze as focused and intense as that of the predator. "Hey," he said, giving that tiny smile that lifted one side of his mouth. The one that always released butter-flies in her stomach. "How are you feeling?"

He stopped just shy of her, yet close enough she felt his heat radiating from his body. A suggestion of his shower gel drifted into her nose—clean, with a slight sandalwood and musk combination that made her want to lean in and sniff him.

"All right." She chewed on her lip, trying to disguise the fact his proximity made it hard to breathe normally. Gesturing to the fridge, she asked, "Are those steaks for dinner? How would you like them cooked?"

God, she sounded like some 1950s suburban housewife with

nothing else to do but guzzle dirty martinis and take care of her man.

This man, except, of course, he wasn't hers.

He said nothing, just stared down at her, their gazes getting tangled up in each other. Then he cleared his throat and stepped to the cabinets. Removing a glass, he placed it under the fridge's filtered water spigot and filled it up. He drank it all before speaking again. "Good to see you up and about."

She frowned, unable to decide if that was a judgment like he thought she was lazy or neglectful of her child. "You're the one who ordered me to stay in bed."

His head tilted. "I did, and by no means does my comment imply that I'm not happy to see you, Dominique," he said quietly. "Nor that I think you've been wasting your days away. No need to get defensive."

Okay.

Yeah.

She'd earned that. "Sorry." She sighed. "I'm in a funk."

"Hmm." He continued to watch her.

"The steaks?" She reminded him because that look was too intense.

"Forget the steaks." Placing the empty glass on the counter, he approached her again. "You haven't answered my question, or at least not adequately. I want to know how you're feeling...in here?" He pressed his finger softly to her forehead, then dragged it in a caress to her temple.

Her lashes flickered at the trail of warmth his touch left.

Funny he should ask. It wasn't like she hadn't been contemplating that question since *the incident* and still hadn't pinned it down to anything other than being completely fucked. But he was taking the time to check in—unlike her dad—and it tugged at her.

"I'm not sure," she whispered.

His hand had dropped to where her neck met her shoulder. He squeezed gently. "Give it a shot."

"I just spent two days crying, but I don't know if I'm crying for myself or for the fact that I killed someone. I hate him." Her voice broke. "And I'm glad he's dead, but that sort of makes me ashamed that I'm glad he's dead. I mean," she sniffed, blinking. "I don't even know if he had a wife or kids. If he's left someone alone in the world to fend for themselves. I'm sorry for that, but—"

"Falk had no next-of-kin, so you haven't left some child fatherless."

That offered a small measure of relief. "How do you know this?"

"I looked into him. All those feelings you're having are natural, and it's good you're letting them out. But let me ask you." Little creases formed at the corners of his eyes, but his gaze was gentle. "Given the chance to protect yourself or your son, would you do it again?"

She took a moment to think and nodded. "No question."

"That's exactly the right answer."

"But—"

"You brought nail scissors to a knife fight, Dominique." He gave her shoulder another gentle squeeze. "You were out weaponed, and the odds were against you, yet you survived. Luca's okay because of what you did."

"I just got lucky."

"Lucky or not, it was justifiable. The man shouldn't have been anywhere near you and now he's never going to hurt any other woman again. You did the world a favor and you should be proud of that."

Her lip trembled, and she bit it. "Then why aren't I?"

"Because you're a good woman." Vasily placed a hand over her heart. The warmth from his palm seeped into her chest and eased her mind a little as her heart beat unsteadily under his hand. "Actually," he paused to take a breath. "Let me rephrase. You're not just good, you're extraordinary. You're beautiful, you're strong and you're brave. Even if you're not proud of yourself, I am."

He must've seen the doubt in her expression because he added softly, "So very proud."

His words weren't many, but they were just enough. The sincerity in them was exactly what she needed to hear. But there was one more issue. A tear escaped.

"And my dad."

He swiped it away with his thumb. "He's a stubborn old bastard, but he's worried about you. Enough to brave coming here, dealing with me and my men. I saw it in his eyes. Just give him time."

"He thinks I've betrayed him by staying here."

"You haven't."

They held each other's gaze for several seconds longer, and there was nothing but concern and candidness in his. She wanted to keep staring at him, drowning in his concern for her, but she had other things to do.

She cleared her throat. "I need to head out for a bit before I do any cooking."

His head tilted. "What needs doing?"

"I have to pick Soren up from the airport. Her car's at my apartment."

"I don't want you driving. You can't wear a seatbelt over your stitches. Yev will do it."

"Vas, he can't. She won't know who he is."

He arched a brow. "She won't recognize her car?"

"Of course she will, but that big mountain of a man driving it will scare the crap out of her."

Vasily smirked. "Or she might find him interesting. He's been accused of that a time or two."

Perhaps she was overthinking it, as she'd made that observation herself not so recently. That big collection of muscle and tattoos could be gentle when he put his mind to it.

Anyway, Soren did not lack experience in bending men to her

will, so what the hell was she so worried about? On second thoughts, if anything, it would be Yev who should be scared.

The thought made her giggle.

Soren would have him eating out of her palm, licking the remnants, and begging for more without him even realizing it.

"I'll send her a text and give her a heads-up."

"Hmm."

He studied her for a moment longer, then sucked in a breath through his nostrils and moved out of touching distance. Something changed about his energy. It became more intense and darker but in a delicious way. He leaned against the counter and folded his arms.

"Tell me," he said, his voice a little husky, "how's the rest of you?"

"The rest of me?"

His gaze dropped slowly to her unfettered cleavage. The heat in his eyes licked over her nipples and set them on fire.

"Your wounds."

Oh, *that* rest of her. Lordy, how to answer that?

"Healing." She swallowed, her own voice becoming slightly throaty. "I shouldn't need any more pain meds tomorrow, maybe just something over the counter."

"Good." His pupils had dilated, turning that silvery gray into something much stormier, making her pulse race and her nipples pebble. "Because I can't wait to get you naked."

She drew in a sharp breath. How could just a simple phrase carry so much weight and turn her on so much? She squeezed her thighs together just as Luca bounced into the kitchen, like a jackrabbit on speed.

"Mom!" His eyes were wide with excitement. He seemed to sense whatever was happening between them and stopped. He looked at Nicky, then at Vasily, and then finally back to her, his face scrunched in confusion. "Why's your face all red?"

Hell's fucking bells.

Being called out by her five-year-old in a sensitive, panty-melting moment wasn't top of her favorite things. Her cheeks burned hotter.

Luca's expression got sly and his tone mimicked hers when she knew he'd done something sneaky. "Were you doing something you shouldn't?"

Vasily's mouth quirked and amusement flickered across his face. "We were just talking about adult things."

"Like kissing?"

Nicky pulled in her lips and looked over her right shoulder at the pantry door.

"Oh, yuck." Luca stuck his tongue out and made a gacking sound like he did when faced with cleaning up one of Marley's hairballs. "Kissing's gross. Can we go swimming?"

Oh, damn.

"Honey, I'm sorry but I just realized I didn't pack your floaties or your swimming trunks."

"Shorts will do," Vasily said. "And who needs floaties, whatever those are."

She gave him a pointed look. "They're inflatable arm bands that keep him from drowning."

Luca bounced on his toes with his little hands clasped in front of him. "Please? You said I could in the car."

"I did, but I can't get my stitches wet and you need your floaties."

"I'm not going to let him drown, Dominique," Vasily drawled. "And though I'd love for you to get wet, there's no need for you to get in."

She looked at him.

He smirked.

Satan.

"Yeah, Mom. You don't need to get wet. I want Mr. Vasily to take me. You just 'lax and get better."

"Are you all ganging up on me?"

"Maybe a little, but some pool activity will get whatever *that* is out." Vasily pointed to Luca's bouncing.

Nicky bit her lip. "You can't take your eyes off him."

"Mommy!" Luca put his hands on his hips. "I'm not a baby and Mr. Vasily said he's not going to let me drown."

"I just want to make sure he knows what he's getting himself into." She turned back to the man in question. "Luca can only dog-paddle so you have to make sure he stays close to the edge."

"If it will make you feel better, come sit with us and watch," Vasily asked softly, his eyes boring into hers.

Yes, why didn't she?

Because seeing him with her son filled her imagination with stupid notions.

"While we build up an appetite," he added. Then, as if to sweeten his proposition, he started pulling his shirt from his pants. He began to unbutton it, slowly, like he was offering her a personal strip tease. Removing it, he gave her a full frontal of his flat abdomen and tattoos. The dip between each muscle made her want to drool, and not just from her mouth.

Before he laid his shirt over his shoulder, she made out an eight-point star on one side and an intricate Russian Orthodox cross on the other. On his left hip, partially hidden by his pants, was a coiled viper about to strike.

Mafia tattoo meanings were not in her cache of knowledge, especially *Russian* mafia tattoos, but she did know that star represented a high rank. But what fascinated her the most, was the barbed wire coiled around the bars on his right biceps. She wanted to trace each point with her fingers, and her tongue.

If she'd forgotten how dangerous the man was, in so many ways more than one, the evidence stared her right in the face. The sick part was, it turned her on, and he knew it. It was in that sexy smirk plastered on his face.

He offered his hand to Luca. "Come on, little man. Let's go

pick out a pair of shorts before your mom changes her mind. I'll teach you how to do freestyle."

"What's freestyle?" Luca looked up at him, hero-worship sparkling in his wide brown eyes as his hand disappeared inside Vasily's palm.

Oh, Jesus, no.

Luca could not fall in love. Or even hero-worship him. It was one thing for her to need an orgasm—okay, *multiple* orgasms after that hot, sex-laden look—but what her G-spot wanted didn't warrant her son's heart getting broken when Vasily inevitably tired of them and sent them packing.

But the sight of Luca's little palm in Vasily's large one was achingly beautiful. The ease with which he offered it made her ovaries weep.

The flesh around the birth-control implant on the inside of her upper arm twinged. She rubbed it with her thumb.

Stop it.

They walked out of the kitchen together, Luca barely containing his excitement, and the way Vasily indulged him caused a deep yearning to flutter in her belly. What a great dad he'd make. He'd shown that multiple times already in the space of just a few days.

But entertaining notions such as those were stupid and unattainable. Foolish.

She sagged against the center island and closed her eyes. There was a soft knock and they popped open again.

Yev walked in wearing black sweats and a tank top, muscles bulging and still a little sweaty from what she presumed was his workout.

"I need the keys to your friend's car," he said, wiping his forehead with an arm almost as thick as her thighs.

"Sure, just give me a sec," she answered, trying not to stare at his glistening, rippling body. He too was covered in tattoos, including on his knuckles but they didn't have quite the same effect on her girl parts as the ones on his boss did.

Retrieving the fob from her room, she placed them in Yev's open palm.

"Your friend is the blonde at the bar?" he asked, his face expressionless as a frying pan. "For that video thing."

"There were several blondes that night the bar." She smothered a smile by pulling in her lips. "You'll have to be a little more specific."

"Sat with a colorful black dude and drank cosmos all night?"

Heh.

"Careful," she warned only half teasing. "Soren eats men like you for mid-day snacks."

Yev bounced the key fob once in his hand, then he gave her a chin nod and cracked a suggestion of a smile.

"I'd like to see her try."

Chapter Nineteen

Despite the problem with Nicky being the top priority on his schedule, there were meetings Vasily couldn't avoid. Like the one he was at the following afternoon.

He sat back in his chair, the black leather beneath him squeaking as he placed his ankle on his knee. He narrowed his eyes at the man sitting on the other side of the desk.

Roger Doocey.

Vasily had gifted the member of the San Francisco Board of Supervisors and his wife a trip to the Maldives, (off the books and illegal as fuck), but he'd also made the maximum donation to his campaign. All for a change in the escort permit requirements.

And now the nerdy prick was backtracking on his promise.

Fucking politicians.

"Am I to understand, Mr. Doocey," Vasily said, his tone dropping to a notch below friendly, "my request has become too difficult for you to fulfill?"

Roger Doocey, either failing to notice the change in tone or ignoring it smirked behind his City Hall desk, then stroked his trimmed beard as if to wipe it away.

The bastard was too stupid, or too arrogant to know who he was fucking with.

He'd learn, as they always did.

"Three simple words," Vasily said, resting his laced fingers on his stomach and tapping his thumbs. "Subject. To. Review. I want those words added to the regulations *or* the requirement of zero prostitution convictions to be removed entirely. That's all."

This was Granger's job, but his lawyer had another priority he was dealing with. One that involved Dean and could not be delayed.

"I apologize, Mr. Melnikov, but unfortunately here's the situation. We *cannot* remove the requirement of zero prior prostitution convictions from Escort Permit Regulations."

"Then add the words." Vasily's tone was that of an iceberg and should've conveyed plenty of warning.

Doocey cleared his throat. "I'm running for Mayor, Mr. Melnikov. Unfortunately, I can't be seen as being soft on prostitution."

Soft on prostitution?

Now that was funny.

Not only had Doocey used prostitutes, but he'd been filmed doing it. *In a hotel room in the Maldives.*

It was Vasily's turn to smirk. Removing his phone from his pocket, he pulled up a video. Turning the volume up high, he pressed start and held it in front of Doocey's face. The unmistakable grunts of sex filled his office.

It took very little time for Doocey's expression or color to change, as the blood drained from his face. "What's that?" he asked in a voice much higher than normal.

"You." Vasily tutted. "In a threesome with two men in a hotel bedroom. Both of which are prostitutes. *Male* prostitutes."

"You set me up?" Doocey choked out the words, looking like he might throw up. "You can't do that!"

Vasily tapped his thumbs together then ran his tongue over his teeth. "I already did."

"Oh, God," Doocey moaned, slumping in his chair. "Oh my God, this can't be happening."

"It is, and I'm sure the voters of San Francisco and your dear loving wife would be extremely interested in your extracurricular activities while she was getting her hair highlighted. Lila looks lovely as a blonde, by the way. Shows off that Maldivian tan."

An oily sheen appeared on the Supervisor's brow, and he swiped a tissue from a box. When he wiped away the sweat, his hands were shaking.

"Fuck." He grimaced. "Please don't do that. It'll ruin my career, not to mention my marriage. I love her, it's just this...this thing I have, I can't help myself."

"You know what to do to prevent me from sharing this with the world. I suggest you do it. And soon."

"I'll make it right, I promise, just don't let that get out. Please, I beg you."

Vasily stared at Doocey, allowing several beats to pass while giving him the full weight of his cold glare. Then, rising, he placed his palms on Doocey's desk and leaned in.

Doocey cowered back, his eyes going wide.

"Get it done," he bit out, "otherwise I'll personally help your wife burn the marriage bed. Have a good rest of your day, Doocey."

Striding to the door he paused before opening it. "And FYI, it's not the only video I have."

The expression on the man's face morphing from frightened resignation to utter horror told Vasily the man knew he wasn't lying.

While the Supervisor sweated and shook in his fancy leather desk chair, Vasily walked through City Hall. It was after closing time, so he encountered no one as he stepped into the early evening exhaust-tainted air. Max was waiting outside by the

Symphony Hall, and he crossed the street. He climbed into the back of the Caddie and rested his head on the leather backrest.

"Where to, boss?"

"Take me home."

To her.

The irony didn't escape him. Doocey's compulsion for dark-skinned, young men had him by the balls, and yet Vasily's own balls were firmly clasped in the hands of one Dominique Marcello.

Ridiculous.

But there it was. He'd kept his distance, choosing to work in his office and giving Nicky time to heal but the compulsion to touch her, and smell her had become unbearable. He needed just one little taste, and the rest could be dealt with by his hand.

His phone rang.

"Yes," he greeted Niccoterra.

"Got a lead on Andretti."

Vasily pinched the bridge of his nose. Though he initiated the search, Nicky's ex was fast becoming his least favorite subject to discuss or even think about.

"Let me hear it."

"Andretti's credit card was last used on Highway 299 about forty miles west of Redding five days ago at a gas station."

Redding?

Northern California again.

Vasily let out a long breath. "Interesting that's in the same corner of California where James Falk was recently released from jail."

"Was just thinking the same thing, and Andretti being a lawyer, I did some digging. Recently filed court documents show he was Falk's lawyer."

Vasily's eyes widened.

Well, well, well. Fucking plot twist.

"The judge agreed to half a million in bail," the Italian went on. "Which would make the up-front ten percent cash payment to the bondsman fifty thousand dollars. Give you one guess who paid it."

No!

"Andretti?"

"Chicken dinner. From his personal checking account, no less."

What?

Perhaps that was why he couldn't afford his kid's fancy preschool tuition.

"This is weird." Vasily scratched his head. "I'm sure it's happened, but lawyers don't usually front their client's bail money."

"Indeed, but I saw a copy of the cashier's check and the bail receipt. Andretti's name is on both of them."

"This whole thing smells," Vasily stated, looking out the window at the city creeping by in the evening traffic. It was starting to come alive. Streetlights flickered on and colorful neon business signs flashed.

"It's safe to assume that if Andretti was Falk's lawyer, he's gotta be connected to Marisol Price. We know that bitch was fucking Falk's brother, but what if she's fucking the lawyer too?"

"Gives a whole new meaning to complicated," Niccoterra said.

No shit.

He'd known enough dirty scumbags in his lifetime, Federov, his old boss being one of them. But the level of which seldom reached this. What kind of man paid his client's bail, then set that man loose on his wife to be raped at knife-point. A wife he wanted back, or so he said.

But there was no doubt Andretti wanted Nicky back.

He'd seen it that night in the parking lot, even through the man's drug-fueled rage. Scumbaggery aside, he was beginning to question if Andretti even knew about the attack on Nicky.

But if the bastard was complicit and orchestrated that rape, he was never more determined to kill the man himself.

Slowly.

"You going to tell her?" Niccoterra broke through his thoughts.

Vasily ticked his jaw. There was no need to worry Nicky over speculation. "Not until we've got something solid."

Max entered the parking garage in his building, and they ended the conversation. Vasily stepped out of the car and rode the elevator up, going straight to his office.

From his desk drawer, he pulled out a burner phone and called Kat, his FBI friend.

She didn't pick up as expected. Nor did he leave a message. Kat would know who the missed call was from and would reach out as soon as she was able.

This Marisol Price person, whoever she was, proved far more elusive than he anticipated. It was time to call on the full weight of the United States government.

He stared at the bar, ten feet from his desk, and considered having a drink.

Fuck that.

He needed something else more than he needed alcohol. Something warm, and soft that smelled and tasted far better than his best scotch. She'd been making his life a living hell since they'd moved in, with her tempting curves, and her soft doe-eyed looks. And tonight it was time to end that hell before he went postal on everybody. A man could only take so much.

Crossing the white rug, he exited his office and walked past the building's main elevator and Yev's apartment. His heels clicked on the white marble floor. A large window near his front door offered a twinkling view of the pyramid-shaped Transamerica building. Usually, he'd stop to admire it for a moment before entering the penthouse, but tonight he didn't.

Nicky lay curled on a couch leaning against a large pillow, reading. Judging by the cover, some romance novel. She chewed on her thumbnail, a habit she'd always had.

The first time he'd seen her do it was in a soapy bathtub. He'd brought her a glass of wine to enjoy with her book, and she'd had one leg bent and out of the water with her foot resting on the faucet.

Unable to resist touching, he'd sat on the edge of the tub and drawn little stick figures holding hands on her inner thigh, making her giggle.

That giggling led him higher up her thigh and to ultimately pleasuring her with his fingers. Before she'd even come down from her orgasm, he'd pulled her from the tub, slippery and wet, and fucked her up against the wall in the hallway, with her legs wrapped around his waist.

He'd never even taken his jeans off.

That was what she did to him.

With that image vivid in his head, the need was as strong as ever—his tightening pants proved as much.

"Hey," she said, a smile starting, but it faded immediately as she took him in. "What's wrong?"

Your ex may be a worse piece of shit than I ever imagined.

But he didn't want to go there.

"Ask me what's right instead," he said softly.

"Okay." She looked at him from beneath her lashes and bit her lip. "What *is* right?"

He was looking at it.

Holding out a hand, he waited for her to put her book down, then place one of hers in his. The resulting warmth of her touch and the softness of her palm sent a pathway of lust straight to his cock as he helped her to her feet.

"Where's Luca?" he asked, his voice gravelly and he entwined his fingers with hers.

"In bed already."

She hummed a small laugh, unaware of, or maybe just ignoring the sexual energy that reached out and curled its tendrils around his swollen dick.

"Seems playing basketball with Yev tuckered him out." She giggled again, showing that little chip in her front incisor. "He almost fell asleep face down in his carrots."

Vasily's lip lifted at the visual of Luca's face in his plate, and at the adorable little laugh lines that formed around Nicky's eyes.

"Yev's a tough opponent."

"Even for you?" she teased, her eyes getting flirty.

He snorted. "Especially for me. But I don't want to talk about Yev."

A moment passed with their eyes locked, and that sensual energy swirled between them. A soft flush brightened her cheeks.

"Are you hungry?" she asked, her voice husky. It did nothing to curb the blood flowing south. He cleared his throat.

"I am."

"I can fix something for—"

"Not for food."

He moved their entangled hands to the small of her back, bringing her closer until their hips connected. The warmth from hers mingling with his ignited his blood further.

He knew exactly where the most sensitive spot on her neck was, just below her jaw and he put his lips there. He touched it with the tip of his tongue, licked a little circle, then murmured, "I'm hungry for you."

The heat from his breath made her shiver. He slid his other palm up her neck and into her hair. Spreading his fingers wide, he cupped her head with his thumb under her jaw.

"Vas?" A shuddery breath escaped her, and her lids lowered to half-mast. "What's happening here?"

What always happened when he was anywhere near her.

"This," he growled, his heart thundering in his ears. Bringing their hands from behind her to the front, he slid them between them, placing them on his cock. Then he squeezed, barely restraining the grunt that wanted to erupt from deep within him at the sensations coursing through his body.

"This is what's happening."

Her lashes flickered a second before his lips took possession of hers. He prompted them with his tongue, and she opened like a flower in the morning sun. Exploring her taste, he found it was familiar, but new, and it ignited his senses, feeding his hunger.

Breaking for air, he groaned into her neck, "I want you. Tonight."

He covered a breast with his large palm. Her nipples were already hard, making little peaks that he pinched and rolled through the fabric. She mewled in pleasure. Unable to hide his need, he grabbed her ass and pressed his hard length against her lower belly.

"I want to make you fall apart on my tongue."

"Oh, God, yes." Her breath hitched as he searched her eyes. They were dark and burning with the same desire he'd known in the past. The memory of which had kept him going during his coldest, darkest days in Russia.

"Bedroom," he ordered before he lost the ability to speak. "Now."

Spinning her, he placed his hands on her shoulders and guided her to his room, then shut the door behind them.

"Tell me you want this, Dominique," he rasped against the skin of her neck, thrilling in the show of goosebumps he elicited. Kissing his way around, he moved to her front again. "Tell me you want me."

"I do," she breathed, dragging her nails up his length. "God help me, but I do. I want this."

He drew in a sharp breath as his stomach muscles tensed and quivered. Then she undid his belt and zipper. Taking his cock in her hand, she rolled her thumb over the tip. It almost made his knees buckle. A deep growl erupted from his throat.

"No touching," he said, removing her hand. If she kept that up, this would be over before it began, and he'd waited too long for her for it to be over too soon.

"But Vas—"

"Shh."

He quietened her with a kiss as he undid the rest of her buttons until her dress pooled at her feet. All she had on were her panties, and the butterfly bandages keeping her skin together. A reminder he needed to be gentle no matter how hard he wanted to take her.

"On the bed," he ordered while unbuttoning his shirt.

Nicky sat on the edge, licking her lips.

"Back, head on the pillows."

Tugging the fabric from his pants, he dropped his shirt on the floor, then pulled his belt.

Nicky was in position, and he moved to the side of the bed.

"Give me your wrists."

"Vas," she said again, "Don't tie me up. I want to touch you."

"Do you trust me?"

"I do, but—"

"Then let me do this." *So he could fucking last.*

She tensed beneath him. "Tell me why."

There was fear in her expression he didn't like. It made him feel like a shit and he didn't want that. "Dom." He took her face gently between his hands, looking deep into her eyes. "We've done this before, remember?"

The pulse in her delicate neck pounded, the rhythm it set was fast and erratic.

"Have I ever hurt you?"

"No."

"Only reason I'm doing this is for you. I'm so wound up and fucking aching right now, if you touch me this will be over in seconds. It's for both of us, and I want to show you can trust me." That he wasn't Falk and if she could ride this road with him, it would help her in the long run. That not every man wanted to hurt her, and never him.

She swallowed.

"Our first time in ten years, and I want more than seconds. I want to make it good for you. But if you don't want it, I won't restrain you."

Her eyes searched his and he waited until the fear slipped away. Until she found what he wanted her to see. That she really could trust him.

Her lashes flickered. "Do it."

"Good girl." He dropped his head for a moment in relief, then hooked the belt around her wrists and attached it to his headboard. "I'll make it worth it for you, but if you need to, you can safeword. Do you remember what it was?"

"Popcorn."

His heart skipped a beat. That she didn't have to dig deep meant the world. That what they'd had before, was close to the surface. It filled his chest with a warmth he hadn't felt in a long time. Since her.

Taking her mouth again, he kissed the lingering doubt away until it turned heavy and wet, and hungry. The desire stoked into flames and set them on fire.

One more time, he broke away, and dragged his lips down to her breasts, breathing onto her skin as she arched and squirmed. He caressed his fingers up her thighs, slowly spreading them. The skin was soft, like velvet under his calloused palms.

Her breathing got faster and shallower and as each second passed, he got even harder, and his own breath rasped in his throat.

Continuing up, his thumbs grazed the outer edges of her sex over her panties. Nicky dropped her head back and whimpered.

He crawled forward, resting his weight on his hands and knees, and took a peaked nipple into his mouth. Sucked and nibbled on it. After a moment, he switched to the other, then blew on it. She writhed beneath him, tugging on her restraints.

"Lower," she begged. "God, I need you lower."

"In good time."

"Goddammit Vasily, don't torture me, it's been a long time."

"How long?" he couldn't help asking as he slipped her panties from her hips, then down her legs.

She kicked them off. "Since...you know, my ex."

He wanted to growl and sigh in relief at the same time. So he was an asshole. But the thought of her like this with any man gave him head-exploding notions of the trigger-finger variety.

Kissing a slow path down her stomach and her mound, he inhaled. Got drunk on her scent as he teased her flesh with his tongue and his fingers. The closer she got to her climax, the harder she panted, and her hips rocked against his face. He held her in place, delving deeper until her muscles tightened, then her hips bucked, and she cried out.

He took her through it until he was about to pass out from his own need—his cock throbbing, and his heart pounding. Reaching for a condom in his bedside drawer, he ripped the foil with his teeth. Stepping out of his pants, he rolled the condom on himself, hands trembling with the effort.

"I'm going to try to take it slow," he said, his voice thick with desire. "But if I hurt you, let me know."

Her face and breasts were flushed, and she was never more beautiful than when she looked at him from beneath her black lashes, her eyes dark and dazed from her orgasm. "Okay." She nodded.

He wanted missionary, skin-to-skin. But that was out of the question. Instead, clasping her by the hips he lifted her thighs, then dropping his head, watched himself enter her. She was tight, and hot, and ready. And so fucking sweet. If this was his last day, he wouldn't have a single regret, only that he wanted more.

He'd always want more.

"Vas," she urged, panting. "Fuck me like I remember. Like we used to."

He lost himself.

Everything faded except for the insane, otherworldly pleasure she gave as he thrust inside her. He tried to make it last, but the moment her inner muscles tightened, pulsing with another climax, he couldn't hold back.

"Oh my God, Vasily!" Her voice calling his name in that hoarse way triggered his unraveling. Gritting his teeth, muttering curse words in Russian, he lost rhythm. It started at the base of his spine and rushed up through every blood vessel, every nerve ending, and every cell. A tingling effervescence that grew with every thud of his heart. It reached his brain and stars burst inside his head.

That exquisite death overwhelmed and destroyed him. Sent him out and beyond for endless moments until his muscles couldn't hold him any longer. Collapsing in a boneless pile next to her, he was functionless. All he could do was catch his breath and hope that when his end finally came, it was like this.

In her arms.

As consciousness began to reemerge, he became aware of the warm sensation in his chest. A gentle burning that, though disconcerting, wasn't unpleasant. A sensation that somehow made him feel strangely...*complete*. He swallowed. *She* made him feel complete.

Brushing his finger over her ribs, tracing them beneath the healing line of her cut, he kissed the round of her shoulder, tasting the slight saltiness of her skin.

"Did I hurt you?"

Shifting, she gazed at him through soft, sated eyes. "Only in the best way."

He smirked, then released her wrists from his belt. However, filled with smug satisfaction that echoed through his body, he comprehended a new problem. He'd hoped to somehow mitigate this chemical compulsion to take her any time she was within yards of his vicinity. To smooth his head of her intoxicating image when she wasn't.

But he hadn't.

He knew as he had always known, he'd just made it worse.

He sighed into her skin while tracing a rough finger along a faint stretch mark on her hip.

"Battle scars," she muttered sleepily. "Sorry if they turn you off."

His finger paused mid-trace as he considered her words. That finger left her hip, slid up her belly, over her breast to capture her chin and slant it towards him.

"Did I appear turned off?"

She met his eyes. There was a glimmer of insecurity that pissed him off.

"Serious question, Dominique."

"You could've been thinking of Sunny the supermodel."

What. The. Fuck?

"Sunny the supermodel could never get me as hard as I just was for you."

Leaning closer, he sucked her bottom lip gently, stroking his tongue along its soft plumpness. "I don't mind them. Your *battle scars* make you more of a woman. Sexier, and much more interesting."

Her eyes shimmered, then she looked away as her throat worked.

He sighed, but taking the cue to give her a moment, he rolled off the bed.

"Be right back," he said and left for the bathroom. Glancing over his shoulder he caught her wiping her eyes with the heel of her palms.

Only one person would've given her shit for stretch marks—the piece of shit lawyer she was somehow still married to. As if it wasn't deep enough, his disgust for the man increased a little more.

At the sink, he removed the condom. Twisted it to tie a knot, then froze at the sticky mess oozing onto his fingers.

Fuck!

He stared at the damn thing for long seconds. What the hell?

The condom had ripped.

Chapter Twenty

Having discarded the broken condom into the trash, Vasily washed his hands, then ran a washcloth under the hot water faucet and squeezed it out. Taking it with him, he went back to the bedroom.

Nicky had fallen asleep hugging a pillow.

He stared at her for a long moment, resisting the urge to move the hair falling across her face or caress her long, smooth leg.

He needed to tell her about the condom, but it could wait until morning. It wasn't worth waking her up. Hopefully, she was on birth control, but if not, he would get her Plan B.

Dropping the washcloth on the floor, he adjusted the comforter around her, making sure she was covered. He leaned over and kissed her forehead, pausing when his stomach rumbled and she stirred slightly. It had been a while since he'd eaten.

Normally he wouldn't have bothered with clothes, but he didn't want to risk a naked encounter with Luca, so he pulled on a pair of sweats and walked to the kitchen. In the fridge, he found the fixings for a roast beef sandwich, which he devoured in a few bites along with a glass of water.

He could've chosen to work. There was enough to keep him

busy, but wasting one moment where he could be close to her wasn't a real choice.

He went back to bed to read.

Or tried to.

He gazed at her sleeping form, her chest rising and falling gently in slumber. She'd kicked off the comforter and his eyes kept wandering to the curve of her breast, to her dusky nipple and the trimmed thatch between her legs.

With her intoxicating scent in his nostrils, her taste still on his lips, just looking at her made him hard. And the longer he looked, the harder he got.

He put the book down and turned on his side, traced his fingers over her breast, circling the areola. Then he circled it with his tongue. Taking her peak into his mouth, he tugged and sucked.

Nicky let out a little moan, and a moment later her eyes opened. The deep blue, sleepy irises called to him in a way no woman had ever done—her gaze summoning him in an ancient and fundamental way.

Despite the things he owned, the power he yielded, or the luxury he lived in, he'd never been materialistic—unlike his brother and so many who were in the Bratva. It's what drove them to do the terrible things they did. To possess that stolen Picasso, or race that million-dollar car. That was *their* weakness.

But Nicky.

She was the only thing he'd wanted to possess, to own fully and completely. And it was only because of her he'd been driven to do some of the things he had. And fuck him, but put in that same position, to see that look in her eyes, he'd do it all over again.

"You sore?" he asked softly.

"Not enough to stop you from doing what you're doing."

He smiled a little, then foregoing her nipple in favor of her mouth, he kissed her. Deep and lingering, a slow burn built into an intense flame as their tongues played with each other.

"I need you on me," he growled when the fire she stoked in

him was an inferno and no longer possible to dampen. Gripping her hips, he rolled onto his back, taking her with him. He helped her mount him, her long legs astride and his throbbing cock standing tall and solid between them.

This time he took more care with the condom and more time with her. Loving every inch of her body until they were riding that wave to its peak. Until they were lost in each other, and it crashed, exploding within their bodies and they were sweaty, breathing hard, and sated, their eyes locked in a moment of pure, sweet intimacy.

They fell asleep, her legs tangled with his, her head resting against his shoulder. Like they used to.

Later, he awoke to find her getting out of bed, her naked silhouette lit by the ambient glow of twinkling city lights.

"Stay with me," he said, reaching for her hand.

"I can't." Her smile was soft and apologetic. "Luca likes to cuddle in the mornings, and I want to be there for him when he crawls into my bed. His routine has already changed enough, and I want to keep this the same."

"Hmm."

Not so familiar with the rituals of what kids did in the morning, he snuffed the pang of jealousy. Her boy got priority, as he should. Though Luca seemed to be adjusting well and hadn't shown any lingering effects of what he'd seen when his mother was almost raped, but Vasily understood her concern.

"Before you go," he tugged her hand, "I want something from you. Come here."

She smiled, then sat on the edge of the bed and leaned over.

Supporting his weight on his elbow, he reached up to cup the back of her head. "We need to talk."

"I know," she whispered against his lips. "We do." Then giving him a last, lingering taste, she drew away and retrieved her dress and panties from the floor.

As she started to put them on, he said, "Don't."

"What?" She looked at him, her brow arched.

"Don't put your dress on. I want the image of you walking naked through my penthouse stamped into my head." Not like he already hadn't fantasized about that already, like all the time.

She chuffed and made an effort at half an eye-roll. "See you at breakfast, gangsta."

To his delight, she did what he asked and left without covering herself. Exhaling, he watched her walk to the door, her pretty ass teasing him. When she moved out of sight, he lay back and dropped his forearm over his face, groaning softly.

Having her again really was like old times—fucking glorious—and as if no time had passed at all.

He took a deep breath and swallowed. Unfortunately, ten years had, and some of it had been ugly. He bore the scars and tattoos to prove it. But that time was over, and he didn't want to resurrect those memories. Being inside her again was a salve to an open wound. One only she could heal.

He only hoped it was sustainable.

Chapter Twenty-One

T he following morning, he found them in the kitchen.

Coffee brewed, filling the room with a smokey, rich aroma along with melting butter and something else. The fat orange fur ball crunched at a bowl in the corner, and Luca sat on the center island, still in his blue one-piece pajamas. His legs were crossed while he stabbed at a bowl with a fork.

"Mr. Vasily," Luca looked up when he walked into the kitchen. "We're making sc'ambled eggs and bacon. Want some?"

"Or an omelet if you prefer," Nicky added, glancing over her shoulder, her gaze soft and lingering. It made his chest swell and his loins stir in his sweats. "I've got mushrooms sautéing in garlic butter."

She wore a pair of peach-colored pajama shorts that landed high on her thigh, showing off her long, sexy legs to perfection. A matching lacy camisole did little to hide her nipples. The same nipples he could still feel and taste on his tongue.

Harnessing his thoughts, he cleared his throat. "An omelet would be great."

Could they look any more comfortable in his kitchen? The picture of domestic bliss, their presence brightening the room, and not just with their colorful clothing. He didn't even mind the cat and the claw indentations it left on his furniture.

Retrieving two mugs from the cupboard next to where Nicky worked, he poured each a cup of brewing coffee. Adding half-and-half, then two spoons of sugar to hers, he stirred and passed it over.

"You remembered," she murmured with a pleased curve to her lip.

Of course, he did. Every little detail. Their gazes stayed caught for a second longer and there was heat in hers, promising more carnal delights, something he heartily approved of. Then before he got a boner and kissed her in front of Luca, he stepped away and ruffled the kid's dark curls.

"Whatup little man? Grown any hair on your chest yet?"

"No," Luca giggled mid-stab at an unbelievably still whole yolk.

"What's that?" Nicky turned, her gaze bouncing between him and her son.

"Mr. Vasily said if I learned freestyle like a man, I'll grow hair on my chest. I think he's just joking. I'm too young. Don't I have to be, like, seven?"

"More like seventeen," Nicky answered.

"Aw, man," Luca whined, looking crushed. "Seventeen? That's so *old*."

Vasily snorted and grabbed the popping toast. He added two more slices, then pushed the lever and began buttering.

"If I'm twenty-nine, what does that make me then?" Nicky quirked an eyebrow at her son as she rescued the bowl from him.

"*Really* old."

"Thanks, Buddy, that's wonderful for my ego." She gave the eggs a brisk whisk before pouring the mixture into a pan. The aroma of sautéing butter, and cooking eggs made his stomach growl.

"But you don't have hair on your chest."

"Thank the gods," Nicky said, flipping the omelet before

adding the ingredients and topping them with grated cheese and folding one side over. "And that's because I'm a girl."

"I bet Wolverine didn't have to wait till he was seventeen. He's got hair all over his face."

"And who is Wolverine?" Vasily asked, his brows pinched together.

Luca launched into an excited and detailed explanation of the hero with retractable blades that sprang from his knuckles. It lasted throughout breakfast.

Then he jumped from his stool. "Mom, can I be 'scused?"

"When you're done taking your dishes to the sink," she answered, finishing off the last bite of her omelet.

"But I gotta poop!" he called, eyes wide and holding his butt.

Nicky made a relenting mom noise at the back of her throat. "All right, go poop. Don't forget to wash your hands."

Luca minced out the kitchen muttering and humming in a strained voice, "Gotta poop, *mmm mm mm m*, gotta poop."

Vasily watched him, chuckling. "Does he need help?"

Nicky shook her head, smiling. "He's fine."

"How long will that take?"

"Depends. He'll probably get dressed after and start playing a game. He knows if he comes back, he'll have to help in the kitchen."

"Smart kid."

Their eyes locked again. Electric heat surged between them, flushing her cheeks.

"Woman, if you keep looking at me like that, I'm going to have to do something about it," he whispered. Semi-tumescent since he'd walked in the door, his cock was now threatening to lift the center island from the floor.

"I can't help it." She bit her lip, which didn't help. "And except for Luca walking in on us, I would highly encourage it."

Vasily almost forgot how to breathe, she was so fucking beautiful, and that she wanted him again too, didn't help matters.

She blinked and was the first to look away, but not before she licked her lips, or how her breathing changed to match his. Placing her cup down, she slid off her stool then collected their dishes, and placed them in the sink to rinse.

Like a bee to the honey pot, he followed, pressing his front against her back. He trailed his hands over the smooth, warm skin of her upper arms several times before slipping an arm around her, then under her top. The flat of his palm lay against her belly. Pulling her closer, he pressed his lips to the curve in her neck and inhaled her scent. Warm and womanly. He sighed into her skin, tracing circles around her navel before moving his hand lower. Slipping it under her shorts, he cupped her sex. She was naked beneath her shorts, a fact he fucking loved. The heat from her core seeped through, making his fingers want more.

"You want me to stop?" he asked, his voice low and gravelly.

She softened and relaxed against him, letting her head fall to his shoulder. "God, no, but Luca."

"If he comes back, I'm helping you do the dishes," he whispered against her ear. "Are you wet?"

"Mm." She closed her eyes, shuddering a little.

He stroked her, working his way between her folds and discovering she was indeed wet. Her clit was hard and swollen. He went further, gathering some of her slickness, brought it up, then alternated between rubbing and teasing her. She hissed and quivered, then parting her legs a little, she allowed him deeper access.

Supporting her weight, he took care of her while kissing and gently biting her neck and shoulders and getting much-needed friction against her ass cheeks.

Watching her get there put him close to the edge himself. Then she convulsed, making a little sound in the back of her throat as she came around his fingers.

It was so fucking hot, he could barely control himself and almost followed her.

When her breathing slowed, he tilted her face and kissed her mouth. Took slow pleasure in the way she tasted. Like breakfast, coffee, and Nicky.

He turned her so she faced him, deepening the kiss while his throbbing erection pressed against her lower stomach. She placed her palm over it, rubbing it up and down. He broke away to look at the ceiling, a deep groan rumbling in his throat as his cock pulsed and jerked in her hand.

"Your turn," she murmured. "In the pantry."

He didn't need to be told twice and led her to the small, enclosed space, flipping the light switch. The moment the door was shut, she surprised him by kneeling in front of him and tugging down his sweats.

"Dom?" He'd expected to turn her around and slide inside her, but damn if he didn't want this too.

"I want to." Wrapping her fingers around his cock she looked at him through her lashes, her pupils dilated. She lowered her hand to cup his balls. "I want to taste you, like you tasted me. Let me."

Christ. How could he refuse her when at this moment he wanted nothing more than to be in her mouth.

"Fuck, yes."

A dirty, sexy little laugh escaped her and a moment later, he slid into the hot, divine depths of her mouth.

And nothing had ever been better—except every other time he'd been with her.

His stomach muscles tensed as she licked and swirled her tongue around the tip, the pleasurable sensations hitting the back of his brain. When she took him in deeper, he gripped her head and began to fuck her mouth.

Slow at first, but it didn't take long to gain momentum as pleasure took control, and she gripped the base of his cock. Hot, transcending, mind-altering pleasure. Then all too quickly, he clenched his teeth and stiffened. His head bumped against a shelf and he bit back a groan as he tapped the side of her head in warning. She didn't pull away, instead took him a little deeper, then he climaxed down her throat.

Shaking from his exquisite release, he used the pantry shelves for support, hoping his legs wouldn't give out as she took everything he had to give. Chest heaving, he dropped his head again and watched her through half-mast eyes.

Christ, he loved her this way, looking so beautiful, her face flushed, his cock in her mouth. Her eyes were glazed like she got just as much pleasure out of what they'd done as he had.

It was enough to drive a man insane.

An ironic chuckle left him as he scraped his hair back from his face. He'd laughed at men who were led by their dicks. Federov, his old captor in particular. Kat had played him masterfully until she got burned.

But here *he* was popping his rocks off in a pantry with the only woman who could make him lose whatever sanity he had.

Nicky wiped her mouth with the back of her hand. She rose and stood in front of him, her lips pink, moist, and puffy while he tucked himself back into his sweats. With his index finger, he smoothed her hair behind her ear, then ran his thumb gently over her swollen bottom lip.

"The condom broke," he said.

She blinked hard. "What?"

"I meant to tell you last night, but you fell asleep."

"Oh." She swallowed, something flitting across her face. "You could've told me when you woke me."

"I could've, but I had other things on my mind if you remember."

"I remember, every little detail, but if you're worried about birth control, it's okay."

She placed his finger on the inside of her upper arm. "Feel that?"

There was something hard and small under her soft skin.

"It's a birth control implant, but I'm more concerned about...
you know."

"I can't remember the last time I didn't use one and at my last
checkup I was clean."

Now that he thought about it, he did remember. It was with
her before he left for Russia. The night they consumed the
whiskey she'd bought and then fucked in front of her fireplace.

"Phew," she joked, putting the back of her hand on her forehead in a dramatic fashion. "Looks like we both dodged a bullet.
No STDs for me and no little Melnikovs in your near future."

He stared down at her, something heavy pressing on his chest
as he spoke. "No little Melnikovs ever."

The words hung between them as Nicky stilled, then slowly
pulled away.

"You mean you've had a vasectomy?" she asked, a frown
forming on her face. It was just a simple expression, but it carried a
weight that told him something had shifted between them. Something monumental and not good. He didn't like it, and it put him
on edge.

"No, I just don't want kids."

"You don't want kids? Ever?"

He took a deep breath and forced the words out that he'd
never had to say to any other woman. "My family is cursed,
Dominique. No child deserves to have Melnikov blood run
through their veins."

She turned her face away and looked at a half-opened pack of
paper towels. Then she pulled in her bottom lip and released a
deep sigh that relayed her disappointment. He didn't know what
to do with that.

"That's so sad," she said, shaking her head. "What about your
mother's blood? All your good parts come from her, Vasily.
Doesn't she deserve to have her legacy live on in a grandchild?"

His mother.

Christ, if she only knew. And though he knew it wasn't her

intention, that was the worst thing she could've said. It was *because* of his mother, and his failure to protect her that he'd made that decision so many years ago. Her beautiful, sad, broken face. Those soulful eyes too often filled with tears of pain and anguish. It was uncomfortable territory, and he didn't like it, but he liked the look on Nicky's face even less.

"There are no good parts of me." He pulled in air through his nostrils, then pushed away from the shelf to open the pantry door. He held it wide for her.

"Sure there are," she said exiting into the kitchen. At the island, she stopped and turned. "Don't sell yourself short like that. Look what you've done for me."

He couldn't deny that by trying to fix the wrongs in her life, he hoped to mitigate the monster in his soul. But the man he'd been forced to become in Russia was a man beyond redemption.

There were special places in hell reserved for men like him and he would not create a child and have it be subjected to the madness that ran latent in his genes. The same cruel ones that had driven his brother to kidnap and his father to crack his mother's skull.

He would not take the risk. "I'm not having kids, Dominique."

She blinked again, then dropped her gaze and stared at her hands.

Picked at her nails.

Several beats went by, when she inhaled and opened her mouth as if to speak, but didn't.

The heaviness between them grew heavier with each moment of her silence.

"Oh, boy. Reality check," she finally said, her voice choked and unsteady. "I'm sorry you feel that way, and I'm an idiot, and I don't know what I was thinking, or what I was hoping for, but in light of what you just said..." She paused and put the tips of her fingers to her forehead.

He felt like a shit, but wasn't it better to discuss this now? Start this new phase of their relationship in complete honesty before either of them got ahead of themselves? But what she said next just about ripped his guts out.

"Then there's no point in us continuing this any further."

No point?

What the hell did she mean "no point?" *Nicky* had *always* been the point. She started to walk away and he reached for her, his fingers wrapping around her wrist. But she yanked it back violently, bringing her arm close to her breast, holding it as if his touch had burned her.

"No! Please don't." She shook her head, her lashes fluttering like the wings of a trapped bird. "You don't understand, I'm not sure I can do this."

Her voice was tight like she was struggling not to cry, and he wasn't a stupid man. But he sure as fuck felt stupid now. He should've figured this out sooner before he'd taken that step of no return.

Nicky was no ordinary woman, but that didn't mean she didn't have ordinary desires. Like wanting to have a family. Another child.

Things *he* should be staying away from. Things a man like him should never perpetuate, and a thing he was adamant would never be in his future. And now it could ruin them before they began again.

He'd been so absorbed in his own selfishness, in his own need to be inside the only woman he'd ever fallen for, not once, but twice—because yeah—there was no denying he'd fuckin' fallen again. Maybe even harder this time, and the thought of losing her over something he would never give her was intolerable.

Like a knife twisting in his heart.

Chapter Twenty-Two

How did a simple joke about STDs turn into something so painful she could barely breathe?

No little Melnikovs ever!

Never had four words been so devastating, so hopeless and so...*final*.

She wasn't one to jump the gun, and it wasn't like he'd promised her babies—promised her anything for that matter—but the thought that the world, (and herself) would be deprived of a beautiful little silver-eyed child just hurt.

So much.

She walked from the kitchen through the halls to her room, her legs leaden and heavy like she wore shoes of stone. With her hand on the brass knob, she was about to turn it when Vasily called behind her.

"Dominique, wait a second!" His voice sounded rough, almost broken, and so unlike him, it made her pause.

"Don't walk away. Let's talk about this."

The lump in her throat was growing bigger as tears threatened to spill over, making it hard for her to get even an ounce of air in. How on earth was she supposed to talk?

Yet she stopped and anchored herself with her palm flat on the wall for support. By the sound of his light footsteps on the hardwood, she knew he approached cautiously. Then his warmth engulfed her as his arm gently circled over her belly from behind and pulled her against his solid front. His other hand came around her chest and rested on the ball of her shoulder. His heart beat in time with hers, but it was at a rhythm faster than normal.

"Please don't walk away from me," he whispered close to her ear, and it was so soft she barely heard it. "I don't want to lose you again."

Lose her again?

But he was the one that left!

Resting his cheek against her hair, his unsteady breath fanned her face while his stubble pressed into her skin. Neither of them moved for several seconds. She didn't know about him, but she was lost in his heat, his heartbeat, and the gentle way he held her. It soaked into her and despite herself, like candle wax beneath a warm flame, she began to relax and melted into him.

"Say something," he said, his voice low and gruff and vibrating through her body.

She swallowed the painful lump sitting at the top of her throat. "What's to say, Vasily? I want another child and you don't want any."

"I hear that, but this doesn't have to be the end. Jesus Christ, I don't want it to end. Let's just take a little time to process."

"Process?"

While getting more invested?

By falling deeper in love only to have her dream of a bigger family squashed like a bug under his boot?

"Let's just give ourselves a minute."

"And then what?" Twisting her neck, she looked at him over her shoulder as tears spilled down her cheek. "You're going to change your mind?"

"Dom—"

"Of course, you won't." She stiffened against him. "You've made your mind up, and it's your right to do so, but you expect me to change mine?"

"I'm not expecting or asking you to change anything right now. I'm just telling you there are reasons."

"I think your reasons are...misguided." She shrugged herself off him, and to her disappointment, he allowed her to, even if it felt like he did so reluctantly. Removing his arms from her body, he separated himself from her. Without him wrapped around her, the chill inside her heart grew.

"They're not misguided."

"I believe they are, Vasily. Even if you don't want a child with me," she paused to swallow at the painful recognition, "your child would have *you* as a dad. You're not cruel and you're not insane. You're kind and considerate, and you'd raise him or her differently than how you were raised. With love, and warmth, and nurturing."

The vision of Luca's little hand in Vasily's big one as he gazed up in hero worship entered her head.

"If you saw what I see when you're with my son, you'd know. I believe you'd make an incredible dad. If you could only trust your-self just enough to consider it for five minutes, I think you'd see it too."

Vasily sucked in a breath of air, a hint of agony crossing his features. "That's the problem, Dom. If you knew the kind of man I am, you would never ask me to consider it."

Was he serious? More tears brimmed on the edges of her eyes and threatened to spill over. "You honestly think I don't know what you're capable of?"

"I don't think you do."

"News flash, gangsta, I have an imagination and I've been immersed in your kind of world since childhood. Believe me, I'm aware of all the violence that can happen, and I've accepted that. And I've accepted you. So, please, don't insult me with any more bullshit. Unless you're telling me you're some kind of serial killer, what are you so afraid of?"

"Dominique, stop." He flinched, then closed his eyes forming deep lines of anguish on his face. He scrubbed a hand over it, dragging it down over his nose and mouth as if to erase the emotions that plagued him.

Suddenly she was afraid of what her words had unleashed. This man seldom, if ever, bared his emotions to anyone, yet something in what she'd said had caused that reaction. A slow, sharp icicle slithered down her spine. It chilled her, causing her to draw in a hard breath.

"You don't know what you're saying," he rasped out.

"God dammit, Vasily. Then tell me." She gripped his forearm, her fingers digging into the solid muscles in frustration. "I want to know it all. I want to know what happened to you in Russia. Most of all, I want to know why you left me."

"That's the thing. I didn't leave you!"

"Then why didn't you come back?" she cried out. "Why did you leave me to deal with what Dean did to my dad alone? You said he was responsible, so why the fuck didn't you help us. Where were you?"

For long seconds he just looked at her, his jaw ticking while he seemed to be gathering himself, gathering his emotions into that tightly controlled box he kept them in. At last, he cleared his throat and said, "I didn't come back from Russia because I couldn't."

What did 'couldn't' mean exactly? "Because you met someone you just couldn't stay away from?" *Some beautiful Russian princess who was everything she wasn't?* God forgive her, but she couldn't help herself from being a jealous bitch. All the mixed, raw emotions and scenarios of that time came bubbling up. The most base of which, besides the fact she'd believed he'd betrayed her was that he'd fallen in love with somebody else.

His head jerked back an inch. "Is that what you think?" Then he wrinkled his brow. That I fell in love with someone else?"

"Well, didn't you?"

"How could I, Dominique!" For the first time, he raised his voice at her, and it shocked her into silence.

"I was fucking head over ass in love with *you*. There's never been anyone else for me, not even close." His words hung in the air, settling like confetti at a wedding. The implications of which were a complete antithesis to what she'd always believed, blurring any thought. Except one.

"Then why?"

His shoulders dropped, almost in defeat, as if he was ashamed of his reasons. "Because I was held captive."

What?

Had she heard him right?

"Held captive?" Her heart raced as she stared at him, trying to process his words.

He nodded.

She gasped, holding her hand over her mouth. Of all the terrible things she'd imagined—besides the ones she'd already acknowledged, countless other scenarios had run through her head. But it had never been that.

"By whom...?" Her voice trailed off, as her lungs were devoid of air, and she was unable to fully take a breath.

"I was betrayed by the man who ran our organization, Leonid." His tone turned dark and somber, and he spoke in a way she knew still bore him pain. "After my dad disappeared, he raised us, and we called him our uncle. His job was to groom us until Dean and I became of age or experienced enough to take the helm." He let out a deep sigh, visibly struggling to find the right words. "Except Leonid developed a taste for the top spot. I didn't suspect it at the time, neither of us did, but he never had any intention of giving it up."

"Oh, my God." Her fingers on his arm tightened as she was barely able to formulate the next thought. "Are you telling me he arranged to have you kidnapped?"

"Not kidnapped," Vasily said, his voice just above a whisper. "Killed."

She exhaled hard as a wave of nausea swept over her and she was ashamed to admit it was one of the things she'd wished for in her darkest moments after he left. And it had almost happened. That she'd once wished him harm or even dead, was now unimaginable.

"But Leonid didn't have the balls to kill me himself," Vasily continued, "so he sent me to Russia. I thought it was to recruit new blood and make new alliances, but what I didn't know was, he had a secret partner. A man named Aleksei Federov who was supposed to do Leo's dirty work for him and dispose of me." Vasily's nostrils curled in disgust. "But Federov was a greedy asshole and had intentions of his own."

Like criminals so often did when it came to money or the promise of greater power and influence. "How did he pull it off?" she asked.

"We always flew private, and about an hour before we landed in Moscow the flight attendant brought me a drink. The next thing I knew, I woke up in a freezing dungeon in a mansion on the outer skirts of Moscow. I'd been stripped of everything. Passport, cell phone, and computer. All I had were the clothes I'd worn when I got on that plane."

He looked at her again. Those silver eyes were a dark gray as they worked, bringing up his old memories. "Federov kept me down there for months. Starved me, took away my dignity, tortured and threatened me. When he thought I was broken enough, he gave me a choice. If I wanted to live, I had to do things for him."

Her mind raced, trying to make sense of everything he was telling her and she became afraid of what she was about to hear—not for herself, but for him having to relive it. And she almost stopped him, having heard enough, but a part of her needed to know the worst.

He paused, looking at a spot above her head as if weighing something in his mind. "You asked if I was a serial killer."

Her eyes widened, then a sharp exhalation left her feeling as though she'd been punched in the ribcage.

Oh, God!

Did she want to hear?

She'd assumed he'd killed before. Men like him, in positions like his, were sometimes left with no other choice. That was knowledge she'd compartmentalized, but was he suggesting he liked it? A cold sweat broke out on the back of her neck and her skin prickled with chills.

"Are you?" She could barely get the words out, and as it was, they came out wobbly.

"Not exactly."

That didn't sound much better, but she couldn't decide if that made her *feel* better. She swallowed.

"I'll spare you the details," Vasily said, "but I was forced to become something I didn't want to be. They called me '*Nayemnik*.'"

The way he spoke, it was like the word left a foul smell in his nose, and she didn't need to understand Russian to know it meant something bad.

"It means mercenary, or hitman," he clarified. "That was my choice. Become one, or die."

The blood rushed in her head, and she rubbed her forehead. It was damp and cold, but she refused to allow herself to indulge in any weakness. She'd asked for the truth, and if Vasily could stand to tell her what had happened to him, she could stand to hear what he had to say.

"Federov gave me targets," he continued, the knob in his throat moving up and down, and even from her position it looked like it caused him pain. "They were Bratva enemies, and it was my job to dispose of them. How I did it was of my choosing, but each one earned me a little increment of freedom."

How could this be happening, and how could she have been so naïve? His words reverberated around in her skull as so many different emotions flooded through her at once. Anger, sadness, disgust at what those people did to him and what they made him do. There was also disgust at her own reaction to him being gone, and the pain she'd experienced.

But mostly she was heartbroken.

For him.

And for herself.

Then she remembered. "Those bars inked into your arm? They're prison bars...from the dungeon you were in?"

He nodded.

"And the barbed wire?"

"Each spur in the wire represents somebody I removed from this planet. I want you to know I'd never...*disposed* of anyone up until that point, but it turns out I'm pretty good at it."

God, she hadn't counted them, but by her memory, there were so many.

Her fingers moved to his shoulder. "But this star, this also means at some point you weren't a prisoner anymore."

His lip curled, but not in amusement. To her, it looked more like he was riddled with his own self-disgust or loathing. Like he thought himself a monster.

"Eventually, I earned their respect and instead of being disposable I became the disposer, an asset and slowly over time rose in rank."

As if exhausted, he leaned his shoulder and head against the wall. For a moment, there was an air of vulnerability about him, it reached inside her and squeezed her heart.

"So you see, Dominique, that's the kind of man I am. A cold-blooded killer, and a target for other cold-blooded killers. Besides the reasons I've already stated, any child of mine would be vulnerable. I'm not even sure I deserve you."

She was stunned, frozen on the outside, but inside she ached.

Not for just those stolen years of his life, or the notion of a family, *but for the fact they'd stolen him from her too!*

And he'd loved her!

All that time was wasted when she'd hated him and none of it was his fault. Tears again seeped from her eyes, and she reached for him, placing her hand on his waist, expecting him to flinch he was so tightly wound. But instead, he seemed to welcome her touch and moved into it.

"Vas, look at me."

She waited until he did, and it took several beats for it to happen. And when it did, there was deep regret in his gaze, and the nurturing, motherly part of her wanted to take it from him and ease his pain.

"Did you enjoy it?" she asked softly.

His brows came together. "God, no."

"Then, that's what makes you different. You were given an impossible choice, one no one should have to choose, and you chose to live."

"I chose to kill."

"In *order* to live. Isn't that what you essentially told me when I killed James Falk?"

He remained silent as he looked down at her.

"How is that any different?" she asked softly. "Your life was threatened, and you did what you had to do, and I'm glad you did because now that we're here again, I can't imagine doing this without you."

Not anymore.

There was a battle happening in his gaze, and she got the feeling he was holding back. Something important, but whatever it was it couldn't be much worse than what he'd already told her.

She slipped her arms around his waist and laid her head on his warm chest. His heart thundered beneath her ear proving, despite what people thought of him and the cold exterior, he wasn't impervious to all the bad things he'd done or gone through.

She understood that now, and even when he hid everything from the world, this man had feelings so deep they cut to the very essence of his soul.

"I'm so sorry," she said on a sob. "I can't imagine what it must've been like for you."

And she didn't want to. It was already too much.

"But it brought me back here," he murmured into her hair. His arms tightened around her, one hand cupping her head to his body. The place where his cheek met her skull, was warm —and wet.

"So, I'm begging you, Dom." His voice shook with the intensity of whatever he was feeling. "Don't make any rash decisions about us just yet. Give it some time."

How could she not after what he'd experienced? Losing something she never had wasn't nearly as bad as losing something she did.

And she'd already lost him once.

There was an ache in her chest that would need to be reconciled at some point. But right now, he needed her.

At her nod, he exhaled deeply. And then there was more wetness on her hair.

His pocket buzzed.

It vibrated against her hip, but he ignored it, choosing instead to hold onto her. It meant everything and flooded her chest with warmth.

After a long while, his heart returned to its normal, steady beat. Vasily released her and cleared his throat, scraped his fingers over his eyes, and removed the moisture that had collected there.

Taking a long, slow breath he fished his phone out and checked a text. He stared at the device as if the words made no sense, or as if he wasn't seeing them. Then, after a moment there was a slight pinch in his brow, so subtle and fast she thought she might've imagined it.

Pocketing his phone, he looked at her again, placing his hands on either side of her face. He leaned in until their lips were just a breath apart. He kissed her in a way he'd never kissed her before. Tenderly. Softly, letting it linger. He tasted salty and he sucked at her mouth until her pulse raced and her knees weakened.

Finally, he broke away and rested his chin on her head.

"There have been some developments," he said with a strange note in his voice. "I'm going to have to leave town for a few days on business. I want you to stay here but I won't be able to contact you. I'll leave a couple of men with you, but I need you to promise me you'll be here when I get back."

She nodded, but he wasn't satisfied with that.

"Say it, Dom."

"I promise I'll be here when you get back."

"Good girl." Then he muttered something in Russian that sounded like it had the word 'blue' in it and kissed her one last time. He left her standing outside her room with a niggling feeling.

One that somehow, given that odd note in his voice, told her the developments of which he spoke had something to do with her.

Chapter Twenty-Three

Three days later, well into the morning hours, Vasily and Vadim quietly approached a large two-storied house in the forest east of Eureka. The area was coated with a thick layer of pine needles and fallen cones. The recent rains had soaked the ground and dampened any sounds they made. Despite the full moon, very little light penetrated the clouds or the tree canopy.

They were here because Carmine's relentless search for the house where James Falk and the rest of the traffickers kept the girls they'd kidnapped finally paid off.

Vadim stepped on a small branch, snapping it. *"Blyad,"* he cursed softly as a nearby owl hooted and took flight.

Vasily glanced over his shoulder and shot Vadim a glare. He was barely visible against a large Redwood, as each man was dressed in unmarked black clothing, gloves, and ski masks, but their eyes had adjusted to the dark.

"Sorry, boss," Vadim muttered.

Vasily shook his head, but at least the young Russian had the decency to look chagrined. Once, when Vasily had gotten over-confident, he'd made the same mistake. One of the few times he'd let a target get away from him, temporarily at least. He'd stalked his prey deep into the Khimki Forest, a green zone near Moscow, until he'd stupidly tripped over a hidden rock, giving up his position and forcing his hand. The prey—Vasily refused to call him a victim—was a pedophile who'd raped the six-year-old daughter of a woman distantly connected to the Bratva. Federov had tasked him with the job, and though he didn't relish killing, he didn't regret the man's fate either. When he'd eventually caught the disgusting piece of shit, Vasily shot the pedophile with the man's own gun and staged it to look like a poaching accident.

Now he and Vadim were almost in position—except for the clearing of about seventy-five feet between the muddy tree line and the back door of the two-storied, slightly dilapidated house. They were the last to be so.

Badger, Carmine's man kept them apprised of everyone's position from the control van several hundred yards to the south of the house. He had patched into the existing surveillance system two days before, allowing them visual access to every room of the house, including the kitchen and perimeter.

Badger had also created a video loop of the outside. Blocking the live feed, he played it, thereby fooling the guard watching the monitors in the security room.

Amateurs.

"Team One, wait for clearance," Badger said into Vasily's earpiece. "Team Two is in the security room off to the side of the house about to take out the guard."

Vasily keyed his mic twice in the affirmative as he waited for Carmine and Yev to complete their job.

Besides the woman and the fat man, Bob in the kitchen, there were two other men inside the house.

"All clear," Badger said. "Approach, Team One."

Vasily led Vadim across the clearing, then advanced to the kitchen, pressing their backs against the ugly brown siding. He tested the thumb press on the ancient door handle. It moved easily, proving the door was unlocked.

"The woman is making some kind of hot drink near the sink," Badger warned. "Beware of boiling water from the kettle. Fat Man Bob is at the table, back to the door checking out his phone. He's unarmed."

There were several seconds of silence, then Badger reported again. "Team Two is in position at the front door. On the count of three, it's go time, gentlemen. One, two..."

Vasily pushed the door and entered just like it was a regular Sunday at church, except it smelled like burnt cheese, old refried beans, and tortillas. The young blonde woman who faced the door gave a stunned blink. Vasily held a finger to his lips, then just as Bob was beginning to turn, he cold-cocked him on the side of his head with the stock of his rifle.

Bob grunted, then toppled onto the floor making a thwacking sound as his large girth slapped against the dirty vinyl flooring. His chair skittered off to the side and bumped into the woman's legs. She dropped her beverage onto the counter. It spilled and dripped down green paint-chipped cupboard doors. The woman backed up against the cabinets, hands clutching the edge of the counter.

"Do not scream," Vasily said softly in Russian. "We're not going to hurt you."

Although it probably wouldn't have mattered if she did. There was a splintering crash, no doubt courtesy of Yev's size thirteen combat boots. A moment later, surprised yells came from the two guards sleeping on the couch, followed by scuffling noises, then silence.

Vasily pressed the barrel of his assault rifle to the middle of Bob's back, making an indentation in the man's sweat-stained white tee-shirt. As extra insurance, he placed his muddy boot on Bob's lower back, just above his rear end. Vadim grabbed Bob's hands and zip-tied them, then did the same for his ankles, and checked for tightness.

"If you want to live, *Bob*," Vasily growled, "stay still and don't fight."

Bob moaned.

"Who are you?" the woman asked in Russian, tears forming in her eyes. "Are you going to kidnap us too, like these men?"

Vasily shook his head. "We're here to rescue you."

Her expression grew wary, then she swallowed. Crossing her arms across her chest, as if hugging herself, she asked, "What does rescue really mean?"

"We're getting you out of here and letting you go."

"Thasnot happenin'," Bob groaned from his position on the floor.

The young woman gripped the metal collar around her neck with shaky fingers. "You have to get rid of these first. They shock us when we get too far from the house."

Vasily's nostrils curled in disgust.

Fucking animals.

"What's your name?" he asked, using his gentlest voice.

"Nadia."

"How many women are in the house, Nadia?"

"Five."

"Where are the others?"

"In the bedrooms, upstairs, sleeping."

"And guards?"

"Four, I think, including him." She looked at Bob moaning on the floor, her lip curling with contempt.

Good. Everything she said matched with what they'd surveyed through the video surveillance system. And based on what they had seen of Marisol Price—which was grainy at best—and if the perimeter collar around Nadia's neck wasn't a clue, this woman wasn't her.

Unfortunately, they hadn't seen anyone resembling the queen bitch anywhere in the house either.

"Where's the woman in charge?" Vasily asked.

"She hasn't been here in days."

"Any idea where she goes when she's not here?"

"Nyet."

Vasily bit back his frustration. He wanted to slam his fist into something. Bob's fat, ugly face would've done just fine, but he adjusted the ski mask on his face instead.

Then Nadia said something interesting.

"Perhaps she went back to Russia."

Wait a fucking minute, *back* to Russia?

"She's Russian?"

"Da."

Finally, they were getting somewhere with her origins. Blowing out a frustrated breath, he nodded to Vadim, and they gripped Bob under his upper arms and yanked him to his feet.

"Watch it," Bob, slurred as the zip ties dug into his flesh.

"Shut up, pencil dick," Vadim growled then ripped a piece of silver duct tape from a roll and placed it over Bob's mouth.

Vasily smirked.

Vadim was of the opinion it was too derogatory of his favorite female part to call anyone a pussy. Vasily had to give it to him—the man had a point.

"Nadia," Vasily said, "my friend is going to take you upstairs to get the rest of the women. Tell them to dress warmly, bring only what they can't live without, and not to panic. We're here to help you, but that does not mean we won't silence you if we must. Understood?"

Nadia looked at the roll of duct tape in Vadim's hand, then nodded. Switching her attention to Bob, contempt written over every inch of her expression, she spat in his face.

Bob reared back, bumping his head on the cabinets. He tried to wipe the spittle from his eyes with his shoulder, but his fat neck got in the way, and he uttered something like a muffled curse behind the duct tape. The effort made his eyes bulge and his face flush red.

Vasily cold-cocked him again. Not too hard, as he needed the man alive, at least temporarily.

"Gnnngh." Bob wobbled, then his legs buckled, and blood poured from a split above his eye.

"You deserved that, *mudak*," Vadim answered as Bob collapsed on the floor again. "And whatever else is coming. Can I have first shot, boss?"

"You're going to need to take a number," Vasily growled. As it was, it took every ounce of Vasily's restraint not to pound *Bob* into the ground—*if* that even was his real name—but he had questions for him.

Vasily keyed his walkie-talkie mic.

"Status?"

"We're in the clear," Badger answered. "All the guards are down."

"Keep an eye on what's happening with the women," Vasily instructed Badger. "Can't have any of them going rogue."

"I'll head up and help him," Carmine added through a little bit of static in his earpiece.

"Roger that."

Niccoterra had his own beef with Bob, and Vasily suspected his hands would be itching to circle the man's neck, and helping Vadim was probably Niccoterra's way of resisting that temptation.

He sent another order to the rest of the team waiting in the wings. "I need the van to the front door and the meat wagon to the back."

Once he received confirmation, he took a breath, then keyed the mic one more time.

"Well done, gentleman. Phase one of Operation Whore House has been a cakewalk."

Almost anticlimactic.

Three days of extensive planning, twenty-three minutes of execution. It couldn't have gone smoother, except for the fact

Marisol Price was still unaccounted for. That's why they still needed Bob.

After he shackled the fat man to a modified meat hook in the old butchery wagon, ensuring escape was virtually impossible, Vasily helped Yev zip-tie and place hoods over the heads of the other three unconscious guards. They dragged them out front and tied them, backs against a large old oak. If they were lucky, they might be blessed with a few birds shitting on their heads.

When they went back inside, the group of women with their eyes as round as the full moon descended an old, scuffed wooden staircase. It had a banister that early in the previous century was probably top of the line. Now it represented the same corrupt decay the people who ran this house had at their moral center.

With Vadim's help, Vasily cut the perimeter collars off the women, then helped them into a van with comfortable seats, heating, and tinted windows.

"Keep an eye on them," he ordered Vadim. "I'm going to do a quick recon of the house, make double sure we're clear."

"On it."

"Coming with you," Carmine stated. "The more eyes, the faster it'll go."

"You should take your men and get going. Lower the risk if anything goes wrong from here."

"Not happening. I'm in it to win it, and recon is my area of expertise."

"This wasn't part of the plan."

"You want to fight about it now?"

Shit.

He couldn't see Carmine's expression. Every inch of him, like all of them, was covered in similar unmarked black clothing and masks. But, he imagined behind those mirrored glasses, the brows above those distinctive green eyes were raised.

The Italian was right. Now wasn't the time.

"Fine. Let's just do it and get gone."

"Ten-four."

The house was old and unremarkable, unlike those grand lumber-baron structures Eureka was famous for. Even though it was big, it took less than ten minutes to clear the top rooms, checking for hidden panels in walls, and closets for crawl spaces in the ceilings and floors. Then they hit downstairs and did the same.

The last room was the kitchen.

Vasily entered the pantry and was about to call that too when something about one of the shelves struck him as wrong. All the others were packed with food items, but this particular one only had a few. Partially hidden behind a dusty can of sauerkraut was a large padlock.

The hair on his nape stood up.

Ah, shit!

Fucking padlocks.

He knew all about those. And on a second inspection, he realized the shelves weren't attached to a wall. They were attached to a door disguised as a wall.

"Gotta be a cellar of some kind," Vasily said.

"Yep, but why's it hidden?"

"Good question. Look for a key while I clear these items."

Carmine snorted, then produced a mini bolt cutter from a utility belt on his black cargo pants. "Fuck the key, use this."

After the padlock was removed, Vasily opened the door. On the inside a couple of inches from the wooden frame he found a light switch. He flipped it, revealing a poorly illuminated staircase leading down. It was dank and musty with an overlying odor of dirt and...something else.

"This isn't good." Vasily exchanged a glance with Carmine. The terrifying prickle down his spine produced by memories of dark tunnels agreed. A prickle he was all too familiar with though he hadn't experienced it in years.

The Italian shuddered. "Agreed. Gives me a bad feeling, man.

Reminds me of a horror movie where the good-looking blonde gets killed first."

"And right behind the blonde is the short Italian," Vasily grunted, turning on his flashlight.

"Good thing I'm not short. Watch out for booby traps."

Heart pounding, sweat popping at the back of his neck and making it itch, Vasily took the lead, testing each step for weak boards.

That smell.

The same one every dungeon had. Decay, human misery, and decades of death. It got thicker as they descended, to the point his lungs could barely handle the pressure.

At the bottom was a narrow, dark, claustrophobia-inducing passage with a metal door on the left. This too was padlocked. Carmine cut it, turned the knob, and pushed the door open with his boot. It gave an eerie squeak, and a wall of different stale air hit them, laced with body odor and the stench of fear.

Vasily's heart rate spiked as he swept the room with his flashlight beam.

This was not his dungeon.

Focus.

This was not Russia. Even so, his breathing sped up, his heart raced and sweat trickled down his back.

Not Russia!

"There," Carmine said, making him focus on something other than his past trauma. "A little to the left."

Shakily, he adjusted the angle of his flashlight and found the foot end of an old metal bed with a thin, striped mattress and a grayish blanket.

It moved.

Carmine added his light into the mix and a shape came into focus.

"Jesus," Vasily muttered, his gut churning with all too vivid memories. This was even worse than what he'd experienced in Moscow.

"Please," a voice croaked. "Wa...ter!"

"Who are you?" Carmine asked, stepping closer, and aiming his beam directly at the form. It cowered against the wall, shielding itself behind the blanket.

Vasily exhaled.

Fucking hell.

Although brief, he'd gotten a glimpse and didn't need to hear the name. The face, though gaunt, filthy, and with maybe a week's worth of beard, was one he unfortunately recognized.

The figure was Anthony Andretti.

* * *

"We have breaking news tonight," the redhead announced on a local news affiliate in Northern California.

"In a bizarre set of circumstances, a man with a hood over his head and in very poor physical condition was dropped at the entrance of St. Joseph's Hospital in Eureka early this morning. He identified himself as Anthony Andretti, a criminal lawyer from San Francisco, who had been reported missing by his estranged wife when he failed to return her text messages. Our reporter on the scene, Nancy Gonzales has the story."

The scene on the television changed to a striking brunette with ruby-red lips standing outside the emergency entrance to the hospital.

"Yes, Lucy and a bizarre set of circumstances is putting it mildly. After he'd been treated for dehydration and malnourishment, Anthony Andretti spoke to the local police and told them he'd been found in, as he put it, "a dungeon beneath a house of horrors", by two masked rescuers earlier this morning.

"These rescuers transported Mr. Andretti to this hospital in Eureka but left him outside the emergency room.

"*During the time he was held captive, Andretti had been beaten and received no food. He'd salvaged water from a dysfunctional toilet tank which ran out sometime before his rescue. According to the attending doctor, his condition is serious, but he should recover with no long-term consequences to his health, thanks to those masked vigilantes. ...*"

"Vigilantes?"

Kat Lewis muted the television and tossed the remote onto the bed of the motel she'd used as a makeshift base of operations—courtesy of the United States government. She slugged her whisky and then turned to glare at Vasily. "You're the Lone Ranger now? What the hell?"

"C'mon, Kat." Stretching his long legs out in front of him, Vasily crossed his ankles and sank into the cheap plaid of the motel's lumpy armchair. "The FBI got what they needed. Those girls are free so why look a career-making-gift-horse in the mouth?"

"I'm not, just...what the hell!"

Vasily smirked and took a long sip of the whiskey he'd bought in the godforsaken town of Crescent City, an hour and a half north of Eureka. It was miles better than the crap in Kat's minibar.

The day before their raid, he'd used the opportunity to visit his brother in Pelican Bay Prison. A good cover story for being in the area if he ever needed one.

"You didn't do this alone." Kat side-eyed him wearily. Who helped you?"

He steadied his gaze on her. "Seriously?"

Kat sighed in frustration. "Fine! Don't tell me. I probably don't want to know anyway, but you better hope that none of those people *or* Andretti can identify you."

"We took precautions."

"I sure as hell hope so."

"Andretti and those girls can give you the intel you need to make your case, but you're going to have to protect them. All of them, Andretti included. He's now a victim, and considering

Marisol Price tried to kill him by thirsting him to death, attorney-client privilege doesn't apply. Give them whatever they need."

"They'll get it. I'll see to it, but those girls, they said there were four men. We only found three."

"Hmm."

"What happened to the fourth man, Vasily?"

Looking Kat dead in the eye, he said. "Maybe he escaped?"

She sighed and shook her head. "You know I can't."

"Can't what?"

"Condone murder."

Of course, she couldn't. But he could. He had an old defunct butchery where Bob would reside until he gave up whatever information Vasily needed. Didn't mean Kat had to know about it.

He shrugged. "I don't know what you're talking about."

"Mmmm," Kat growled and screwed up her face. He watched her debate with herself. If only she'd do it faster. He'd stuck around to have this debriefing with Kat, but he had a woman to get home to. A woman he missed and couldn't wait to slip into bed with. He sniffed his whiskey and wondered what she was doing at that very moment.

Finally, Kat relented and waved a hand, dismissing the subject of Bob. "You know Andretti wasn't the only person they kept in that cell."

A chill ran down his spine as his eyes met Kat's.

"They found more bodies, Vas. Well, skeletons really and by the early looks of it, they're female."

Fuck. Of course, they did.

"I can't even, Kat." He shook his head and dragged his hands through his hair. "That's the FBI's problem. Mine is Marisol Price. I have to focus on her. Have you found anything?"

Kat shook her head, frustration forming little lines around her mouth. "We might be able to identify her fingerprints from the house. Once we've isolated all the others, we could get lucky if hers are in the system. My team's already on it."

"How long will that take?"

"Depends. There could be dozens, possibly hundreds of prints. I won't know until I've had a chance to properly interview the girls and get an idea of who has been through that house."

Weeks then.

"We do have a place to start, though." Vasily's lips parted in one of his rare smiles.

Kat's eyes jerked to his, surprise glinting in hers. "Where's that?"

"It seems our mysterious and ghostly Marisol Price might be Russian."

"Oh, for fuck's sake." Kat rolled her eyes. "Why does that not surprise me? Which reminds me." She put up a finger in a *give me a minute* gesture. "I have something for you."

Kat moved to her briefcase sitting on top of a desk. After rustling inside she produced a thumb drive. The one he'd given her with the video of Bob and Marisol Price herding the girls into that house.

"I couldn't email what's on this to you, because we don't need the electronic paper trail, but I managed to get it cleaned up a little better, thanks to the latest gazillion-dollar technology the agency just acquired."

She shoved it into her laptop, pulled it up, and clicked on the little triangle.

She was right.

The house was clearer and so were the faces.

"Unfortunately, it's not clear enough for facial recognition," Kat continued, "but there's something familiar about that woman. She reminds me of someone, but I just can't put my finger on it."

Jesus fucking Christ!

Vasily's heart dropped into his stomach, his blood running like shaved ice through his veins.

There was no need for facial recognition technology. Kat wouldn't know her because she showed up after Kat's cover in

Russia had been blown and she'd already left the country. The woman's hair was different. She'd worn it shorter in Russia, and here it was pulled into a long, dark ponytail. But he knew that angle of her jaw, the way it jutted forward. He knew it because he'd once spent a couple of nights in her bed. The thought that mouth had been around his cock made him want to throw up.

"The reason she reminds you of someone, Katerina, is because she takes after her father." Vasily scrubbed his hand over his jaw. "That's Oksana Federova. Federov's daughter."

Then he rose and went to the bathroom and threw up.

Chapter Twenty-Four

"Please, Nick, I need you." Anthony's voice sounded hoarse and weak over the phone, and not filled with his usual smug arrogance. Since their separation, that lack of smugness would've been enough to make her run to his side. Well, maybe not run—perhaps a slow walk at best—and only for the sake of their son.

She leaned her hip against the window and stared down at the city, feeling disconnected from the world. A light fog swirled, allowing her occasional glimpses of the other buildings. Vasily's apartment was beautiful, luxurious even, and she had every material thing she wanted at her fingertips, but it was lonely. She hadn't seen him in four days, hadn't even heard from him for that matter. Not even a text.

Those four days may as well have been four years. Not even Marley, who'd wrapped himself around her head at night and purred her to sleep had helped. Or, sad to say, Luca and the constant bodyguards, which seemed to have doubled since the day before.

"I want to see you and my son." Anthony adopted that *I feel so sorry for myself* tone when he wasn't getting his way. It drove her nuts.

"There are armed guards outside my door. They won't let anyone in who isn't staff or family."

Armed guards?

Nicky huffed and rolled her eyes. "Aren't you being a little dramatic? They're probably just the hospital's security or local cops."

"They're not. These dudes are heavy-duty and serious. They check the ID of everyone entering. And the Feds didn't put them there either."

"Well, who else could it be?"

"I asked the Special Agent in charge when she interviewed me. I have an anonymous benefactor."

The FBI agent, Kat Lewis, had been the one to notify Nicky that Anthony had been found. After that, there had been a series of phone discussions with his doctor and the hospital administration seeking his health insurance information. Anthony had never changed his emergency contact and since she was still legally married to the man, she became it.

But an 'anonymous benefactor?'

Probably one of Anthony's well-connected clients who still needed him to represent them in their criminal trial.

Whatever.

She didn't have space in her head to consider it any longer.

"In that case, since there are armed guards outside your door, I'm definitely not bringing Luca to visit you. I'm not exposing our son to any more danger." *Or guns.* "You'll be back in the Bay Area in a few days anyway."

And just because she couldn't silence her inner bitch, she had to ask. Surely, he didn't expect her to believe there was no one else who could visit him? "Why aren't you asking your latest to pop by?"

There was a long pause, and she could hear Anthony's deep,

uneven breathing. Had he fallen asleep? His doctor had said he'd been sedated, so perhaps that was it.

"Anthony?"

He made a strange noise, sort of a combination of a snort and a sob. Against her will, her chest twinged with sympathy, but not enough to make her want to forgive him just yet. Or fly to Eureka.

"She's the one who did this to me," Anthony said.

"Excuse me?" Nicky blinked in surprise.

"The woman's a monster. But I didn't know when I took her on as a client."

"Good grief, Anthony." Nicky placed her palm on her forehead and blew out a long breath. "You sure know how to pick them."

"I was...conned into taking her on, Nick."

Conned? Maybe as a client. But as a lover?

"Conned how?" At gunpoint? By her phenomenal beauty or her skills in bed? Though, honestly, she doubted a woman's skills in bed had anything to do with his cheating. More that it was just Anthony's nature to cheat.

"Marisol needed one of her associates out on bail. She persuaded me to put up the bail money and I managed to get him out, but once I realized what her real business was and who she was connected to, I tried to sever her as a client. I tried to get our money back, but things sort of spiraled out of control."

Marisol?

Something tickled at the edges of her memory banks. She'd heard that name before. The more she turned it around in her head, a sensation that fluttered across her skin, like an unpleasant cold breeze sneaking through a drafty door.

But it also shook something loose, and dots started connecting. Anthony was imprisoned in Northern California. According to Detective Fetzer, her would-be rapist also came from Northern California.

And where had Vasily gone for business?

Northern California!

She knew this because she'd overheard him giving instructions in Russian to Yev. They almost always spoke English unless he didn't want her to understand. Which further solidified that lingering feeling his business in the northern part of the state had something to do with her.

That conversation may have been in Russian, but she had understood one thing. He had specifically said Eureka. Were all these pieces of information somehow linked? The goosebumps on her skin tightened.

"Who's she connected to, Anthony?"

"Dangerous people, Nick. Trust me, you don't want to know about them."

Nicky bit back a frustrated growl as she tapped her phone on her head. Why did everyone think it was necessary to keep things from her? This was her life, dammit. And it was *her* body that had been violated by a fucking hunting knife.

James Falk's pale face came into her head as he lay dying in her closet, accompanied by his last lisped words.

Mathol's gonna kill you.

She hadn't registered them at the time, thinking Falk's oxygen-starved brain had misfired, made his tongue thick and tied. But could he have meant...?

Fuck. What had her lawyer said?

"Are these people you're talking about as dangerous as human traffickers?"

Anthony's intake of air was loud. The heaviness of it reached through her cell phone, causing her to almost drop her device. Somehow, she kept it glued to her ear even as his non-answer solidified her suspicion. But she had to be sure.

"And does the name James Falk mean anything to you?" she asked, her voice trembling.

"Falk. Jesus," he rasped. "How do you know that name?"

287

Oh, good God, this couldn't be happening. It was all connected.

"What happened, Nick?" Anthony's tone was now urgent, bordering on panic. "Tell me. Did he hurt you?"

Nicky felt her blood pressure drop. White spots formed behind her eyes and her world started to spin, but she managed to sit on the edge of her bed when her legs went weak. Setting her head between her knees, she forced the blood into her brain.

"Nick, answer me." Anthony's voice penetrated through the rapid drumming her heart made in her head. "How do you know that name?"

"He tried to rape me," she croaked out.

"Ah, fucking hell." His heavy breathing filled the cellular space between them. "That bitch. That fucking bitch!" His voice was trembling as much as hers. "Are you okay?"

"I'm alive."

"That's not what I'm asking, Nick."

"He didn't succeed, but, Anthony, James Falk's last words to me were 'Marisol's gonna kill me.' What if he meant it as a warning?"

"It *was* a warning, Nick. Those people are dangerous, and none more so than Marisol. I'm checking out of this hospital today. You can't be alone."

"You don't need to do that."

"Fuck that shit. I'm checking out."

"Anthony, no!"

"Why not?"

"Because I'm safe where I am, and I'm not alone. That's all you need to know."

"Nick—"

"But what *I* need to know, is who this Marisol bitch is. And you're going to tell me everything you know, or God help me, Anthony, I will come up there and personally let an air bubble into your IV."

Chapter Twenty-Five

Plausible deniability.

Nicky wrapped her arms around her waist and rocked on the edge of her bed, trying to calm her breathing.

Was that why Vasily kept her in the dark about his *business trip*? It was the only explanation that satisfied her in any way.

Knowing how his world worked, she'd long ago accepted things got done in ways that skirted the edges of law enforcement. She was still processing, trying to stitch the pieces together when she heard Vasily's deep voice seeping through her bedroom door.

He was home.

She stopped rocking and focused on its warm timbre, allowing it to calm her as a schoolgirl buzz of excitement washed through her veins.

Vasily was speaking in Russian to Sasha, and despite her irritation at him keeping her out of the loop, her relief and happiness that he was home safe were greater.

She waited until she heard the voices quiet, and after a quick check in her mirror, went to find him. He sat on the black couch in his bedroom, elbows resting on his sculpted thighs, hands hanging loose between them. The floor seemed to fascinate him, but when he heard her footsteps, he looked up.

His mere presence strengthened the longing she'd fostered for the last four days. His smell, his deep voice, and the way he looked at her. Hungry. As if he could never get his fill. That was the look she craved and lived for. It stoked something inside her—something she realized had been dead for a long time when she was with Anthony. That wasn't to say Anthony hadn't looked at her the same way...in the beginning. The reaction it evoked, however, had never been equal.

How had she existed without Vasily for ten years? She'd been a mere shell of herself, and how could she choose to exist without him now? Given the choice between another child or him, she'd choose him, if he wanted her.

Studying him, she noticed the tension lines corrugating his forehead highlighting the dark pewter storm brewing in his eyes. He looked exhausted...and worried.

She paused at the entrance to his room and offered a small smile, wondering if she should give him his space. "You're back."

His eyes sparked, drinking in the length of her bare legs, like a parched flower after a desert monsoon.

"Hmm."

The lines in his skin smoothed as his face relaxed. The school-girl buzz of excitement changed to an electric jolt and zapped through her system. Still, she hesitated inside the threshold, unsure. Arching an eyebrow, she asked, "You want to be alone?"

Giving a single shake of his head, he curled a finger and beckoned her closer.

Her chest swelled with relief, and warmth that grew with each step. Stopping a foot away from him, she asked, "How was your trip?"

"I accomplished what I needed." He straightened in his seat, looking up at her. He was so tall, that even sitting, he didn't have to crane his neck very far. Then he winced, and grimaced, rolling first one shoulder, then the other as if the muscles in that area were giving him trouble.

"I'm sensing a but," she murmured.

He gave a slow, tired blink and then rubbed his shoulder. "It was productive and... informative."

"Informative, hm?" Even weary and intense, the man did things to her. The way his muscles bunched as he manipulated his shoulders beneath that gray sweater. Nicky licked her lips and moved closer. "I don't suppose you want to share the details with me?"

Perhaps she could lessen the burden that seemed to weigh his shoulders down. The one she was sure he carried for her.

"Business, Dom." He placed his hands on her hips. "You know I can't speak about it."

"Not even a little bit, especially now that Anthony has been found?"

There was the faintest of questions in his eyes. Perhaps if she didn't know him like she did, or if she wasn't as close in proximity as she was, she might not have noticed it. But the slight silver shimmer told her that her suspicions were correct.

If her intuition had smoldered before, now she could no longer dismiss it.

"It was you, wasn't it?" She placed her hands on his shoulders and felt the tight knots in the muscles as her gaze raked his face for any outward sign of confirmation. At her scrutiny, the tension lines in his face deepened, but he couldn't block the knowledge from showing. It was as if she'd unmasked him, stripped him of the one defense he was always so good at. His ability to hide his thoughts and feelings.

It made her ache for him even more, and she touched the side of his face, then ran her fingers through his thick hair, gently scraping her nails along his scalp.

"I talked to Anthony today. He told me about a woman named

Marisol Price, and how she conned him and set Falk on me. Did you know about her?"

The faint lines fanning from his eyes twitched and it was all the confirmation she needed.

"Just figured that out recently. I'm still looking for her."

"Thank you," she whispered, nodding. "For everything you've done for me, and for whatever you did to get Anthony out of that situation."

"Dom—"

"Shh." She put a finger to his lips. "I don't need to know the details. Not yet, if ever. And Anthony doesn't suspect it was you, and he'll never hear it from me. I just wish you'd shared more with me."

He closed his eyes for several long beats and during this time he swallowed. When they opened again, the storm in his gaze had calmed and was replaced with a softness and a measure of awe. A slight upward tilt of his mouth happened, making her lips tingle with the need to kiss him.

"You're the only person who's ever been able to see through my wall. Why is that?"

"Maybe it's the awesome power of my vagina?"

He chuckled. She was struck by how beautiful he was when he laughed. How the indentations in his cheeks creased, and how he brightened with an inner light. All of which made her heart clench, and ache pleasantly. She made a vow on the spot to always endeavor to make him laugh.

Then he winced again.

"Want me to help with that?" she asked softly, removing the hand from the side of his face and placing it on the rigid cords in his shoulders. She squeezed. He sighed and she began to knead, using the rolling technique Soren had taught her.

A tired groan left him, and he dropped his head forward, resting it against her chest. She continued for a few moments, before kicking off her sandals. Pushing him 'til he rested on the backrest of the couch, she settled on her knees, one on each side of his thighs.

"Mm, that feels good." He breathed out a long breath of air, relaxing. "Don't stop."

His words licked her like a cat lapping up cream. "I have no intention of stopping," she murmured near his ear. "It's the least I can do for what you've done for me." Slowly, the tension drained from his shoulders, and she moved to his neck and scalp as his palms caressed a slow, warm path up her legs until they clasped her buttocks.

Another groan escaped him, but this time it resonated with the very core of her womanhood.

"Luca around?" His voice was husky and hot against her skin.

"He's with my dad."

Without warning, he pulled her closer until their groins connected. "Give me your mouth," he growled.

She didn't hesitate, and there was nothing tired in his kiss. It was hungry and demanding. His tongue took command, seeking her surrender, which she gave willingly. He kissed her like she was oxygen, and his lungs were starved. It was amazing, thrilling, and hot. His lips moved to her neck as his hands plunged under her panties, engulfing her ass cheeks, and yanking her even closer.

"You're so hard," she panted as his cock, a solid shaft of granite strained through his pants. It rubbed her most sensitive parts just right.

"Been hard since the moment you laid your hands on me," he answered, his voice carrying the rough edge of lust. "I love that you wear dresses." He rocked her, stimulating her just enough it encouraged that urge between her legs that was now bordering on fire. "And I love that you're not wearing a bra. Undo your buttons for me."

Breathing hard, pleasure surging through her, she undid enough of her dress that it fell off one shoulder, exposing a breast. He took her nipple between his teeth, alternating between nibbling and sucking, coaxing little whimpers from her. Panting, she tried to increase the speed of her hips, urging him on but he controlled the pace. She was so close. Just a little more pressure, just a little more speed and she'd get there.

Releasing her pebbled nipple, he pulled away and demanded, "Look at me."

"Vasily," she gasped. "I'm so close, I need this."

"*Look* at me." When their gaze met, his was dark and burning. "I love your eyes when you're about to come. Keep looking at me. I want to watch you."

She was panting, but she nodded, unable to think of anything better than him helping her come. Nor could she help to note all the times he used the word *love*.

He relinquished control, letting her dictate the speed and pressure, and within moments it built, and then her body tightened.

"Oh my God, oh *fuck*," she cried out in a sob as her climax rushed through her in waves, setting every nerve tingling and every cell on fire.

He watched her go through it, that hard jaw clenched, yet with a wonder in his eyes that burned through her and stamped itself into her memory. It was something so profoundly there, so deeply seated, so... *shattering*, she wondered how she managed to stay whole.

Still twitching and buzzing with her orgasm, she shifted, reached between her legs, and pulled the zipper of his jeans, releasing his cock from his briefs. It sprang free, hot, and hard.

Gripping him, she pushed her hand slowly down his shaft. A shudder shook his body, and he gritted his teeth.

"You're so fucking gorgeous, I want to fuck you until I break you," he growled, strangely echoing her earlier thoughts. "Until you come apart, all your pieces unraveling. Just so I can watch you come back together again. It's the most exquisite thing I've ever seen. And it only happens with you."

His words stunned her.

They were so violently beautiful, so wrecking, she absorbed them, making them a part of her.

He undid the rest of her buttons and then pushed her dress off, letting it pool on the floor. His eyes roamed an indulgent path from her breasts to her panties. Exhaling a long, slow breath he began to kiss and taste her, along the sides of her breasts to the hollows in her shoulders and neck, building a new inferno inside her. She squirmed in his lap while he took his time, savoring her, nibbling at her jaw, licking the corner of her lips. Possessing her mouth again with the same passion, he kissed her until they were panting.

He rolled her from his lap onto the couch and pulled her panties down. From somewhere, he'd produced a condom and within moments of rolling it on himself, he guided himself to her entrance.

When he entered her, it was slow, almost reverently, his gaze burning as he waited for her to absorb him. Then he moved, purposefully, and maddeningly. Punctuating each thrust with kisses below her ear, her neck, and her shoulder. Each teasing, torturing stroke rubbed that sensitive spot inside her exactly right and her pleasure built again.

Just as it was about to overtake her, the words tumbled from her mouth before she could stop them. "God, I love you so much."

Vasily stilled, suspended on his arms above her mid-stroke. Staring down at her, a terrible awe clouded his eyes.

Oh no.

What had she done?

She'd ruined it, this wonderful, tender moment. While he stared down at her she clung to his hips in case he left her.

"Vas," she implored, wishing she could go back a few seconds in time. "I'm sorry. I shouldn't have said that."

That awe in his gaze sparked into something fierce.

"Yes," he ground out. "You should've. I've waited ten years to hear you say that."

Silent tears poured from her eyes and ran down her cheeks.

"You are beautiful," he whispered, his voice ragged. "So fucking beautiful, I think you've just broken me."

Then he unleashed himself, his rhythm speeding up and each thrust got deeper and harder. Like a slow-burning ignition cord finally reaching its point of combustion, her orgasm reignited as he pounded her into the couch.

With a low, guttural noise that vibrated through her body he tensed, gave several hard thrusts and a moment later he climaxed, his breath stuttering.

When he dropped his head to her shoulder and buried his face in her hair, the tide of raw, unfettered emotion welled up inside her. As his harsh breaths seared her tender skin, more tears rolled down her cheeks.

Still draped around her, Vasily moved a hand to her throat, then slid it up, cupping her jaw. The other, he skated underneath her and pulled her close, turning her face towards his. He touched her tears away with the tip of his tongue, then kissed her again, sucking tenderly on her top lip. It was a little salty, yet sweet and full of heartbreaking, beautiful emotion.

When it was over, their lips separated, but their noses remained connected. He gazed at her with so much of something in those darkened eyes. Something she'd just put a name to, but swallowed the disappointment that he hadn't said it in return.

Would he ever?

"In the interest of sharing, I need to tell you something," he said, pulling a fraction away. "It's about a woman in Moscow."

Her lungs froze.

God, she didn't want to hear about this!

"Vas, you don't need to."

In fact, please don't.

"Hear me out," he said gently. "It's not what you think." He rolled off her, shifted into a sitting position and removed the condom, tied a knot in it, then stuck it in his pocket. After he tucked himself away, he adjusted his jeans appropriately back on his hips but left his fly open.

If she was going to hear about another woman, she was going to do it covered. Leaning over him, she snagged her dress and panties off the floor. Vasily took her underwear, but instead of hooking them over her feet, he wrapped them around his fist.

"Her name is Oksana," he said with a slight twist of his lip as if the syllables left a sour taste in his mouth. "She was the boss's daughter and went to school in the U.K., then after that spent most of her time in Europe and the U.S., so I never met her until later after I'd weaseled my way into Federov's inner circle."

While he spoke, his face had hardened, but his gaze seemed distant and focused on a big abstract painting in front of him.

"By doing what he asked of me, those...kills, I proved my loyalty. But I never forgot or forgave him for imprisoning me and turning me into something I didn't want to be. Outwardly, I appeared cold, but resentment burned inside me, and I knew a time would come that I'd act on it." Vasily brought her panties to his nose and inhaled like he was anchoring himself—to the present —and her.

"The last year I was there, Federov threw a party. It was in honor of Oksana finally returning home. Everyone who was anyone was there. Politicians, and oligarchs with their single sons. He'd hoped to marry her off to one of them. But for some reason, Oksana ignored them all and decided she wanted me that weekend. She was attractive enough, and I'd consumed enough alcohol, so I indulged." Vasily closed his eyes and pulled in air through his nose. "It was a stupid move. Mostly I spent that weekend with her to get under Federov's skin."

Nicky picked at a button on her dress. "Did you...care about her?"

He gave her a brief, sideways glance. "You don't need to care about someone to fuck them."

No, she didn't suppose it was a requirement, and words

couldn't describe the level of relief that surged through her. She understood she was being selfish. It was none of her business what he did before he came home, and he was a man. Men did what men do when women present themselves to them, but the thought of him harboring feelings for someone else hadn't stopped the twisted tendrils of jealousy from spiraling through her.

"How long did it last?" she asked, hating how fragile her voice sounded, and curled her fingers into the fabric of her dress like she needed her own anchor to steady herself.

Vasily gave up his spot on the wall and turned his head to make a point of looking her in the eye. "Just that weekend. For me, anyway."

She wanted to ask why, but at the same time didn't want to hear the lurid details of his sexual encounter with a mob princess.

"The woman was entitled, and cruel. I saw her throw a bottle of vodka at a servant when she dared to enter the room without knocking. It cut her head open and after that, I was done. But Oksana wasn't. I tried blowing her off, but that backfired. She began to obsess and caused a scene in front of her father." He sighed and dropped his head back to rest it on the backrest. "Things with Federov had become fragile enough but they took a nosedive from there. I had earned my place, and I had the respect of the other men. Some of them considered me a leader and there were...rumblings within the ranks. Federov began to feel threatened. Oksana's constant poisoning didn't help, and I realized that the guarantees he'd given that my life was no longer in danger didn't apply anymore."

Hell hath no fury.

Nicky sighed and picked at her thumbnail. She'd once been close to becoming that woman but for such different reasons.

"Then there were a couple of incidents."

Nicky's hand stilled and her eyes widened.

Incidents?

"The brakes on my car failed. Somebody had messed with

them, but when that didn't kill me, there was an explosion in my apartment. Supposedly my housekeeper had left the stove gas on and when she lit a cigarette, it blew her to hell and back. Thing was, she didn't smoke. Even if she had, she wouldn't have smoked inside because I didn't allow it." He paused again, his throat bobbing. "That one hurt. She was a good woman with six grandkids."

Suddenly the air felt oppressive. Nicky's chest rose and fell in a series of heavy breaths. How close she'd come to losing him forever. How close they'd come to never reuniting, even if at the time all that happened, she hadn't even known he *was* still alive. The thought was frightening as hell.

"Can I ask you something?" she asked after a long moment of her heart pounding against her ribs.

"Hmm."

"I guess I don't understand why you hadn't left Russia before that point?" she asked. "You said you'd earned your freedom, so why did you stay?"

Vasily inhaled, then let it out. "Freedom is relative, Dominique. And one doesn't just *leave* the Bratva. Generally, there is only one way out, and that's in a coffin."

He brought a knee up and shifted on the couch to fully face her. Then took her left hand in his, massaging her ring finger. "Anyway," he said softly. "I had no pressing reason to come back."

Her jaw went slack, then she searched his face looking for something to contradict what he'd just implied. But it was there, in the stormy gray of his eyes.

He didn't come back because she was married.

The knowledge both made her belly twist and flutter and crushed her in equal measures. Her throat tightened as she struggled to contain her emotions.

"And there was something else." He lowered his gaze to their hands and his fingers entangled with hers. "Early on, Federov put measures in place that ensured I would do what he wanted. He had leverage."

"Of you killing people?"

He didn't answer, just sat silent for several seconds. "After the second attempt on my life, I knew my time was up. I didn't know for sure who was behind the threats, Oksana or Federov, but it didn't matter. And as it happens, that's when Dean got arrested. That's when I decided to leave. But before I did, I had to ensure that leverage was nullified."

Nicky couldn't even begin to name all the emotions swirling inside her. They jumbled together in a messy recipe of foreboding, relief, horror, and countless others. Her lungs felt stifled as she waited for him to continue.

"Federov made his money with drugs and weapons. The short version is I had some knowledge of his distribution routes and who the players were. I tipped off a friend in the FBI and she contacted Interpol. There was a sting. Federov and a few of his soldiers were arrested. Then his assets were seized, and his international bank accounts were frozen. Last I heard, his ass got shanked in a German prison."

"So, he's dead?"

Vasily nodded.

For the first time that evening since her phone call with Anthony, she felt there was room for hope. That her situation would improve. That the threat that hung over them would dissipate and they could go back to their normal lives. "And the leverage, is it gone too?"

He shook his head, then rolled it to face her. "To the contrary. That leverage has only increased."

What?

Her brow wrinkled. "I don't understand."

"Oksana."

The way he dragged that woman's name from his mouth obliterated the moment of hope she'd experienced, making her chest feel as if it was collapsing inward. Nor did she have to see the fear in his eyes to know it wasn't fear for himself.

It was fear for her.

"Oh, my God." Her fingers in his went taught. "She's here, isn't she?"

He nodded. "That woman you mentioned, Marisol?" She and Oksana are the same person, and she's bent on destroying me, however that may happen. I'm worried she's coming for you."

Chapter Twenty-Six

V asily was not a patient man. He didn't have to be, given his position of power, and neither was he one who tolerated tardiness in the best of times.

These were not the best of times.

It was just after lunch the following afternoon. Vasily nursed a whiskey watching Steph Curry score a three-pointer while he waited at Zander's bar—one of two things that kept his irritation in check. The other was the man he was meeting was Nicky's father.

He wanted this to go well, which was why he chose neutral territory. It didn't require a high IQ to suspect Marcello wouldn't set foot at his restaurant as it was hard enough getting him past the lobby of his apartment. It also didn't require a high IQ to assume Marcello would try to control the situation by showing up late.

His big toe tapped inside his leather boot when he finally caught sight of the man entering from the street through the main door. A brief glimpse of weak sunlight backlit him, but not enough to hide his face.

The scowl he wore indicated Marcello's level of pissiness was way up in the high digits, but that was his usual lately.

It was hurting Nicky.

"This better be good, Melnikov," the ornery old fuck grumbled as he stepped up to the stool next to Vasily. After slinging his leather motorcycle jacket over the back, Mario took a seat. "I don't like being summoned, least of all by you."

Vasily took another sip of his drink, allowing Marcello a moment to stew in his self-righteousness, then dipped his chin at Barney to pour whatever he wanted.

The silver-haired gent looked at Nicky's dad, his fists resting on the bar, waiting.

"Yo," Marcello said, offering a fist bump to Barney. "Long time no see. I'll have a beer."

Barney produced a sideways grin that lifted his graying goatee, then said, "Coming up."

Marcello traded pleasantries with Barney while he pulled the lever on an amber ale, then removed the excess foam. He placed it in front of Marcello on a coaster stamped with the bar's motorcycle wheel logo.

"I'll give you two gentlemen some privacy," Barney said, then moved to the furthest point away and continued to clean the shelves containing the expensive booze. Besides them, there were only two others in Chuck's, far enough away that lack of privacy wouldn't be an issue. Steppenwolf's *Born to Be Wild* added extra insurance so that no one would hear their conversation.

Nicky's dad took a tug on his beer. He wiped his mouth of the excess foam that got trapped in his mustache with the back of his hand, and asked, "So what's so damn urgent?"

The need to knock some sense into you, you stubborn old fart.

But Vasily didn't share that thought as he wasn't here to fight with the man.

"When was the last time you had an actual conversation with your daughter?"

"Really?" Mario smirked. "My relationship with her is why you called me here? It's none of your business."

Vasily exercised his jaw for several beats while he stared at him. "I suggest you make it my business, Marcello. Her happiness is my goal, and right now, her only parent is being an ass because he doesn't like that we might want to be together. It's making her miserable."

Mario's thick brows rose then they dropped again when he narrowed his gaze. "I oughta knock your block off for calling me an ass."

"But you won't, and except for the fact you got a bad heart, I would knock yours off. But that's not why I asked you here."

"Then stop wasting my time and get to the point."

"I'm here to appeal to your better angels."

Mario scoffed and shook his head.

"I ain't got no angels on my side. That was made clear when I went to prison for nine years for something I didn't do."

"And that's one of the reasons I called you here," Vasily said. The letter he had in his back pocket burned like a hot poker on his ass. "Information has come to light that is not good. Information that I need you to consider real hard on how you are going to handle it moving forward."

"What information?"

"It has to do with the safety of your family."

"I've already accepted your goddamn babysitter when I spend time with my grandson. What else do you want?"

Patience, Melnikov, he told himself. His knuckles turned white, and for a moment, the safety of the glass he held between his fingers was threatened. He made a conscious decision to relax them.

"This is not about what I want," he said. "Though I'm asking you to put that stubborn Italian pride aside for one minute. I wouldn't be here if it wasn't a matter of life and death. *Your* life and death."

That got the man's attention.

"Mine?"

"In case you haven't figured this out already, I have enemies that are using Nicky to draw me into the open. It's the reason she was attacked in the first place."

"And that," Mario stabbed a finger into the bar, "is *one* of the reasons I don't want you near her."

Vasily had to concede the point. He'd considered for half a second putting distance between himself and Nicky. But the reality was, he was selfish. He wanted her close, in his bed, where it was much easier to protect her.

"That aside, the threat to Nicky extends to you too, and she would feel a whole lot better if you weren't in danger and close by. She also needs you, by the way. Considering all the time you've lost, I'm proposing you stay at my penthouse until this is over."

Genuine puzzlement colored Mario's face as the man's interest was finally piqued.

"And if I don't?"

"I'd think you'd want to do it to put your daughter's mind at peace, but if that's not enough, then let me sweeten the deal. You do what I ask, you get this."

Vasily reached behind him and pulled the folded piece of paper from his pants pocket. "This is a copy." He slid it along the bar. "My lawyer has the original."

"What's this?"

"Won't know until you open it."

Marcello twisted in his seat, then fumbled in his inside jacket pocket, snagging a pair of gold wire-rimmed readers. He perched them on the end of his nose.

Vasily took a small amount of satisfaction as shock registered, then disbelief and confusion in equal measures played over Marcello's face. The emotions went through a second cycle until finally, Marcello turned to look at him, his throat bobbing. The letter in his hands shook. "If this is a joke, you're a sick son of a bitch."

"No joke. My lawyer is in the process of taking all the necessary steps with the court to have your conviction vacated."

Marcello continued to stare at him over the top of his glasses, his deep brown eyes wide with shock. "You'd do this?"

Vasily shrugged. "It's the right thing. Dean is doing life anyway. I have the D.A.'s assurance in writing that if he pleads guilty to the murder of your partner, Pavel, saving the State the cost of a trial, the death penalty stays off the table."

"How the fuck did you convince him to do that?"

"The D.A. or my brother?"

"Either...both."

Vasily would've enjoyed taking credit, but he didn't. "His confession can't make up for the years you spent in prison, I know that." He shifted on his barstool to face Marcello fully. "But I was hoping it could be a start to fix what he did to you."

Marcello stared at the piece of paper for a long time before placing it on the polished wooden slab.

"Nine years, Melnikov." His voice was thick with emotion. "Nine. Fucking. Years I lost with my daughter. Missed my grandson's birth, and his infant years. Missed walking Nicky down the aisle. Missed being there for her when she left Anthony. My business gone, my land gone and in case you didn't fucking get it, *nine fucking years* of my life gone." Mario Marcello swiped a thumb and finger across his eyes, erasing the trace of tears that had seeped out. "How does anyone make up for that?"

Vasily sucked in a slow breath. He hadn't expected this to come easy. He still bore a grudge against Federov and now Oksana for the life that had been stolen from him, so he got it.

"I understand."

"Do you?" Mario's eyes narrowed as he glared at him.

"This is going to sound self-serving, and I don't expect you to believe me, but it's the truth and it's all I can offer. I was never on board with the plan to take your business. My brother had approached Pavel, your partner, and made him an offer to sell. He agreed."

Mario stared at him. "You're lying. Pavel would never have agreed to something like that without talking to me first."

Vasily glanced around. The couple on the far side were absorbed in their own thing, holding hands across the table and staring into each other's eyes. Barney had moved to the back, and the music had changed to John Fogerty crooning *I Put A Spell On You.*

"Pavel had debts. He owed us money and had no way of paying."

"What the fuck you're talking about?" The disbelief in Marcello's voice curled his nostrils. "What kind of debts?"

"Gambling."

A flicker of something moved through Mario's eyes and Vasily knew he'd hit a memory. The old man ran a hand over his still-thick hair.

"Damn. I knew he played cards, but are you telling me Pavel played at *your* underground poker rooms?"

"He dropped thousands, then took out loans using his half of the equity on the scrapyard as collateral. Then dropped thousands more."

Mario slumped against the bar, his expression contorted from the information Vasily had just shared.

"Dean planned to take his share of the business in exchange for nullifying his debts. Problem was, part ownership wasn't enough for my uncle. Pavel was supposed to convince you to sell. He and Leonid had a deal. Then Pavel changed his mind and somehow came up with the money. You know what happens in our world when deals are shat on. I was already in Moscow and didn't know of the retribution Leonid and Dean cooked up. If I had been here, I would've stopped it."

"Why should I believe you?"

"Because I didn't want a war! I wanted to rebuild into something better than what my father created. Other properties would've done just as well."

"Then why the fuck didn't they?" Marcello's tone suggested his question was only half rhetorical, but he'd give the man all he knew anyway.

"You were fencing stolen car parts for the Cadora Family. Leonid had a beef with them, and he wanted to edge into the black-market car parts business. He figured if he took profits and territory away from the Italians, he would kill two birds. It was never personal towards you."

"Jesus." Mario took a long slug of his beer, then placed the glass down carefully. "Collateral damage. Sucks when you're it."

Vasily could relate to that more than the man could fathom. "My point of all this is, I'm willing to make amends."

"That's fucking great, Melnikov, but what exactly does making amends mean?"

"That." He pointed to Dean's confession. "To begin with. And I will fund whatever you need to start a new junkyard if that's what you want."

"How about giving my nine years back?"

"If I could, I would." And he wasn't lying. He'd shift continents to make things right. "I don't want you as an enemy, and I'm willing to do my part in fixing that. For Nicky's sake."

"Yeah, about that," Mario growled, staring at him, his jaw working and his lips pressed in a thin line. "Why her? You're a good-looking son of a bitch, with money, and power. You can have your pick, but you had to sniff around her like a stray mutt."

Vasily chose to ignore Marcello's disrespect. The man loved his daughter, and he couldn't fault him for that.

"Because I love her," he answered simply. "I always have."

Marcello's eye twitched as he continued to stare at him. "Then answer me this, Melnikov. And be truthful or despite this" —he waved Dean's confession in the air— "there's no point to you and

I ever getting along. Why break her heart the way you did? Do you have any idea what that did to her?"

Yeah, he did. Though Nicky wasn't responsible for it, his heart had been broken too. An invisible band tightened around his chest. He'd been honest with her the night before, but there was one small question she'd asked that remained unanswered. It weighed heavily yet, it was a burden he was happy to carry.

"I had no choice," he answered, rubbing the space over his heart to ease the sensation.

Marcello scoffed. "There are always choices for men like you. Some of them shitty, I'll give you that, but they're choices none-theless."

Right.

He didn't want to do this with Nicky's father, but if he wanted any chance of having any kind of a normal relationship with him, he had to give him something.

"I was betrayed too."

That ant-like sensation he experienced each time he thought or spoke of that dank hole prickled down his spine. He proceeded to give Marcello the CliffsNotes version of his imprisonment and life under Federov but left out the choice he was forced to make. That would surely be a bridge too far for the man to take.

When he was done, Marcello leaned forward and rested his weight on his elbows. His prison-weary brown eyes had that look as if he'd just dropped a live hand grenade on his ass. But for once, it didn't feel hostile.

"Jesus," Mario murmured, scrubbing a hand over his stubble. "I wasn't expecting that. Fuck my daughter's taste in men."

"Never professed to be a prince, Marcello. But, I'm sure there's shit you had to do in prison you're not proud of either because such is the life we live."

Faced with that reality, Marcello grimaced, confirming Vasily had hit on some unknown truth.

"You hurt my daughter again, and given the odds she hasn't

already done it, I'll shank you in your sleep. You have my word on that."

Their eyes met and Vasily smirked. "Only way that happens is if you move your ornery ass into my apartment."

Marcello held out his hand. "Then I guess we have a deal."

Chapter Twenty-Seven

ne month later

"Morning, Beautiful." Vasily's sleep-deepened voice penetrated the haze of a dream almost forgotten. Something about her walking across the street with a pink cockatoo on her head. It had been singing *Baby Shark Doo Doo Doo Doo Doo Doo*. Why that song, she couldn't fathom as she hadn't heard it a while. After the thirty thousandth time Luca had listened to it, she'd banned it from their household.

Vasily brushed the hair off her face, then tucked it gently behind her ear. The dream faded as his finger traced a slow line down her neck, across her collarbone to her nipple.

"You awake?"

"Mm," she murmured, wriggling a little as his nail raised goosebumps on her skin. She lifted one heavy eyelid, then the other, and tried to focus on the beautiful man in front of her. "If you want me to be."

The sky was streaked with orange and red, and usually by now in the pre-Vasily days, she'd be up and getting Luca ready for school. Though lately, she'd been spoiled and didn't have to. Vasily paid for a temporary tutor who wouldn't arrive until 10 a.m. to give Luca the schooling he'd otherwise be missing. That didn't mean there wasn't still a small amount of guilt involved. What Luca lacked in socialization and learning in an environment with other children his age was more than made up for in the diminished worry her son wouldn't be kidnapped. There was also the occasional play date with his friend Charlie from Tiny Titans while his mother went through chemo.

Her eyelids, in the meantime, had gotten used to not opening at the first crack of the sun. It was a luxury she was enjoying.

Vasily lay on his side facing her. An arm was tucked beneath his head on the pillow, his hair mussed and sticking up in places. It made him look younger...and even sexier if that was possible. A lazy, slightly amused smile curved his mouth as a finger circled her nipple.

It apparently didn't mind waking up. In fact, *it* was getting excited.

"Seems your brain might not want to be, but this"—he tugged on the hardened bud— "is definitely awake."

A jolt of pleasure along with a small jolt of pain shot straight to her core, stirring up fires that only a few hours ago he'd sated. Repeatedly.

She closed her eyes and marveled at her inner insatiable nympho. So much sex in such a little time. How could a girl get so lucky?

She hesitated to count, but very few surfaces in his apartment or his office had escaped their righteous carnality in the last month.

Orgasmapalooza!

Vasily moved closer, then pleasured her nipple with his tongue as the tips of his fingers moved slowly down her belly making her quiver inside. They roamed over the roundness of her ass, then behind her thigh to her knee.

"Lift your knee," he murmured, then he continued up between her legs, his rough palm, like the finest of sandpapers, sent amazing sensations throughout her body. When he got to her center, he groaned in appreciation at the fact she was already wet.

"I guess another part of you is awake too. But I don't know, perhaps I should let you go back to sleep."

Her eyes sprang open. "What?"

Vasily shrugged, his expression making the dimple in that Russian chin deepen. She'd become very familiar with the texture of his morning stubble and how it felt against her skin in sensitive places. "I need to work out with Yev, anyway."

"Don't even think about leaving me now!"

A half chuckle rumbled from his chest and wrapped her in its warm deliciousness. Then he sucked air in between his teeth. "There's that enthusiasm I love so much."

"Mm, well." She produced her own lazy smile. "There's a sexy man in my bed, and he's doing all kinds of bad-boy gangsta things to me. What's not to get enthused about?"

Vasily's eyes turned dark at the compliment, and before she could think or even protest, he rolled her onto her back pinning her arms above her head. Positioning himself between her legs, he rested his weight on his elbows. In a thick Russian accent, he asked, "Who is sexy man? He touch my woman, I *rrrip* toenails out."

Nicky burst into giggles as he lowered his face to her neck. God, she loved this playful side of him.

His deep voice and hot breath sent shivers cascading down her spine and changed her giggles into mewls of pleasure. His solid body on hers felt good and right and she relished he no longer treated her like a delicate flower now that her wounds were healed.

"I don't doubt you would for a second," she said, biting her lip to keep her giggles from getting out of control.

"I'll tell you what *I* don't doubt."

"Yeah?"

"This." He nudged himself against her. "Us. We're indisputable. Now that I have you exactly where I want and your full attention, there's something we need to talk about."

"Seriously?" A little line formed between her brows, but it wasn't one from worry. It was one caused by the amazing sensations moving through her center. "You want to talk now?" she said, arching her back and looking at him from beneath her lashes.

"No time like the present." Vasily adjusted his weight and slid a hand under her back. Hers went to his buttocks where she spread her fingers over his skin.

He tilted his hips and eased deeper inside her. Heat twisted up from her stomach as she met his slow thrust. "Before I get distracted again. When this shit is finally over, I want you and Luca to stay here with me."

"Just me and Luca? What about Marley?"

"Marley can stay. That monster has grown on me, even if my furniture is suffering. How much hair can a cat shed anyway?"

She smiled. "A lot. You don't know how many vacuums I've killed."

"Hmm. Your dad, however." He arched a brow and shook his head, but there was a spark of amusement in his expression. "Not so much."

Nicky chuckled and lifted her knee to wrap her leg around his waist. "You're just sore he beat you at poker last night."

Vasily scoffed. "I let him win." Then he slid another inch further into her, closing his eyes briefly as he let out a low, satisfied groan. When he'd settled, he said, "I'm not going to say you can't go back to your job at the bar, but just so we're clear, that's what I'd prefer."

Was he joking?

Nicky went still beneath him. That was exactly what Anthony

had done. He'd insisted she not work, and it had been a mistake. "Vas, I need to make my own money. I can't be a kept woman."

He gave her a pointed look. "Semantics. Any way you look at it, you're going to be kept because *I'm* keeping you."

"That's not what I mean, and you know it," she said, jerking her hips beneath his and laying a spank on his ass.

His eyes widened, then he made a sound that could be interpreted as shock. "You did not just spank my ass."

"Hm-mm, I think I just did," Her eyes glistened with mischief. "That's what you get for telling me not to work."

"Oh, you're going to be punished for that," he growled. "The only person who does the spanking in this house is me." Then he began to tickle her under her arms.

She squealed in laughter, clenching her leg around his waist as he laid merciless onslaught to her side.

"Stop," she squeaked between giggles.

"I'll stop when you apologize."

"I'm sorry...I won't..."

"Won't what?"

"Spank...you...again."

Those silver irises were dark and burned with amusement as he looked down at her. "Have you learned lesson?" he said in that exaggerated Russian accent again. Which only made her laugh harder.

"Yes!"

"No more spanking?"

"I...promise."

"Thank fuck, because all that squirming has made my dick even harder and if I don't get moving inside of you in the next five seconds, my balls are going to explode."

She hissed and strained against him, angling her hips to meet his. "I rather like those balls."

"Good thing you do, because they're the only ones you're

getting." With that, he pushed even further into her. Then he got to the serious business of thoroughly fucking her. All thoughts of being a kept woman evaporated from her brain. Every nerve ending in her body lit up like Las Vegas on New Year's Eve, and instead of his balls exploding, her mind pleasantly did.

Chapter Twenty-Eight

"**G**od, it feels like ages since I've seen you," Soren eyed Nicky over her espresso cup. And it had been, since before Soren left for her conference in Phoenix.

It was later that same morning, and they were seated outside in an enclosed patio of a busy breakfast bistro half a block from Soren's spa. The tall, painted white wooden fence surrounding them was trimmed with a dark pink climbing rose, its fragrance filling the outdoor space.

"It's no excuse but I've been swamped," Soren continued. "It's getting close to the holidays and the spa is hella busy. Plus, I'm a woman down with one of my girls on maternity leave, so I have to pick up the slack. But now that I've had a real chance to look at you..." Soren pointed a frosted pink fingernail at her. "You look even more gorgeous than usual. Her blonde brows pinched together as she tilted her head slightly. "What are you doing differently? Are you cheating on me and letting someone else give you a facial?"

Facial?

Nicky almost burst out laughing at the semi-worried look on Soren's face. "You know I'd never schedule one anywhere else." She stuck a forkful of frittata in her mouth to avoid answering that it was probably all the sex hormones coursing through her system. Soren's incessant need for details on her sex life wasn't something she wanted to discuss. Yev sat a few tables away, probably out of earshot, but she wasn't taking a chance. Twirling the fork in the air, she said, "But now that you bring it up, I could use one since I have all this free time."

"Well, girl, get it on the books already. But tell me something." Soren's smile faded into a low-level scowl as she glanced at Yev. His gaze was on the large, ornate iron gate and any malignant characters who may enter from the street. "What's up with that?"

"Ever since...you know...I have a constant shadow until my circumstances are better."

"Circumstances, huh? We'll discuss your *circumstances* in a minute. But that man." She dropped her voice and flicked her blonde hair in the direction of Yev. "He's no shadow. He's a freaking thunderstorm without the lightning on a cold-as-hell night. I mean he's interesting to look at. I'd even go as far as to say he's kinda sexy, but does he ever talk?"

"What do you mean?"

"He didn't say two words to me the whole ride home from the airport other than grunting 'get in.'"

"Did you try making conversation?"

Soren's head shot back a couple of inches. "Have you met me? Of course, I tried making conversation, and I might've even smiled a time or two just to diminish the buckets of testosterone I was drowning in." Soren paused and blew out a tiny breath behind her cup. There was an odd look in her eyes, one Nicky seldom saw. Despite the confident shield her friend hid behind, there was a tiny amount of doubt written on her face.

"And?"

"I got nothing. Just a jaw tick and the odd grunt. He didn't even look at me!"

Nicky grimaced on the inside. Was it horrible she hadn't

owned up to the fact she'd pre-warned Yev about Soren's man-eating abilities?

"Maybe he did, you just didn't see it behind those mirrored sunglasses?"

"Trust me, babe, I was right next to him, and I know when a man looks at me. Most of the time, I can feel it, and he didn't. He just sat there ignoring me and it kind of made me wonder if I'd aged twenty years during my flight from Phoenix."

Crap. Now would be the perfect time to fess up to what she'd said to Yev, but for some reason, Nicky couldn't seem to do it. But she did offer one helpful nugget. "Even if you had aged twenty years, which you have not, you'd still be gorgeous. I'd bet he's just playing hard to get."

"Well, whatever." Soren waved a hand in the air. "His loss." Then her voice changed to wistful. "Though judging by what's in those jeans, it might be mine too."

"Oh, honey, stop. It's not like you lack for interested men. You don't have anything to worry about. I'd say he was probably intimidated by you. I'm guessing he doesn't know how to handle all that wonderfulness."

"Intimidated? Him?"

"Why not?"

"Pfft...hardly." Soren waived a hand. "I'm thinking I'm the one who is intimidated. I mean, look at him. He's huge and rugged, and so..." She left that thought unfinished but gave a little shudder that had probably nothing to do with them being outside.

Nicky smothered her smile. She had to give it to Yev. The man had chops if he had Soren in a twist. It was always her gorgeous friend causing the twisting. Unless, of course, Yev wasn't interested. But that wasn't the impression she got in her kitchen prior to him picking Soren up from the airport. He'd noticed her at Chuck's. And anyway, straight men not noticing Soren just went against nature. It was why she got bored with them so easily.

It was probably just his play—and it seemed to be working. So, she was going to leave them to it and enjoy the show.

"But, change of subject. I'm not here to talk about him. At the risk of poking the tiger, are you sure you know what you're doing, staying with Satan? The man broke your heart and now you're back there? I'm not getting it."

"He had his reasons, Sor, and he's trying to make up for it."

Her brows arched higher. "And you're satisfied with those reasons?"

"I am."

"But you're not willing to share them with me?"

"I can't, babe. If there's anyone I trust in this world, it's you, but it's not my story to tell."

How could she explain without further cementing Soren's negative opinion of Vasily what he'd done to save his own life? Soren was no prude, and she hadn't grown up sheltered, but her family had no ties to the criminal element that Nicky's dad had. She hadn't been exposed in the same way and was a lot less forgiving of criminal acts that sometimes were spurred from self-defense or pure survival.

Soren squinted, then pursed her lips as she tapped at her espresso cup with a nail. "Not to say *I* don't trust *you*, or what you have to say, but I'm reserving judgment for now. Just know I'm here for you if you need me and afford me the luxury of saying I told you so."

"I know, and luxury granted."

The slight breeze shifted. Nicky caught the whiff of coffee from the little espresso cup between them. It smelled unusually strong, and not particularly pleasant. She swallowed and sat back in her chair, then grabbed her fork to pick at her frittata. "But speaking of Vas, this may help you look at him in a different light. I didn't tell you what he did for my dad."

When she was done reporting on Dean's written confession, Soren stared at her from across the table, her mouth hanging slightly open. "Okay, now I'm not going to lie. That *is* impressive. And getting your dad to stay at his apartment, even more so. But I'm still skeptical of you moving in with him. A bit soon, no?"

"We missed out on ten years together, Sor. Years we'll never get back and I don't want to waste any more time."

"Look, I'm not trying to be Negative Nelly, and the gods know I want you to be happy, but you're not even divorced yet. Have you even found a lawyer?"

"Uh-huh." And it was true. Granger, Vasily's lawyer, had come through for her and found a woman willing to take her case. Having heard who some of her clients were, and the success rate she'd had, Nicky would say Granger knew his stuff.

"Anthony isn't going to fight it anymore. I guess after what happened to him, he's had a little time to reflect, and he's realized what a dick he'd been. He even apologized, Sor."

"Good. I hope his new attitude lasts. It sounds like all your dominoes are falling in the right direction."

Indeed, except for the matter of Oksana. That had still to be resolved.

The breeze shifted again and Nicky wrinkled her nose. "Is your espresso okay?"

Soren looked at her cup, then back at Nicky. "It's fine. Tastes great. Why?"

"Smells weird to me."

"Hm, maybe you're coming down with something."

Nicky placed her fork on her plate, her appetite gone. Perhaps Soren was right, but she'd felt great this morning. In fact, better than great. She'd left their bed tingling with happiness and by the satisfied and relaxed look on Vasily's face, so did he.

"Why aren't you eating?" Soren asked, breaking into her thoughts. "You've barely touched your frittata. Usually, you devour that shit. Does it not taste good?"

Huh.

Soren was right. Usually, she did. It was her favorite item on the menu, and it *didn't* seem to taste the same. A bad batch perhaps?

"Oh shit, Nick." The cup Soren held made a clattering sound as she dropped it back into its saucer. A small amount spilled.

She looked at her friend, who was staring at her, a strange look in her eyes.

"Do you need me to point it out?" Soren asked.

"What are you talking about?"

"Sensitivity to coffee smells? No appetite? You're glowing like a fucking chandelier in Buckingham Palace? Does any of this sound familiar?"

And her raging horn-dog libido!

Nicky's heart stopped, then she blinked.

Because...oh...Jesus!

She felt the blood draining from her head and her skin turned cold and clammy.

No.

It wasn't possible.

"Girl," Soren said, grabbing her hand from across the little table, her voice dropping to a whisper. "I have to ask. When did you have your last period?"

Chapter Twenty-Nine

"We need to make a quick stop at the drugstore," Nicky told Yev when they were on their way home from brunch with Soren.

To his credit, the big man looked impatient at the detour but didn't complain as he made a few extra turns before heading to a CVS near Vasily's apartment. Pulling behind a white truck, he tapped a steady rhythm on the steering wheel with his thumb while they waited for the spot next to the truck to become available.

Gathering her hippie-style suede purse and adjusting the strap around her shoulder, Nicky put her hand on the door handle.

"Wait." Yev frowned at her.

Nicky looked at Yev, then at the woman who was taking her time loading her items into the back of an SUV. She held her phone in one hand and talked at it, while her other fumbled for one of the many shopping bags still in the cart.

"I'll only be a minute." Nicky pointed to the person through the windshield. "By the time that lady has unloaded her shopping cart, I'll be done."

The lady dropped her phone and it skittered under her car. She

ANN HOWES

dropped down to her knees and sticking her ass in the air went searching for it. Nicky looked at Yev and gave two slow, exaggerated blinks.

"Boss said not to let you out of my sight." He glared back at her. The muted sunlight cast through the tinted windows highlighted the scar across his eye, making it look harsher than usual. "And that means, *I don't let you out of my sight.*"

"Seriously?" She twisted in her seat to meet his glare. "I only need a few feminine products. I'll be in and out in no time."

"Not happening."

"Fine!" She rolled her eyes and folded her arms. "Follow me in but keep a little distance. I need privacy."

"To get tampons?" Her mountainous bodyguard smirked. "Not unfamiliar with what you ladies need at a certain time of the month."

Had any of his ladies needed a pregnancy test? It was a question she wasn't going to ask because it would raise all kinds of red flags which he would undoubtedly mention to his boss. But she was willing to bet this hulk of tattooed muscle had a stash of the Morning After pill taking up space in his medicine cabinet. Her eye began to twitch. She pressed a finger to it and tapped her foot as they waited.

Finally, the woman having recovered her phone and disposed of her cart, climbed into her metallic orange Kia and pulled out. Yev pulled the Caddie in and before he'd even turned the engine off, Nicky began to exit the car.

"For fuck's sake!" he growled.

The Caddie door slammed, and the alarm chirped at the same time angry footfalls crunched on the gravel behind her. "I said wait up!"

Damn. She'd hoped to get some distance between them, but Yev's legs were as long as a tarantula's if one took scale into account, and probably just as hairy. Though that was Soren's fantasy to ponder. She had other things to worry about, like proving her friend's suspicion negative.

She was not pregnant!

"What's the damn rush?" Yev grumbled as he slowed his pace to match hers.

Nicky craned her neck and offered a smirk of her own. "I thought you said you were familiar with what ladies needed at that time of the month. Sometimes Mother Nature sneaks up on us, you know."

Okay, technically not a lie. Pregnancy snuck up on women all the time, *not* that she was pregnant. Perhaps it had been the chicken they'd eaten for dinner the night before that was disagreeing with her. Though nobody else had complained about their gastronomical constitution. Nor had anyone else developed a sudden sensitivity to smells.

"*Blyad.*" Yev's eyes widened a second before he rubbed that giant bear paw over his jaw. "Okay, didn't realize it was an emergency."

More like a red herring, and hopefully, if she was really lucky, he wouldn't pay too close attention to her purchase.

But that was why she had a plan B. She snickered. *Plan B.*

A metallic crashing noise diverted Yev's attention somewhere to their left. It was followed by the sound of glass hitting metal and a muttered curse. An elderly gentleman had run his grocery cart aground into the curb, and it quickly became obvious why.

Her wing woman had arrived.

The gentleman had paid more attention to Soren's bouncing bosom than where his shopping cart was headed.

She sauntered across the parking lot, hips swaying and blonde hair blowing gently behind her. The only thing needed to complete the scene would be Def Leppard's *Pour Some Sugar On Me* blasting from somewhere.

Yev's lips twitched at the old man, whose color was one shade lighter than the toppled gallon bottle of burgundy lying on its side in his cart.

Soren stopped to help the man untangle his cart's wheels from a small fallen tree branch, and in doing so unintentionally gave the old codger a bird's eye view of her plump cleavage and her perfectly formed derrière.

Yev's lip twitch slowly turned into a flat line, which then further turned into a scowl as Soren straightened and gave the old man a big smile and a soft touch on his arm. She straightened and closed the distance to meet Yev and Nicky at the entrance to the drugstore.

"What's up, Cowboy?" Soren greeted Yev with just the right amount of indifferent friendliness. Then with barely a sideways glance, strutted through the sliding door and entered the store.

Yev's gaze followed her tiny waist and round, swaying rump. *There's my girl.*

Nicky pulled her lips in, smothering a chuckle. Lordy, this was going to be fun. Perhaps it was time to break out the popcorn.

"Cowboy?" Yev muttered, two lines forming between his thick, dark brows. "I don't look like a fucking cowboy."

Nicky cast her gaze downward, to the pair of well-loved black leathers covered by his True Religion jeans. "I think she's referring to those."

They had that in common, an old and lingering penchant for cowboy boots. Nicky had in fact seen Yev in several pairs, from super scuffed to freshly polished and silver-tipped, depending on the occasion. The ones he wore now were somewhere in the middle.

He grunted, then held out an arm and allowed her to precede him through the automatic doors. Grabbing a basket, she dawdled to the candy aisle and hovered over the different brands of imported chocolates and bags of hard sugar candies.

"You want anything?" she asked Yev, turning over a packet of chocolate squares and pretending to read the ingredients.

"Don't eat sweets." Yev gave a pointed look at the fat, platinum Cartier on his wrist, then back at her. "I thought you said this was an emergency?"

Nicky scoffed. "First things first, *Cowboy*, and by the way, chocolate is always an emergency. Another thing you apparently are not familiar with during a certain time of the month."

Yev's head tilted towards the ceiling. He closed his eyes for a few seconds as he shook his head.

Nicky giggled, then Soren moved into view at the end of the aisle and gave her a thumbs up. She then headed to the front of the store and the checkout line.

Mission accomplished.

Nicky wasted another minute waffling between the bag of chocolate caramel squares and round mint thins giving Soren time to complete her purchase. Settling on the squares, and with Yev still on her tail, she wandered to the feminine products aisle and snagged a box of tampons.

They joined the checkout line. Soren was a few customers ahead tapping her credit card on the machine and chatting with the young male associate behind the register. A barely audible rumble escaped that impressive chest directly behind her head. When she glanced up and back, Yev's gaze was glued on a box of extra-large condoms the flushed associate handed Soren, along with a small brown paper bag.

Nicky's shoulders shook gently with silent laughter.

Score one to Soren.

They went through the line then met outside. Soren hugged her and when Yev turned away for a moment to check on a passing car, she lifted the tasseled flap of Nicky's purse and dumped the contents of the brown-paper bag inside.

"Call me later, yeah?" she said, looking Nicky in the eye.

"Will do." Nicky closed the flap and settled the purse on her hip.

"Later, Cowboy." Soren tossed her flaxen locks over her

shoulder and sauntered away, the puffy-but-empty brown paper bag still in one hand and the box of condoms in the other.

Yev mumbled something in Russian.

"What did you say?" Nicky asked, giving him a wide-eyed innocent look.

"Never mind." He jerked his head in the direction of the car. "Time to go."

She could practically hear his molars grinding over the sound of Kaleo's growly voice singing *No Good* over the Caddie's speakers as he navigated the traffic home.

Twenty-five minutes later Nicky rested her arms on the toilet seat and spat out the last of the bile and frittata she'd eaten for brunch. She pressed the handle down to flush the foul mess away.

No more denying it—it was official.

If those plastic doodads hadn't confirmed she'd soon be eating for two, her sudden bout of vomiting did.

One test, maybe two could be a coincidence, but all three?

Just to be sure, Soren had bought different brands. Two showed double 'positive' lines and the third, a blue plus sign. All three mocked her from the bathroom vanity counter.

"How is this happening?" she asked Marley, wiping her mouth with toilet paper. Up until the first one showed positive, she'd still been convinced she had nothing to worry about.

But now, the hollowness in her chest and the slight sensitivity in her nipples forecast doom and heartache. It was accompanied by the sick feeling in her stomach.

The cat sat next to her, swishing his tail and guarding the bathroom door. For some reason, Marley had a habit of doing this. Anytime she had to use the facilities, he insisted on entering with her. Usually, it was a bit of an annoyance, but now she was grateful.

"How am I going explain this, big boy?"

Marley turned his head to that impossible degree only animals seemed to be capable of and looked at her. He gave a slow blink of his lone amber orb as if to say, "I got you."

She scratched behind his ears. He reciprocated by pressing himself against her side, his purr magnified by the acoustics of the bathroom. Though comforting, it did little to squash the million thoughts and questions swirling around in her head.

This should've been a happy moment.

A celebrated one.

One she'd wanted for so long, yet given Vasily's position on having a child, it could only be described as...desolate.

What was she going to do?

Nicky wiped more tears from her eyes with the heels of her palm, then blew her nose again and tossed the toilet paper into the bowl. What were the odds—a broken condom *and* her birth control failing? One in a billion? Two?

And why in the name of all that was holy, did this have to happen *now*? They'd just come back to each other, *and dammit*, she wanted more time!

She flushed the toilet again, then pushed herself up to rinse her mouth with cold water before guzzling some straight from the faucet stream. The coolness felt good going down and helped calm her a little. When she'd sated her thirst, she patted her face with cold, wet hands to bring color to her complexion.

If Vasily asked her to, could she terminate this pregnancy?

God, no.

She couldn't even if he wanted nothing more to do with her. Just contemplating the thought hurt beyond measure, because the fact was, even though she'd only known for sure for a few short minutes, she was already in love with this baby.

With Vasily's baby.

The question was, would he ask, and would she feel the same about him if he did? She wrapped her arms around her waist, rocking as she hugged herself.

Would he blame her and believe she did this on purpose? She didn't break the condom, but he'd probably think she lied about being on birth control.

Oh, God, what a monstrous fuck-up.

Telltale excess saliva pooled in her mouth again, but this time she skipped the toilet. The water she'd drunk exited her stomach and splashed into the marble sink, to be joined with a fresh flood of her tears.

Chapter Thirty

That same afternoon Vasily stood in the middle of the main dining room of *The Happy Clam* and stared at the bottle of Beluga Noble vodka in his hand. An icy shiver ran down his spinal column and left an unpleasant feeling in his gut.

The vodka had arrived in a black, glossy box, adorned with a black silk ribbon tied in an elaborate bow. There was no note, and no return name or address on the gold label, just his own name in bold, black lettering.

Yet he knew.

It wasn't the most expensive Russian vodka, but it had been favored by his old nemesis, Aleksei Federov. The man had drunk it by the liter, and sometimes when aggravated, straight from the bottle.

"When did it arrive?" He glanced at Jones, his restaurant manager.

"Last night." Jones scratched his balding head, displacing a few light brown hairs and making the fine strands point skyward. "Someone left it at the bar. At first, I thought it was from a rep leaving us a sample. But then I saw it was addressed to you.

331

Thought I'd give you a call right away instead of waiting for your regular visit. Is it your birthday?"

Vasily shot him a glance but didn't bother explaining. "I need to see the surveillance footage from last night." Perhaps Oksana had dropped it off herself instead of a lackey. But would he be able to pick her out of the crowd, or had she disguised her appearance as cleverly as she'd disguised her identity?

"Anyone act out of sorts or cause problems?"

"Just your average night." Jones pursed his lips and shook his head, then led the way to his office. He pulled a set of keys from the pocket of his brown chinos and let Vasily inside. The room was small and plain and lit by a single fluorescent tube above the desk. A gray metal filing cabinet stood against a white wall that hadn't seen a coat of paint in a decade. The wall was covered in awards from the culinary industry, including the coveted Michelin Star. Copies of those awards adorned the walls of the restaurant itself. They approached a long desk that took up half the space in the room. Scattered on top were papers, menus, and two computer monitors.

Jones jiggled a mouse, and one of the screens lit up. It was split into four images showing footage of the restaurant lobby, the main dining room, the patio, and the bar. He tapped on a keyboard and minimized three of the images, leaving the one focused on the bar.

"Our barkeep said it was sometime after 10 p.m. when he first noticed the package."

Vasily sat on Jones's chair and studied the steady stream of patrons placing orders and leaving with their drinks. He'd been at it for about forty-five minutes when he saw her. Her appearance was brief, and she didn't stand out. Except for the black box she carried he would've had difficulty spotting her. Her dark hair hung loose around her shoulders and covered most of her face.

He watched her place the box in the middle of the bar, then turn to walk away. After three steps she stopped as if having a thought on which direction to take. But then she turned and looked directly at the camera pointing at the bar, staring into the lens for about five seconds. Then she smiled.

Fuck. She'd known exactly where that camera was. Vasily paused the footage and used the mouse to create a square around her face, zooming in as much as the program allowed without the image becoming too pixelated.

His fingers stiffened around the mouse, and tension tightened his knuckles. Unpleasant goosebumps broke out on his flesh, and the hair on the back of his neck stood to attention. There was nothing amiable in that smile, and by all appearances, it just looked like any other. But that wasn't what scared him.

It was something he'd seen before. The kind of soulless, unfiltered evil so clear and forefront in the eyes of men who had done unspeakable things to other humans. The kind one would expect to see in the eyes of people like Charles Manson, the Son of Sam, or Richard Ramirez, *The Nightstalker*.

That visceral evil, sometimes hidden just one layer behind charm, was there in Oksana Federova's eyes, plain and for all to see. And those eyes carried a message.

They'd be meeting soon.

Chapter Thirty-One

"Dad, would you mind giving Luca his bath?" Nicky asked as Mario cleared the last of the dinner dishes from the kitchen island and placed them in the sink to rinse.

"Sure, Stick." He glanced at her over his shoulder as he opened the dishwasher. "You didn't eat much. You alright?"

"I'm fine." She offered him a weak smile. "Just tired."

This wasn't a lie. Well, the *tired* part wasn't, but as for the rest, she was far from fine. She'd faked it all day since she'd found out and considered making prime rib for dinner with mashed potatoes and sautéed Brussels sprouts with bacon. But Vasily had texted saying he was in meetings and wasn't going to make it in time for dinner. And anyway, knowing what she had to do when he came home would most likely ruin prime rib for her for the rest of her life. This was why she'd ordered Chinese and met the delivery person down in the main lobby of the building. If one didn't have the correct thumbprint programmed into the little digital pad, one did not get access to the private elevator that led to the penthouse.

She'd only ordered in a couple of times. Once when Vasily was in Northern California rescuing Anthony, and today because she couldn't face cooking.

How was she going to tell him?

This was the question she'd asked herself for the thousandth time as she faced the floor-to-ceiling window staring at the tail-lights of the evening traffic crossing the Bay Bridge. She could hold off telling him, but that would only delay the inevitable, and there was no way she could fake it for long, anyway.

Not the way she felt.

Ominous gray clouds dimmed the horizon of the North and East Bay, threatening a storm. The sun had already set but Nicky couldn't find it in her to turn the lights on. The gloom inside matched the darkening horizon and mirrored her emotions. Aerosmith's *Sweet Emotion* pumped through the speakers. Ironic, as there was nothing sweet about hers.

In some respects, Vasily not being around for dinner had been good. It had given her time to get herself sorted. But in others, it unfortunately gave her head the space to envision scenarios she didn't want to envision.

Her shoulder rested against the bookcase in the corner of the reception area, and her head leaned on a leather-bound copy of an expensive novel written in Cyrillic. She wrapped her arms around her waist, trying to mitigate the hollow in her stomach and the sting of tears at the back of her eyes.

She'd come alive when Vasily had re-entered her life. She'd vibrated. Felt feelings she hadn't since he left for Russia ten years ago. It sounded cliché, but colors were brighter and more vivid, and her smile was wider. Food even tasted better. Well, it had until this morning. And now, because of one little swimmer in a hundred million that had found its way past a broken condom *and* her birth control, she was about to lose all of that.

Again.

The elevator doors swished, and her breath stopped short. A small square of light reflected in the window and Vasily entered the lobby. His suit jacket was draped over his wrist, and his hand was shoved into his trouser pocket. He'd rolled his sleeves up and muscles in his forearms flexed as he held a phone to his ear. He was talking in English, his tone clipped and bossy, but as he caught sight of her in the gloom, his step faltered and he switched to Russian.

A debate had been running in her head. Should she give him time to settle into his evening? Let him have a glass of wine and delay the inevitable, or should she rip the gag off and vomit the news out first thing?

Vomit—hah!

Interesting choice of words, given she'd wrapped her arms around a toilet bowl more than once that day. Though how much of that had been due to hormones, or the desperateness of her situation, she couldn't begin to guess.

At the reminder, the sting behind her eyes sharpened, and her throat tightened as if a large boa constrictor had wrapped itself around her neck.

Maybe it would be okay. This was another thing she'd wondered about for the thousandth time. Maybe somehow, he'd changed his mind, or at least softened his position and would accept the news about this baby. Reluctantly at first, sure, she'd give him that, but in the end, he'd look forward to and love their baby as she would.

Then again, maybe his position hadn't softened. Maybe it was the opposite.

His reflection showed his gaze was focused and intense as he studied her. "*Spasibo*," he said into his phone. There was another brief exchange in Russian, then, "I've got to go."

He hung up and slid his phone into his pocket. His head tilted, and the invisible energy around his body seemed to electrify, arcing across the room, but it wasn't the usual pleasant electricity that happened between them. This was tense, and wary, on edge.

"Dom, what's wrong? Why are you out here in the dark?"

Still facing the window, she drew in a shaky breath and wiped the tears from her eyes with her thumb. It trembled, as did her bottom lip.

This was it. Their final moments of being together, and she wanted to take in his beautiful face before it turned hard with what he would probably perceive as her betrayal. She turned slowly to face him.

"Is Luca okay?" he asked, his brow furrowed.

She sniffed and cleared her throat. "He's good. He's in the bathtub. My dad's watching him."

"Then, baby, what's wrong?" Tossing his jacket onto the cream couch, he closed the distance with those long, strong legs. "Talk to me."

Baby.

A wry giggle almost escaped her, but she drew in a sharp painful breath instead. He'd never called her that. It was an unexpected gift and she clung to it, committing the gentle, slightly worried timbre of his voice to memory. There'd be dark days ahead and she'd need to recollect that precious gem and play its music in her head. The last note of what they were.

She stepped closer and wrapped her arms around his waist, laying her head on his chest fighting that damn boa constrictor around her neck. He was warm, his arms strong around her upper back and shoulder, his heart beating steadily beneath her ear. And his smell...God, she loved his smell. She'd make a point of stealing one of his un-laundered shirts before their inexorable ending and he kicked them out.

He held her tight, kissing the top of her head but saying nothing until finally he drew back a little, his expression soft and tender. The arm around her shoulder moved, but the hand attached to that arm came up to cup her jaw.

"Dom," he said, tilting her face upwards.

Knowing she was about to lose that look, that amazing, beautiful, soft look, the dam broke, and her breath hitched. "I have something to tell you." Her voice trembled and came out tight. "You're not going to like it." Tears rained down her cheeks. "You're going to hate it, and I'm so, *so* sorry but I don't know how it happened... I mean, I do know, it's obvious how, but I..."

The furrows in his forehead deepened, and two lines formed between his eyes.

"First, I want you to know...um, you're not obligated. I will understand as you've made your feelings exceedingly clear. I didn't plan this, I swear. You have to believe me."

He squeezed her gently. "Dom, you're killing me. I don't know what you're talking about, and I need you to get to the point."

"I'm...um." She sniffed and another sob wracked her chest. "I'm pregnant." This last came out barely a whisper.

He stilled, then his entire body stiffened. Then she lost his warmth, and his strength as his arms and hands dropped from her completely and he stepped back. The cold that suddenly surrounded her wasn't just physical. A hand came up but paused on its way to his face. "What?"

Then that hand completed its journey in his hair, to be joined with the other. He scraped them back across the sides of his temples to meet at the back of his head, elbows pointing outward. "You said you were on birth control."

"I am."

"Then how did this happen, Dominique?" His voice got low, his tone cold and hard. "Did you lie to me?"

"I didn't lie," she whispered, her arms crossing her waist again. "I really didn't, I swear. I don't know how... somehow it failed."

He stared at her for a long time, his face like granite, his lips tight and pressed together. Some sort of scenario seemed to be playing out in his head and his eyes, but she didn't want to imagine what. In the last month, she'd become accustomed to his gaze being less guarded. But given what had to be going on inside, the negative things he had to be thinking, she now wished she'd never seen the softer side to him. It was too much to lose.

"Please say something," she whispered.

"Jesus, fuck," he murmured. His breath punched out, then a guttural growl rumbled from his throat. For a long moment, he didn't draw another one in. When he did, it was long, measured, and through his nose.

"I know this is a shock, and I'm so sorry. It is to me too."

"Shock?" he barked, looking at her as if she was a piece of filthy gum stuck to his shoe. The lines around his eyes deepened in a squint, then he turned his body so he was facing away from her and put a hand on his brow. He shook his head. "Fuck, I can't do this right now."

"Vas—"

Then that hand left his forehead and suddenly faced her, palm forward. Though it didn't touch her, it felt like a battering ram pushed her away. "Don't speak."

"I understand—"

He whirled to face her again. "No, you don't, Dominique. You don't understand a damn thing, but I'm not discussing this with you right now." He made a fist and with the flat part tapped his skull a couple of times, his face screwed up like he was in pain. Pain she'd caused him. "I don't want to say anything I can't take back."

She stared at him for a long moment, not breathing, but nodded. She understood that at least. Finally looking away from his anger, she gazed at the sparkling city skyline and bit her lip. It was trembling, like the rest of her. Tightening her arms around her waist to control her trembling, she swallowed down the huge knot in her throat and fought the urge to sob.

This was worse than what she'd anticipated. His anger had always been cold and controlled, which she could handle. But this was far from cold and the effort he showed to control it clearly cost him. He drew in another long breath through his nose, then snagged his jacket from the couch, flung it over his shoulder, and started to move. But instead of going through the arched doors in the bookcase to the main apartment and his bedroom, he continued to the lobby and the elevator.

"Vas?"

"Don't wait up for me." His tone was curt as he stabbed the down button with his index finger. In the moment it took for the doors to open, she observed his jaw was set tight, and his cheeks were more hollowed than usual like he'd sucked them in.

Without looking at her, he stepped inside. By some weird coincidence, the music had changed to Chris Cornell's *Black Hole Sun,* and as the doors closed, that small square of light disappeared into the gloom, along with the rest of the light in her life. And in the dark of that formal reception, her feeling of loss was like no other she'd ever felt. It was so much worse than when her dad had been sent to prison and the first time Vasily left her. She didn't know then what she knew now. That he'd loved her, and it wasn't his choice to leave.

Now it *was*. And he was the one who felt betrayed. She'd give almost anything to go back in time and take a damn morning-after pill, but she couldn't.

Covering her face with her palms, she planted her butt against the couch, the same one Vasily had bent her over and kissed her that day she came to his apartment and accused him of blowing up her car.

She burst into tears.

Chapter Thirty-Two

Vasily slammed his car door, then sat back in his seat, covering his face with his hand. The roar in his head from the blood rushing through was only slightly muted by the thunder of his heart kicking against his ribs. He felt as if he was standing on the edge of a cliff, not knowing which way was up, or which direction to take.

Tightening his fist, he held it in the air. With immense control, he restrained himself from punching the window, or his steering wheel. Everything weighed down on him, pressing him into his seat, and making it hard to breathe. Like a caged animal.

"God-fucking-dammit!"

At last, he uncurled his fingers and raked his hands through his hair, gripping his roots until they stung.

Ice baths.

Breathing in, he imagined himself plunging deep into a narrow lane cut into the ice of the Irtysh River. The excruciating, tiny daggers slicing through his arteries, penetrating his brain and extremities. The intense, single-purpose struggle it took to move one arm in front of the other and drag it through the water to reach the shore and stay alive. Then the euphoria fueled by endorphins afterward flooding his system. Except now, no endorphins were rushing through his veins, only acid.

He breathed out.

Fuck, fuck, *fuck!*

Had she lied to him?

Would she even do that? Her denial was emphatic and believable, but the tears streaming down her face didn't stop an invisible harness from squeezing his chest at the possibility she'd played him.

For a few weeks, he'd believed she was willing to put having a child aside for now, but had he been wrong? Could he have become too comfortable, too happy, too...*in love,* he'd overlooked her real agenda?

Which was what exactly?

To trap him?

Christ, she didn't need to trap him. She already owned his pathetic ass, his heart, and what was left of his soul, so why...?

A blast of air left his lungs, and his stomach sank to meet his reality somewhere in the vicinity of his shoes.

Nicky didn't break the fucking condom.

Goddammit, he was an ass!

She thought she'd been protected, and *she* couldn't control if her implant failed. Vasily scraped his hands through his hair again and let out a groan loaded with self-directed anger. This wasn't on just her. It was on both of them.

He stilled himself, breathing hard, and stared unseeing through the windshield at the stained concrete wall in front of his car. Taking in several more deep, slow breaths, he blew them out slowly, then wrapped each finger individually around his steering wheel and gripped it.

A baby.

Fuck.

A tiny human sired from his loins with his blood, his genes. *His family history.*

He needed this like he needed a shank in his side, which would more than likely be his end if Oksana got to him first. And where would that leave Nicky? He didn't have to imagine. He knew.

Finally, after what seemed like an eternity Vasily pushed the start button. He slid the Mercedes into reverse and backed out of his parking spot. Took the sharp corners, and the sound of his tires squealing echoed off the solid concrete support columns as he drove up the ramp. At the top, he waited for the electronic gate to rise, his big toe bumping against his shoe. When there was barely enough room, he scraped beneath the gate with inches to spare. With no destination in mind, he entered the gridlocked evening traffic leaving the motor-oil-tainted air behind him.

* * *

"You wanna know what I think?" Zander asked him two hours later, twisting his neck and giving him that cocked-head, squint-eyed look they'd all inherited from their father.

There was no judgment in his brother's look and for that Vasily was grateful. On any other day, he wouldn't have given a Russian rat's ass about what anyone thought about his personal life. But an hour of aimless driving around the city while he regained his calm had somehow brought him to his brother's parking lot.

Somebody explain that one to him.

He'd sat there like a tool in the dark, staring at his hands on the wheel, until Zander tapped on his window. "You've been here for an hour, brother," he'd said. "Normally I'd boot your sorry self for trespassing, but you look like a man who could use a drink."

So he'd followed Zander upstairs, and now Vasily took a slow sip of his third whiskey before shifting his glance to meet his brother's. "I just stepped on an IED. There are bloody pieces of me stuck to the walls of my penthouse. You think I have any brain capacity, or any fucks left to give to process what you think?"

Zander snort-smirked. He turned his side to the protective barrier around his rooftop patio and rested his jean-clad hip against it.

"But," Vasily added, jabbing his index finger for emphasis before Zander could offer more snark. "I got a feeling you're going to tell me anyway."

They'd been staring at the city view for the length of the time it took for him to spill his guts. About the pregnancy. About his reasons to remain childless. About some of the dangers facing them. Something he rarely did, especially to someone outside his very small circle of trust. Again, someone explain that to him.

The rain that had threatened all day never materialized and had passed through, leaving a clear sky and a bone-chilling cold that seeped through his suit jacket. How much of that chill was due to the remaining humidity in the air, he wondered.

"I think," Zander swirled the whiskey in his glass making the ice tinkle, "if you never wanted kids, you would've had that tube in your balls cut a long time ago, eliminating any possibility of that risk. Yet you didn't, which leaves me to wonder if you weren't totally committed to remaining rugratless."

A shiver ran through Vasily. He pressed his thumb and finger to the bridge of his nose and squeezed. Yeah, he couldn't deny he'd thought about having a vasectomy, but he'd never been in a situation with a woman where it had even been close to a question. Nor had he ever been that out of control with one that he'd forgotten to pinch the tip of the condom and it had ripped.

Fuck, there might be some truth to what his brother said.

And Nicky.

A sharp, painful sensation pierced his chest at how he'd left things. In his initial anger, he'd blamed her, but that initial anger was self-directed and came from selfishness. This was his fault, no way around it. And he'd left in a manner that implied it was hers, something he needed to fix.

Once he'd fully processed the news.

In his defense, he'd been shattered, fucking obliterated. Before he stepped into that elevator, through sheer force of will he'd kept his legs from buckling. The moment he was out of her view, he'd almost lost that battle and had gripped the brass railing for support. His fingers, which were now cradled around his whiskey glass were still stiff from the effort.

"Having just explained my situation, I shouldn't have to remind you how dangerous my life is, and never mind having a kid with our blood running through his veins could potentially be even more so in the future, little *brat*. A potential bomb waiting to explode."

"Just because *the asshole* and Dean were off their rockers, doesn't mean we all are."

The *asshole* Zander referred to was Dmitri, their father. Zander refused to even acknowledge him as a parental figure and Vasily couldn't fault him for that. He barely did, and he'd thought of him at one time as "Papa."

Pushing his dark, wavy hair off his forehead, Zander scratched the back of his head. "I'm not gonna lie, it does worry me a little. But *our* childhood was beyond fucked." Zander zig-zagged a hand between them. "Neither of us turned out like him. I think the odds are leaning in our favor, and it's not like you would do anything to deliberately harm that girl. Am I right?" Zander gave him a pointed look, a warning rang in his tone which Vasily both respected and appreciated, even if it irritated him at the same time.

"Of course not." *Other than what he was doing to hurt her right now.* Everything else he'd done had been to protect Nicky. *Every fucking thing.*

Zander tipped his chin. "Well then, there you have it. And don't forget, brother, Dmitri's only half of your makeup. The other half comes from your mother."

Interesting. Vasily straightened his posture and squared his shoulders. Nicky had said almost the same thing—that all his good parts came from her side. He narrowed his gaze in suspicion. "You've been talking to her?"

"To Nicky?" Zander's brows furrowed, then he shook his head. "Not since she told me about the dude who tried to rape her. You're thinking she asked me to talk you down?"

Did he think that?

No.

He hadn't even known he was coming here until he pulled into his lot. But Zander knew Nicky. They had a working relationship and a friendship that predated all of this. He also shared blood and a similar, unfortunate life experience with him. They'd both lost their mothers to Dmitri's cruelty.

Anyway, Nicky fought her own battles and by all indications, she hadn't even been aware she was pregnant just that morning. At the memory of that beautiful moment, Vasily's heart squeezed, his mind spinning with the worst scenarios cascading through his thoughts.

What had he done?

Nicky didn't deserve this. Waking up to her every day, those gorgeous eyes taking him in and lighting up like she'd won the man lottery was the best damn thing that ever happened to him. And now he'd gone and ruined it.

The thought of losing her after finally having her back? It was too painful to even think about. He discreetly wiped away a tear that had slipped down his cheek.

He'd make it right somehow. He had to, as there was no point in anything without her.

While he stewed over that realization, they were silent, staring at the bustle below, the small crowds forming as they waited for their stamps to enter Zander's bar. Occasionally they'd catch a riff of whatever music was playing, and now it was "Thunderstruck" by AC/DC.

Then he asked his brother the question he'd never thought would leave his lips. "You want kids?"

Zander's expression softened with a smile. "Terra does. There's a hole that needs filling from losing her mother and her unborn baby brother, and if I can do something about that, I'm gonna. And," Zander chuckled, "if I don't produce babies, Ginny, my grandmother will haunt my ass for the rest of my days."

A strange, sharp pang of jealousy stabbed at Vasily. Not that Zander'd had a loving adult to help him through the worst nightmare a kid could experience, but the stark, bitter reality that he and Dean hadn't had one. And how much more that had messed with Dean's head and turned him into the ruthless asshole he'd become. Vasily's throat bobbed as he swallowed the tightness that had formed. "You were lucky to have her."

"Yeah."

Zander caught his eye, the truth he'd had been given much more not lost in his expression. And even beyond that, was his acknowledgment of what it had cost himself and Dean.

"And Chuck," Zander added. "The man who owned this bar before me. That old fuck was hard-as-nails, an outlaw biker who did some horrible shit in his time. Never had kids of his own. Took me on as a son and kept me in line when Ginny couldn't. Also showed me what was possible in how much he loved my grandmother with *everything* that was in him." Zander paused, then a moment later cleared his throat. When he spoke again, his voice was huskier than before. "Cancer took her, and it killed him along with it."

This information was new to Vasily. They hadn't been close as kids, as it was only after Dmitri had crushed Vasily's mother's skull and taken the only good thing that mattered in his and Dean's lives that they'd learned they had another brother.

"We never knew what happened to you after Dmitri died, little *brat*. And it didn't mean I never thought about you, we were just too busy trying to survive our own deal. In all sincerity, I'm happy you had it better than us." He looked at the man next to him, a small smile tilting his lips. "But is there a point to all this sharing?"

Zander chuckled. "Always the motherfucker."

Then he moved and took a step closer so they were standing shoulder to shoulder, but facing opposite directions. Vasily continued to look straight ahead, but Zander angled his head to look at him. "My point is, family is what you make of it. It's not just the blood that runs through our veins that forms one. It's the love you have for people who you choose to include in your family. If you love Nicky half as much as I think you do, and knowing the love she will pour on your baby, you're ninety percent of the way there. Barring shit you have no control over, you make her, Luca, and this new little Melnikov your family, the rest of your days will be like a layer cake stuffed with all your favorite fillings. Nothing but sweet, man. Nothing. But. Sweet."

Zander's words, and the support emanating from his body where their shoulders touched, both warmed and stunned him to stillness. Who knew a descendent of Dmitri Melnikov could wax so...*beautiful?* Perhaps there was hope after all.

"I hear you," Vasily turned his head to catch his brother's eye. "It's selfish, I know, but I just wanted more time with her. Alone, unshared." *After ten fucking years of being denied.*

"You're already sharing her."

"Hmm."

Somehow, he never thought of it that way. Luca was an incredible kid who didn't demand her attention every second. But when her child did, Nicky gave it to him one hundred percent. She'd once told Vasily, 'quality over quantity.'

"Babies are different." Well, he assumed they were, given he'd never had the opportunity to deal with one. Never mind the one-in-a-hundred-million crap shoot that could end up being Dmitri two-point-oh. "Who's to say this new little fucker's genetic code isn't as bad as it could get?"

"Get the fuck out of your head, man." Zander frowned. "Dmitri was weak, Dean even weaker. Neither are as smart or controlled as you are, and they allowed their demons to dictate how things went." Zander bumped his shoulder with his whiskey glass. "You're not weak. Whatever demons you may have, they don't hold so much as one of those tiny birthday candles to you. And, never forget, you'll have Nicky. Together you'll raise that child with love and none of the bullshit we went through."

Again, Vasily was reminded of Nicky's words and repeated his narrowed glance. "You sure you haven't been talking to her?"

"No, brother, but it's a given. If that's what she said, she's a smart woman. Now get the fuck over yourself. Don't you think you deserve something good for once in your miserable, lonely life?"

Did he?

Christ, he hoped so. "It's not a question of what I deserve." Zander had no concept of the sins he'd committed or the people he'd assassinated. Granted, they were the sludge at the bottom of a garbage can, who deserved much worse than the quick, clean death he'd given them. But those sins were coming back to haunt his ass. If Oksana somehow managed to get to him first that would leave Nicky unprotected and vulnerable. If anything happened to her... *to them...* it would kill him a thousand times over if he wasn't already dead.

That band around his chest tightened and this time he rubbed it. "It's a question of what I need to protect. I might not be able to."

"Doesn't mean you won't die trying, and that's all anyone could ask."

Truth be known, he'd crawl over rivers of lava or acres of razor wire to lay down his life to do just that. But he couldn't express in words that he'd never been more terrified that what was about to come wasn't up to him.

And the stakes had risen. Should things go to hell, he now had one more person to lose.

His child.

Chapter Thirty-Three

Shitty didn't begin to describe the rest of Nicky's evening.

From deep inside, she mustered the strength most mothers found in times of adversity and put her child first. While reading to Luca at bedtime, she faked a brightness she didn't feel, kissed his forehead tenderly, and tucked him in tight. Then she did the dishes, packed them away, and wiped down Vasily's gorgeous highly polished wood counter, her fingers tracing the natural grain that shone through.

She really would miss this kitchen. The space, the modern appliances, the gadgets...and the *pantry*. The memory of giving Vasily a blowjob in it that fateful morning when he'd told her "no little Melnikovs ever" surfaced.

"Oh, little Jelly-Bean, I've fucked this up, haven't I?" Tears pushed to the front of her eyes, making them burn as she put a protective hand on her belly. "Your mom's a class-A idiot when it comes to men, but I promise I'll do what I can to have your daddy in your life."

She snatched a daisy-patterned paper towel from the roll hanging beneath a cupboard and blew her nose. "He's pissed with me right now, but once he meets you..."

She paused. Would he though?

Or would he be one of those men who'd support his offspring financially but not emotionally?

God, she hoped not.

If his interactions with Luca were a clue, he'd adore this baby and be a good dad. But he'd been so angry, and the only thing she could hope for was he would eventually forgive her.

She wiped her tears, tossed the rolled-up paper towel into the garbage bin under the sink, then made a cup of ginger tea, wishing it could be a choice bottle of red from Vasily's extensive wine collection.

With her cup in hand, she went to her room. Somehow going to his just didn't feel right in the situation, yet she still paused just outside the threshold contemplating the thought. Eventually leaving her door slightly cracked, she climbed into bed, sipped her tea, and waited for him to come home.

He'd told her not to wait up, but since when had she been known to follow orders she didn't agree with? She lay against the headboard picking her nails and trying not to cry.

At some point, she fell asleep—alone—for the first time in well over a month. She'd dreamed of Vasily spooning with her, his warmth against her back, a protective arm over her waist and against her stomach, a hard, firm leg nestled between her thighs. The soft hairs of his body brushed against her skin, creating a sense of peace that lulled her, and she'd slept hard.

When she woke, she reached for him, her fingers touching the cold sheet, but disappointment crashed through her. The pillow where his head would've been was smooth and untouched, as was the comforter. Yet she imagined she caught the faintest hint of whiskey and his enticing shower gel. She breathed in deeply to get another hit, but it was gone, along with her sense of peace.

Probably just wishful thinking.

Nicky rubbed the sleep and the remnants of the tears from her eyes then glanced at her phone.

It was well past eight, later than when she normally woke. Though she'd slept, she felt unrested and dragged her feet through the emotional tornado surging through her to the bathroom and took care of her needs.

"Well, fuck it," she murmured to her splotchy-faced reflection as she brushed her hair. "Time to deal with whatever treasures today will produce. Maybe Zander will give me my job back."

First, she had to feed her son.

When she left her room, she hesitated a moment outside of Vasily's closed bedroom door. It hadn't been shut the night before. She raised her hand to knock but paused short of making contact with the wood. Did she want to face him just yet? Her head wasn't in a good place, so perhaps after she'd consumed some tea.

Luca sat alone on a stool at the kitchen island in his Wolverine pajamas, eating from a bowl of Cheerios. His face was still flushed from sleep and his curls were mussed into his mini 'fro.

"Morning, Buddy." She approached him from behind and wrapped her arms around his little shoulders, kissing the soft, warm spot on his temple. "Did Vasily help you with breakfast?"

"I did it myself. I'm not a little kid anymore, Mom."

"I know, honey." She smiled. "I was just wondering."

Like if it was just a dream Vasily had crawled into bed with her, or if he was even still home.

She clung to Luca for a moment longer, absorbing the heat from his small body, letting it permeate her own. After letting go, she grabbed Marley's kibble from the pantry and poured it into his bowl.

The breakfast bell rung, the cat zoomed into the kitchen making his loud and bratty displeasure known at having to wait for his meal.

"Oh, cut it out, you little monster." She gave him a quick rubdown and scratched him behind his ears. It's not like you're starving, chubby man." Then to Luca, she asked, "Daddy will be here soon. Do you have big plans this weekend?"

Since Mr. Matthews, Luca's tutor didn't come on Fridays, Anthony had started taking them off to spend more time with his son. So far, he'd kept to the plan.

"He said we're going to the 'Sploratorium."

"That's great, baby." Nicky flipped the switch on the electric kettle, then selected a bag of Rooibos herbal tea from a ceramic jar that contained her stash. "The Exploratorium has a lot of stuff about comets and space exploration. Maybe you'll get to see a really good image of Betelgeuse. Just always make sure you're near the bodyguards, okay?"

"'Kay," Luca answered around a crunchy mouthful of Cheerios. It never ceased to amaze Nicky how easily he'd adapted to having big, burly Russian badasses constantly in his space. He'd even learned a few phrases of the language and insisted on saying *spasibo* instead of thank you.

Mario entered, dressed in faded jeans, a thick red and black winter plaid shirt, and carrying his leather motorcycle jacket and helmet. "Yo, family." The simple phrase made her heart trip, as her family was going to be bigger in a little over seven months.

He went straight to Luca and ruffled his hair, making his curls even wilder. He looked at Nicky, then at her teabag, and frowned. "Coffee ready yet?"

"Morning, Pops. Would you mind making it?"

"Sure," he agreed, however, the way his thick, straight brows came together suggested he wasn't so sure. "Cutting out caffeine?"

Nicky faked a smile. "Something like that." Fortunately, he hadn't been around for her last pregnancy so her sudden coffee aversion shouldn't ring any alarm bells. At least not yet. And if he noticed her red and puffy eyes, he chose to keep quiet. And for that she was grateful. His position had mellowed towards Vasily. They had developed a mutual respect for one another, and she didn't want to be the one to change that, although soon that may be out of her control.

"By the way," Mario added as he hung his jacket over the back of a stool. "I'm heading out on a hog ride with some of my old buddies. Won't be back 'til Sunday evening."

She breathed a sigh of relief, as whatever blowout was brewing between herself and Vasily would at least be in private.

"Please be careful, Pops, and make sure you're never alone." Pouring boiling water over her teabag, she pressed it down with a teaspoon and let it brew before she added a little sugar and milk and stirred.

"I'm not the target of those sickos, Stick. Melnikov is."

"We don't know that, Dad." She removed the teabag and squeezed it out before disposing of it. Then she tapped the spoon on her cup and dropped it into the dishwasher. "And it wouldn't hurt for you to be careful, that's all."

"Stop fussing, girl." Mario spooned coffee into a filter and shut the lid. "I survived prison, I think I can handle a ride with five of my Harley buddies."

She sighed and wrapped her fingers around her cup. "Alright, I'll shut up now." He was right. Nine years of being locked up with hard-ass criminals had taught him a thing or three. A little freedom ride with his biker friends wasn't so bad, was it? Harley men were tough, and most weren't afraid to get their hands bruised or bloodied defending a fellow biker brother. Her black thundercloud didn't have to hover over everybody else's head.

She kissed his cheek, then murmured with fake enthusiasm, "Enjoy yourself. I'm going to get dressed so I can be decent for Anthony when I meet him in the garage."

When she reached her room, Vasily was just exiting his and her heart jumped into her throat.

He examined her for a second, his expression changing from stoney to stormy or maybe...tormented?

God, had it already come to the point he couldn't stand to look at her? Her throat clenched at his obvious dismay, and any hope she might have had of his mellowing to their situation disappeared like a feather in a hurricane.

The ache twisted further into something almost unbearable, stopping her ability to breathe. Before she made a fool of herself, she turned towards her door and put her hand on the knob.

"How long have you known?" The unevenness in his voice was so unfamiliar it stopped her. But he seemed to hold himself away as if the very thought of her coming close or touching him was unwelcome.

"A few hours before I told you." She bit the inside of her lip, and he dropped his gaze to focus on it. "I know you're angry—"

He pulled his head back an inch, then rubbed his freshly shaved jaw. "I don't know what I am right now. I haven't wrapped my head fully around the implications of this yet."

A long silence followed while he stared at her, appearing to be sorting out some inner struggle. But what? Her imagination produced all the worst scenarios she didn't want to voice. But she had to. She forced the next words out over the tight lump in her throat.

"Do you...want us to leave?"

He blinked and tilted his head. "Excuse me?"

"I can start packing and we can be out by the end of this weekend."

"Are you fucking kidding me?" He stared at her, disbelief flickering in his gaze. His lips flattened, those silver eyes hardened, and the old, scary Vasily appeared. In a move so fast she barely comprehended it, he stepped forward and grasped the back of her neck. Turning her doorknob, he pushed her door open and her inside. Nicky's heart raced as she stumbled a little, not knowing what to do or say at his sudden anger.

"Is that what you want?" he growled, shutting the door behind him. "To leave?"

Her lashes fluttered as she grappled with how this was going to turn out. "I just thought...I didn't..."

Vasily's hand on her neck went away, but his stare was intense and unsettling as his eyes roamed over her face and body, before landing on hers again. "Didn't what, Dominique?"

"I didn't think you'd still want me here."

He watched her for several more heartbeats, which should be noted were not slow in the least.

"Unbelievable."

Anger radiated off him and she was beginning to feel a little uncomfortable when his fingers circled her teacup and he pried it from her. Placing it on her nightstand, he then dragged one hand through his hair, while the other went to a place low on his hips.

"I feel like I'm walking on a tightrope made of dental floss," he growled. "And that's what you ask me? Jesus Christ. A second ago you asked if I was angry, Dominique. Well, I wasn't then, but I'm sure as fuck getting there now. Do you think I'd kick you out onto the street during all this bullshit? Where do you think you're going to go?"

Wait...did he? Her chin lifted an inch. *He considered her pregnancy bullshit?*

What the actual fuck?

Every maternal instinct, all the emotional turmoil and tears she'd been drowning in came rushing up and shifted into something much more primitive, igniting her temper like he'd tossed a match into a can of firestarter. Nicky raised her chin even higher to glare at him.

"I'll tell you what's bullshit, Vasily. And it isn't having a baby. There's a future human being inside me." She slapped her palms against his chest hard enough that they stung. "*Your* future human being. Don't speak about her like that."

He caught her wrists, holding them midair between them, and glared down that handsome Slavic nose, his eyes flashing silver fire. "That's not what I meant. I'm talking about Oksana, woman!"

Oh.

She swallowed and tried to back away, but his hold on her was unrelenting. The clarification may have doused the flames of her temper, but his attitude sure didn't. And she was sick of feeling as if she'd done something wrong, like everything was her fault. Pregnancy hormones aside, facing his disapproval was the final stake in her heart and she was done.

"Well, whatever." Again, she tried to free herself but failed. "The fact is I'm pregnant and you need to learn to deal with it or get out of my way so that I can do it in peace."

"The only damn thing I can deal with right now is how to keep us all safe. The rest can wait."

Thwarting any of her attempts to pry her wrists free, he brought them closer to his chest and pressed her palms to the spot in the solid muscle she'd just slapped.

"To answer your question, there's no way in hell you're leaving now," he added. "What did I tell you yesterday morning?"

She didn't have to think too far back, because it had been on a constant loop in her head. "You said you wanted us to stay."

"I meant it."

"But things have changed since yesterday, and it's a change that you have made very clear you don't want."

"I am still processing."

"Well, while you're processing, if you want to keep protecting us, fine. But I'm asking you to find us a different place to do it in. I won't subject myself or Luca to this...this disapproval or anger."

Nor her dad. Mario would likely break his parole, go Tony Soprano on Vasily's ass, and shoot him. She could bear her pain in silence, but she'd be damned if the two men she loved would be enemies again bent on destroying each other. She'd rather be alone and a single mother than let that happen.

Finally, Vasily let one of her wrists go. He squeezed his eyes shut, then pressed his fingers to the outside corners, and dragged them towards his nose. After clearing his throat, he dropped his voice low but there was no softening of his tone. It vibrated against her palms on his chest. "The time for that has passed. You'll stay here, and that's final." He dropped her hand, but her fingers continued to tingle from the contact. "Now, I've got shit to deal with. You'll have to excuse me."

He walked passed her to put his hand on the doorknob.

"Vasily."

He stilled, and when he turned to look into her eyes, she felt as if she was being stripped bare, piece by piece. "What?"

"You need to understand I won't be just an obligation."

He squinted at her from over his shoulder as if she'd lost her mind.

"I told you I loved you," she said, and waited for some sort of reaction, but all she got was a deepening of the scowl on his face like he was bracing himself against something.

"You never said it back. You said..." Her voice broke, and she stopped for a second. "You said you loved me ten years ago, but I have no idea if you still do. And honestly, I don't know if this has been ruined to a point there's no coming back from, but either you're in, or you're out. That's where I stand. Now it's up to you to figure out where you do."

For several seconds he didn't move while he took in her ultimatum, and from her point of view, it didn't do anything to lessen his anger. If the way his jaw ticked was any indication, it increased it. But she wasn't backing down. That he understood where she came from was too important.

"You're right about me needing to figure this out, but you're wrong about something else." He leaned in, looking directly into her eyes. "I have said it." Then he straightened and continued with his quest to open her door.

He had?

"When?" she asked, shocked.

"The morning before I left for Eureka. And more importantly, Dominique, I haven't just said it, I've fucking well shown it. The fact that you don't see that I have, is more hurtful than anything you just said."

He dragged the door open and stalked away, leaving her staring at his back, her heart aching like it had been sprained. She pushed the heels of her palms to her eyes to staunch her tears. But then his words truly penetrated through the fog of her anger and frustration. She brought up the memory of that morning when he'd told her what he'd done in Russia. He'd said something to her in Russian. She remembered it because it sounded like it had the word 'blue' in it.

Grabbing her phone from her nightstand, she pulled up the Google Translate app, found the English-to-Russian version, and entered *I love you*.

The result was *ya tebya lyublyu*. It was a tongue-twisting mouthful, but her heart began to pound at what she thought she knew. To be sure, she listened to the audio.

Lyublyu.

Blue.

Her breath hitched and fresh tears spilled down her cheeks. It felt as if the weight of the world had lifted from her shoulders because, with that final parting shot, he'd give her something she didn't have earlier.

Hope.

Chapter Thirty-Four

An obligation?

Goddamn, the woman pissed him off beyond belief! Hadn't he done everything he could to show her she was more than that?

Vasily slammed his office door shut, hard enough it shook the walls. He stalked to his desk and had a moment where he considered snapping the fucking thing in two. But he dropped into his chair, placing his elbows onto the thick glass and his head into his hands. And let out a deep growl of frustration.

No woman had tested him the way she did, got under his skin or twisted his head into a slinky so he couldn't think or act straight.

What the hell was wrong with him?

Yeah, okay dammit, so he had a moment of insecurity after he'd told her what he'd done in Moscow, and his stupid, stubborn pride had dictated he say he loved her in Russian.

He'd known she wanted him, that was never in doubt, but he hadn't been completely one hundred percent sure she felt the same as he did. Especially as he'd only just convinced her that it was Dean who was responsible for what had happened to her dad.

Then she'd said those words. Ones he'd longed to hear, and he'd done the thing she'd just accused him of not saying it back. Because of his fucking pride again.

He sat backing his chair and grimaced, rubbing the area on his chest where she'd slapped him. It had stung. An ironic chuckle bubbled up from deep inside. Any man had done that to him, he'd have dropped them in a second with a fist to the nose and made them lick their blood from the dirt.

He had half a mind on going back to her room and fucking the stupid out of both of them. They were acting like teenagers, for Christ's sake.

But the despair on her face. That she'd been crying had stripped him raw, and he'd let his emotions take control. The pain and disappointment he'd caused her, he just couldn't stand it.

He should've fixed it last night. When he'd found her asleep in her bed, he'd hated she wasn't in his. He'd watched her for several minutes, debating whether he should wake her and hash it out, before he'd finally undressed and crawled in with her. Just listening to her breathing, and feeling her silky skin against his had calmed him. His baser instincts had wanted to wake her, make love to her, but she'd slept like the dead.

That he hadn't followed through with that one small action was his mistake.

He glanced at his watch—he was out of time. It had taken some wrangling, but Granger had set up a Zoom meeting with the San Francisco Prosecutor about Dean's confession to begin the proceedings of clearing Marcello's name. Unfortunately, getting through to his woman, and how much she meant to him would have to wait.

Vasily silenced his phone, then wiggled his mouse and woke up his desktop. Once connected, and the initial pleasantries done, Derek Granger went straight to business. They were halfway through the allotted thirty minutes when Vasily's office door slammed open.

"Boss!" Yev skidded across the hardwood floor into the room.

Vasily didn't even have the chance to be annoyed at the interruption. His bodyguard's wide eyes, ashen face, and the fact he brandished his gun told him everything he needed to know. Ice-cold fear slithered down his spine, mirroring the shock in Yev's eyes. He felt as if he'd been punched in the gut.

No.

Fuck, no.

"There's been a breach." Yev rasped, out of breath. "That bitch has Nicky!"

Chapter Thirty-Five

Nicky and Sasha escorted Luca to the private parking garage where they met Anthony, who was waiting inside his car, listening to some legal podcast. Then Sasha left to retrieve one of the Cadillacs.

Anthony gave her a sad smile in greeting as she pulled open the door, and a small part of her felt sorry for him. He'd made his bed and she'd forgiven him, but her own problems were bearing down on her. Despite this, she still managed to give him a small smile in return.

She let Luca climb in first, then set a knee on the seat as she helped him into his car seat, Nicky secured his straps then took his face between her hands and kissed him on his forehead. "Have a good time, Buddy."

Luca, in his infinite sweetness and five-year-old wisdom touched her face with his little fingers and said, "I love you, Mommy."

Her heart just about burst wide open, and she swallowed the sudden lump in her throat. "I love you too, baby. See you on Sunday night."

She shut the door and stepped back. Anthony tooted the horn

and drove off. Nicky waved and blew her son a kiss. His little face peered through the car window, grinning and waving back.

Anthony's Porsche disappeared up the garage ramp, followed by Sasha in a white Cadillac.

As Nicky turned to press the elevator button, a slim-ish woman dressed all in black, knee-length leather boots, skinny jeans, and a crewneck sweater, rounded one of the massive support columns and stepped into the light. Her face was shadowed by the visor of a baseball cap bearing the logo of a popular food delivery company. Her long, dark ponytail had been pulled through the gap at the back and hung over a shoulder.

It struck Nicky as odd. How did she get down here? There were only two ways to enter the private garage. One through this elevator, and the other through the security gate for which there was a code.

"Can I help you?" Nicky asked assessing the woman. She was attractive. Just a smidge taller than herself, with curvy hips and biggish boobs. "Are you lost?"

"No, not lost." The woman's lips twisted into a smile, then she raised her arm, pointing a gun at Nicky's heart.

Jesus, what?

The air left Nicky's lungs in a short, explosive burst. She raised her hands and took an unsteady step back. "Oh, God."

"Don't move," the woman ordered. "I wouldn't want to shoot you so soon. It would be a waste and I still need you. But it is so nice to finally meet you, Nicky. I'm Oksana Federova. Perhaps you've heard of me, hm?"

Ohgodohgodohgod!

How did this happen?

She looked around. Were any of the badasses down here to help her? The woman jerked her chin. "If you want to keep that pretty little thumb, I suggest you put it to use and take us up right now, darling. Vasily and I have business to attend to."

She had almost no accent. And what accent she did have

surprisingly wasn't of Eastern Europe. In Nicky's mind, she'd pictured this ogre-like woman with a thick Russian growl, but this was almost charming and generically American.

"How did you get in?" Nicky asked, her voice cracking. And she didn't only mean how had this woman slipped past security at the gate. What level of hell had this bitch portalled from?

She put her shaking thumb on the pad and the doors opened.

"Step inside." Oksana twisted her cherry-red lips and lifted a slim shoulder. "Where I came from is neither here nor there. Let's just say, men are easily distracted. Honestly, they're like horny little squirrels with ADD sometimes. Show them a hint of underwear, or a decent pair of tits and they just can't seem to help themselves."

The doors swished closed, and the elevator started to rise.

Oksana smiled, looking her up and down. On the surface, that upward movement of her lips looked pleasant, but the accompanying assessment gave Nicky the shivers. Her skin prickled as if something creepy and ugly like a centipede or a hundred tiny spiders crawled up her.

"You know," she drawled, her eyes glittering with malice. "I never could quite figure what he saw in you, but now that we're close up..." her voice trailed off. "I can finally appreciate your looks." In the enclosed space, Oksana's perfume, though expensive, was cloying and caught in Nicky's throat. "You're prettier in real life." Her lips pursed. "We have much in common, don't you think?"

Oksana paused for effect as if weighing a question in her head and letting the tension mount. "Did Vasily tell you we had a... something?" Then she chuckled, the sound almost jovial, but it was loaded with venom. "Well, technically I had a *something* with both men in your life. And of the two, Vasily is the better lover. Though Anthony, to be fair, isn't bad. Just not quite as well-endowed, but he does know how to work it. I rather enjoy a man who knows his way around a woman's body, don't you?"

Nicky swallowed, fear slithering through her like a snake in a slime patch. This woman was fucking crazy, chatting like they were old friends and this was nothing more than a chance meeting in a private parking garage. Never mind the cruelty she'd shown by tossing Anthony into a locked dungeon and virtually throwing away the key.

What had either of them ever seen in her?

Nicky pressed her back against the elevator wall, putting as much distance between herself and the woman as possible. The only thing keeping her calm was the hidden camera she knew was directly above her head. Please God, hopefully someone in the security room was paying attention.

The elevator came to a stop and that friendly electronic female voice sang "Penthouse." The doors whooshed open, but Nicky froze as her legs were like noodles and didn't want to work. Oksana raised her brows and gestured Nicky forward, waving the gun in a circular fashion.

Nicky stepped out, fear tightening her chest as adrenaline coursed through her veins. All too aware of the gun pointed at her spine, she fought to keep her legs from buckling. The click of her cowboy boot heels sounded as wobbly as her legs felt, almost as if the sound was laughing at her as it bounced off the marble floors.

"Hm." Oksana hummed, dipping her finger into the tinkling waters of the fountain and tracing a random pattern. "I'm impressed. It's not as stylish as my father's penthouse in Moscow, but it's not bad. Although, sadly, my beautiful home now belongs to one of Putin's oligarchs. The *mudak* doesn't deserve it, but thanks to Vasily's betrayal, there you have it." She shrugged. "Keep going."

Her carefree, singsong tone stoked Nicky's fear as she led her through the arched door between the bookshelves. There was no telling what evil lay behind that tone, or what was going to happen next. If Nicky could just get to a panic button without alerting Oksana, she might survive the insanity of this moment. They not only alerted the security room but also activated the cameras situated throughout the apartment.

There was one behind the bar.

"Would you like something to drink?" Nicky asked, looking at the beautifully carved wooden wet bar stocked to the hilt with all kinds of expensive liquors. She hated how her voice trembled, but there wasn't much she could do about it.

"So early?" Oksana arched a brow. "Sweet Nicky, please tell me you don't have an alcohol problem."

"I meant water. I need some. Would you mind?"

"I would." Oksana's tone suddenly hardened. "Now stand over there." Using the gun to point, she indicated a place next to one of the couches.

Marley lay in his favorite spot at the end of the backrest, sleeping in a swath of sunlight. Nicky stood, her spine stiff and straight, facing the front door. The cat yawned but barely lifted his lone eyelid.

Oksana took a position behind Nicky but slightly off to her side, and she didn't have to see it to sense the gun was pointed at her temple.

"Now stay still, I wouldn't want you to accidentally trip any buttons now, would I?"

Oh, fuck.

Nicky glanced at Oksana.

The bitch smirked and gave a delicate wave. "Hello, *bratva* princess here. My father had the best security money could buy so I know all about hidden cameras and panic buttons behind bars and under coffee tables. It will do you well to never forget who you're dealing with, darling."

Nicky felt all her hope collapse as Oksana moved until she was directly behind her. She jumped when the cold metal of the gun barrel made contact with her neck just to the right of her spine.

God forgive her, but she wanted to shit herself she was so terrified. Tears burned her eyeballs but she refused to cry in front of this woman. On some level, she felt compelled to beg for her life, tell this woman she had a child, another on the way, but that would only give the bitch more leverage. Her breath shuddered in her throat as she gripped her dress at her sides. "What do we do now?"

"We wait. And if he's paying attention, it shouldn't be too long."

It wasn't.

A couple of minutes later, the front door opened. Vasily's expression was cold. His gaze grazed over Nicky, lingering only a fraction before he focused on the woman behind her.

"Well, look who finally made it," Oksana purred. "My, my, aren't you as handsome as ever."

Vasily said nothing in response, his expression as inscrutable as a mask, and his eyes were as hard as steel. Nicky felt a wave of relief wash over her and she prayed that he wasn't alone, that Yev was somewhere close, and that he could get them out of this mess.

"Let her go, Oksana," he commanded. "Your beef is with me."

"And ruin my fun?" Oksana laughed, the sound grating on Nicky's nerves, like fingernails scraping down a chalkboard. Then the woman tutted. "Not a snowball's chance in hell. Are you armed?"

"*Nyet.*" Vasily shook his head, then held his hands in the air.

"English, Handsome. We wouldn't want to be rude in front of Nicky now, would we? Turn around. Let me see what you have behind your back."

Vasily gave her a hard stare that was punctuated with ice, then shook his head but complied. Keeping his eyes on Oksana when possible, he made a slow circle, displaying nothing in his waistband.

"Show me your ankles," Oksana demanded, suspicion coloring her voice.

Again, he complied, lifting his pants' legs to show dark blue Argyle socks.

"Good boy. Now don't do anything stupid, and that goes for your henchman, whom I'm sure is lurking nearby." Oksana took a step closer to Nicky, using her as a shield. "One wrong move and this sweet little girl's spine gets smooshed into ground beef."

Vasily's jaw flexed as his gaze caught Nicky's. In the brief moment their eyes connected, his softened. There was a message there, though she couldn't determine if he was offering an apology, or if he was asking her to trust him. Perhaps it was both.

Yes, she trusted him, but she couldn't say the same about the woman shoving a gun against her vertebrae. Her lashes flickered in answer to whatever his message was.

He seemed to give a small nod, then shifted his gaze from her's and refocused on Oksana. "What do you want?"

"A little loyalty would've been a good start but that's no longer an option, am I right?"

He stayed silent. Only hardening his glare, those normally silver eyes now a ruthless, gunmetal gray.

"Oh, come now," Oksana accused. "You took everything from me, and now I'm going to take everything from you. Starting with this pretty little thing. We're going on a trip, but first, you and I have things to discuss." Oksana jabbed the barrel deeper into Nicky's flesh. She tensed at the bruising pain and breathed in hard through her nostrils.

A trip? Oh, God, to what part of hell was she going to take her?

"You want me," Vasily growled. "Let her go."

"Sorry, no," Oksana singsonged. "I've been planning for this very scenario for weeks, finding ways to get close to you, and waiting for my moment. Therefore, darling, like the finest of Russian caviar, I'm going to savor it. And your pain when this lovely girl gets sold to some poor, ugly man who couldn't find a woman otherwise."

"So, you trafficked in humans to get my attention?" Vasily

advanced a step. "How typical of the kind of woman you are. Tell me, was it everything you dreamed of?"

"Not a step closer!" Oksana barked and pressed the weapon even deeper into Nicky's flesh. "Or she dies."

Vasily shrugged, his expression impassive. "And deprive yourself of your leverage, and the fee you'd get for her? You know me, Oksana. Except for the mess it will make on my couch, do you think I care?"

The air thickened. Nicky's breath stopped in her throat. Even Oksana seemed shocked by his statement as Nicky felt the tension vibrating through the nose of the gun into her muscles.

"You haven't really thought this through, have you?" he added. "Up till now, I have to admit you had the advantage. But you're overestimating what she's worth to me."

Then Oksana gave an ugly, harsh laugh, and suddenly Nicky felt the heat of her breath near her ear. It was tainted with the evil spewing from her.

"Always so cold, this one. He could crack an iceberg with those eyes and that voice. But I don't believe him for a minute that he doesn't care. Because you see, I know him better than he thinks I do. Did he tell you what he did for my father in Russia?"

"Yes." Nicky swallowed.

"Oh, do elaborate, darling. I can't wait to hear what he told you."

"He said he became an assassin." Her throat was like sandpaper and there was no saliva left in her mouth. She fought hard against her instinct to jerk away from Oksana, but she didn't want to incentivize the bitch to pull the trigger.

"Ah, but did he tell you *why* he became an assassin?" Oksana purred into her ear.

"So he could live."

"So *he* could live?" The bitch laughed again, this time it was high-pitched and bordered on madness.

Dear God, this insane woman was losing it.

"Oh, darling Vasily, surely you can't be that naïve thinking I'm going to buy that?"

"Oksana!" Vasily's tone was thick with a warning as he moved a step closer. "Stop."

Oksana's cheek vanished from her peripheral as she straightened and moved behind Nicky. Her tone turned harsh. "No, you stop. I'm warning you, *Nayemnik*!"

Vasily halted, and he held his hands up in the surrender position. "Don't, please," he said his voice suddenly cracking. "I'm begging you. Whatever you want, it's with me. Leave her alone."

"Oh, Vasily, Vasily, *Vas-i-ly*." She tutted again.

Nicky looked at him with a growing sense of dread. What had him so worried that it turned his expression to one of fear?

Confusion was followed by the icicle in her spine sliding down as she watched their interaction. And it suddenly dawned on her, he wasn't just worried about what Oksana might do—he was also worried about what she might say. Nicky's mind raced at all the possibilities, that perhaps he hadn't been honest with her. Her stomach plunged, and despite the tiny life growing inside her, she felt suddenly hollow inside.

Her breath hitched as she stared at him.

Oksana chortled, and it was a sound that was way too jolly for the situation. "Oh, Nicky. You're so precious, but you should know, he didn't assassinate those people so that he could live. He assassinated them so that *you* could live."

What?

"Think back to all those years ago, darling. Didn't you ever get the feeling, that prickly sensation at the back of your neck that you were being watched?"

Nicky gasped. She had! There was a time in the months after he'd left and before her dad's trial that she'd felt she'd been watched. Sometimes a stranger would be too close, invading her personal space. It happened often enough it couldn't be a coincidence, but when she'd turned to confront them, they'd moved away, as if nothing was meant by it.

It had been *them*. Oksana's people! Goosebumps broke out on her flesh and her blood turned cold.

Vasily's throat bobbed. "Please," he implored Oksana. "Do whatever you want with me, just don't."

"Vasily darling, I love when you beg, but you don't get to give me orders. And she deserves to know, doesn't she?"

Nicky twisted her neck to look into Oksana's muddy brown eyes. Her throat burning, she asked, "What do I deserve to know?"

Oksana smiled but kept her gaze on Vasily. That skin-crawling sensation rippled over her again. "Vasily is more stubborn than a mule. It's quite entertaining actually. And the only way my father convinced Vasily to do his bidding was by threatening your life. He showed him photos of the stranger next to you with a dirty hypodermic needle. Who knows what was in there?" Oksana smirked again. "My guess was blood tainted with Hepatitis C, HIV, or a cocktail of something far worse. Something that would make you terribly sick. Maybe even die a long, horrible death."

They what? Fury at how they'd manipulated him boiled up inside her like a volcano about to blow. It overtook her.

"You fucking *bitch*!" Nicky snapped, stunned at their cruelty. She spat in Oksana's face and somewhere in the echoes of her rage, she heard Vasily yell. "Jesus, Dom, no!"

Oksana's head reared back, her eyes widening in surprise before her face twisted into an ugly mask and she grabbed a handful of Nicky's hair. Then she pulled back hard, and Nicky yelped at the sudden pain stinging her scalp.

A vague, familiar growling filled Nicky's head, but she couldn't tell where it was coming from, if it was internal or external. But then an orange and white blur flew over her face.

Marley's ear-splitting, pissed-off alley cat yowl filled the room, and it was quickly joined by Oksana's hoarse scream.

A loud boom rattled her brain.

Instinct made her recoil away from the sound, and she toppled over, falling onto the couch on her side. Curling into the fetal position, she covered her face with her arms. Time seemed to slow down, and everything went deadly silent for several long seconds like she was sucked into a vacuum. Then a high-pitched ringing and the *whoomph, whoomph* of blood rushing through her ears filled that silence.

After what seemed like an eternity, but was only a few seconds, there was a second gunshot. This one was accompanied by a fine mist of red.

God, was she dying?

A sharp, acrid stench invaded her nostrils confusing her, and mentally, she tried to take stock. She felt nothing, except for something warm on her cheek, and her hair was obscuring her vision. She reached up to push the strands aside. Only it wasn't her hair. It was a furry curtain of orange and white...*and red*.

Marley?

Fuck.

No, no, no, no, no, no!

A sudden surge of energy and a second round of rage pulsed through her veins. Nicky leaped to her feet and looked at her hand. She was clutching half of her cat's tail, and it wasn't connected to the rest of him. There was no sign of Marley anywhere. Her frantic eyes darted around, skimming over Yev who was crouched on the floor leaning over a body.

Where had he come from—the lobby perhaps?

Vasily was still standing, and relief added to the other emotions flooding through her that it wasn't him lying on the floor. A small sob escaped her, and she ran to him.

"Are you hurt?" Vasily demanded as he yanked her into his arms. His voice sounded raw, a low growl as he pressed her head into his chest, holding on to her with a fierceness she was grateful for. His body trembled with the aftershocks and the slow, unsteady beat of his heart throbbed beneath her ear.

"I'm okay," she sobbed, looking past his arm. "But I can't see Marley."

"That was stupid, Dom, antagonizing her like that. So fucking stupid, but that damn cat..."

Nicky gave another half sob, which was also a half laugh.

Yes, her damn cat had saved her again.

Then she took in Oksana. She lay on her back, and even in death, her eyes were cruel. Blood seeped into the rug from a gaping, bloody hole in her chest.

Yev still had his gun in one hand as he looked up at them and shook his head. "Sorry that took so long. Couldn't find the right angle where I wouldn't put Nicky in danger, but I think I might've hit the cat." Then his eyes widened. "Boss!"

Yev dropped his weapon on the corner table. It made a dull thud as it connected with the wood, then he lurched forward. It was his tone that alerted Nicky and suddenly she realized the heat coming from Vasily's body was sticky and unnaturally hot.

Something was very wrong.

She looked down at the spreading patch of red staining Vasily's formerly pristine shirt. He staggered as his legs gave out and he began to slump in her arms.

She braced herself against his weight, but he was heavier than she could handle. Yev helped her catch him and they guided him to the couch.

"Fuck," Vasily groaned as he sat. "I feel kinda dizzy." His eyes seemed slightly unfocused as they ran a slow, worried path up her body. He attempted to reach out to her. "Dom, you're bleeding."

He thought it was her blood?

"It's not her boss, it's you," Yev said, curling his fingers in Vasily's shirt. He ripped it open, making the elegant buttons ping off the coffee table. The wound was high on his left side, and nowhere near anything vital, but it was oozing blood. Too much blood.

"Call 911," she ordered Yev, then snatched a small throw cushion from the corner of the couch.

Vasily slumped sideways onto his back, his head rolling as if he no longer had the strength to hold it straight.

"Ugh, fuck, that hurts," he groaned between clenched teeth when she pushed the pillow to his side to staunch the blood.

"You're going to be fine," she sniffed using her knee to help apply pressure. "You have to be, you hear me?"

His smile was weak, and barely lifted the corner of his lips. "Not going anywhere, but what she said..." He took a series of labored breaths followed by a grimace as a wave of pain overtook him.

Nicky grabbed his hand and squeezed tight as he fought against it.

"Shh, it's okay. Don't worry about that. It doesn't matter now. You just stay alive."

"Why I did it...never wanted you to hear...to live with that kind of guilt."

His gaze locked with hers as he took a couple of hard swallows. It hurt Nicky to see him struggle like that. It hurt her, even more, to know that he'd carried that burden by himself for so long.

"Shoulda said it earlier." His fingers entangled in hers, and he gently squeezed her hand back. "Stupid I didn't, but I'm in. Nothing else makes sense. Need you...want this baby." He groaned against the pain again, and it was evident he was fading as the color drained from his face.

"Vasily, save your strength." Though his words inspired an avalanche of happy emotions to tumble inside her, they were mixed with worry. She needed him strong. "This can wait 'til later."

"Need to say it." It was costing him, but he held her gaze and all the hurt from his tortured past was there for her to see. "Love you, Dom. Never stopped...loving you."

"I know that now Vas." She sniffed. "And I love you back, so very much."

Like a light being switched on, Oksana's revelation had made it clear exactly how much he loved her. And that he'd sacrificed his soul so she would remain unharmed. Pain twisted her heart at how much had been hidden for so long. Tears rained down her cheeks but as both her hands were occupied, and she had no desire to break contact, she made no move to wipe them away.

"I know what you've done for me, and I'm so sorry I doubted you," she whispered. "But don't you dare think about leaving me alone again."

"Never." He exhaled, but his eyes were becoming unfocused. "Not in this life...or the next."

Then he allowed himself to succumb, and his eyes rolled halfway back as he lost consciousness.

"Vas?" She shook his leg, panic creeping into her voice. "Oh, fuck no, Vas, wake up."

"Let him sleep," Yev said from behind her. He was watching her with his phone pressed to his ear. "It's just a flesh wound, but that hole in his side hurts like a motherfucker."

"You sure?" She sniffed again. "Because if you're wrong or lying to me, I'm going to shoot *you*."

"Trust me." He offered her an assuring look. "I know when a man is dying, and he isn't. He's strong and he's survived worse."

Then as if he couldn't control them any longer, Yev's lips tilted upwards, and his eyes went all melty and soft.

"So that's what that trip to the drugstore was all about," he said. "Pregnancy tests?"

Nicky wiped her tears with her shoulder and nodded.

He looked at her for a long moment, then he bent down to her level. A thick, strong arm curled around her front, and an enormous hand cupped her face as he kissed her forehead. Perhaps it was her imagination, but when Yev pulled away and Nicky caught his eyes, she was sure his looked suspiciously wet.

"I'm ecstatic for both of you," he said in a voice that was gruff and a little uneven. "You're exactly what he needs."

Epilogue

Eight months later, Nicky entered their bedroom carrying a tray that contained Vasily's breakfast. He lay against his pillows, his perfect, naked chest and washboard stomach bearing one more scar on his left side. The bullet from Oksana's gun had passed through his flesh just below his ribs but did no substantial or long-lasting damage to any of his organs.

For this, she thanked the gods every single morning. The sight of him stole her breath and made her heart do that jumping thing, as it did each time she looked at her man.

But this morning it was especially poignant.

She stopped at the threshold, taking a mental snapshot of the moment. Her throat thickened from suppressing tears of joy, and her heart just about burst open from happiness.

Vasily was reading to Luca, who was on his side in the middle of their bed, head propped in his hand. He was engrossed in every word that her new husband spoke.

On Vasily's chest, lay their three-week-old daughter, Angelique Marie Melnikova. They'd named her after his mother, and though it was too early to be certain, all indications were that she'd inherited her father's silver-gray eyes. He gently patted her diapered butt as she made happy little baby gurgles and clutched her tiny fists into the sprinkling of hair on his chest.

To complete the picture of her version of heaven, her fat, one-eyed, half-tailed ginger cat had curled himself around Vasily's head and was making biscuits in his hair.

As she approached their bed, to take her place next to Luca and complete their beautiful family, Marley lifted his eyelid, yawned, then proceeded to accompany Vasily's reading with his loud purring.

It was one of the million perfect moments that life continued to gift them since the minute Vasily reentered Nicky's world. A life that lasted well into their eighties and left a long string of Melnikov descendants, none of whom showed any signs of the madness Vasily had been so afraid of.

***

If you enjoyed this book, please rate it or leave a short review using the link below. Thank you!